EXCHANGING

by

K. E. Brungardt

Cover designed by Kat Domet/Domet Design

ISBN: 9780578892733

For my husband, Larry, whom I love more than all the stars Jessi sees from the spaceship on her way to Amorpha.

For my readers, because why write a book if no one is there to read it?

Table of Contents

CHAPTER ONE

When I first arrived on Amorpha, the only Human in a city of a million Amorphans, the name-calling, fist-shaking and heckling I received at the University shocked me. I understood, then, why the rules forced us Exchange students to have bodyguards. After hearing threats on my life, voices disparage my parentage and screams for my removal from their world, among other things, I regretted for a short time being fluent in their language. On the other hand, the majority of Amorphans were interested in Humans and curious in a friendly way and their kindness offset the angry voices.

However, over the first few months, most of the angry Amorphans calmed down once they realized I didn't eat their precious progeny for breakfast or practice other horrid human rituals on my fellow students. Finally, the Zatro—equivalent to a Governor President Dictator of his city—used his power voice to calm the population, so going to classes and home again became routine and no more exciting than any other University student's life. Except for the bodyguards and their weapons, of course.

A slight breeze cooled my face as we–me and my two bodyguards–left the University building, stepping outside into a sunny, warm day to go to the hovercar. Sunlight sparkled off their refractory skin in rainbows of colors as their glittery eyes looked around, watching everything with suspicion. I felt shorter than usual sandwiched between the two tall, willowy Amorphans in their uniforms, one on either side of me. Amorphan students, professors, and visitors streamed around us, some in a hurry for their next class, others rushing to get home or to a job, I guessed, although my day was over. Several nodded my way as they passed or raised a hand in greeting and I did the same with a smile on my face, carefully not showing my teeth, which could be misunderstood as a gesture of aggression. Getting through the crowd felt like a dance, one I enjoyed each time.

When a hand clamped itself around my right forearm, pulling me so hard I stumbled and lurched, confusion was my first reaction; I thought I'd tripped over something. Myometo, reacting to my stumble, grabbed my left arm to steady me as he pivoted, placing my back against his front, trapping my hair between us, shouting, "Let her go!" while his other arm encircled my chest, squishing my boobs painfully. Zaleander, my other guard, turned to get in front of me, or tried to, anyway, as someone jumped on his back, going for his weapon. Whoever had my arm in a death grip yanked hard enough against Myometo's solid hold to dislocate my shoulder; I felt the pop of it being forcibly removed from my joint. I added my scream to a sudden upswell of cursing and yelling around me.

I couldn't bite the offending hand--even if I could reach it—because he wore a metal-reinforced glove, explaining why his grip hurt so much plus Myometo had me pinned against his torso. Amorphans have boneless hands and fingers, with surprising strength even without any reinforcement. *Maybe he's heard I'm trained in fighting dirty.* A different hand lifted a blaster into my peripheral vision on my left side and discharged, a loud buzzing sound clapping against my ear as laser energy shot over my head, my ears ringing from the noise. Dots of light danced in front of my eyes from the sudden flash.

Someone in the crowd screamed, or maybe more than one person, it was hard to tell in the confusion and clamor. The Amorphan still clamped my arm in an unbreakable hold as he jerked me again and I nearly fainted as agony in my shoulder rocketed up from a ten to a million on the pain scale.

A wild noise came from my mouth, tears flooding my eyes but not before seeing my attacker wore a head-to-toe camouflage suit, his face covered with a shiny, mirror-like surface. It seemed impossible to inflict any harm to him physically and using a blaster was extremely dangerous, with the bodies crowding around us. It would be too easy to hit an innocent person and, possibly, already had. I did wonder, for a fleeting second, why the male had grabbed me and not shot me with a stun gun. On the one hand, I was relieved to not have been shot; on the other hand, the intense discomfort in my dislocated joint almost made me wish he had.

I yelled, "Let me go! My shoulder's out of place!" Myometo ignored me or didn't hear me, seeing as how he was too busy preventing me from being abducted. He kept me held tight against his own torso with one arm as he wrestled with the intruder with the other, keeping the offending hand now holding a stun gun from being pointed at me.

Zaleander grappled with another Amorphan in a camouflage uniform, trying to keep control of his own weapon while fighting his adversary. It must've been Zaleander's weapon discharged over my head, his aim knocked off when his assailant jumped him.

My attacker took an unexpected step forward, no doubt shoved by the bodies pressing in on us, others trying to help–or hinder–so I slammed my heel into his shin area as hard as I could. My voice hoarse from shouting, adrenaline pumped through me as all my years of self-defense training kicked in. My hair, suddenly released from its trapped position against my back as Myometo was jostled enough to open a gap, unraveled from its complicated braid, sending out shafts of hair to join the fight while staying discreet about its actions.

Yeah, my hair has abilities and opinions, one of my secrets, and I'm not sure I still know the full extent of what it can do. Right now, though, my hair had my full blessing to do whatever was needed to my assailants as the strands of hair snuck between fibers of the attackers' outfits, driving into skin like needles.

Between my repeated kicking of the guy's shins and my hair doing its thing, plus my guards beating at the assailants, finally, *finally*, he dropped his hand from my arm.

The one in front of me shouted, "Retreat!" as he tried to move back to leave, finding he was hemmed in by a crush of bodies around him. A blaster appeared again in my side vision, going off at full volume next to my ear before the unknown male could take more than a step. My attacker dropped like he'd stepped into a gravity well. The pressure of bodies around us released as fast as he fell to the ground. I felt, more than watched, people rushing away, but not really being able to see through the tears in my eyes, the ringing in my ears and the agony in my joint.

I gritted my teeth, cradling my right arm with my left to relieve the pressure on my damaged shoulder joint. Myometo kept me upright but I couldn't talk through the intensity of my discomfort, could only gasp in small breaths. He barked orders into a comm unit while Zaleander secured the person on the ground before he regained consciousness. I didn't know what happened to the other person who'd attacked him, and I didn't have the strength to ask.

My hair fell back into place so no one would notice its participation in this fight. I squeezed my eyes shut as tears continued to leak down my face.

Thanks, Queenie. Glad you could finally make it. I panted, trying to distract myself from focusing on my injury.

HMPH. WAS TRAPPED. AND NO, JUST NO.

Yeah, yeah. Even in the midst of chaos and my pain, I felt the desire to try out yet another name for my hair, which it flatly refused, for the trillionth time. *Can we fix my shoulder? Like, now? This hurts as bad as changing shapes does, only this is lasting way longer than a minute.*

My other huge secret is I'm the only shapeshifter in all the endless universe, a supposedly impossible happening. Not to mention discovering I had mental telepathy while on the journey here. Oh, and that I really wanted my hair to have a name, other than 'it'. I'd been trying out names since my hair and I first became aware of each other as I entered puberty, aka the Transition Years. So far, it has refused all my offerings, serious or otherwise, and if I persisted in using a disliked name, I got stung for doing so. One time, I'd liked Latifa and used it for a day before I couldn't take the pinches anymore.

STOP RAMBLING! WHEN BONE IN PLACE, ACCELERATE HEALING.

Myometo's face loomed before me, stopping my internal conversation, the pressure of his arm around my chest disappearing as he grabbed my upper arm on the good side. "Madam, are you all right? Madam Jessi?"

My head swam and my vision wavered as dizziness and lightheadedness fought for number one position. "I need to sit." I shook my head, hoping to clear it, gulping in air against sudden nausea from the motion. "My shoulder's dislocated."

"Are you sure?"

"Oh, I'm quite sure. It came out of place when that guy yanked on my arm." I sucked in a breath. "It really hurts. And you're hurting me, too, so please let me go. Thanks."

I yelped as he dropped his arm, jostling my shoulder and I staggered. "This. Hurts." Myometo helped me down to the ground, my Amorphan robes bunched up around my knees, revealing I wore jeans underneath and tennis shoes. I rested my arm gingerly against my bent knees.

The crowd gathered around us and I recognized a few of the faces, fellow students staring with horrified expressions, head feathers upright in alarm. A few held a hand over their mouth, while others exclaimed and pointed. *Lookie-Loos are in every society, alien or not,* I thought as I ignored the crowd, concentrating on evening out my breathing so I could deal with the intense throbbing in my right shoulder.

I heard the whine of a hovercar approaching, chirping a siren to announce its arrival and everyone in the crowd moved back to make room for landing. A taller than normal Amorphan—and they are quite tall by Human standards in general—stepped out the door of the craft, hurrying over to kneel in front of me.

"Madam, I am Physician Kenonaki. I am here to assess and treat you."

"Dislocated shoulder." I said through gritted teeth. "Are you familiar with Human anatomy?" Sweat beaded on my forehead but I didn't have a hand free to wipe it away. I blinked as one droplet rolled onto my eyelashes but before it could sting my eye, the lashes flicked it away.

"Yes, our skeletal structures are quite similar. Let me just feel...here." He looked off into the distance as he gently probed my shoulder area. He nodded. "Yes, you are correct, the arm bone is out of its socket." He rummaged in a small bag slung over his torso, pulling out a tube. "Let me administer this into the joint area to numb it and then I will put it back like it should be." He looked at me with compassion on his face, his skin reflecting colors of concern and sympathy.

"You're sure it is safe for a Human?"

"Yes, I'm quite sure. I am the assigned physician for you, you see, and I've been prepared since before you arrived for most emergencies. I've been studying your anatomy, physiology and biology for many months. Plus, I've reviewed many months-worth of hours on different procedures on the Human body, including this."

Well, how about that; my own personal physician no one thought to tell me about.

He held up his bag. "This is my travel equipment for Humans, approved by your world and the Imurians."

"Okay, then." I squinted at the tube, trying to read the label. "What's in there?" My mother, being a doctor herself, taught me a lot over the years, including being cautious about medications. Although I just wanted my shoulder back in place, Mom would *not* approve if I didn't vet the medication first.

"Lidocaine, imported from your world." He held the tube for me to read and that is, indeed, what it said, along with a human laboratory and pharmaceutical name.

"What? No morphine for my pain?"

He quirked an eyebrow ridge at me. "I am sorry, but we cannot have you disabled right now in the midst of danger."

"Of course. You're right," I said. "Go ahead."

He placed the tube against my exposed skin with a light pressure; I grimaced as he activated the device to deliver the medicine into the joint space. Thank the purple panties of an angel, no needles were needed. Within a few seconds, the biting pain started to abate, and I drew in a breath of relief. "It's working."

The doctor nodded. "I'll give you a minute more and then I can put you back together.

A resounding "thunk" as he replaced the ball joint back into its socket and a sling later, I felt so much better. I knew I'd heal faster than normal; my top-grade nano system's that good, plus my own unique ability to heal fast, but for now, being back together was good enough.

CHAPTER TWO

I'd been hustled into the armored hovercar as soon as the physician gave the all-right sign, surrounded by five guards this time. *Huh, seems like overkill now. Don't think those males are coming back right away. Well, at least they didn't kill me, or try to overkill me, haha.*

"Why'd those guys grab me?" I said, my tongue thick and words slow from the pain med I'd finally convinced the doctor to give me. My eyes closed as I leaned my head against the headrest behind me. I nestled into the hovercar seat as they prepared to lift off the pavement to take me home. The whine of the engine startled me, my eyelids flying open, but they drifted shut again as soon as my brain caught up to knowing the noise as benign.

"We don't know just yet, Madam Jessi, but we'll find out." Zaleander said in a grim voice. From his tone, the one male they'd caught would be having a very bad day. I preferred not to think about what the officials would do to gain the information; I couldn't do anything about it, anyway.

I fell asleep as an overwhelming tiredness washed over me, waking up some time later when the hovercar landed in front of my house. "Madam Jessi, we'll check first to make sure all is safe before helping you out. Please stay there."

"Okay." I yawned. Wrapped in a cocoon of fuzziness, I vowed to avoid future pain tabs, hating the feeling of lassitude and fuzzy mind.

HATE IT, TOO.

Yeah, I'm not taking another of those. Sorry, won't happen again.

BETTER NOT. My hair's huffy tone annoyed me.

Okay, Buttercup. I used my snippiest tone to answer.

The door swung open, Myometo's face looking in at me. "Ready to go to the house?"

"Yes. I think. That pain med made me very tired."

"It'll do that." He reached in with his hand, offering it to me and I grabbed his hand with my left one. "How's the arm?"

Without thinking, I shrugged, then winced. "Ah—not healed yet." I drew in a breath, waiting for the surge of discomfort to recede. "Have you told Matra what happened?"

He grinned, the skin around his eyes crinkling. "Yes. She's not happy; thank the universe we have the male in custody, not her. Nothing worse than a mad, scared mother on a rampage."

I smiled at that. "I think you're right." I sighed. "Okay, I'm ready to try again." Once again, I took his helping hand

and managed to climb out of the vehicle onto the pavement without further problems.

"Jessi! Jessi, are you all right? I'll kill them, I'll flay them with my own teeth, I'll tear them from limb to limb!" Matra shouted in a fierce voice as she rushed in front of Myometo, shoving him out of the way with her hip. "How dare they hurt my child! I'll show them pain like they've never had before!" She reached out, cradling my cheek with a gentle hand, tears sparkling in her eyes as she bared her double row of sharp, pointed teeth. "Here, let's take you to the house and into a chair. My goodness, child, you're as pale as a mushroom!"

I snorted a small laugh. "Gee, thanks, Matra. Your mushroom is ready to find a chair or a bed, I'll admit, but really, I'm okay. My shoulder hurts, yeah, but it'll be fine by tomorrow. Or maybe the next day." I yawned then.

She smiled at me, her sharp teeth disappearing as she patted my good shoulder. "I only speak the truth; you're very pale and that's saying something, since your skin is so white and lacking color." She tsked, so like my human mother, tears welled in my eyes from a sudden rush of homesickness. "Come now, child of my heart, let's go inside."

Bodyguards fell in around us for the few feet to the front door of the house. It opened as soon as it sensed Matra's and my biometrics, and she ushered me ahead of her into the front room.

"Matra Teatriana," Myometo said, "we'll have an extra detail assigned to your house for the next several days. Rest assured, we will make sure Jessi is fully protected, along with all of you."

She paused, looking back over her shoulder. "See that you do so." She shut the door behind her with a firm click, looking over at me. "Good. You're sitting. I'll bring you a drink and then you'll tell me exactly what happened."

I nodded. When Matra spoke like that, the best thing to do was agree. After she returned with my cold drink, I told her everything I remembered about the attack.

"The thing I don't understand is why it happened or what those males wanted with me. Things are going so well with school and living here. I haven't made anyone mad–that I know of–so what could I possibly have done to cause this?"

Matra reached over, smoothing hair away from my face and my hair let her. No one on Amorpha or most of the known universe knows about my abilities or about my hair, and I intended to keep it that way. Having sentient hair and being the only shapeshifter ever–something generally accepted as being completely impossible–is something I must keep secret, for my own safety, if nothing else. A part of me wondered if anyone did know about my specialness and perhaps that trigged the kidnap attempt. Immediate worry leapt into my brain, heart rate speeding up in response.

STOP. NO PROOF OF THAT.

Matra stroked my cheek with a loving touch from her thumb. I closed my eye to soak in her caress; I needed a loving touch right then and I shoved my anxiety out of my head. For now.

"You did nothing wrong, Jessi. Nothing! Do *not* think for one nano-second that this is your fault in any way. We'll know soon enough why; they will not be gentle in finding out the answers from the prisoner." Colors of anger flashed through her glittering eyes, red twinkling over her skin.

I saw fury on her face and shivered a little. I wouldn't want her expression directed at me. Amorphans are beautiful people, with skin that refracts sunlight and colors according to their moods, their multi-faceted eyes glittering whenever light hits them. Feathers adorned their heads like hair and their tall, willowy forms were graceful. Thinly lipped mouths hid very sharp teeth and they had eyebrow ridges but no eyebrow hair. Amorphan hands and feet were boneless as they could change their shape at will but they weren't true shapeshifters.

Right now, Matra bared her shark-like teeth again, echoes from their violent, messy past. For a second, I visualized those teeth ripping and tearing and goosebumps raised on my arms. Amorphans had an edge to their personalities, a bit cold-blooded and pragmatic when dealing with lawbreakers, reminding me of our legendary sharks from old Earth. I didn't pity my attacker, but maybe I should. I flinched away from her expression.

Matra snapped her mouth shut, her eyes softening as she gazed at me with a tender look. "Oh, my child! I'm sorry; I didn't mean to upset you." She reached out, snagging a light blanket from the couch. "Here we go." She placed it around my shoulders with a light touch, being sure to not jostle my sore shoulder. "Is that better?"

I smiled at her, loving her concern and protectiveness. "It's perfect. Thank you." I laid my left hand on top of hers. "I'll be better by morning, you know, but I'm so happy you're here."

She smiled, teeth hidden now. "I'm glad to be here for you."

An unexpected yawn surprised me and I covered my mouth, muffling my voice. "Sorry; it's the pain med, I think."

"Jessi, lie back and take a nap. It's not just the medication; being in a fight like that, being hurt, all that adrenaline, no wonder you need to rest. Don't worry, I'm here to watch over you and I'll be sure to wake you in time for our family meal." She patted my cheek and stood to walk off toward the kitchen but turned back to look at me. "You'll be okay here? Can I do anything else for you?"

I shook my head. "I'm fine, I'm safe. Please, go do what you need to do and I'll be right here."

She nodded, moving toward the kitchen. "I'll be close by if you need something or want anything."

I took her advice, working myself into a comfortable position for my shoulder, then closing my eyes. I heard

Matra's voice murmuring in the kitchen as I drifted off, wondering whose ass she chewed as I fell asleep.

CHAPTER THREE

Loud noises startled me out of my nap and I flinched, reminding me of my injury. "Wha–what?"

"Jessi! I heard you had a fight today and you won!"

I opened my eyes all the way to see my little Amorphan brother standing in front of me, grinning, showing all his pointed teeth.

"Did you? Win, I mean? I bet you did!" He said with pride as he puffed out his chest.

"I'm not sure I'd call it winning, exactly." I rubbed my nose. "I mean, I have this now," and I waved my hand at my other arm in its sling. "But they failed so I'd say that is the win. Myometo and Zaleander did most of the fighting."

"Was there shooting?" He said with eagerness, eyes sparkling.

I rolled my eyes. Just like a boy. "Yes, but not by me. Zaleander shot the guy tugging on me."

Datro hurried over to us, grabbing Simatrao by his shoulder. "What did I say, son? Something like 'do not wake your sister if she's asleep. She's had a tough day.' Isn't that what I said?" He said in a sharp tone. Then, looking at me, he gestured apology, his head feathers drooping a little. "Jessi, I'm sorry he woke you but now that you're awake, I'm so relieved to see you looking well. Matra said you were very pale, although I'll be truthful in saying I don't know how she can tell that, but you look incredibly good to me." He pulled Simatrao to one side to move up next to me where I reclined on the couch. He patted my head.

"I'm so angry this happened and I'm so relieved you're home here with us, safe now. Matra has already been stripping hide from officials, as you can well imagine."

I smiled, nodding. "Yeah, I think she was doing that as I fell asleep. I don't envy whoever was at the other end of her PerPad communicator."

He nodded, his feathers more alert now. "So true. If I'd been able to be here earlier, I would've done the same but no need to call now, I think. I was tied up in meetings all afternoon and didn't find out about this until I left. I'm terribly upset with my office people for not telling me sooner."

"It's okay, Datro. There's nothing you could've done but I'm happy you're here now. I feel better knowing you and Simatrao are here, secure, and we're all together." I looked at my brother, wrinkling my nose. "I may not be much fun tonight, though."

He said in a bright tone, "Oh, I'll help you. I can cut your food for you, even place it in your mouth, help you to bed. Anything you need! Wait until I tell my classmates tomorrow how you fought off all those attackers!"

I held up my hand. "Whoa, Simatrao, slow down. I didn't fight off any of them, actually. I did fight back, yes, but my shoulder was pulled out of place early on, Myometo had me in a tight hold and it was really Zaleander who stunned the guy so he could take him prisoner."

"But you did fight, right?" His excited voice touched me, the shine in his eye more than its usual glitter. If I'm not mistaken, there was a little hero worship going on here. Oh, dear.

YES, HE LIKES YOU. My hair made a kissing sound.

Oh, stop that, Petunia. He just has a little crush on me; remember I'm many years older than him.

MWAH. Sometimes, I wished I could slap my hair, but my hair is also me, so I restrained myself.

I shook my head, grinning a little. "Yes, I fought. I kicked his leg–a lot. Not much else I could, since Myometo had me clamped against him *and* my joint was out of place. Trust me, that really hurts."

He pumped a fist. "Yeah, sorry about that, sister Jessi. But you fought back and that's what my friends want to know." He beamed again, with teeth. "None of them have believed you could do anything like that because you're so little and, well, you know, human and have your skin and eye deficits."

"Simatrao!" Matra and Datro spoke at the same second, shock, and displeasure in their voices. "You did *not* just say that!"

He blinked a few times. "But it is only the truth, Matra."

I laughed, I couldn't help it. "It's okay, Matra, Datro. I know about my deficits and I'm not insulted." I sketched a salute to Simatrao. "I'm glad to impress in spite of my shortcomings." I grinned. "Get it? Short coming?"

He laughed. "I get it. And you are for sure short, even for Humans, yes?"

"Yes." I nodded. "It's an odd thing, but not even the best doctors could get me to grow taller."

TOO HARD TO CHANGE TO SMALLER IF TALLER.

I know that now but no one, including me and you, knew that then. Some of those treatments hurt if you remember; I was sure happy when the doctors finally gave up.

Datro said in a firm voice, "While you are diminutive, it's of no importance to us. We love you, you are part of this family forever and size doesn't matter."

Laughter bubbled up in me, but I managed to squelch it to a snort. Datro wouldn't have any idea why I'd find that statement funny and I didn't want to explain, especially in front of my brother.

To change the subject, I said, "Thank you, Datro, I love you all, too. Now, I hope our family meal is ready because I could eat an entire chicken, I think, I'm that hungry." I patted my stomach. "And have dessert, too."

Simatrao brightened up. "Yes, dessert!" He turned a hopeful face to his father. "Could we start with that, just this once?"

Datro smiled. "No, son, we must eat our food in its proper order. You know that. Perhaps for your born-day celebration, we can go backwards just that once."

"I think it'd be fun." Simatrao announced, giving Datro a thumbs-up move, learned from me. Datro shook his head at the motion but smiled a little wider.

Simatrao, true to his word, cut up food for me but I convinced him I could feed myself while thanking him profusely for helping me. Matra and Datro watched our interaction with pleasure, smiling as Simatrao fussed over my plate. I ate well, although not the entire bird like I'd threatened. When we were finished, I said, "That was delicious, Matra, but I need to go to bed now. I'm so tired all of a sudden."

Matra stood in a flash of movement. "I'll help you get ready for bed; I'm sure you're quite worn out. How is your discomfort? They gave me some meds to give you if you need it."

I shook my head. "It's uncomfortable but I can manage. I don't like how I feel with that stuff, so I'll just muddle through on my own. But thanks, I could use your help getting into my night clothes.

Once tucked into bed, I smiled up at her. "I was assigned the best family of all five of us exchange students. Thank you so much for making me truly a part of your family."

She laid a soft hand on my forehead, leaning in to kiss me on the cheek. "We are the blessed ones. We miss our older son, of course, more than I can really impart, but I know he's in a good family, too, on New Eden with your parents. And I know that, because of how much we love you and how well you've fit in here with us." She smiled, a tender look in her eyes.

I reached up to squeeze her hands. "I agree; we are blessed."

She stood, turning a little to head to the door of my bedroom, but hesitated, turning her head to look at me. "You do know, Jessi, you can tell me–us–anything, anything at all. All families, especially us Amorphans, can keep secrets when needed. I want to be sure you know this."

I nodded, panic surging up. *Does she know my secrets? How could she know? I've been very, very careful when practicing shifting shapes.* "Yes, uh, thank you for reminding me, Matra." I held my breath, waiting for her to tell me she knew what I did in the privacy of my room at night.

She nodded. "It is, perhaps, something you wouldn't necessarily know so I wanted to be clear. Not that you have anything to hide from us, I'm sure, but, you know, if there's a boy or friend trouble, you can talk to me." She gave a firm up-down with her head, leaving my room and clicking the door securely into place.

I blew out a breath. *She doesn't know. She's talking about relationship stuff.* I grinned to myself. *Like I have a relationship to even talk about.* I thought about Keaton, then, wondering how he was getting along in his own Amorphan city, family and University. Longing swept over me; I'd love to see another Human face about now but that wasn't possible until our six-month mark in the program. I brightened; our six-month reunion was only a few weeks away.

CHAPTER FOUR

I slept well, waking up to a deep ache in my right shoulder but the intensity had greatly diminished already. Just to be sure, Matra came back to my room last night with a med film, insisting I take it, so I gave in. As a result, I felt very refreshed this morning, feeling grateful for her insistence.

I rolled my shoulder a little, sling still in place, and although it protested, the discomfort was tolerable. I managed to brush my teeth but knew I'd better ask Matra for help getting dressed.

CAN HELP.

Yeah, of course you can but it would be odd if I didn't ask for her help, Doris.

OH. TRUE, JUNE.

I opened my door to call for Matra and discovered her hovering in the hallway, duster in hand. Delight lit her face when I said, "Matra! There you are. I sure could use your help in getting dressed."

She tossed the cleaning tool onto the floor, hurrying to come into my room. "Did you sleep okay? How is your pain? Do you need more medication? How about breakfast?" She gripped my good forearm to look me full in the face.

"I slept great." I gingerly raised my shoulder up. "It still hurts but I'll tell you this, it's nothing like it was yesterday. I'd say it's at least 50% better and I think I'll be close to normal tomorrow."

"Praise the universe for that!" She exclaimed as she removed my sling and helped me out of my nightgown. "Your nanny system is a really good one, I'd say."

"Top notch, only the best for us Exchange students." I smiled at her. She helped me with my bra, then my jeans, although she shook her head at them. I sighed. "The leggings are over there."

"We don't wear clothes like this below our robes." She said for the umpteenth time since I arrived to live with her.

"I know. It's just, well, I'm more comfortable with jeans or leggings on, that's all." The Amorphan robes were diaphanous and floaty and see-through to a degree of discomfort for me, so I liked to be dressed underneath. I shrugged, then winced. "Oops. Not ready for that yet."

"Sit down now so I can put your shoes on for you."

"An injury like this sure makes you realize how much you depend on two arms," I remarked as I sat on the bed's edge. "Thanks for helping me, Matra. I really appreciate you."

She nodded, her head feathers waving side-to-side, a sign of pleasure, I'd learned.

"Oh, pixie poop!" I said without thinking. "I just remembered I'm supposed to go to Karantina's house tonight for a party."

She looked up as she slipped my shoe on my foot. "You cannot go. There's too much risk and I won't allow it." Her lipless mouth set in a tight line.

I heaved a sigh. I knew that look; my mom looked the same when her mind was made up about something, too. Some things were the same, no matter the species. "Yeah, you're right. I do want to go, of course, but I'll stay home, instead."

She stood. "Good. Now come to breakfast."

I followed her out the door and down the hall to reach the eating room. I climbed up onto my chair with its booster seat, and Simatrao snickered even as he gave me a hand up, as he always did. "I can't help it if you all are too tall, including the table. It's either this seat or my chin will be below the tabletop."

"We are not too tall." Simatrao intoned. "You are too short."

I barked a laugh. "Yeah, well, I've heard that most of my life." I scooped scrambled eggs onto my plate, grabbing a piece of toast to go with it. Everything on the table could be eaten with a spoon or a fork in deference to my injury.

"Thanks for the easy eating."

"I wanted to feed you," Simatrao grinned, "but Matra was afraid I'd poke out your eyes or something else important with the eating fork."

I wrinkled my nose at him in mock anger. "Yes, I think she's right to be scared, so I'm really glad she thought ahead to save my life." We all laughed, Simatrao waving his fork around in the air like a toy hovercar, making zooming noises.

Love for this family washed through me even as I felt the grief of never knowing my human older brother, Devon. He'd died on the starship, StarFinder, when my parents emigrated to New Eden while Mom was pregnant with me. The scientists aboard experimented on Devon and all the pregnant women on the ship without permission or forewarning and Devon died as a direct result.

It's also the reason I'm the only shapeshifter in all the known galaxies, an ability I didn't know I possessed until my own journey on the StarFinder. Now, I hoarded my secret with a tight grip for fear the scientists who'd killed my brother found out and took me for their own purposes.

"Jessi? Jessi, come back!"

"Uh, what? I'm sorry; I was lost in thought for a minute."

Datro said in a wry tone, "We could tell."

I made a face. "Sorry, I'm listening now. Did you ask me something?'

"Well," he said, "we have been in discussions with your Chief Bodyguard and the officials for the Exchange program. And–"

I interrupted. "Did they find out who was behind the attack? Why it happened? Who are they? Will they be back?"

His head feathers laid back a little as he shook his head. "No. The male who injured you died in custody."

My mouth fell open as my eyes widened. "Did they–tell me they didn't torture him to death. He didn't deserve that. I mean, yeah, he hurt me, but it wasn't on purpose or anything." I covered my mouth with a hand.

"No, he chose to die rather than talk."

"Chose to die?" I shook my head, not understanding. "You mean they gave him a choice?"

"No, child," Datro said in a gentle voice, "he chose to take his own life rather than answer questions. He asked for water and a Personal Legal Representative; when the guard stepped out to pass on the request, he swallowed poison. They couldn't save him."

Bile rose in my throat and I swallowed hard. "He died because of me? Why? What's so important he chose suicide?" I laid down my utensil, feeling sick to my stomach, putting my hand to my belly. "Who was he so afraid of, more than the law, I mean? Or what was he so scared of happening, he took his own life? Or what information did he have that was worth giving his life for?"

"He picked death, Jessi, not you and it's not because of you. He picked that path to go down when he agreed to his involvement." Datro looked at me with sadness in his eyes.

Matra pushed her chair back, rushing over to put her hand on my good shoulder, giving me a squeeze of reassurance. I gripped her hand for the reassurance. Simatrao patted me awkwardly from my other side.

I shook my head in denial. "Did he have family??"

Datro tilted his head to one side, head feathers slicking back. "No one knows, yet, who he is."

I furrowed my brow. "They don't? How can that happen? I thought there's a, you know, database or something?"

"There is." Matra spoke from behind me. "He's somehow not in it."

Datro said, "It is not supposed to be possible but, of course, money or power can make many supposedly impossible things happen." He fiddled with his knife. "There's not many on this world with the combination of power and money so it should be only a matter of time before the Officials figure out who and why."

"I..it feels like my fault. I mean, if I hadn't come to Amorpha, he wouldn't have wiped his existence from the records and he'd still be alive. Like, if I wasn't here, he wouldn't have taken the job. Right?" I frowned as I looked at Datro.

"No, Jessi. These types of Amorphans..." He sighed. "He would've found some other illegal job to do and probably would've died because of that. Some people want the criminal life and others are forced into it. We can't know which for him but," he pointed a finger at me, "It. Is. Not. Your. Fault."

"I hear what you're saying, I really do and I appreciate it. It's hard to accept, though, since I'm the one he tried to take and no one knows why." I gasped at a sudden thought. "What about my classmates? My Human ones, I mean? Are they okay? Did anyone try this with them?"

Datro swung his head back and forth. "I asked about that, in case it was a coordinated attack, and so far, they are fine."

"You're telling me the truth?"

"Yes." He looked at me in the eye with a grave look on his face.

His simple answer convinced me. *So, I'm the target, at least for now.* "Will they increase the guards with them now?"

"Yes, because we do not know more than we did earlier. There is no way to know if this is a bigger plan than just you or not. So, guarding increases for all five of you."

I breathed out in relief. "Well, that's good, anyway." I tilted my head up to smile at Matra as I dropped my hand. She smiled back, her feathers moving in a gentle wave, as she stepped closer to my back instead of away, keeping her hand on me. I appreciated her presence.

I pushed my plate of food away; I couldn't eat right now, not with my queasy stomach. "Will they be told why?"

"They are told the need for another guard to be assigned is due to rumors, that kind of thing. They will not be told about the abduction attempt on you. The officials want to keep their anxieties low and this occurrence kept quiet for safety reasons."

"Oh. Okay." I didn't think it the right thing to do but I didn't have a way to change it, not now, anyway. "So, what's next? I can go back to classes on Firstday, right? Today's what...Worship Day? So, there's Second Rest Day tomorrow and I'll be good to go in time for Firstday, then."

"Datro, can I tell her? Please?" At his father's nod, Simatrao turned to me, excitement radiating from him. "We get to go to the Kelvactian woods, all of us! I mean, I'm sorry you got hurt, of course, but in a way, it's good because we get to go camping. In the woods! Just us–well, and all the guards, too–but it's going to be so much fun!"

Blinking from surprise, I felt Matra patting my left shoulder and I looked at Datro. "What? Where? Why?" I felt like a journalist channeled questions through me but those words spouted from me in my bewilderment. "What's a Kelvactian woods?"

Datro held a hand up. "This is what we wanted to tell you before we got diverted into the bad information. Because you're injured," he pointed at me, "and yes, we know you heal fast. But no one's completely recovered from an injury like that in two days, so the officials and us," he swept a hand to include Matra and Simatrao and me, "decided going to a secret remote place for a week would be a good idea. Capturing you from the middle of a remote, wild, wooded area with a dozen guards around will be much more difficult." He smiled. "And we'll have a family vacation at the same time. Matra and I both will have paid time off." He raised his eyebrow ridges. "You'll get to experience more of our wonderful world and be safe from danger while they investigate deeper into the attack."

My mouth dropped open somewhere in the middle of all that in complete astonishment. "The woods? In the middle of nowhere?"

"The Kelvactian woods, to be precise, but yes, I suppose the definition of the area would be 'the middle of nowhere'."

CAN PRACTICE BETTER!

Huh? Oh! Yes! We can try out our DNA cache for real, not confined to my small bedroom, so we can really learn what each species is like. We hoped for an opportunity like this!

WITH BAD OFTEN COMES GOOD.

When did you get so philosophical, Socrates?

PHBBT.

"Middle of nowhere. Hmm." I nodded, flashing a grin at Datro, feeling cheerful for the first time since the meal began. "You know, that actually sounds surprisingly good to me. Let the dust settle, let the investigators do their job so we all come back to peace. I can go back to classes without a lot of fuss and it'll be safe for—wait a minute, what about my tests?"

I rubbed my nose, then my mouth. "I can't skip those; I need high marks in these classes to get into medical school."

Matra spoke over my shoulder, still behind me. "You will be granted special testing time when we return from our trip to the wilderness. It is arranged already with your professors." She chuckled. "Also, just because we are taking an unexpected trip out of the city doesn't mean you, and I mean both of you, get to skip your studies. Yes, I mean you, Simatrao." She thumped the side of his head. "We are taking your class work with us so you can keep up with class knowledge."

Simatrao groaned and I made a face, but truth be told, excitement started to build inside me at the thought of going somewhere so different and isolated. So what if I had to spend a few hours each day with textbooks? Not like there'd be a lot else to do out in the middle of nothing but trees.

"At least I can keep up, then, with my classmates. Will there be computer connections out there? I could sit in on my classes in a virtual way." I remarked. "Are we taking a tent or are we sleeping under the stars, I hope not?" I'd had enough of that type of camping when I was a child when my human Dad drug me out to the woods way more often than I thought reasonable. My mom wrung her hands every time we left, camping gear in the back of the vehicle, telling Dad, "You be careful out there! You bring her back in one piece, no injuries, no traumas!" She'd never come with us, saying her idea of camping was a four-star hotel, and made sure she was on call at the hospital when there was any planned camping trip. Ultimately, Dad and I would have a great time out in the woods, just the two of us. He taught me a lot about survival skills, starting fires with a flint, gutting a fish and other rugged stuff and I smiled at the memories.

"No tent or star sleeps!" Matra exclaimed. "We're going to a cabin with all the amenities—except computer connection." At Simatrao's groan, she thumped his head again, then smoothed his head feathers. "We can be disconnected without ill effect, my son. It'll be good for you to do plus it's for security reasons; can't have anyone tracking our location. It's a good thing we're not going to truly camp." She made a huffing sound. "As if I'd sleep in a tent or under the stars. What a silly idea."

CHAPTER FIVE

An hour later, standing with our suitcases inside the house door, we waited for our transport vehicle to arrive. I still felt unsettled from hearing about the male's suicide but also excitement at going someplace new, out of the city, bubbled up and I had to smile at the thought. Extra guards milled around in the yard and curious neighbors came out to see if they could join our party.

"Hey! Where's Myometo and Zaleander?" I didn't see them anywhere in the crowd.

"They'll come later, after they heal."

"Heal from what? I didn't know they were hurt, also."

"What happens to you also happens to them. It is their punishment for not protecting you better."

I whirled to face Matra. "*What?* Tell me they didn't have their shoulder dislocated on purpose!"

She shrugged. "It is our way. It's their penance and must be accepted. They'll recover. When they are healthy again, they'll return to their duties as better bodyguards." She glanced at me, then back out the front window. "Do not think of it, Jessi."

"It's not right! You're telling me, that, for instance, if I died while they were guarding me, they'd be killed?" I clenched my hands.

"Yes." Matra said in a matter-of-fact voice. "It's our law from millennia ago and is as appropriate today as it was back then. You, and your classmates, are very precious to Amorpha and you must be kept safe by the best protectors possible." She looked at me with a questioning look on her face. "Why are you upset about this? It is our law, and it's effective. For instance, when I was young and looking after my younger brother, if he got hurt, then I received the same, just like I told you. It made me very diligent about my care-taking."

Times like this shocked me back into awareness of the aliens I lived among. Their ways are not Human ways and I'd become so used to being here, I'd think of me as one of them, until something like this jarred me out of complacency.

"Well," I said, "It's not right. We Humans don't do things this way; we suit punishment to the deed and not everything is someone's fault. Like, Myometo and Zaleander didn't know someone would try to grab me like that, so they shouldn't be hurt because I was. It wasn't their fault."

"It is their job to protect you from all things. Their diligence was less than stellar or they would've prevented it. They'll be better guards when they return."

I opened my mouth to argue some more, anger curling in my stomach, fighting with queasiness over imagining their arm being pulled out of its socket, but our vehicle dropped to the pavement in front of the house. Guilt at being the cause of my guards' injuries settled in beside my anger, but I knew I couldn't change what had happened and maybe I couldn't change their law. I would try but it had to be a different time.

Larenteno opened the door, holding up a hand to stop us from swarming out as a group. "One person at a time, please." He nodded to Datro. "We will start with Datro Lariendo." I peeked around Larenteno to see two rows of uniformed males, all holding blasters in their hands, flanking our walk to the vehicle.

Wow. They're really not taking any chances.

AS THEY SHOULDN'T. HMPH.

My hair's still miffed at my injury, even though when I shapeshift, all my joints dislocate, rearrange, dissolve to be reshaped, and oh, I don't know what all goes on, actually. I'm in too much pain to pay attention to how I get reshaped. It's way more agonizing than having my arm pulled out of its socket, to tell the truth. The difference is, I only have to endure shifting for a minute or less while a shoulder injury takes days or weeks to recover.

Datro made it safely out of the vehicle and Larenteno gestured Matra out next. *Huh. I guess if they make it there safely, we'll be okay. I wonder if they're taking them out first to make sure.*

MAKES SENSE.

"Are they taking Datro and Matra first to be sure it's safe?" Simatrao whispered to me. "Looks that way to me." He lifted his hand to wave back at Matra, who smiled our way.

"Yeah, I guess so." I whispered back. "Question is, who do they take next? You because you're younger? Or me because I'm more valuable?" I grinned.

"Hey!" He protested but couldn't retaliate because Larenteno pulled him out the door next and quick walked him to where Matra and Datro waited in the air van.

I called after him, "I guess the treasured one comes last!"

He made a face at me over his shoulder just before Larenteno shoved him through the open door before running back to where I waited. The guards, who were all facing outward, turned to position themselves so some faced in, some out, and some sideways. They tightened up, shoulder to shoulder, while Larenteno opened something like an umbrella, beckoning me out of the front door. I stepped out and he hustled me down the walk to the waiting transport.

Matra said. "Here, come sit by me." She patted the seat next to her and I plopped into the space.

"Wow." I said, looking around, seeing several vid screens, a rack of headphones to plug into it, a small refrigerator tucked under the seat across from me, and enough room for maybe five more people. It looked like a toilet room was snugged into a corner "This is pretty nice and comfy seats. This isn't a hovercar, is it?"

"No, it's a shuttle van and it'll take us all the way to our cabin. Might as well get comfortable, it'll be hours before we get there."

"Really? It's that far away?"

Simatrao answered. "Oh, yes! It's a long way there; I looked at the map, like two thousand miles or something. It's been explored, I guess, that's why it has a name and such, and they have cabins for rent. It's a popular place when it's Vacation Time." I could hear the capital letters. "And we get to go there during the off-season! No one else around so we can explore and have fun and maybe even sleep under the trees one night! Right, Datro?"

I chuckled. "I tell you what, little brother, you and Datro can sleep outside; I think I'll stay in the cabin with Matra and a comfortable, no-bugs-allowed bed."

He turned big eyes toward me. "Oh, please?" he said in a wheedling voice. "It'll be fun and Datro will be there."

"And the guards, no doubt." I shook my head. "Sorry, my brother, I prefer to sleep inside."

Datro said, "Simatrao, while I'd like to persuade her to stay outside with you and me, it won't be allowed for any of us." He patted Simatrao's knee as he saw his crestfallen look. "There are wild animals in the forest, maybe drones sent out after us so they won't take any chances at all, since we'll be the only people there for miles around."

Matra sniffed. "You already know I won't sleep outside. I'm glad to have a daughter to agree with me." She smiled at me. "Now, look around. There's the waste room and it has a modification for you, Jessi. The refrigerator is under here," she tapped the door, "with drinks and snacks. As you can see, there are several vid screens so we don't all have to watch the same program. You can move to a different chair if you want. However, we always need to be harnessed in, except for using the toilet and changing seats."

Datro said, "Jessi, if you want to move to a window seat to look out, do it now before we take off. Same for you, Simatrao."

We looked at each other and nodded. I moved to a seat on the pilot's side so my sore shoulder would be away from the side of the craft as my brother moved to the opposite side. Matra buckled my safety harness for me since I still wore the sling. I really thought I wouldn't need it by now, since I have fantastic recuperative abilities, but my joint still felt better in it. I settled back to check my view out the window, Matra placing a pillow under my right elbow for comfort as we heard Datro speak into his PerPad. "We're settled."

The door opened and four guards entered the shuttle, each taking a chair in the corners of the seating area. They were familiar faces; we each lifted a hand in greeting as they buckled in. Something was different about them today and I looked more closely. They held blasters in their hands, not safely holstered like usual, and a cold chill whispered down my spine.

"Zarilayo?" When he looked at me, I continued. "What's the word? Any answers about what happened? Do you know who the male is yet?" I pointed at his blaster. "Is there something we should know before we take off?"

He looked at me with a steady gaze. "You all are safe." He swept his look around to include my entire family. "That is what you need to know." He looked at something on his PerPad, ignoring the rest of my questions.

Datro said in a quiet tone, "Jessi, they will tell us if there's anything more to know. Now, settle back and enjoy the trip."

I watched the ground recede below us as we gained altitude. The view of the city from up high was enthralling with the geometry of the lay-out, what was hidden in people's back yards, and all the greenery. I picked out my university, amazed again at how much ground it covered, and watched as the homes shrank into a series of doll houses, then became covered with clouds. *So much for my view.*

Turning away from the window, I looked to see what everyone else was doing. Simatrao was playing a game on his PerPad, Datro napped, his head tilted to one side on a pillow, and Matra watched the vid screen across from her. The guards sat, relaxed, in their chairs, each holding their Perpad in front of them. I liked being on my Personal Pad, too, but my shoulder ached, and I didn't want to push it too far too soon.

Our pilot's voice came over the speaker. "We have gained altitude and you can move around back there if you need to. Do not stay standing and always wear your safety harness while seated. There might be bumps in the air so be cautious moving around."

Datro startled awake at the sudden voice intrusion, but fell back asleep, judging from his head lolling again on the pillow. Matra lifted one side of her headphone, saying, "Jessi, are you all right? Do you need something?"

I nodded. "I'm going to change seats so I can watch a movie."

"Of course; let me pause this and I'll help you."

"Oh, no, that's okay, Matra. No need. Larenteno can help me buckle back in, right, Larenteno?" He had the grace to nod.

She hesitated, then acquiesced. I smiled at her as I unbuckled using my left hand and moved to a chair with a vid screen. Larenteno came over to help me with the harness and as he bent forward, I whispered to him, "Now tell me the truth. Is there any more information? I need to know; after all, it's me they came after. I need to know why."

He gave me a long look as he fumbled with the buckler. "There is little information to give, Madam. The male who died was hired, we know that, but we do not–yet–know by whom or for what purpose. He was paid in cash; we found large denomination bills in his uniform," and he named an astounding figure, "but we don't know much else. We have run all the biometrics on his body but his identifying information has been completely wiped." He shook his head, then looked at me with a tiny smile. "This is a classified trip in case you wondered. No one knows where we are headed."

"Yeah, I figured as much." I raised my eyebrows. "Someone has highly placed friends or bosses, I suppose, with lots of power and money, to be able to completely wipe a person from all data bases. Are you looking for people like that?" Then I grimaced. "What about our teachers? Someone needs to tell them we'll be gone, since Simatrao and I are both missing a week of classes."

"The teachers were told there's a family emergency, requiring a week away."

"Are Myometo and Zaleander along for this trip? I haven't seen them since that day."

"They are not yet healed but will join us, perhaps later in the week."

My jaw clenched. "It's true, then? Their shoulders were dislocated because I was hurt?"

He gave me a puzzled look, eye ridges pulling together. "Yes, of course. How else could it be?"

"That's not *right*. It wasn't their fault."

"It is the right thing under our law and we all know this. It is part of the job, which we accept." He tugged on my harness until it was snug. "If you will excuse me, I must return to my seat."

They're aliens. I need to remember that. Their laws and ideals are not mine. It's ingrained in their society, so I have to find a way to live with it. Thinking about living with such a barbaric thing didn't make it any easier to accept. I'd have to make sure I didn't get hurt again, that's all. Unless I became their Zatro, I couldn't change the ancient law, and perhaps, not even then, since a Zatro only controlled one city. I realized then I didn't know if they had a council of Zatros who made universal laws.

I'd better watch a movie, maybe that'll distract me.

I flicked through the menu, finally settling on a comedy imported from my world. Placing the headphones on one-handed was a minor challenge but I settled them into place, snuggling into the soft upholstered seat, placing my injured arm on the pillow on the arm rest. *Well, poopie-dooples. Wish I'd brought some snacks with me. Yeah, I don't want to get up again.*

My hair blew a raspberry. PHBTTTT.

What? Like you can eat crunchy stuff, Murgatroyd? I puffed out a small annoyed sound. Since I couldn't find a good name for my hair, I'd decided to go with ridiculous ones for a while.

LIVE VICARIOUSLY.

Startled by the comment, I chortled out loud and the guards looked over at me as did Matra, with identical puzzled looks on their faces. I waved my good hand in the air. "Funny movie."

Matra's mouth lifted upwards. "I'm happy you found something to help you laugh. How about snacks, shall I bring you some?"

Simatrao's hand shot into the air. "I'll take some, Matra!" When she looked his way, he tacked on a hasty, "Please?"

"Me, too, Matra. Please?" I grinned.

She unbuckled, grabbing an armful of tasty treats before standing to bring them to us. She brought me a drink, also, the fizzy kind she knows I like, and I thanked her profusely.

Ok, get prepared to live a little. I smirked as I snapped open a bag of deep-fried crunchy leaves with the salt-and-vinegar flavor I loved.

THAT'S MORE LIKE IT.

Several hours passed by with minor turbulence, a few visits to the bathroom and two movies watched and one nap taken. I stretched my left arm over my head, restless, wanting to move around more than just to the cramped toilet room and back.

"Are we there yet?" I asked, almost whining the words. An instant memory flashed in my head of asking the same thing, over and over, as a child on a trip, Mom and Dad laughing a little as they answered the same thing every time. "We're almost there, little one, it's over the next hill." Only the next hill never seemed to quite arrive until, suddenly, we were at our destination.

Larenteno answered. "Yes, Madam Jessi, we will touch down in thirty minutes. If you're interested, you can move back to the window to watch the scenery below; we'll be dropping our altitude in fifteen minutes."

"Thanks. I'll do that." I unbuckled, decided one last trip to the toilet was a good idea, and when I came out, I returned to my original window seat as did Simatrao. Impatient to see something other than clouds, I tapped my fingers on my knee in a rhythm, my leg jiggling up and down a little.

"Are you anxious?" Datro asked. He'd slept almost the entire trip and I started, not expecting to hear his voice yet.

"Uh. Yeah, I guess, maybe a little." I drew in a breath to calm myself, stopping my foot from jittering and fingers from tapping. "I also want to see something besides clouds outside."

The engine started easing back on the throttle, starting our descent, and the clouds thinned until a large expanse of green could be seen. Simatrao and I exclaimed at the same time, "Look, there it is!" I sat forward as if I could see better that way, and Simatrao did the same thing.

Our pilot announced, "We have begun our landing sequence; please remain in your seat with the harness on and we'll be on the ground in a jiffy." Homesickness washed through me at the words; my Dad pilots shuttles as his job and I'd often gone with him on trips to one of the moons and back when the load was light. He said almost the same words, only in English.

I watched the trees, at first a huge mass of intermixed greens, become more distinct, separating into several types, like pines mixed with oaks and other trees I couldn't name. A large clearing abruptly appeared and, in the center, stood a two-story majestic looking house. "Ha. You all might call that a cabin. I call it a mansion."

CHAPTER SIX

Settled into our rooms, mine with the modified toilet for Humans, we gathered again for a full meal. Lunch had been snacks so I was more than ready for something cooked. Turns out one of our guards, Farayeno, loved to cook and made a delicious meal for everyone. Afterward, we sat in the rocking chairs on the porch to watch the sun go down.

I drowsed in my chair, relaxed and ready for bed but I didn't want to move. Sitting here with my exchanged family both delighted me and helped to fill the chasm caused by unexpected homesickness. Comfortable in my chair, I listened to Matra and Datro murmur to each other, laughing now and then, and even Simatrao stayed quiet, watching the tree line for wild beasts to come by.

That would be totally cool if something wandered out into the clearing for us to see. As long as it's like a deer or a hopper, that is, something cuddly without big teeth.

YES. NEED DNA.

Sarah, don't we have enough?

NO, GERTIE.

I snorted, a soft sound in the dusk. My hair had a fixation on gathering DNA from anything alive. *How about a tree? Or the grass? They're alive.*

NOT THE SAME. YOU KNOW THAT. Said with huffiness.

Just teasing. By the way, I'm too tired to 'play' tonight plus too many people around for true privacy.

AGREED. This time, disappointment came through. MAYBE ALONE IN WOODS TOMORROW? Hope in the words.

As if!

HMPH.

The last light of the day disappeared, leaving a sky full of wonder, with millions of twinkles and occasional last-minute chirps of birds. Darkness settled over us, so complete, I could hardly see my own hand, much less the guards patrolling the edges of the clearing. A rocking chair to my right creaked and Datro's voice said, "I'm going to bed. How about all of you?"

Simatrao protested. "Aw, Datro, I want to stay up and play some games."

Matra answered him. "We have plenty of time for that tomorrow and the rest of the week. Off to bed with you. Now."

"I'm all for bed, myself." I yawned out the words. As soon as my teeth were brushed, I sank into bed, pulling the covers around my neck, as sleep closed around me in a warm embrace.

I looked around, seeing thick tree trunks, a leafy canopy high overhead, azure blue sky peeking through here and there, tangled underbrush with bushes and wildflowers blooming erratically in a wild explosion of colors. "Where am I?'

'You are in a pocket of reality.'

'Who's speaking?' I gazed around me. 'Where are you?'

'I am speaking. I am within you and around you. I am the Universe.'

I rolled my eyes. 'Yeah, right.'

'I tell the truth.' Slight huffiness in the tone of the imaginary voice.

I rolled my eyes again. 'Of course you do.' I shook my head a tiny bit. 'I'm dreaming.'

'Not quite a dream, Jessi. You live in the Universe and the Universe lives within you and the dream realm is part of the Universe. When you take a breath, you pull the Universe in and you breathe out a measure of Universe.'

'How very poetic.' I remarked.

'Breathe in the good and breathe out the bad. Your body knows how to do it.'

'Then why are you instructing me if I already know how?'

'It is something you must remember.' Aggravation laced the imaginary voice. 'Everything is connected throughout the Universe. Different shapes, different colors,

different societies and species all with varying beliefs, but it is all one Universe and there is no end.'

'Like a circle.' I commented as I turned slowly around. The scenery didn't change and I didn't know how I'd gotten there, so I didn't know how to leave.

'Except a circle has an outer edge and an inner edge. The Universe is infinite in all directions, all dimensions, all times, all ways possible and impossible.'

'That is difficult to fathom, having a finite mind.'

'Yes. A limited mind cannot understand, not until you enter other layers of being. You can, however, remember to breathe in the Universe and breathe out the unwanted. Practice your forms but, above all, remember to breathe in the Universe always.'

I made a face. 'Yeah, yeah, okay, I get it. It's a no-brainer; I have to take in air so I'll breathe in the Universe. From what you're saying, that's what we all do anyway.'

'You more than most.'

'The Akrion particle inside me? Is that what you mean?' A flash of intuition helped ask the question as I reached out to touch a tree trunk, my hand going through it. 'What is this place? That tree looks solid and yet it isn't.' I wrinkled my nose as I pulled my hand back and passed it through another tree, fascinated to see how swirls, sparkles and colors followed the movement of my hand. I fluttered my hand around, happy from the light show following my movement.

The voice sighed. 'Yes, the Akrion. It is beyond special and granted to very, very few who can assimilate it.'

'It killed my brother.' I remarked.

'It was his time.'

'His time? He was a child! How can you say it was his time? He never had a chance at a full life!' I felt unutterable sadness pour over me and tears leaked from my eyes. I didn't bother to wipe them away as my emotional reaction made me feel weak and listless.

'His purpose was at an end; he was the vessel needed to get the Akrion into you. He has passed on to a better level of being.' The voice sounded nonchalant, irking me. 'It is not your fault.'

'It was my fault. I took it from him. And he died!' I shook my head, denying the voice. 'I'm not exceptional. I don't deserve it.'

'You are special, my child, and you are the chosen vessel. Take care. I cannot protect you from everything but I tell you this: you carry the Universe within you.'

I bounced out of bed the next morning, totally refreshed in spite of a lingering feeling of something weird in my dreams. I shook it off as I headed downstairs in search of breakfast. "That fresh air sure gives me an appetite," I said, as I entered the kitchen to find a large array of breads, sweet pastries, and scrambled eggs hot on the stove. My stomach growled in anticipation and I settled at the table with a full plate. I sucked in a large breath of air, feeling my lungs expand with a need I didn't understand, holding the air in for a few seconds, then blowing it out, puzzled at the urge to do so.

CHAPTER SEVEN

We spent the day exploring the grounds and the trees, penetrating the gloom under the branches as far as our guards allowed. We laughed and chased each other, threw handfuls of leaves in the air and down neckbands–if I could catch someone to do so–and exclaimed when finding a walking path. There were few of those, perhaps four that we discovered, but Matra declared following the paths would wait for tomorrow or the day after. After playing all morning, burning off our excitement and energy, we returned to the cabin for lunch and study time for my brother and me.

He sat at one end of the large table in the eating area, his PerPad in front of him, snacks and drinks stacked to his left. The solid wood table was centered in the middle of the spacious room, windows spanning the expanse on three sides of the area, promising to be very distracting. Large, tall wooden chairs marched down each side of the table, brightly colored cushions on each seat. The lighting was superb with all the windows and a lot of inset overhead lights.

No curtains adorned the windows during the day, but at night, shutters lowered over the reinforced panes and locked into place. I watched guards moving around outdoors, carrying rifles, looking at ease. Matra was in the cooking room, putting together snacks and a drink for me and Datro had stepped outside, talking to one of the male guards. I wondered for the umpteenth time why there were no female guards. I'd asked several times but all I would get was a strange, puzzled look back. Apparently, there was no need to explain as it was quite obvious–to them–only males were guards.

I chose a chair in the main room with a large side table, mainly so I wouldn't have to use a booster seat on the tall chairs at the oversized table. Well, okay, it's only oversized for me. I needed pillows behind me on the chair to be comfortable and a booster seat with my legs dangling and I'd had enough of that, especially with a sore shoulder.

I tested my shoulder, rolling it around while Matra wasn't looking. The deep soreness had changed to a lighter ache and the looseness in the joint was gone. Matra, with her mother instincts, said, "Jessi? How is the shoulder? Is it hurting now?"

"Actually, it feels much better. The soreness has gone down by at least 75% and it's not loose in the socket anymore. I really want to get out of this sling."

She strolled over to my position and laid a soft hand on my shoulder joint. "Move the joint to your tolerance."

I schooled my face to keep any potential cringes of pain off it and slowly went forward, then backwards with the shoulder. To my delight, although tender, it felt almost normal. A big smile spread across my face.

"Now up, then down."

I shrugged, as requested.

"Hmm," she said, tapping her lipless mouth with a finger. "Not today but," she smiled, "looks like tomorrow."

I nodded with enthusiasm. "I agree!"

She pushed my food stash within easy reach of my left hand, patting me on the head and left me to my studies. Simatrao said, "Hey, if I run out of food, I'll come get some of yours."

"Ha. Only if you don't mind losing fingers."

Smirking at me, he waggled his hand, folding his first finger down as if missing, making me chuckle. The Amorphans are unique in that way since they can actually change their hands and feet to other shapes for whatever purpose they needed. Studies showed it to be an evolutionary thing for survival; they could also alter their sexual organs if needed. It took time, effort, and concentration for them. Also, like some Earth lizards I'd read about once, if they lost a digit, it eventually regrows. Amorphans were as close as anything came to being a shapeshifter in the Universe but they couldn't change into other forms and they couldn't change fast.

Unlike me, who can change shapes, following the DNA pattern of whatever species I wanted to be and I've been practicing on reducing my change time to less than a minute. It leaves me breathless for a bit afterward, but we'd made a lot of progress.

My hair and the Akrion particle were a large part of being able to do this, the bulk of my hair needed to add height and weight for larger forms. I only discovered this talent while on the ship ride here so I had a lot of learning to do and there are no teachers for this.

We didn't have internet connection out here but our lessons were pre-recorded for this outing. I fiddled with my PerPad, wishing, again, I could text my co-exchange students but it was strictly forbidden and our devices disabled from doing so. Not being a techie, I didn't know how they could exclude just us five from contacting each other, but it was true. Ever since arriving on Amorpha and being separated from each other to our own city, Amorphan host family and University, I'd tried and tried to contact Zoe through mind-whispering. I failed each and every night at the agreed-upon time, remorseful at not being able to connect with her.

We were frenemies, mostly, but I had saved her life on the StarFinder on our trip here by giving her my blood. A surprising connection developed between us as a result; I would never have guessed that could happen in a gajillion years. Along with that, an ability to mind whisper awakened with extraordinarily little time to teach her how to use her new mental telepathy safely before we disembarked the ship. Perhaps my hasty lesson on shielding her mind resulted in her keeping her mind too tightly shuttered for me to get through.

Or—more likely—we were just too far apart from each other for brain waves to travel. I'm new at the mind whispering game, too, actually, but at least I'd had Si'neada to teach me the basics and some of the more advanced stuff in our time on the starship. There's a lot I didn't yet know about it, like how distance factored in, but it seemed reasonable being really far apart would be a major detriment.

Another possibility is she'd reverted to her normal self, the one who snubbed me or bullied me whenever and however she could. Being separated for months could mean she'd forgotten my intervention or she didn't want to be reminded of how the scientist Imurian had used her for experiments and then wiped her memory of the events. Well, except the last one, because I rescued her before she was given the med to destroy her recollection of the evening.

I dragged my thoughts back—again—to my studies of Amorphan physiology, a class I really needed, especially to be the first ever interspecies physician. I backed the vid up until I found where my mind had wandered away so I could start memorizing the nervous system.

The next morning, I took off my sling with glee, reveling in the freedom of having my right arm back in use. A little stiffness and a tiny bit of soreness remained but that would stay my secret. I stretched through all the ranges of motion, feeling satisfaction at being able to use it in a normal manner.

I whistled an airy tune as I entered the kitchen, joining three guards and my family. They all stopped in their tracks to stare at me, frozen in place from whatever they were doing, like a painting. A cup half-way to the mouth, a fork with food stopped in mid-air, water splashing out of an over-full cup. I wrinkled my brow. "What? Do I have something crawling on my hair?" As if my hair would allow a hitchhiker.

"That." Matra said. "That sound." She spread her hands apart. "What is that?"

My mouth opened a little in surprise. "You mean whistling?"

Simatrao said, "Is that what it's called? I've never heard anything like that, have you, Datro?"

"Judging by your reactions, I'd say no one has heard whistling before." I said in a wry voice.

Datro tried out the word. "W-w-w-ist'lin."

"Close enough. There's no word in Amorphan for this."

"Do it again!" Simatrao begged. "Show me how! Please?"

I shrugged, pleased my shoulder barely noticed the motion. "Well, first you have to purse your lips, or mouth, then your tongue has to narrow the opening and you blow over it." I demonstrated the sound. I'm not the best whistler in the world but I can carry a tune, so I whistled a little bit of an Amorphan song, blushing when they all applauded.

Simatrao tried and I did my best to coach him, but their anatomy didn't seem compatible with whistling, although we had fun trying. Maybe because their mouths didn't have lips like ours, or I couldn't show him how I held my tongue, or whatever, but it was good for laughs. No one even noticed I didn't wear my sling between eating, drinking, laughing and trying to produce a whistle.

I snapped my fingers and again, everyone froze in place, looking at me with wide eyes. I gazed around, "Don't tell me you've never heard someone snapping their fingers before, either."

They shook their heads no in unison. I grinned. "Well, not sure if you all can do this one, either, because it might require bones for enough pressure." I held up my right hand and demonstrated the move. They all tried this one. They could produce a soft snap but not the full-bodied one I could make, so I'd say bones made the difference.

Matra exclaimed as laughter died down, "Your sling! I knew something was different about you this morning, besides the wistlin and snapping."

I beamed at her. "Yup, all healed, doing fine, feels so good to be out of the sling."

Simatrao bounded out of his chair after shoving the last of his food into his mouth. "Let's go explore one of the paths." He grabbed me by my right hand to pull me out the door.

Matra gasped. "Simatrao, let go of her arm right this instance!" I guessed she saw my wince when he put a sudden tug on the joint.

Shame-faced, he dropped my arm. "Sorry. Sorry! I wasn't thinking; I won't do it again."

Laughing, I said, "I want to explore the paths, I do, but can I at least get some food first? Just because you ate, doesn't mean I'm not hungry." I patted my shoulder. "Don't worry, it's just fine, took me by surprise, is all."

"Oh." He said, with an abashed look. "Sorry. Sure, have some breakfast."

After eating enough to satisfy my stomach, we stepped outside. Two of the guards from the kitchen said they'd go with us, so Simatrao and I discussed which path to start with. Since I didn't really care, I let him win the choice after a game of "Rock, paper, scissors." I had to explain what paper was first. He caught onto the game with enthusiasm and said he'd make all his choices that way from now on. At least it was something any Amorphan could do, unlike whistling or snapping.

As we moved toward the trees and our designated trail, two more guards walked over to join us. Two would go ahead of us and two behind, but we could take all the time we wanted. Matra and Datro had declined today's jaunt in the woods, Matra explaining she was still itching from yesterday's bites. Good thing for me the bugs preferred Amorphans and not Humans.

We stepped into the shadowed gloom under the trees. Overhead, branches crisscrossed the sky, leaves of all varieties and colors rustling in the soft breeze, and the slight smell of pine sap pleasant to my nose. "Funny how many trees here are so much like the ones on New Eden, and, I'm told, on Old Earth."

"Really?" Simatrao said. "I'd think the trees there would be all alien and, you know, different. Like they can walk or talk or something or do magic." He fluttered his hands in the air, imitating tree branches. I think.

I nodded. "Yup, you'd think so, but maybe there's only so many ways the Universe can make trees." I swiveled my head. "Like that one there," I pointed, "looks something like an oak and that one is a lot like a pine tree we have at home. Those over there, well, I have no idea what they are so those are alien to me." I fist bumped Simatrao's shoulder. "Maybe they'll get up and walk away for us."

"Yeah, that would be chill if they did."

We continued walking the path, examining shrubs, tree bark, watched insects scuttle around on the forest floor, and listening to bird calls. I tried to imitate some of them but even the guards laughed at my attempts, while remaining attentive to our surroundings. I knew Simatrao hoped to see wildlife but doubted we would, not with all the noise we made as we strode along.

About the time my bladder started to get my attention, the pathway came to the edge of a clearing. "Oh." I said. "It goes in a loop." The cabin was directly ahead of us although we were coming out on the west side. "Good to know we won't get lost with that path, anyway. I wonder if the other trails we found loop around, also?"

Simatrao said, "I thought we'd get to go deeper into the woods, not come right back to here. And I really wanted to see a forest beast." He pouted.

I patted his back. "Brother, to see a wild beast, we'd have to be much quieter than we were today. We could be heard for, like, two miles, because we made quite a racket while walking." I smiled at him. "Maybe next time, we'll be sneaky so they don't hear us and we'll get to see something bigger than a beetle."

His expression brightened as he gave me an 'okay' sign and a cheeky grin.

CHAPTER EIGHT

The next couple of days went by, slow and carefree, and we relaxed from the lack of danger. Mornings were spent playing outdoor games or taking the trails, afternoons Simatrao and I spent studying and the evenings were reserved for family games. Off-duty personnel joined us for those, laughing and joking as much as we did.

Midway through the nine-day week, the guards hid their yawns behind hands as they sauntered around the clearing on their patrols. When Simatrao and I wanted to go outdoors into the woods, they perked up and scrambled to volunteer to go with us as a welcome change from their routine. They wouldn't let us deviate from the paths nor forge our own way. Matra and Datro took turns strolling with us, educating us about different plants, trees, and birds. I treasured this time with them to remember in later years as a tranquil period in which we all bonded tighter as a family unit.

My Amorphan parents hadn't ever treated me as a foreigner or alien species, which I appreciated, and in turn, I treated them with the same respect and love I did my own biological parents. While I could change into an Amorphan body—and I did at night in utmost privacy to keep up the practice—looking like one is different than truly being one. This trip to nowhere really helped me live and breathe as a different species, even in my Human shape, almost forgetting my natural parents were Human.

Fifthday, halfway through the Amorphan nine-day week with four more weekdays to Firstday, dawned bright and cheerful. I woke early and got up to get some private time before others joined me. Although I enjoyed the heck out of this retreat, I felt antsy with the 24/7 companionship wearing on me a bit. I dressed in jeans today with a long-sleeved green pullover patterned with leaves for my top and sneakers to complete my outfit.

Leaving my robes in my room felt good; they were easy to wear but I didn't need to dress like an Amorphan out here in the wilderness. I felt a deep desire to dress like someone from my own world; I knew Matra and Datro understood that now and then, I just needed my own clothes. I slipped downstairs without noise, clutching my PerPad, grabbing food and a thermos of coffee with cream from the kitchen so I could go outside.

Settling into a rocker on the porch, I sipped coffee and ate my pastries. Too early for anyone to have cooked eggs and I didn't feel like doing it, so pastries were my choice. *Sheesh, I was fluffy before this trip. I'm happy my jeans still fit after all this rich eating.* I contemplated the sweet roll in my hand, thinking for a split second of placing it back on my plate, then stuffed it into my mouth instead, enjoying every bite.

Glad for my long sleeves because of the chilly morning air, a mist wreathed the ground near the trees. The guards looked blurry when they passed through it as they roamed the grounds. The gray sky lightened with each minute as the sun strove to climb into the sky and I imagined its rays as beams of light coming down to burn off the ground-hugging fog. Mesmerized by the monotones of the early morning and reluctant to move from my spot, an idle thought popped into my head.

The guards aren't spaced as evenly as they used to be. There's a gap now and then when no one is in sight. Guess they feel we're pretty safe here, too.

COULD EXPLORE WOODS. BY OURSELVES

Huh. We could, at that. I'm fidgety today, anyway, and need something different to do.

YES.

Acting on impulse, I stood, stretching both arms over my head, nodding to the guard strolling by. He stopped to look me over, decided I wasn't in danger, so he inclined his head to me in acknowledgement and started walking again. We were too far apart to speak but he could see my smile. Walking down the front steps, I stood in front of the quiet house, looking around, tucking my PerPad in my back pocket. I patted my specially made bra to be sure my forbidden gun stayed secure between my breasts, an absent-minded habit I needed to break. Anyone watching would think I checked to be sure I hadn't somehow lost the girls.

I've trained from childhood to use a weapon safely, my Dad made sure of that, so my Imurian trainer on the starship decided, because I'm so petite and already trained to use firearms, I needed a weapon for self-defense. It's our secret and against all the rules, even though it's keyed only to my DNA for use. No one on Amorpha knew I had it and I wasn't telling. I wore it all the time, tucking it under my pillow at night, just in case someone decided to go through my belongings when I wasn't around. This gun would get me sent back to New Eden pronto and all my plans for the future would die, just like that, if it was discovered, so I stayed super cautious about hiding it.

I saluted the next guard walking by, further out by the tree line, and he held up a hand in response. I moved at a slow pace toward the tree line, looking as casual as I could manage. I stopped to pluck a little flower from the ground, making it look like I wanted nothing more than gathering enough blooms for the table vase. Within several minutes, I'd meandered close enough to the trees to dash into them when the next absence of guards occurred and it was tough to be patient until the gap occurred. I grasped my small bouquet in my hand, now and then lifting it to my nose, scanning the ground for more blossoms.

NOW.

Without looking, trusting my hair, I melted into the forest, trying to make as little noise as possible. *Hope they didn't see me come in here.*

THEY DIDN'T. LISTEN. Said with confidence.

I held my breath to hear better but heard nothing more than a small breeze teasing the mist into tendrils around my ankles. *You're right, they don't know I came in here. Hopefully, they think I went back into the house with the flowers.* I grinned. *Let's explore somewhere not on the trail.*

A hank of hair pointed ahead and to the right. *As good a direction as any, I guess.* I moved into the brush, squinting into the low lighting, moving branches carefully out of my way, still in stealth mode. *We won't go too far, I think. Will have to come back when the family is up because they will notice I'm not there. I doubt we have much time but at least we have some.*

OKAY.

I doubted I'd see anything different than being on the trails, but it felt good to be out alone, doing what I wanted, at least for a short while. A bird cheeped ahead, sounding sleepy, as the gloom brightened a little with the rising of the sun; soon there'd be a chorus of bird songs as they woke up to face a new day. I gulped in a large lungful of fresh air, holding it for a second or two before releasing it, as had become my morning habit.

Maybe, if I stayed quiet enough, I'd see something like one the of the graceful deer-like animals or maybe something small and fluffy, like a hopper. Usually, my hair clamored for

DNA samples but unless it was a sentient species, collecting the DNA wasn't useful. Too much danger of losing myself and my ability to return to my own shape when becoming something that could only use instincts to survive.

Dad taught me from an early age how to move through the woods. New Eden, like Amorpha, wasn't fully settled, being early in the Rent-to-Own program for each planet. There were lots of unexplored areas on either world and I was comfortable being alone out here because of him. He had been very particular to make sure I could manage in the wild, if needed. The forest floor, still damp from the mist, meant I didn't have to test every step to avoid cracking a twig, giving away my location and, perhaps, drawing fire from a trigger-happy guard.

A few more sleepy bird calls started around me and I grinned. I succeeded at being stealthy if the birds didn't startle at my movements. Dad would be proud. I slipped from tree to tree, reawakening my rusty woodsy skills, although when damp leaves slapped me in the face, it was a reminder to be more watchful. I wiped my face, grimacing, hoping it wasn't something like the poison sumac on New Eden. If it were, I'd know soon enough.

HERE.

Huh?

CHANGE TIME!

It's all the warning I got as agony gripped me in its teeth, bones snapping and reforming, skin crawling, breathing coming in hitches. I didn't even know which DNA was being used but I'd find out in less than a minute. Practice time in my bedroom at night was all I'd had before today. Since I had to stay quiet in my room and couldn't really explore using my different aspects, we–my hair and I–worked hard on reducing change time and also incorporating whatever I wore into the changing.

It took quite a while to figure out how to break inanimate things like guns and clothes into molecular components to be added into my new shape. We had to experiment a lot and there were some rather amusing and sometimes terrifying results, like one time, the handle of my secret weapon became my nose.

Being the universe's only shape changer means there's no owner's manual and no instructors so it's all trial and error. There were times I wondered if I'd survive my own self-directed training but suspected the Akrion particle liked me so far and wouldn't allow my death just yet. I'd take reassurance wherever I could manufacture it.

I looked down to check out what I'd become and made a wry face. *Okay, a Chee:long'a. Well, four hands could be, well, handy.* I snickered even as a strand of hair stung my cheek in disapproval. *Oh, stop that.*

I stood about the same height as my Human form, still humanoid in shape. The biggest differences were the scaly skin, two sets of arms on each side with three-fingers and one thumb per hand and wrap-around eyes, giving me a 360 view of the forest. Switching to use the new form's instincts and brain could be a challenge plus keeping my own Human thoughts; it's like having a split personality. I guess, anyway.

Now the birds noticed me, and all sound stopped like someone sliced wires. I didn't move, letting them adapt to me, projecting non-threatening thoughts outward. Speaking of thoughts, I opened my internal mind shields, slowly, to check for sentient thoughts. So far, I hadn't ever connected with any Amorphan, wondering if none of them were capable of mind-to-mind communication. I listened with both ears and mind for a couple of minutes, imagining my mind going up and down frequencies.

Sounds resumed around me as creatures decided I wasn't a threat, insects scuttling under leaves and birds starting to call again. Turns out a Chee:long'a has superb hearing; I heard a small moth fanning its wings and other tiny sounds mixed with the larger noises of birds and small animals, brain busy sorting the sounds into categories.

Then I heard a high-pitched whine, barely there at first, but gaining in intensity as if something approached. My head turned instinctually to pinpoint the source of the annoying whine even as I shook my head to dislodge the sound, but it didn't go away.

What is that?

AIRCRAFT.

Oh, yeah, you're right. I didn't know one was scheduled to come today. Maybe we ran out of supplies or something. Or they're checking on us to be sure we're all right.

MAYBE. It sounded uneasy.

I shrugged. *Relax, Aloysius. Guess we'd better go back; no way the family would sleep through a shuttle landing and I don't want to be classified as missing.* Disappointment washed through me. *Didn't get to be a Chee:long'a for very long.*

After becoming Human again, I started back toward the clearing, the dental drill whine becoming a little more intense. I still practiced moving quietly through the forest, with careful foot placement and gently moving small branches out of my way, this time not letting them snap back at me, feeling pleased with my skills. The trees thinned a little as I approached the clearing just ahead. I could see the sky, surprised to see thunderheads piling up over head and heard the rumble of thunder.

STOP!

I froze in response to the urgency in the word, hearing a commotion ahead of my position. Shouting voices, was that anger or panic I heard? I couldn't understand the words because I wasn't close enough yet and I only had my human ears now. What was going on?

ZZZZZzzzzzzt. The sound sizzled through the air and I smelled burned ozone as my instincts screamed at me to duck. *BOOM!* My heart pounded as the air shivered around me from the force of what sounded like an explosion and I instinctually flinched away from the sound, crouching to avoid being a target. Thunder rolled, static electricity made some of my hair lift away from me. That lightning strike had been dangerously close.

EXPLOSION, NOT LIGHTNING.

You sure?

MOSTLY.

I had to get closer to see what had happened, to see if everyone was all right and determine what action to take. My heart hammered in my chest, my breathing so quick, I thought I might pass out from lack of oxygen. Making myself take slower, deeper breaths, I began creeping forward. Anxiety screamed at me to move, move, MOVE but I forced myself to stay slow, all my years of training reminding me that being careful meant staying alive. Being amongst the trees was not reassuring, however, since lightening could strike again and this time, choose a tree next to me. If it had been lightning.

The commotion and decibels increased the closer I came to the open area, thick smoke or fog in the clearing adding to the confusion. I smelled smoke and tasted ash on my tongue and panic threatened to overtake my emotions, and I barely managed to shove it aside. After all, as a future physician, I had to learn how to be calm in times of disaster and stress.

I stepped to the edge, hugging a tree for cover, peering around it to see an unimaginable tableau in front of me. Black, oily smoke roiled in the air, flames reaching hungrily upward as they ate at the cabin, my mouth dropping open in shock. What happened here? Did the fireplace catch on fire or the furnace explode? Did lightening hit the cabin and cause the fire? Only a minute or so had passed since I heard the strike; it was hard to believe the ravenous flames ahead of me could be that big already unless something fueled it. Or perhaps someone had already set a fire and the lightening was pure coincidence.

A shuttle like the one we arrived in sat at the opposite side of the opening from where I stood, door open, as did our own shuttle where it sat diagonal to me but adjacent to the new one. People ran around the area, shouting and gesturing, shooting at others with guns, a few people holding hoses directed at the flames, looking ineffectual against the immensity of the fire. *Where is my family? Why are they using blasters? Are they trying to create a firewall or a burn back area? I don't understand! Did all those guys come here in response to the fire? Oh, my Gods, I hope everyone in my family is safe on that shuttle!*

I tried to suck in a big breath but the air was so thick with smoke, I choked instead. I couldn't stand there any longer; I had to get out there to find out what happened and help put out the fire. I took a step forward–or tried to, anyway. Somehow, I was tied to the tree and I couldn't complete one step even though I did my best to do so. *What in the blazing fires of hell...?*

DANGER.

I know that! I need to be out there to help!

NO. The single word said with a firm Mom-style voice, brooking no arguments.

That's when I discovered a lot of my hair had wrapped itself around the nearest tree trunk to hold me in place. I opened my mouth to shout for someone to come get me and hair shoved into my mouth, acting as a gag. As soon as I thought about yanking the lengths of hair from the tree, more hair pinned my lower arms to my torso.

LET ME GO!

NO. MEGA DANGER. CANNOT ALLOW.

Untie me right now! I mean it.

NO. Implacable tone, laden with stubbornness and refusal to reconsider. I knew I'd lost this battle—for now.

Unbidden tears dripped down but I couldn't wipe them away, not with my hands bound to my side. Through the haze from the smoke, I couldn't tell who anyone was from where I stood. Heat batted at me; wind fueled from the monstrous blaze. Sparks showered over the area, setting small fires in the severely cut grass; chaos reigned in the clearing. Streaks of light from handheld blasters suggested fighting among the people out there and I still couldn't tell who was an enemy or who was a friend.

For all I knew, it could be mistaken identities fighting it out or it could be my bodyguards trying to keep everyone safe. Crap on a door handle, I wanted to scream from the frustration of not knowing any facts about the bedlam I witnessed but my hair held me mute and helpless.

A thunderous crash shook the ground as the roof fell in and people fighting the inferno dropped their hoses and ran for safety. The small blazes in the open area raced toward each other as if wanting to unite into their own conflagration and bodies dodged those flames as people dashed for one or the other shuttle. As soon as everyone was on board, the crafts lifted into the air, leaving me alone in the forest, tied to a tree with my own damned hair. My hair and I would have ugly words later.

The intense heat beat at me even from this distance, the fire roaring as if a beast, hungry for all it could consume. My hair gave up its tangled grip on the tree trunk, knowing I couldn't go forward against the blistering heat from the enormous bonfire ahead. I cried, shaking from the force of my sobs, my nose running and my eyes swelling to slits. If my family had been in that cabin...No. I couldn't think that, I couldn't bear the pain of them burning to death. I had to believe they were all on one of the shuttles, on their way to safety and treatment for smoke inhalation. My own throat felt raw, each breath raking over my throat; I had to get away from the smoke.

CHAPTER NINE

I moved into the brush behind me, stumbling, not caring where my feet went or who or what might hear me. Any animals would have already fled this area and I'd watched two shuttles fly away without me.

Alone. I'm completely alone in the woods and the only thing I have are the clothes I'm wearing and my gun. And my hair, but I wasn't speaking to it right now. I could've made one of those shuttles and been taken to safety, but my hair had bound me hand and foot with a gag and I was helpless against it. Anger burned through me and if I'd had clippers, I'd have shaved my head to the skin.

"How could you?" I screamed into the air, hands clenched, wanting to hit something. "We could be on that shuttle with our family right now if you hadn't kept me prisoner! You–you fracking ugly mass of curls! Don't you dare, *ever*, to do that again. Do you hear me? Never do that again!"

SAVED YOUR LIFE.

You don't know that! I could've made it to one of the shuttles. When they saw me coming, they would've helped me!

WHICH THEY? YOUR GUARDS OR THE OTHERS?

The guards, of course. Who were the others? Do you know? Cuz I sure couldn't see through all that smoke to recognize anyone.

NOT FRIENDS.

How do you know that? I bit out the words through the storm of rage still surging in me.

SHOOTING AT EACH OTHER. FRIENDS DON'T.

Okay, that was a fair point but damned if I was going to concede anything just yet. I stomped forward, breaking twigs under my feet, not caring who or what heard me. Replaying the scene in my head, I didn't see anything around me except for noticing when to dodge a tree or a bush. The smoke had been so thick and black and oily looking, I didn't have a clear look at anything from where I had been standing. The noise had been incredible, flames roaring like an angry herd of dinosaurs on a stampede, drowning out any other sounds. A wind whipped the fire high into the air, perhaps caused by the fire itself, with smoke churning and swirling, creeping along the ground, boiling up to obscure the shuttles and figures running around, with some of it escaping upward to be whisked away by the wind.

I stopped dead in my tracks. "I have to go back. I have to see if they came back for me and to see if I can figure out what happened." Pivoting in place, I started to make my way back to the clearing, already sick to my stomach at what I might find. I knew I'd poke through the remains of the cabin as soon as it cooled enough to do so; I had to know if there were any bodies in the wreckage. Besides that, I had nowhere else to go. I heaved a sigh and set out to follow my path of destruction back to the clearing.

I stopped at the tree line when I reached it, holding my hair in both hands to prevent it from roping me to a tree again. Yeah, still pissed about that.

SAVED YOUR LIFE. It actually made a 'hmph' sound.

You don't know that for sure. You might've condemned me to dying in the forest instead.

DID SAVE YOUR LIFE. CAN'T DIE IN FOREST. HAVE AT LEAST THREE SPECIES THAT CAN SURVIVE IN WOODS.

I blew out a breath, then realized how heavy the smoke smell was in the area. I drew up my shirt to cover my nose as a sort-of mask so I didn't choke on every breath. My eyes burned, not only from the crying I'd done but also from the acrid odor and the thick haze I peered through. The outlines of the remains of the cabin were out of focus because of the smoke; the grassy area separating the cabin from the trees was blackened and charred but no trees were on fire. Apparently, there had been enough of a clearing around the building to act as a very efficient firebreak. I had a sudden surge of gratefulness that I didn't have to run from a forest fire.

I pulled my PerPad out of my back pocket to check the time, shocked to see only an hour had passed since I first witnessed the fire. Frowning at the number on the screen, I checked for a signal, hoping against hope there would be one. Nope, of course not. I shoved it back in my pocket, then pulled it back out to turn it off. I could charge it with solar energy if needed but without any signal, there was no reason to keep it on, so might as well conserve my battery power.

Fatigue chewed at me and I sank to the ground. I was already covered in ash from earlier so what was a little more soot on my jeans? I felt something strike my head and I turned my face upward to realize it had started to rain. *Just what I need now is to get wet and cold with no way to get dry again. Can this day get any worse?*

YES.

I wasn't asking the peanut gallery, which is you, by the way. It was a rhetorical question. So don't be jinxing us. Wish I had something to collect the rainwater for drinking. Huh. Might as well wish for an air car to arrive and whisk me home again while I'm at it. I scooted back into the brush until I was more or less protected from the falling drops.

At least the rain will cool down the remains of the cabin so I can go through it.

My hair tightened on my head. **DANGEROUS.**

Yes, it will be. But I have to know–we have to know if anyone was killed in that fire. Also to see if there's any way we can figure out what really happened. That fire wasn't started by any lightning strike, unless it hit the fuel tank or something but even then, that fire had been going for a while.

NOT A FIREFIGHTER.

I rolled my eyes. *I know that but I do know a few things about fires. They don't just go from a spark to a monster blaze in a couple of minutes. At least, I'm pretty sure they don't. From the oily look of the smoke, I'd bet the cabin had been treated with fire retardant for safety so it would've taken something big to make it burn like that. And if someone set it, which I'm betting on, they'll be blaming the fire on a lightning strike. They might've waited until a storm built up to swoop in. It's what I'd do although any examiner worth their salary could tell the difference, if anyone comes to examine it, that is.*

For the first time, I thought about the shuttles. What if they got into an air fight and shot each other down? Or one of them went down? What if my guards had all died? What if my family had been with them? What if my family was with the other shuttle? My heart constricted in my chest, a sharp stabbing pain shooting through me at the thoughts.

STOP THE WHAT IFS! WILL KNOW WHEN WE KNOW. UNTIL THEN, SURVIVE. Several strands of hair flicked my cheeks, the equivalent of a slap to the face, as I shook my head like a horse getting rid of a horsefly. It worked, however much it annoyed me, and brought me back to my senses. Dammit, it was right. First, I needed to stay alive so I could find out what happened and why. A certainty settled into me that this was all directed at me, another failed kidnapping attempt. A very bold, dangerous action on their part, where I could easily have been killed instead of captured.

Time enough to figure that out later. For now, going through the heap of what used to be a dwelling to find out what I could was my priority. Until it cooled enough to work my way through it, though, there was nothing to do except keep an eye on the sky to see if any shuttles arrived. If they did, I'd have to figure out if they were friend or foe before announcing my presence. My hair was right; there was danger out there with my name on it and it hunted me.

CHAPTER TEN

I stared into the gloomy clearing, storm clouds low and heavy with rain, blocking out the sun. I shivered as a cold wind blew through, and rain pattered down, tap-tap-tapping on the leaves overhead and around us. I rubbed my arms with my hands to warm me, as if that would help. I sighed. "Guess I'd better find a place to shelter from the rain. Perhaps I should think about changing to something with fur for warmth."

A hank of hair pointed off to my right and a little behind me. Shrugging, I followed its direction and moved off into the trees, where the darkness gathered in spite of being daytime. The rain had trouble penetrating the leaf cover this low so staying dry was easier until a leaf tipped its watery contents down my neck. I swear the leaves aimed for me. I funneled water from the leaves I could spot into my mouth, first making sure there were no drowned insects in it.

I'd guess we only went about twenty yards into the woods when my hair pointer dropped back into the mass, so I stopped where I was and looked around. It looked like any other part of the forest, trees all around, low bushes, plenty of leaves and twigs and small branches scattered around. I heard distant thunder rumble and I hoped that meant the storm was moving out of the area.

So, what's here? Why did you have me stop here?

LOOK UP.

I squinted as I surveyed the upper tree trunks, looking for whatever I was supposed to find. I saw an opening rather high up in the tree ahead of me, one with a big, thick trunk. *You really think I can climb that tree and fit into that space?*

NOT AS YOU.

I restrained myself from smacking my forehead. Certainly not as me. I thought through the list of DNA species I carried inside me. I needed something that could climb a tree and fit into that hollow. Somehow my brain blends with the brain of the new species so I can act on their instincts, but I still needed the ability to think things through so had never changed into something like, say, a squirrel. I'd never tried becoming something non-sentient and being all alone in the woods was not the time to start experimenting.

Melakew? This species was sort of an 80/20 cross between a large dog and a rabbit, sporting long, long ears and a twitchy nose. I was pretty sure it could scale a tree because its fingers and thumbs had very sharp claws, as did the back feet. Raindrops struck me on the top of my head and face and I knew I'd better get into shelter soon.

Without advance warning, wrenching pain cascaded over my body as I dropped to the ground to writhe through the change. Species aren't built overnight, I suppose, so changing into one in just shy of a minute was doing damn good. I wished it could be instantaneous, especially because of how much it hurts to do this, but as my dad would say, 'If wishes were fishes, we'd have a fish fry.'

Raindrops became heavier, now striking the ground, coming through the foliage and thunder rattled nearby. I opened my eyes, sitting up to see my four-fingered hands and thumb with long, curving claws, feeling my ears droop down my back like long hair as I slowly stood up to stand. This form was bipedal like a Human so balancing wasn't a worry.

Wrinkling my nose in distaste, the smell of mustiness and wetness fresh in my now-sensitive nose, I walked, a little unsteady on my new legs, to the chosen tree and started to scale it. As I'd thought, the curving claws were really good at this endeavor and I made it to the hollow in pretty good time. I sniffed at the opening before sticking my head in there; I sure didn't want companionship, so I made sure it was empty before committing myself to climbing into the opening.

I smelled the dryness of old leaves and bark, dried out scat and the wetness of the falling rain. I tried to lift an ear but I wasn't quite in control of them yet, so I used one hand to lift it up to listen for sounds outside of the pitter-patter of rain drops and heard nothing more than that. Other than the drips of rain, the forest had that expectant stillness, like it was holding its breath until the storm left..

I dropped into the hollow, curling to conserve body heat, thankful this form had body fur, facing the opening. Then I thought of something.

Where's my gun? I might need it if something wants to join me in here, you know, Matilda.

HUH. GET IT FOR YOU.

After some weird gyrations in my body and the sensation of something opening and then closing in my abdomen, something dropped beside me. I picked up the gun, checking to be sure these fingers could pull the trigger while holding the weapon, making a face at the dampness on it. I really hoped it was from rainwater. I didn't want to know how it had been incorporated or expelled; thinking about it was enough to give me the willies.

My mind whirled with worry: Where was my family and were they safe? Did they make it back home? Did they find a different place to stay and everyone would be back later to get me? Did they even know I was missing? Did they think I was dead? I started imagining different scenarios, my heart growing heavy with the thoughts. Finally, I shook my head with a sharp motion, trying to wipe the pointless worries from my mind. I didn't know any of the answers so instead of chewing over my fears like an old bone, I should probably come up with plans, instead. I drew in a long breath, held it, then let it go. *Breathe in the universe and then let it out.* I wrinkled my snout. Now where had that thought come from?

I started thinking about what it meant to breathe in the universe; did that mean every time anyone breathed in, the galaxy became a part of us? When we let out a breath, were we replacing that tiny gap of missing universe with what we expelled? Was it a one-for-one exchange? Or was this just some random thought? I mean, after all, wasn't the atmosphere of a planet peculiar to itself and not really a part of the universe as a whole? Or...was it? What generated the atmosphere in the first place? I know what the scientists would say and the churches would say something different, but couldn't it be both?

After a few minutes of these heavy thoughts, my eyelids half shut as my body relaxed a little. Even flopped over my back, my ears heard everything, from a raindrop striking a leaf to the soft rustle of the wind working its way through the forest, the creaking of a branch, two twigs rubbing together. Thunder still sounded in the distance and I discerned the tiny background noises of insects rustling through debris in the hollow, making me grimace. *As long as they're not spiders. PLEASE don't let them be spiders!* I shuddered at the thought.

I tried lifting an ear to see if I had better control yet but the snug hollow didn't allow me to extend it all the way. I examined my hands, admiring the curving claws with their razor tips, and how the soft, thick mottled-gray hair grew down to the first knuckles with a heavy pad of skin on the palmar side.

The universal thing between sentient species, besides the ability to do math and laugh, is the thumb. All the alien cultures killed off by the Imurians had thumbs, the ability to reason and build cultures, if not civilizations, and do math, no matter how rudimentary. I am the only being in any galaxy anywhere in the universe that can become one of these murdered species.

The Imurian scientists had no problem committing genocide when it served their own purposes. If the world was needed for a new population to buy through their Rent-to-Own program, and the existing culture wasn't advanced enough, well, wipe them out. That's their motto, as far as I know, and one I'm determined–somehow–to stop. There is an underground movement among the Imurians to put a stop to such practices. It hadn't gained much traction yet, still being very secretive. Putting together a strong enough group to make a difference was proving quite difficult. The Imurians essentially lived their lives on starships, exploring galaxies, new worlds and contacting newly discovered advanced civilizations, so contact among each ship traveling the galaxy can be limited, even with faster-than-light engines.

I gritted my teeth, feeling the back flat molars touch. This mouth had frontal sharp teeth for tearing and ripping meat, but the back teeth were designed as chewing surfaces. I thought back to the DNA blurb I'd memorized for each lost species I carried within and remembered this form as omnivorous. Well, if the rain ever stopped, I could eat leaves and berries for a meal and my stomach helpfully rumbled in anticipation. I wasn't sure of the time but it had to be mid-morning or later, I'd guess.

Well, let's make some plans. After the rain stops, I can find something to eat, since this form can eat vegetation. Then we'll go back to the cabin and see if it's cooled enough from the rain to go through the remains to see what we can find. After that? Guess I'll give it a day or so to see if anyone comes back to look for me.

GOOD PLACE TO START.

If nothing else, we'll have time to practice a few more forms, as long as I'm all alone in the wilderness.

TRUE.

Be careful what we wish for, right? I certainly didn't think we'd be stranded in a forest somewhere on Amorpha.

TAKE ADVANTAGE. My hair shrugged. It's hard to explain how I know but I do, even stuffed into the hollow like I was. Rain splashed in the opening now and again onto my face and I licked off what I could reach with my tongue. Oh, well, it was still better than being out in the open and sopping wet. I yawned and out of nowhere, a spider dropped in front of my open mouth.

"AAAAAAAAAAAAAGH!" I screamed with zero control over the volume while the force of my exhaled air blew the spider so now it swung through the air. Absolute fear made me push my body back, like there was someplace to go, my heart hammering, my eyes riveted on the creepy thing. Logically, I know I'm so much bigger than a spider, but emotionally, they're all the size of a space shuttle, especially when they come out of nowhere. Logic had no place here right now. What I know is they have way too many legs and they always come right at me. No, really, they do.

The horrible little monster appeared to take offense to my presence or, perhaps, my scream or it was getting seasick from swinging back and forth. Whatever it was, it scuttled back up its self-made string and disappeared from my view. I moved into hyper-alert status, feeling like millions were scampering over me at that very moment.

"I don't care if we get wet, I'm getting *out* of here, like, right now."

True to my words, I poked my head out far enough to look around for the 10-legged monsters but couldn't see anything. Then I exploded my body outward and literally ran down the tree trunk. I think I went so fast I didn't have a chance to fall because I sure wasn't using my claws and, somehow, I ended up standing on the forest floor with my gun in my hand. I had no memory of grabbing it before ejecting out of the opening.

I looked around to see if anything bigger or badder than me had come to investigate my armor piercing scream. I had control of my elongated ears now, and they stood like antennas, swiveling back and forth to catch the sounds of any immediate danger. Raindrops hit my head and the ground was damp, but it wasn't raining heavily like earlier when I took shelter.

"Well, I can only get so wet. I'll think of this as equivalent to a cold shower." I took a step and stopped. "Uh, which way?"

SHHH! If it actually had a voice, my hair would've hissed the sound.

Okay, okay, I get it. Danger and all that. At least there's no fricking spider in front of my face. Grimacing, I looked around me. A nearby bush looked rather tasty and my stomach gurgled in anticipation. Stepping over to it, I pulled a tiny piece of leaf off, placing it on my tongue to process. I waited several seconds. *Well?*

SAFE AND DIGESTIBLE.

Nodding, I stripped leaves off the bush, sticking them in my mouth and the flavor of cherries hit my taste buds. Mmmm, *these are good!* I ate until my stomach quit complaining before taking care of other bodily needs.

I huffed out a satisfied breath. *Okay, back to my original question. Which way?*

Without my input, one ear lifted from its relaxed position down my back, pointing off to my right. *You think you're funny, don't you? Couldn't you have just, you know, told me?*

SNRK, SNRK. FUN.

Rolling my eyes, I smiled. *Yeah, everyone needs a little fun now and then.* I started walking in the correct direction, my woodsy skills coming to the forefront. At least I didn't have to worry about cracking a twig or rustling leaves; the rain had wet everything enough to dampen those sounds. My Melakew senses became alert as I made my way with care and as much stealth as I could muster back toward the cabin.

At least you can't tie me to a tree this time. And, by the way, I'm still mad about that.

SAVED YOU. Funny how my hair didn't sound contrite at all.

From what, exactly?

BEING TAKEN PRISONER.

Startled, my mouth opened in surprise. *How, by the seven gates of hell, do you know that?*

A hesitation. Finally, it said, COMPILATION OF THINGS. BUT CORRECT.

I knew I wouldn't get a better explanation. I wondered what time it was but, first of all, my PerPad was turned off and second of all, I had no idea how or where it was assimilated into this body. I mean, there's no biological parts to a PerPad so how can it be incorporated, even on a molecular level, into a new form? Build strength into bones, perhaps, like an artificial joint would be? I decided I'd only get a headache if I tried to figure this out, so I put it aside as a discussion for another time. I knew the Akrion inside of me, a god-like particle, had a big hand in all this but I also suspected I wouldn't get any answers.

The trees thinned ahead, telling me I was almost at the clearing. I estimated it was late afternoon by now; I didn't know how long I'd slept in the hollow before the ten-legged monster came along but long enough to move the day along.

I crept to the edge, all senses–Melakew and Human–alerted for anything menacing. Other than the soft patter of rain onto the ground, the air was still and nothing moved. There were no shuttles in sight although, surprisingly, there was still a small amount of smoke drifting up from the pile of rubble that used to be a cabin.

My ears returned to their relaxed position down my back and I inhaled the fresh smell of cleansed air from the rain with pleasure. I pulled in a few big breaths, holding each one for a second or two before releasing it from my lungs. *No time like the present and there doesn't appear to be anything around except me. The real question is, do I go over there as myself, as this Melakew, or something larger and more dangerous looking?* I frowned as I thought about this. *As myself, if an enemy comes back, I'm vulnerable but if my guards or family come back, they know it's me. If I go as this form, I'm small enough to hide in the rubble, I suppose, until I knew if anyone returning is friend or foe. If I go as something large, strong but dangerous looking, there's a good chance they'd shoot first and then ask questions, no matter who they are. Okay, rule the Xingian form out. Looks too much like an old Earth grizzly bear.* I tapped a claw against my lips.

RADIR FORM.

Now, that's a thought. It can run fast on its four legs, has arms from the upper torso with those five-fingered hands and, of course, the all-important thumbs. It wouldn't look dangerous to anyone if they do see me. Okay, ding ding, I think we have a winner.

CHAPTER ELEVEN

Moving back into the foliage to hide my writhing through the change, I found a small, protected area in amongst all the scraggly bushes. I couldn't help it; I scanned the area closely to make sure no webs were present before I waded in and hunkered down to the ground.

Switching to a new form is always disorienting, having to figure out how to use the new body with efficiency. I struggled to my new four legs, feeling like a new-born calf finding its balance, shaking out my arms and hands, looking like what I imagined a centaur to be. I felt around my face, feeling an elongated muzzle with a large, moist nose, and big upright ears on top of my head. I smiled to feel hair flow down over my shoulders while my eyes took in more degrees of vision than human eyes as I waited for my human brain to integrate with the Radir brain to make sense of what I saw around me.

After what seemed like eighty years but really, only a couple of minutes or so, I moved, working hard to hold my human brain out of the way to let the radir's instincts take over walking. I hoped, with more practice in each form and experience, that eventually, while I couldn't speed up the change any more than we already had, perhaps using the new body would be within a few seconds. Having been there and done that, as it were. Well, only time would tell.

Again, I paused at the edge and checked the area with my new keen senses but heard and saw nothing to worry about. I moved with caution into the open, sniffing the air, ears swiveling as I swung my head back and forth, my arms crossed in front of my upright chest, mostly to hide the gun I held. It was lucky for me that not all the wildlife on this world had been catalogued yet, so I'd look like just another undiscovered type of animal out here.

I felt vulnerable out here, my anxiety high, but it looked more natural to be moving with slow deliberation. Being a shape-changer wasn't a deluxe package. That is, the transformation doesn't come with language skills, knowledge of their society structure, how far they had advanced in math or reading or whatever. It didn't provide personal memories, so it was all up to me to figure out how to fake it, as I sauntered toward the rubble.

My right ear alerted on a soft buzzing sound, swiveling toward the source as my head whipped to my right. My nose picked up the teensiest bit of metal smell as I sighted on the fritterer drone that was examining me. What would this form do? Ignore it? Swat at it? Run from it? Swatting seemed the most likely, so, transferring my gun to my left hand under cover by my mane of hair, I slapped at the small flying thing, as if it were an insect. After all, a Radir didn't know what a drone was so the logical thing to do was try to shoo it away.

It ignored my flailing hand in the air, dodging any contact, while filming me. This could spell trouble if someone got excited about a new species out here and came to check it out.

We need to destroy the little bugger.

AGREED. My hair whipped out a hank of hair faster than I could follow, grabbing the drone out of the air and held it for a couple of seconds. **STOMP IT NOW. REMOVED RECORDING.**

Okay, let me have it. I placed it on the ground, feeling it straining to fly again. My feet had thick, hoof-like coverings without toes and I raised my right front leg, and as I pulled my hand away, came down on the drone with all my might. I stomped it a few times to be sure it was completely broken. I crossed my arms again on my chest, my hair returning the gun to my right hand while keeping the movement concealed. After all, if there was one drone, there might be more. I just hoped this was one left behind by my guards and not being monitored. Yeah, and pies are made of stardust.

Okay, let's get this over. I resumed moving toward the rubble, kicking into a trot to cover the ground faster and within a minute or so, was at the pile of debris. If I hadn't actually been staying here, I would never have taken it for a ten-bedroom cabin. I'd thought of it as more like a dormitory, comfortable in every way. I looked at the wreckage, noting where thin tendrils of smoke spiraled upward in spite of everything looking soaked. I held my hand over the burned boards but didn't feel any heat emanating from them so it was probably safe to explore.

Abrupt emotions swept over me: loneliness, sadness and guilt mixed together. What if I was the only one who survived from my Amorphan family? I could never forgive myself if they had died because they thought I'd still been inside when the fire started and tried to come back in and save me.

A sob escaped my throat as I wiped my eyes with my hair, and, for once, it didn't object. I heaved a breath in and out while I looked it over, mapping in my head where the door had been and the bedrooms we'd used. I would start with where Simatrao had slept. I had to know. Sorrow constricted my throat, making it difficult to swallow for a few seconds. *Hey, silly girl, you don't even know that he's dead. I need to go on the theory they all escaped,* I chided myself. *Take my gun, please. I can't dig my way in there while holding it.*

YES.

Now with two empty hands, I bent down to move a few burned boards out of my way, hoping to clear a path to walk. It was hard work, moving boards, testing to see if it were safe, avoiding as best I could the upright parts that might fall over on me if disturbed. I'd never been at the site of a major fire but I knew enough to be very careful in how I moved through it. I wondered if a fire expert would come to determine whether the fire started from a lightning strike or something man-made. Or, I conceded, it could be a combination of both.

Sometime later, I stood where I thought my brother's bedroom had been. I couldn't squat in this form and didn't want to kneel so I bent forward, using a thin sturdy board to move things out of the way, kicking things out of the way when I could with my sturdy hoof-life feet. Talk about labor intensive work; everything had to be examined and there were clumps of who-knows-what that I couldn't identify. Every time I saw something small and bone-like, my heart constricted with pain until I ascertained it wasn't a body part.

My eyes stung from the acrid fumes when I disturbed dry ash under piles of debris and it all smelled of burned wood overlaid with a strong chemical smell, making my sensitive nose sore. I tried to wave away the odor, but it was too strong. *I wonder what the chemical is that I'm smelling. If it was fire retardant, it didn't work very well.*

COULD BE ACCELERANT.

Well, there's a cheerful thought. But, yeah, it could be. I guess you could analyze it and tell me but what am I going to do with the information if it is? If it is, were they trying to kill all of us? If so, who? More importantly, why?

SOMETHING TO FIND OUT.

First, let's get back to civilization but it's too far to walk back there. I continued poking through the boards, moving things around, thankful the heavy rains had turned the ash into sludge instead of puffing into my face with every move.

I finally straightened, putting a hand to my lower torso where it joined the long portion of my body. *This is really hard work but I thank the twinkling stars that I'm not finding anything that looks like people. Of course, I could've missed something, too.* Feeling depressed, I gave up on this area and moved on to what I thought might be Matra and Datro's room.

It took a lot of time to thoroughly go through each area; I knew I wouldn't get it all done today. I hadn't found anything like charred bones so I was relieved by that. I was startled to see the daylight waning toward dusk as my stomach pointed out quite rudely how hungry it was and my tongue felt like sandpaper. Looked like I'd be alone all night, so might as well go back into the trees for safety and return in the morning to sift through the dining area and kitchen.

Starting my careful path to the perimeter took energy I didn't have but it had to be done. I forced myself to pick up one leg at a time, even though all I wanted to do was lie down in the rubble and sleep. I neared the edge of the burned cabin, gloom gathering thicker around me, rain pelting down suddenly from the sky, when my ears picked up a distant sound. *What is that sound? Is that thunder? I can't hear it very well through the rain.* The sound was distant but continuous and then I noticed it getting steadily louder at a rapid rate.

A few beats of silence.

AIRCRAFT. RUN!

Adrenaline flooded my system and I discovered I could leap far and long on these springy legs, clearing the rubble and landing on the grassy area. I continued bounding toward the trees, too many yards from the tree line when the aircraft arrived to land in the clearing. I glanced over my shoulder to see something a little larger than a hover car, smaller than a shuttle, settle onto the grass, its lights shining out into the twilight all the way around its perimeter. Hard driving rain slapped onto its metal sides as my body became drenched.

One more leap brought me to the edge of the trees where I had difficulty slowing my approach, crashing through bushes, breaking off small limbs, until I slowed enough to stop. I bent over from the torso, panting for breath, ears laid back, willing my heart to slow down. I shivered, cold and wet, wishing I had a fireplace and a towel.

NO TOWEL. NEED THE WATER. ABSORB TO USE.

That's a handy piece of information.

NECESSITY.

Oh. This is a brand-new talent, then. I knew I should melt deeper into the woods for safety but curiosity turned me around so I could sneak back to see what was going on out in the clearing. And my hair let me go.

I realized how dark it had become; I could see shapes but not details. The rain clouds obliterated any moonlight or star light, so it was darned black under the trees. *Hey, do we have something that sees really, really, good in the dark? I mean, like maybe an owl can do?*

HIDE. WILL MODIFY EYES.

You mean I'd stay in this form? Is that a good idea? Those people out there could very well be hunters; after all, that drone got a good look at me before we destroyed it. Even removing the vid feed before stomping it, it would've sent back info as it took it. My ears twitched back as I twiddled the hair hanging over my shoulder in uncertainty. *I think I need to change.*

NEED NEW BODY, YES. MODIFY THOSE EYES.

Agreed. I need to be small enough to hide but able to fight, in case they're not friends. I think becoming a Melakew again is the best choice for now; it's a small form and has that mottled fur, making it much easier to blend into surroundings. I'd love to be something big and strong and scary, I tilted my head to one side, *but I don't want them shooting me, either.*

GOOD CHOICE. FIND PLACE.

I peered around, trying to see through the thickening dark for a possible place to hide. These eyes did see better in the dark than my own since they'd adjusted to the gloom and I frowned as I saw my rather obvious trail where I'd run into the woods. I needed to move away from this area and find a place somewhere else.

Even feeling better from absorbing rainwater into my system, my energy was still low and I would've given a big thumbs up for a full night's sleep right then and a banquet. I blundered through a bush or two, as leaves over my head dumped collected rainwater onto my head and my body. *By the pink panties of a demon, that's cold!*

It still rained hard enough for water to drip through the canopy overhead, finding ways to splash me on the face and head. I could hardly wait to become a Melakew again, with its thick fur warming me right up.

My left ear turned toward sounds wafting into the woods from the clearing. I continued to pick my way through bushes as I listened hard. The falling rain and rustle of foliage interfered with hearing clearly, frustrating me. Male voices shouted as they crashed through the brush, no thought given to being stealthy, as I shivered from abrupt fear. I held a leafy portion of a bush aside so I could step through it when some of the hair hanging over my shoulders tapped my arm.

HERE.

Huh?

HERE! Impatience.

Looking down, the branch I held covered an open area under the bush and would act as good cover for changing shapes. Folding my knees, I sank into the sparse opening with my legs tucked under. The branch snapped back into place, hitting me on the back of the head.

Ouch! I wiggled and scooted around until I was covered by foliage every which way, hoping I wasn't waking any spiders or other despicable bugs to crawl over me. I shuddered at the thought but my shape changing started and bugs didn't matter anymore as pain churned through me.

Grateful now for the heavy fur covering me, I regained my composure as I adjusted to the new shape, faster than before. I peeked through the leafy branch over my head as I moved it ever so slowly and gently to provide an opening. My newly enhanced vision allowed me to see even better in the dark with startling clarity.

Thank you!

MMM-HMM.

A light beam swept across the area and I instinctively ducked low, holding still, not daring to breath. How'd they get this far into the woods without my hearing them? It had to have been while I switched forms. I'm so darned vulnerable during transitions and open to attack or whatever, but they didn't find me, for which I was grateful...and still alive and free.

A crackling sound alerted me; of course, they wouldn't have good reception out here, either, except for local signals between devices. I flinched as a voice out of nowhere startled me.

"Have you found anything, Baleanden? How about the others?" A male voice muttered, sounding too close for my comfort. A bright beam traversed the area in a slow and careful arc, almost painful to my night-vision eyes, making me squint.

"Not yet." The answering voice sounded metallic and familiar. "We found broken twigs and disturbed bushes from where that animal ran. The odd thing is the path just—quits. Return to the clearing and we'll start at first light. This cursed rain makes it almost impossible to search." The answering voice was soft and, if I hadn't had these ears, I would never have heard the conversation.

"Of course. Let me try my goggles first, okay?" He murmured into a device on his wrist. My eyes had adjusted enough to the sudden light to see an Amorphan form standing still, wearing clothing that blended nicely into the surroundings. If my eyes hadn't been enhanced, I wouldn't have seen him. *He's smart enough to not advertise his presence in the woods, although the light is kind of a give-away.*

As if hearing my thought, he snapped off his light device, making spots dance before my eyes. I blinked several times as my eyes adjusted and I saw, to my horror, he now wore night vision, body heat sensitive glasses. He turned in tiny increments as he examined everything around him.

I didn't dare move, hardly dared to breathe, making sure I didn't rustle or jostle the bush I cowered within. *I wonder how many of them there are? At least two, anyway.* Worried, I chewed at my lower lip as anxiety ratcheted up, making me want to fidget. *I know! I'll try mind whispering; maybe a Melakew has different frequencies than humans do and I can actually hear an Amorphan. Hey, you are lowering my body temp? I feel cooler.*

WELL, OF COURSE. HMPH. Roberta—**NO!**—sounded insulted.

In all my months so far on Amorpha, I'd never been able to hear an Amorphan's thoughts, no matter how much I tried. Every night in the privacy of my room, not only did I change shapes for practice, I opened my mind shields, as Si'neada had taught me on the StarFinder spaceship, to quest for others' thoughts. Lowering my shields incrementally, I began "listening" on higher frequencies than my human brain could go. I can't explain how I go through different frequencies, I sure couldn't tell anyone what "station number" it is, I just can. It's slower than I'd like, as each time I slide to a different 'setting', I "listen" long enough to know if it's being used or not. Well, hell's pitchforks, I had nothing better to do right now and if I could listen in on this male's thoughts, that would be mighty handy.

I 'listened' hard, hoping to catch some of his thoughts, squeezing my eyes shut in concentration. I ran through the frequencies faster than I ever had; I felt circumstances pressuring me to hurry and hurry faster. That was a mistake.

CHAPTER TWELVE

Even my hair was taken by surprise.

He loomed over my bushy hiding place and his presence pushed against me.

HE'S HERE! My hair sounded frantic and shocked.

He is? I peeped open my eyes as the hairs on my neck stood straight at attention and my skin crawled from his proximity. *Poop on a popsicle stick. Ohhhh, crap.*

I held perfectly still, not twitching so much as a whisker. I felt his arm come over the bush and I knew, I just knew, he would move the branch covering my spot and me hunkered down. I could only think of two choices. The first was to stay still and hope he somehow missed seeing me or wouldn't bother with me. Or second, boil out of this bush like my ass was on fire and attack.

I only had a split second to decide. Let me think, yes, we'll fight.

My heart jackhammered in my chest as adrenaline flooded my system. I watched through narrowed eyes as I saw darkness reach forward, then drop to grasp the branch with his left hand. As he pulled it up, his right arm came forward, holding a short-barreled gun.

I leaped up , which I didn't know I could do, yowling at the same time, razor-sharp claws fully extended, aiming for his face. He flinched back, flinging an arm up to ward me off in an instinctual move. My stomach hit his forearm as my hand claws sank into his scalp, my back legs windmilling in an effort to catch his body. Curse the universe, he was strong and kept my lower half pushed away. He yelled, a sound mixed with pain and anger. I hoped no one else was close enough to hear him and come to his aid.

GUN!

His free arm came around, the one with the weapon in his hand. He only had to turn his hand to shoot me which would be fatal—at least to me. Probably would hurt himself, too, from that close. I snapped sharp teeth at his nose area, but an Amorphan's nose is flat and hard to catch with teeth. Snarling, my legs kicked in a desperate effort to snag the gun or at least kick his aim away.

One foot connected with his gun hand, shoving it away from me just as he pulled the trigger and a searing pain went across the top of my rump. I screamed at the pain but continued clawing at the male's face, now slick with his blood.

He brought his hand back toward me as I used my other arm to claw through his sleeve, cutting deep into his skin. He shouted in pain and dropped the gun as he tried to grab me with that hand; I heard it thud on the forest floor. He somehow managed to yank his other arm out from underneath me, grabbing me by the ruff of the neck, wrenching me free of his body. His arm swung around with enough impetus to fling me through the air.

I hit a tree trunk hard, something snapping in my arm and maybe a couple of ribs, my body falling into the foliage below. No time to think or take care of injuries. I had to skedaddle and find safety somewhere he couldn't find me. I had no doubts he would kill me at first sight.

As I hit the foliage, my body twisted like a cat's so I landed on my feet. Springing onto the nearest tree trunk, I climbed the tree as fast as I could go, and a Melakew could shimmy up a tree faster than anything I've ever seen. I went high, maybe higher than it was safe to do, but fear drove me upward until I found a branch to take to the next tree. I ran down the branch on three limbs, cradling the broken arm against myself for security.

When the branch started bending under me, I vaulted for the next tree, latching on with my free hand and snagging the bark with my hind claws, my fractured right arm screaming in pain. It was guttural, intense pain, especially when the broken ends ground against each other from my frenetic pace. I shoved the agony aside with gritted teeth, however, as being dead would be infinitely worse than being broken.

I scrambled up as high as I could go with three limbs, trying to hold my broken arm still, which is impossible while climbing a trunk. An energy bolt whizzed nearby, aimed where I'd just been on the other tree, energizing me to scramble upward even faster. Once there, I again leaped to another tree, repeated my actions, and kept going in a rinse-and-repeat scenario. Many, many trees later, I clung to the bark, exhausted, panting for breath, wondering where I was, but more importantly, where my enemy was by now. Each breath was agony, a sharp, stabbing pain with each breath in.

HOLD STILL. MUST STABALIZE BROKEN RIBS.

I almost whimpered out loud. *Camouflage?*

DO I LOOK STUPID OR SOMETHING? HOLD STILL AND YOU WON'T BE SEEN.

Yes, your majesty.

An undignified snort was my answer.

I'm pretty sure I outdistanced him by going through the treetops; he had to fight his way through foliage and branches and bushes, slowing him down. As soon as Queen Hairy let me move, gaining me another snort of derision, I crawled my way up, *just a little bit more, just a little bit further,* until I reached a sturdy branch. I collapsed onto the junction of branch to tree.

Unless a light beam hit me directly and I moved at the same time, no one could tell me apart from the tree trunk, except, perhaps, for looking like a funny type of bump.

Agonizing pain pulsed from my injured limb. Now that I could stay still, perhaps my body could start healing it. I was used to feeling tortured during a shape change but that only lasted a minute or less. This didn't stop. *It has started healing? Right?*

PREPARING. MUCH DAMAGE FROM RUNNING AND CLIMBING.

Is it a bad break?

BAD ENOUGH. NEED TO WORK.

The dismissive tone made me feel like it had hung up on me. I closed my eyes to rest a little while listening for the approach of anything or anyone. I switched directions so much while jumping from one tree to the next, picking the trees only for proximity, I didn't know which direction I faced nor where I was relative to the clearing.

I really hoped my assailant would put the experience down as an attack by a wild animal and resume looking for the Radir, which didn't exist now. That frackin' drone had sure ruined my evening.

The air was still and cool; the rain had stopped at some point in my escape and the woods was about as silent as it can get. My heart lurched as I remembered I had been mind-whispering when the male Amorphan found us. I wondered if I somehow alerted him while going through frequencies, hoping to find his mind voice, or anyone's, really. I didn't think I'd projected out any thoughts, but I was no expert at this telepathy thing and might have done so without even knowing it. *Jessalya Lilienthal, stop it! It doesn't matter right now.* I scolded myself as if I would stop self-recriminations.

Staying completely still is a hard job but an important one when you're pretending to be part of a tree trunk. My arm protested even the tiniest of movement, my fear kept me glued to the bark I sat against, and every breath hurt. I thought of my family and felt sharp, emotional pain go through my chest because I missed them so much. I also feared for their safety, worrying about them so hard, I almost forgot to breath.

Somewhere while wallowing in my misery, I fell asleep. I don't know how long I slept when noises below startled me awake, heart hammering. Gray light filtered through leaves, branches and twigs, so it must be around dawn, I figured. Like any hunted animal, I used my senses–smell, hearing, sight–to discern what rattled around below me.

I risked a quick look downward as I heard leaves being ripped from a bush. I frowned; I didn't see anything until it moved forward to reach for more leaves on a different part of the bush. *Huh. Whatever that is, it's pretty. Don't think I've ever seen a warm-blooded animal with mottled green hair before, but it sure does blend in that way. Especially from above.* A long neck led up to two pointed, swiveling ears off center from its roundish head and a long muzzle. Big eyes sat more to the outside of the head, suggesting this animal was a prey species. My viewpoint was from high, so I didn't know what kind of legs it had but it appeared to have at least four and no hands. My hair longed for some of its DNA.

If I didn't know better, I'd say it looked a lot like the deer imported to my world of New Eden, if you ignored the green coloring. I watched it mosey through the forest below me, in no hurry, its long, hairy tail switching its sides now and then. I shifted a little; my butt felt numb and slowly, ever so slowly, stretched out my limbs, one leg at a slow, cautious time. When I lifted my right arm to do the same, the throbbing, screaming agony of hours ago was greatly reduced and I heaved a silent sigh of relief. *Oh, my glory, that feels better. Thank you, thank you, thank you. You're the best doctor ever, Betsy.*

JUST DOING THE JOB, BETTY. Another way I knew it didn't like the name I'd chosen. It sounded modest, but I knew it was pleased to be thanked even if it didn't like the name.

How far from the cabin do you think it is, anyway?

NOT SURE. HARD TO MEASURE IN THE DARK GOING FAST.

Yeah, I know what you mean. How about which direction we should go to get back to the cabin?

CLIMB HIGHER TO SEE THE SUN.

I almost groaned at the suggestion. I double-checked and triple-checked our surroundings below and outward and even above me. The deer-thing still meandered around down below and all was serene, with a few birds chirping and twittering as they started their day. My stomach grumbled about being hungry and my mouth wanted water. Since a

Melakew was omnivorous, I reached above me and plucked a leaf from a low-hanging twig, placing a small piece of it on my tongue. *Are the tree leaves okay to eat? Will it give me the moisture the body needs along with sustenance?*

I'd give a gazillion dollars, like I have any money, to know what exactly went on inside my body to do all this stuff. I'd give more than that to know how it does a chemical analysis of things like, oh, I don't know, leaves. I flexed muscles in my limbs while waiting for the answer.

After a few long minutes, I got my reply.

SAFE TO EAT. ENOUGH WATER TO SUSTAIN.

Heeding my self-preservation training, I moved at what felt like a snail's pace to pull down reachable leaves and eat them, stuffing them into my mouth, forcing myself to eat them slowly. I kept a careful eye out for incoming danger. When nothing happened to alert the creature or the birds or me, relief washed over me. One good thing about hiding high in trees is people usually don't look up. I knew this about Humans, and I'd observed the same tendency with Amorphans, another thing we all had in common.

I scooted up the trunk to the next branch to continue my meal since I'd run out of leaves to reach, my injured arm protesting and weaker but usable. I ate until I felt full. I inched my way higher and higher, heart thumping in anxiety at how high I'd gotten. I was so happy to see a glimpse of the sky, I would've clapped my hands in joy, but they were busy holding onto the now slender, swaying tree trunk. Besides, I was too old to act like a kid.

CHAPTER THIRTEEN

Once we glimpsed the sun, I knew which way to go. Again, I had a choice to make. Change shapes to something that could make good time on the ground or go from tree to tree in my current form. Since I didn't know if the hunters were still out there, I decided to stay as I was and travel through the treetops. Good thing this species seemed to have a little bit of monkey in it.

In the daylight, it was a lot easier to decide which tree to go for and I made really good time back toward the clearing. I paused now and then to shinny higher to scope out how close I was getting. Finally, after several more trees, I spotted it, feeling glee at the sight. I slowed down my approach even though eagerness urged me to hurry; I didn't need a revengeful Amorphan shooting me down because of carelessness.

Several trees later, I was close enough to look over the lay of the land as I clung to the side of the tree, my right arm shading my eyes. Looking toward the burned-out building, a shuttle squatted near the remains. The craft was small, painted a dull collection of browns and greens, a few antennas on the roof and the door closed in the belly. No signs of life around it so I didn't know if this was the craft for the hunters—which I thought it was—or if they had returned and were inside sleeping or if they were still in the woods. Then the hatch opened and stairs descended.

I counted five Amorphans, carrying weapons and dressed in camo-cloth although one of them had bandages over his face, head, and arm. My eyes narrowed as I watched them. Somewhere along the way, my eyes had added a telescopic feature, like a bird of prey, so I could focus in on the group. *Wow, this is so cool! Love my new eyes, Davida.*

YOU'RE WELCOME, BERTHA.

I hoped it was only those five and not more of them in the woods still searching for little ol' me. Now and then, the wind carried words my way, but they were only snippets. My best guess was they were discussing the fire and deciding what to do. They looked like a bunch of uncertain people, reluctant to leave but equally reluctant to stay. There was a lot of gesturing going on and some shouted words that I could understand.

"...gone..."

"...back later..."

I'd say they were arguing. The guy I'd disfigured seemed to want to leave, probably wanting better medical help, and kept pointing at the shuttle and his face while talking. Some of the others wanted to stay and hunt for exotic species they'd never find, from what I could read from their body language, gestures and longing looks they cast at the trees.

With the acuteness of Melakew ears, I was the first to hear the high-pitched whine of an approaching aircraft engine. Who was coming to this blasted—perhaps literally—clearing now? I voted for it to be my bodyguards returning to look for me, although it could easily be more hunters or my enemies. Or their enemies. Well, guess I'd find out soon enough. I stayed where I was, motionless, to be hidden in plain sight if they bothered to scan the trees with their scopes.

I almost laughed at the people on the ground when they finally heard the arriving aircraft, now in view. I squinted, wishing I had sunglasses against the glare of sunlight glinting off the metallic shuttle, trying to find any identifier painted on its side. Although, to tell the truth, I probably wouldn't know what it meant, anyway, but I'd bet a berry crumble with cream my hair would remember any call sign if it was the same shuttle we took to come here.

OF COURSE WOULD REMEMBER! It sounded offended.

Don't get your knickers in a knot, Nancy. It's a compliment.

OH. YES. IT IS. THANKS, ANDREA.

The problem is I can't see anything painted on its side except a camouflage pattern. That could mean military or someone here to check those guys' hunting licenses. I breathed out a silent sigh. *I suppose it's too much to hope they're friendly to me. Hey! Maybe they're bringing my family back here to help find me!* That thought brightened my attitude. *Well, all I can do is hang here and wait to see what happens.*

YES. WILL KNOW SOON.

Yup. Then a thought occurred to me; I couldn't believe I hadn't noticed my gun missing before this. I imagined my former trainers glowering at me, arms akimbo. In my defense, I'd been a bit busy scrambling through treetops to escape the guy who wanted to capture or kill me.

Where is my gun? Hell's tinkling bells, did I lose it? Did I leave it in that fracking bush? My heart lurched with sudden panic. *Did that hunter guy find my gun? If he did, he'd know I'm not an ordinary woodsy creature.* My breathing turned ragged and my stomach dropped like it was in freefall. *Although maybe he'd think it was coincidence? Or that I'd found it and dragged it to my nest as a plaything?* My limbs trembled so hard I thought I might lose my grip.

HAVE GUN.

Where??? How?

GRABBED GUN BEFORE ATTACK.

My body shuddered with the force of my relief and I closed my eyes in gratitude. *Why didn't I use the gun on stun?* All my self-defense training should have led me to automatically using my weapon.

MELAKEW'S INSTINCTS TOOK OVER.

My mouth opened in surprise and snapped shut again. *That makes sense.* Profound relief and gratefulness saturated my emotions. *Oh, Gawds and their garters, I'm grateful you saved my gun.*

MIGHT NEED LATER.

I made a face of agreement. The arriving shuttle squawked a warning to the shuttle on the ground, making me jerk in surprise. Then, I watched as the hunters ran to their craft, disappearing into the maw of their vehicle, door shutting tightly as soon as the last one was in. Their engine revved in preparation to lift-off, but the other shuttle now hovered over it, demanding identification over their loudspeaker. The craft on the ground didn't respond, at least not over their loudspeakers, as the newly arrived vehicle stayed in place.

A couple of tense minutes went by; I started to feel the strain of holding so still against the tree trunk. *What do you suppose is going on over there?*

CHECKING AUTHENTICITY.

Which makes the new guys some kind of authority. I blew out a breath. *Well, if we don't know them–and we probably don't–we'll just stay in the woods and figure out how to get back to our city. Maybe we can sneak onto their ship without them finding us.* I grimaced at the thought of those hundreds of miles I'd have to traverse, without food or water. Yeah, being a stow-away had to be better. The abrupt thought of a hamburger with pickles, mustard, ketchup and all the fixings made my stomach gurgle and my mouth salivate. Like I'd find a hamburger on Amorpha. Or coffee with cream in the wilderness.

An itch started between my shoulder blades, in a place I couldn't easily reach under the best of circumstances. *Make that stop!*

DON'T BE SNIPPY.

I'm tense, my muscles hurt from hanging onto this fracking tree, and I'm worried. Worried about my family, worried about finding my way back, worried about, well, everything! I have a right to be crabby. And I want a hamburger, dagnab it!

HMPH. The itch stopped, anyway, despite its opinion.

Sure wish Si'neada were here. He'd help me find my family and find out what happened to that cabin.

YOU'RE WELCOME.

Oh. Sorry. Thank you. I appreciate the itch being gone.

MANNERS ALWAYS MATTER.

I rolled my eyes. You'd think my hair was some prim old lady lecturing me at a state dinner or something. While having this conversation, the two shuttles, one hovering over the other, had been stationary; at least there wasn't any shooting. As I thought that, the airborne craft moved to the side and settled on the ground while the first one rose in the air and took off to the south.

Guess they had the right credentials. Relief washed over me as they left; now I didn't have to worry about revenge or capture from any of the hunters. However, I sure wished the other door would open so I could see who came out of the craft. The suspense was almost worse than holding still.

I didn't dare move because I figured they had top-notch surveillance equipment on their ship, and I didn't want to be seen yet. The minutes crawled by and I felt pretty antsy about my position. Then, just as I decided to hell with it, I was changing positions, the door opened and the steps came down. I clenched and released muscles to help relieve the tedium of holding still.

Then the hatch on the side of the craft slid to one side and metal steps unfolded until they touched the ground.

I forgot my discomfort as I clutched the tree tighter in my anticipation, wishing they'd hurry up. *Where in the pits of hell are they?* My hair wisely didn't answer.

The doorway darkened and a flash of excitement swept over me. *Finally!* An Amorphan figure in a utility uniform stepped onto the top step, looking around, a rifle-type weapon held at ready as he inched his way to the next step. His head swiveled back and forth, scanning for danger—or, perhaps for me in some form or other, using the scope on his gun. I used my new telescopic vision to watch his activities. When he didn't see anybody, he called back something over his shoulder.

Two more males came onto the stairs after the first guy, holding assault style weapons. They approached the ground with caution; any little sound and their heads whipped around to find the noise, rifles pointing at the source.

With their helmets on, I'm having trouble seeing who they are.

SAME HERE.

Five more Amorphans exited, making their way to the burned ground when they got the all-clear. Three of the eight held shovels and other tools instead of weapons.

They must be here to go through the debris; maybe looking for bodies?

OR EVIDENCE.

The three males with the shovels walked to the edge of the debris, pointing and conferring, looking to a projected holographic image that must be the floor plan of the cabin. The other five spread out, ringing the cabin area, facing the woods, clearly on guard duty.

As the one facing my position settled into place, my eyes zoomed in to examine him more closely. I almost fell out of the tree in surprise. *That's Myometo! I thought his walk looked familiar. I need to get down from here and change back to me so we can let him know I'm alive! And he can get me back to Matra and Datro.*

Longing to be with my Amorphan family hit me hard again, making me gulp as tears sprang to my eyes. Unexpected homesickness followed on its heels, and I felt like my heart would tear in two between both my families as my yearning to see all of them deepened. It took all my strength to swallow back tears so I could make my cautious way to the ground for changing shapes, keeping the tree between me and the clearing for cover.

WAIT FOR BREEZE BEFORE MOVING.

And how long will that take? I can't wait that long; I've got to get down now. Even if they see me, by the time they get to my current position, I'll be well into the bushes and halfway through the change.

WAIT----!

A blaze of energy zipped through the leaves above me and a small branch fell to the ground. My heart stuttered in terror, my lungs paralyzed as I clung to the bark near the base of the tree. *Crap on a cracker, that was close!* Limbs trembling from fright, I felt a little faint.

TOLD YOU TO WAIT! My hair snapped at me, true anger in the words. GO NOW, HURRY, GO FAST! Urgency to the words.

I didn't argue, I complied. Dropping to my stomach, I made my way through the bushes, ignoring the scratching twigs and sharp edges as I went. Sometimes, life sucked.

I heard soft sounds behind me, my ears telling me Myometo had reached my former position. I slowed to a crawl to keep my movements quiet, knowing he'd come into the trees next once he decided there wasn't anything in that tree or on the ground underneath.

THERE, TO YOUR LEFT.

The dark mouth of a burrow beckoned. *Sure hope nobody's home. Like spiders.* Shuddering at the thought, I scrabbled with my hand for loose debris to toss in the opening to see if anything responded, like, you know, with teeth or growling. I flung a loose handful of pebbles and dirt into the dark with as much force as I could in my current prone condition, which wasn't much, then held my breath.

I heard—nothing. No snaps, growls or big teeth. I turned so I could enter feet first, not knowing how big the dugout was or how far it went. I didn't have time to worry about that, anyway, so I scuttled into position, pushing myself backwards into the hole. My feet caught on some roots and dangling tendrils of plant roots swung over my head and face but I was able to scooch back deep into the tunnel so I was fully encased but could still see out the opening.

I did have the presence of mind to obliterate my entrance tracks with my hands as I went. It was hasty and wouldn't stand up to serious inspection, but it was the best I could do for now. My instructors would've been pleased for me remembering to do that.

Crappy diapers of a demon, I hope there's no spiders in here with me. Let's see. Dark, damp hole in the ground? Yeah, there'd be hideous many-legged things in here, but I couldn't afford to panic over that right now. *Can we change now?*

NO.

Not enough room in here?

WAIT. THEN CHANGE. TOO NOISY, TOO MUCH MOVEMENT.

My hair was certainly a better strategist than me. However, it was right; there was a lot of involuntary movement as my body structure shifted and he'd almost certainly hear that, even if he didn't hear me moaning through the agony. I always did my best to be silent, but, well, cut me some slack here.

I hoped they stayed long enough so I could safely join them. Judging from their tools, and the fact it was still morning, most likely they'd stay all day poking around in the rubble. I'm not sure what they were looking for, but I suspected, at the least, it was my remains, and, perhaps, also my Amorphan family's remains. And evidence of what caused the fire. I hoped.

Vibrations through the dirt made me twitch; he walked nearby, and even though his steps weren't easily heard, I was surprised at how much I felt his movement. I stayed as still as a monument, knowing I matched my surroundings, even my irises. I closed them, anyway, in case he shone a light in here and noticed a glint off my eyes.

He felt close, very close, and I didn't dare breathe or twitch, even as I felt something small scamper across my face. I whimpered but not out loud and had to forcibly refuse to swat at it. Finally, he retreated after rustling through nearby foliage; I felt small branches swishing back and forth as he moved them around. When I was sure he was far enough away, I sucked in a much-needed breath, along with a little dirt, after swiping a hand across my face. I almost choked on relief as he left although I kept still for several more minutes to be sure he was gone from the area.

CHAPTER FOURTEEN

CHANGING NOW.

At least my hair gave me warning even as action followed on the last word. I barely had time to grit my teeth to keep my gasps and groans internal as much as possible. The confines of the burrow made this a difficult shift; dirt rained down on my body as I writhed. I wished I didn't stay so aware through all this. If only I could snap my fingers and be something else in an instant. Yeah, and if I had a feather in my ass, I could fly.

When done, as usual, I needed a half-minute to recover. At least, recovery was getting faster, especially returning to a shape I've done before. It's just that it feels funny for a few seconds to have a body with different placements of stuff, like arms and legs and too many eyes.

Pulling myself out of the dark, now small and tight tunnel into the daylight made me blink until my eyes adjusted. I surveilled the area with a keen eye, listening hard, before poking my head out of the foliage, following by standing. Nothing reacted so I started for the meadow, brushing dirt and moldy, damp leaves off my restored clothing. A small squeak escaped my lips as I felt something move under my fingers and my arm flung it away hard. I did *not* want to know what it was.

I sidled up to a tree trunk before stepping into the opening when I reached it, since I didn't feel like being shot before they identified me. Cupping my hands around my mouth, I called out to Myometo.

The wind was blowing toward me, snatching my words away, although I was glad to see blue skies and a bright sun instead of rain clouds and gloom. Taking a big breath, I shouted Myometo's name with all my might. This time he turned his head toward my position but didn't move. Instead he swung his assault weapon to his shoulder, sighting in my direction through the scope. I yelled his name again, throwing in a wave of my arm back and forth, shielding my body behind the thick trunk.

After what felt like years, he lowered his weapon and waved back at me, then made a "come to me" gesture. A huge smile split my face as I stepped forward, happiness at my rescue putting a spring in my step. He kept the rifle trained on me as I started my approach. When it lowered, I knew he'd positively identified me.

I broke into a run; I couldn't wait any more to get to my guys. Myometo started toward me and we met somewhere in the middle. I threw my arms around him in a tight hug, making him say, "Oof".

"I'm so, so glad you are here. It's been very scary out there by myself and then those other guys arrived and one of them shot at me and I was so afraid but," I gulped in air, "you're here now and I've never been so relieved."

He patted my back awkwardly, standing stiff under my hug assault. I stepped back, grinning up at him. The corners of his mouth actually tilted upward, just 1.5 millimeters each, as he looked back at me with his glittery eyes.

"How about Matra and Datro and Simatrao? Are they okay? When can I see them? Did you bring them with you?" I dodged to one side, trying to see if they were coming down the steps, but there was no one. "Who are those people in the ruins? Are they looking for the cause of the fire?"

Putting my hands to my cheeks, I squeaked out the words. "Oh, crap on a cracker, don't tell me they didn't survive. I couldn't stand it if you tell me that, I just can't." Tears sprang into my eyes.

He held up a hand in a 'stop' motion, saying, "They are alive and unhurt but they are not here." He looked over his shoulder at the people poking through the crap that used to be a cabin. "Most of them you know as your bodyguards and one is the fire inspector." Frowning a little, he asked, "Do you know what caused the fire?"

I shook my head. "There was a lot of lightning and thunder and one strike in particular hit damn close or maybe did hit the cabin. I didn't see it happen, only heard it. However, the fire got huge in a big hurry even with all the rain and that's when I ran for the trees." I wiped tears off my face. "There were two aircrafts here and that didn't make sense to me. One was the one we arrived in, but I don't know when the other got here or who was in it." I searched his face. "Do you?"

"We will talk more once we get you to the med unit and make sure you're healthy and without injury. Have you eaten anything?"

My stomach protested its hunger loud and clear. "Not really," I admitted. "I looked for berries and stuff in the woods, but I didn't find much." My meal of leaves had long worn off but I wasn't mentioning those. "And I'm *thirsty*. I couldn't find a water source so I got my drinks from where the rain pooled on the bigger leaves."

"I will walk you to the shuttle to feed you and get you medically checked out." He placed a gentle hand on my shoulder. "We will talk later about all this." He nodded toward the fire area.

True to his words, after medical cleared me, I scarfed down a hot meal, drinking lots of cold water, at the galley table. I'm not even sure what I ate but nothing had ever tasted so good. Even using the bathroom and washing my hands seemed like the most luxury I'd had in my life, since peeing in the woods left a lot to be desired, especially for a Human girl without toilet paper...or a Melakew, either.

I patted my stomach after cleaning my plate. "Okay, I feel so much better now." A huge yawn surprised me, and I patted my open mouth until it was gone. "I think I need a nap. I didn't sleep well in the wild, especially after those hunter people arrived. They scared the everlasting poop out of me and I spent most of my night awake worried they'd shoot me first and ask questions later."

He tilted his head to one side, standing across the table from me in guard mode. "How did you know they were hunters?"

Think fast, Jessi. "Ah, I heard them talking about having seen some unusual animal in the area from a drone and they had flown there to capture it plus they dressed like hunters, at least to me." I shrugged. "I personally never saw any animals, but they seemed convinced. I ran to get away from them since I didn't know if they knew what a Human looks like and might mistake me for an exotic animal."

I spread my hands apart. "I watched from the edge of the trees to see if it was you all coming back for me, but when I didn't know them, that's when I ran and hid. After that guy yanked my shoulder out of place at University, I wasn't too eager to reveal myself to strangers."

I rubbed my shoulder for emphasis and to cement my story. I'd better not mention the broken arm and bruised ribs. Besides, they were mostly healed by now.

"I'm pleased you thought ahead to that. They have licenses to hunt and collect unknown animals for study and cataloging and for our zoos. They proved they had the proper credentials."

After that, I took a refreshing and much needed shower before going back to the tiny galley to get something to drink. As I entered, Myometo slapped a folder shut, pinching his mouth into a tight line.

"What's wrong?" I asked him, wrinkling my brow in puzzlement.

"Nothing is wrong." He barked out the words although the colors of guilt flashed over his exposed skin on his neck and face. "Nothing for you to worry about."

I rolled my eyes. Right, uh huh. That usually meant something was out of whack and it probably involved me. I pulled out the other chair at the table, sitting, then leaned forward on my elbows. I pointed at the folder. "What's that? Some kind of report?"

"Yes, a report." His clipped answer meant he didn't want to talk about it.

"What's in it? Is it about me? My family? Why is it on paper?"

"I cannot discuss such matters with you, Madam. These," he tapped the folder with one boneless finger, "are not your business."

"But my name is right there." I reached over to place my finger on my name.

"It is only a report to my authorities to tell them we found you alive."

I narrowed my eyes at him as he stood. If that was all the information in there, why was he being so possessive? And more than that, why was it on paper and not on his PerPad?

I rose to step over to the small fridge and removed a bottle of water. "Oh, okay." Then I glugged water, keeping my eye on him. He picked up the folder as if it were precious jewels, inclined his head toward me, and took a step away. He turned back. "Oh, Madam Jessalya, when everyone is back on board, we'll have several hours ahead of us for the trip. You can stay onboard for now or you can watch the others search."

"How long before take-off?"

He shrugged, a commonality between our species. "Hard to say. When the fire inspector has his data, I think."

"Are they looking for bodies in the rubble? My family?"

"I told you your family is alive. You were the only missing person. We are looking for any indication of what started the fire and it takes many people to make searching time shorter."

"I'll come watch. Maybe I can learn something or tell what something is if it's intact enough. I could even help look."

"You are not trained nor qualified for that. You may only watch." Narrowing my eyes, I stuck out my tongue at his back as he walked away.

A couple of hours later, I was beyond bored. They didn't find anything to ask me about and it was slow, tedious, meticulous work. I wandered away to walk around to see if I could wake up. As soon as I took a few steps towards the woods, though, a guard hurried over in front of me to politely, but firmly, shoo me back.

Accepting that I must stay close, I thought of something to ask Myometo. I hurried his way, a bad feeling in my stomach.

I cocked my head to look at him. "I have a question for you."

He raised an eye ridge. "I have an answer; let's see if they match."

I almost smiled at that. He wasn't known for jocularity so this was a rare display, and any other time, I would've laughed. I had a private bet with myself I could make him laugh–or at the least, smile–someday but other than the tiniest motion toward a smile when I ran up to him earlier today, it hadn't happened.

Suddenly nervous, I rubbed my lips. "Ah, uh, that is, I'm just wondering something."

He continued to look at me with his eye ridge raised, holding still with a long stick in his hand he used to poke through the debris. He wasn't going to make this easy.

I expelled a breath, then sucked one in. "Okay, well, I'm wondering if I'd been killed, would you all have been killed, also?" I grimaced at the words.

He didn't answer right away, pressing his lips together, weighing me with his alien eyes. "Yes. We all would have been put to death for not protecting you. They would need proof of your demise first, however, before convening to impose our just punishment."

"What if it was completely accidental?"

"That would be taken into consideration."

I shook my head. "It isn't right to do that. It just isn't. What a horrible law you have. How can we change that?"

Myometo twitched one end of eye ridge upward, just a millimeter. "It is what we believe, Madam. I, and all of us," he gestured around him, "knew this risk when we accepted this assignment. It is certainly in our best interest to keep you alive, no matter the cost." He nodded at me. "If you don't like this consequence, then make sure you stay alive so we may live."

"How can the law be changed?"

"It cannot. It is more than a law; it is part of us and has been for millennia. It is logical so we may do our best job."

"I'll do my best to stay alive, then. How is your shoulder?"

"It is fine. And yours?"

"Just peachy-keen." I twitched a smile at him; I wondered how his internal translator interpreted my words, since I'd used Standard for the phrase.

Someone shouted his name, grabbing our attention, as he waved to us, beckoning us over to the wreckage. Well, perhaps they were only summoning Myometo but I tagged along to see what had been found.

CHAPTER FIFTEEN

From my viewpoint, it looked like ashes, sludge, burned unidentifiable things and not much else. *Like when I poked around in there.* I wasn't surprised; it had been one heck of a conflagration, fueled by the energy source of the house when the fire reached it.

We waited at the edge while one of the blackened people picked his way toward us. "By the stars, they're filthy." I remarked. "Sure glad that's not me in there in all that nasty stuff."

Myometo gave me a slanted look but said nothing while he waited for the other person's arrival. When the male reached the edge, he hopped over the last of the debris to stand on the clear ground near us and gave me a puzzled look. "Is this…?" He pointed at me with a very dirty finger.

"Yes, this is Madam Jessalya. You will not find her bones in there, after all." Myometo said with a grave look on his face but I thought I saw colors of amusement flit across his face.

"Yes, yes, I know that." The male said with impatience. "You reported that already." He stared at me up and down with an appraising look. "So...this is what a female Human looks like in person. Up close and personal like." He reached out to touch me or my hair or whatever so I stepped back.

"Please don't." I said. "Your hand is filthy."

"The female is fluent in Amorphan?" He sounded amazed.

"Yes, I am. I have a state-of-the-art translator and I have learned your language. I even dream in Amorphan now." I raised one eyebrow at him.

He looked back and forth between Myometo and me. "Well, this is astounding." His face broke into a big grin and then he bowed toward me. "I am Fire Inspector Xaleander and I am very pleased to meet you in person." He raised his hands in front of his face, looking surprised. "Oh, by a hat full of stars, my hands *are* filthy."

I bit my lip to stop myself from laughing at him. Myometo let out a big sigh. "Yes," he said, "you and everyone is covered in soot and ashes. Have you found anything important? What do the instruments say?"

Xaleander cut his eyes toward me. "Perhaps we should discuss this after I clean up?"

"We can discuss this in front of her. Perhaps she saw something that might be pertinent to your investigation."

Xaleander nodded. "I see. Well, I'd like to clean up first, then talk to my crew about their findings so I can collate all the information. I'd also like to interview Jessalya, with you present, of course, Myometo."

"Certainly. You know where the showers are." Xaleander headed for the aircraft, shouting to the others he was ready for a shower. The ones in the rubble started making their way to the cleared ground to do the same plus get a meal. The two remaining guards tightened their positions around us.

"After everyone has cleaned up, we'll depart." Myometo said, watching the workers climb the stairs into the craft.

"How long will that take? Do I have to get on the transport now?"

"What do you want to do out here?" He gave me a suspicious look.

I shook my head. "Enjoy the sunshine while I can? And the fresh air?"

"I'd prefer you safe inside." The look he gave me was almost pleading. "Please."

Twisting my mouth in disappointment, I nodded. *Hmm, maybe I can look for that folder when he's busy. Surely, picking the lock on his lockbox won't be difficult. Right, Rapunzel?*

SURE, MILDRED.

Boarding the transport, I was disappointed to find Amorphans, showered and clean, crowding the small galley and the tiny sitting area. They looked at me as one and, bending my arm up, I lifted one finger to acknowledge them as I realized I knew one of them from my night guard duty detail.

Farayeno stood and stepped aside from the chair. "Please, Madam, sit. May I get you something to drink?"

"Coffee?" I asked, ever hopeful but not surprised when he shook his head. Wel, at least I was almost past the caffeine withdrawal headaches. "Yeah, not surprised. I bet you didn't think you'd find me alive. Am I right?"

They had the grace to look embarrassed, shuffling their feet and not quite meeting my eye. "Iyah," Farayeno said, "we were, of course, hopeful we'd find you alive."

"But not hopeful enough to stock coffee, I think." He looked abashed at my words. Smiling at him, I reached over and patted his arm. "It's okay, I understand. Just think, since I'm alive, you all can make plans for the future now."

They stared at me with their glittery eyes, making me feel a little uncomfortable under their intense gaze. I held my hands up, palms out. "I know your laws about this. I'm more than happy to save your lives, believe me. I can't believe you even have a law like that and I'd change it if I could."

My statement startled vehement words from all four of them at once and their iridescent skin started flashing yellows and greens. Mostly what I heard were variations of "It is our way!" "It cannot be changed!" "We accepted this!" If they'd been water in a pot, they'd be boiling.

My eyes widened as I stepped back from them, holding my hands up, waving to get their attention. "I'm sorry! I didn't mean to ruffle your head-feathers, honestly." I rubbed my hand over my mouth. "It seems I have no choice but to accept your Law of Consequences."

Myometo entered the small space at that exact moment. His skin flashed in a variety of greens and yellows, colors, indicating being upset or annoyed. *Yeah, I'm betting on annoyed.*

"Why are you upsetting Madam Jessalya this way? She is our responsibility, not a debate opponent." He glared as he snapped out the words. "All of you are hereby assigned to clean this galley, the showers and waste room, starting now. And you'll be working the midnight to six shifts for the next two weeks." He flashed his sharp teeth at them and they flinched back. "Go now and be out of my sight."

"But–" I started but Myometo turned his angry eyes toward me.

"There are no 'buts', Madam. They will learn to behave with manners and treat you with the respect I expect from them. They will do as ordered." Looking at his face with his nostrils flared, eyes narrowed and teeth showing, I knew this was not the time to argue with him.

He made sure I was comfortably settled in a flight chair and I sank into the plush, soft chair, the kind that conforms to your body and you feel like you could stay there forever. He buckled me in with the safety straps, making sure I was comfortable. I was grateful I'd used the waste room on our way here since I now was secured every which way from

Sunday—or Worship Day, as the Amorphans named it. Since I had a vid screen to use and a source of snacks and drinks at my left hand, I wouldn't lack for anything on this trip.

Several hours later, two trips to the waste room (I really needed to learn to drink less on a long journey), and one fruitless interview later, I heard the engine's tone change, indicating a start to a descent. I looked out to see a cluster of single-story buildings surrounded by a nasty looking fence. A handful of people were barely visible on the grounds, as we were still high up, and they didn't seem overly concerned about an incoming aircraft. I watched as they grew larger and more identifiable as Amorphans, especially when a couple of them turned their faces up toward our descending vehicle.

What is this place? It looks like a prison. Are they going to jail me for something?

DON'T KNOW. IF DO, WE'LL ESCAPE. Said in a matter-of-fact way like we did prison breaks in our off time as recreation.

Twisting in my seat for a better viewpoint, I saw outlines of buildings in the near distance, suggesting a town nearby. I felt a little better knowing this place was close to larger populations and not in the middle of nowhere, like the cabin had been. Maybe my family was being held here for safety until they could be reunited with me.

Rustling noises drew my attention back to the sitting space. The few guards sitting with me were up and moving toward the front of the craft, even though we hadn't landed yet. As far as I could tell, we were hovering in the air right now.

"Hey!" I called after them. "What about me? Should I come with you?"

The last one in line turned his head to look at me. "No, Madam, you stay here until Myometo comes to escort you." He stepped out of the room.

I pushed on the release latch on the body harness but I couldn't get it to move. I wrinkled my nose and pushed harder with my thumb. That didn't work, so I used both thumbs on it. It still didn't budge.

"What the frack...?" I muttered.

WON'T RELEASE UNTIL LANDED.

Seriously? I was able to get up before to go to the bathroom and there wasn't a problem with the buckle then.

There was no one in sight to ask and I didn't want to use the comm button on the console of the chair. If they were busy with landing procedures, it wasn't right for me to intrude right now. My pilot dad taught me that from a young age, explaining how dangerous it could be to be interrupted while landing a craft. *Guess I can wait until we land. After all, what would I do differently, anyway? Nothing, that's what, so might as well look out the window to see what's happening.*

Within a few minutes, the pilot brought the shuttle to rest on the ground, and I watched as armed people in uniforms surrounded it. They looked more like soldiers than bodyguards; their jumpsuits were a different type of material and colors and their postures were more erect and precise. I was quite startled when one turned to look at me staring out the window, lifting his hand in a wave with a smile on his face. Before I could smile back, he'd turned back to watching the perimeter.

All was quiet around me. *Has everyone left? Did they forget I was here? Or is this just a stop-over and I'm not getting off here?*

I tried to undo the buckles again but it was still a no-go. *Can you help me undo them?*

WHY? NO PLACE TO GO.

I was saved from an argument when Myometo walked through the door from the front area. "Hey, am I glad to see you!" I indicated the harness around me. "I can't get these to release. I mean, what if there were a fire or something, I'd be trapped here."

He raised both eye ridges. "You cannot release those because I have the control. We needed to be sure everything is safe and everyone is who they say they are before I allow you to leave. We will be staying here for a while."

"Where is 'here'? Why are we staying? Is my family here? How soon can I see them?"

"It is my job to make your safety one hundred percent certain, so we have brought you here to this facility. Let's get you out of the harness and into the building, then we can talk more."

I noted he hadn't answered my questions but let it slide for now. Standing, I shook out my arms, then gathered up my few belongings, sticking my Perpad in the back pocket of my jeans. I grimaced. "I hope I can get laundry done here, my clothes are filthy. Oh, and a charger for my device."

"We have robes for you. And a charger."

"In my size?" I'm absurdly short by Amorphan standards for an adult and even for us Humans. If I were a child, my size would be okay, but I'm not and nothing the doctors could do made me grow any taller. I know why, now, but it was a large source of angst during my growing years because I didn't yet know about my shape-changing abilities. A smaller overall size is easier to reform into another shape while the volume of my hair adds bulk when I need to be bigger.

"Yes. We had them brought from your house in the city."

"Did you include my under garments? My human ones, that is?"

"Yes, Madam."

"Sweet! Thank you. I'm looking forward to clean clothes." *And I can change bras; this one really needs washing. Plus, these are the ones Si'neada made special for me to conceal my weapon.* I almost touched it through my clothes to be sure of its presence but stopped myself. Just in case Myometo noticed me doing it and wondered about it.

CHAPTER SIXTEEN

Being in clean clothes is wonderous and does marvelous things for one's mood. My grimy clothes were taken by a soldier to be washed, but I didn't let him take them before extracting all kinds of promises they would be returned to me as soon as they were clean. I wasn't taking any chances of losing my only pair of jeans.

In the meantime, I felt airy and fresh underneath my Amorphan robes. There's something about the floaty, gossamer-like material that makes me feel very feminine and I indulged in a few twirls just so it would flow around me.

I'd also been very happy to have someone clean my sneakers while I was given privacy to shower, brush my teeth and get into the robes. Sneakers aren't standard for any Amorphan, but we Humans had been given special permission to wear our own style of shoes.

"Okay, you can take me to Myometo now. He and I need to have a conversation." I nodded at the soldier standing with stiff posture at the door of the changing room.

"I cannot at this time do that." He said, eyes looking straight ahead, posture stiff.

"Why not?"

"Those are not my orders."

"Well, what can you do?"

"I can accompany you to the entertainment area, the eating hall or to your assigned quarters."

Since I wasn't hungry, not after all the snacks onboard, that ruled out eating. I'd also watched enough vid shows to last me a few years, so that was out, too. Sighing, I said, "Okay, I guess it's my quarters, then. When will I see Myometo again?"

"Later, Madam. When he is done with his duties."

"I thought I was his duty."

"Yes, Madam, you are. He has reports to file."

"Oh." It seems the military isn't so different among species. Reports must be reported and boxes must be checked and protocol must be followed. "Is Myometo in the military? I thought he was only in the bodyguard business."

"He is. It is a branch of the military but soldiers volunteer for the jobs."

Well, ruffle my fanny feathers. Who knew? I guess it made sense, in a way; after all, they'd be well-trained for the job this way. And they'd do the job for more reasons than just money or because of orders. I found that rather reassuring.

"Well, lead on, McDuff."

He gave me a sideways glance with a tiny furrow of his eyebrow ridges but he refrained from asking who or what McDuff was. Stepping behind me, he directed me verbally until we arrived at my assigned room. I made note of the door number—W257—since all the doors looked alike to me. He opened the door, then made sure I palm-printed the door mechanism so I could control it. I suspected I wouldn't be the only one who could access it, however. After all, I was now on a military base.

I also had to wonder if the room was under surveillance, by sound and/or camera. I knew I couldn't risk changing forms here nor could I risk my weapon being seen. *I need to be very circumspect about things while in this room. Actually, anywhere on base.*

TRUE.

I sat on the edge of the bed, looking around at the small but excruciatingly neat room. A single person sleeping bed on the left wall from the door, a small window on the wall across from the door with a small desk and chair under it. The wall to the right had a closed door and I pointed at it. The room was painted military gray.

"The waste room?"

"Yes, Madam."

"I hope a Human can use it?"

"It has been modified to accommodate that need, yes, Madam."

I nodded. "Okay, I guess I'm safely ensconced in my room now. I suppose all I need to do now is wait for Myometo."

"This is true. There is a vid screen," he pointed at the control that would bring it out of the wall, "and comm pad here. Please remain here until someone arrives to escort you wherever it is you are needed. There is an alarm that will sound if you leave without proper guidance."

"What if I get hungry?"

He gestured toward a small refrigerator I hadn't yet noticed. "Snacks in there and drinks." He nodded to a cupboard on same wall. "Dry snacks in there."

"I guess a girl has everything she needs here, then. Except answers. Is my family here? You know, my Matra and Datro and brother Simatrao?"

"I must return to my other duties. Make yourself comfortable."

"Why doesn't anyone want to answer me about my family? Were they killed and no one will tell me?"

The door was closing behind the departing soldier so I barely heard him say, "They are alive, Madam."

"Well, that's at least a consistent answer." I growled to myself.

Flopping on the tightly made bed, I put my hands under my head as I stared at the ceiling to think things over. Without meaning to, I fell asleep.

I startled awake, heart pounding, as I bolted straight up to a sitting position, my breathing harsh and fast. What had awakened me? Where was I, for that matter? Why was I even asleep? Daylight still brightened the window, although not as bright as before, so either it had clouded up or it was late afternoon.

IN ROOM. MILITARY BASE. SAFE. NIGHTMARE DURING NAP.

Okay, that answered those questions. I had a now-vague memory of dreaming about Amorphans being shot in front of a firing squad. Someone then tapped on the door. Still a little shaky and wary, I called out, "Who's there?"

"Myometo. Check your vid screen."

Why hadn't I thought of that? Answer: because I'm not used to being on a military base. At my Amorphan home, the door announced visitors and automatically showed who was there, needing verbal permission before allowing anyone outside of family to enter.

"Um, okay. Give me a minute." I shook my groggy head, rubbing my eyes, and yawned. I hate napping for this very reason. I wake up grumpy, out of sorts, not feeling rested and it takes me a few minutes to shake it all off. I fumbled around until I could push the button for the vid screen to descend from its hiding place. Then, I had to figure out how to switch it to the 'door' view. When I did, I saw Myometo standing outside my door, face upturned to the camera, arms crossed on his chest. A soldier stood behind him but facing the hallway, like a guard would do.

Pushing my volume of hair back over my shoulder, I thumbed open the door, trying to cover yet another yawn with the back of my hand. "Sorry, I was asleep when you knocked."

Myometo nodded, lifting a hand in a gesture of apology. "I thought perhaps you'd like to come to the exercise area for a workout."

Well, that was about the last thing I wanted to do in life but getting out of my room for a while would feel good and less like I was a prisoner here. I lifted my index finger in a 'wait one' motion. "Let me put on some exercise clothes. Be right back with ya."

He nodded again, widening his stance as if he were settling in for a long wait. I noticed, for the first time, he was dressed in soldier clothes and not his bodyguard jumpsuit thing. Two guns, one per hip, were visible and a rifle was slung across his back. My eyes widened a bit at all his armament as he gazed at me with a somewhat cynical look.

I closed the door before anything blurted out of my mouth, changing my clothes in record time. Getting in and out of an Amorphan robe wasn't the quickest thing to do, what with all the internal straps and stuff. I made sure my gun was secure in my special bra holder thingy before opening the door to join Myometo in the hallway, happy my sneakers looked brand new again. "Do I need a towel or do they have them at the gym?"

"There are towels there. And water."

I pointed a finger at the soldier walking ahead of us. "Who's that?"

"My underling."

His what? He had underlings, like, what, minions? Just what was his rank, anyway? I couldn't make sense out of the patches they wore to designate rankings and all that stuff. "Really? You have an underling? Do you have more than one?"

"In a manner of speaking, yes."

"Why is he here with you?"

"Guard duty, of course."

We walked at a brisk pace down the hall, turning a corner and going a few more yards when Myometo came to a stop. We weren't that far from my quarters, I reckoned, and I could find this on my own. If I was allowed to be on my own, that is. I sniffed in the distinct odor of a workout gym, a mix of sweat, grunts, farts and wet towels.

The floor mats were a familiar sight along with a rack of weights against the wall opposite us. Some of the machines were odd looking and I hoped I didn't have to figure them out. I'd stick to what I knew and call it good.

Myometo, it seemed, had other plans. "While you are here, I will drill you on self-preservation techniques so you may remain healthy, hearty and alive."

Crap on a crutch. Really? "You know I've taken self-defense classes for years on New Eden, right? And on the StarFinder on my way here."

"Yes, I know. And yet, someone dislocated your shoulder while walking *with* us bodyguards. I also know you didn't defend your body at the time. It is now part of my job to make sure you leave here with that skill set."

"I had no chance to fight him! You had me pinned to you, remember?"

"Nevertheless, you will receive more training."

I curled my lip. "No way out of this?"

"Orders from the Zatro himself."

I threw my hands up in defeat. "Okay, okay, if the Zatro says so, it must be." I poked a finger into his chest. "But when are we going to talk about my family? When are you going to tell me where they're at and when I can see them?"

"Later." He said in a clipped tone. "For now, training."

When he finally–finally!–called a halt, I dripped with sweat and my legs shook while I panted for breath like a running dog. I felt as wrung out as a wet rag and doubted I could walk more than the few steps to the towels and water bottles. "When you...said...training...," I gasped, "I...didn't know...you meant...kill me."

His wimpy excuse for a nose flared wide in the middle of his face and the corners of his lipless mouth twitched. "You, Madam," he pointed at me with an imperious finger, "are woefully out of shape. I plan to make sure that changes. You will be in great condition when you leave this base."

"And...when...will that be?" I was starting to get my breath back, which I thought was a good sign. Perhaps I wasn't quite as out of shape as he said.

He shrugged. "I do not have that information yet."

"And my family...?"

He looked around in a very pointed manner. "It's time for the evening meal."

"Yeah, yeah, I know. We're standing in a corn field."

He looked taken aback. "What is 'corn'? Is the word short for something else?"

"No, it's a type of crop grown for us Humans and certain farm animals to eat. The stalks of the plants grow the corn, and those are called 'ears'. It's a joke." I cleared my throat. "Obviously, only a Human joke."

"Obviously." He muttered but I heard him. Then, louder, "Then you understand why not here."

"Yeah, I get it." *But it sure feels like he's stalling and putting me off. I wonder what he doesn't want to tell me.* "Do I have time for a shower before the meal?"

He swung his head back and forth for a negative answer. "Are you hungry?"

My stomach growled. "Yep, I believe I am."

CHAPTER SEVENTEEN

After a filling dinner, I felt somewhat refreshed and my legs didn't feel as wobbly. My body begged for sleep and when Myometo noted my yawns, he assigned two guards to escort me to my room. I thanked them, closed the door, and sat on the edge of my bed. *I'm sure there's something Myometo doesn't want me to know. He keeps deflecting answers about Matra and Datro and Simatrao. What is he hiding?*

My hair shrugged in a 'who knows' kind of way. FIND OUT.

Well, duh, Einstein. Where would we look? I don't know what he did with that folder and if he has it in his room, there's no way to get at it.

Too bad I can't just send a few of you out of here to slither around and get information. That would be a lovely solution but my hair didn't survive leaving my head.

BECOME MYOMETO, MYRTLE.

Now why didn't I think of that? Ok, I'll become Myometo, then I can gain access to wherever I need to search. And hope no one wants to talk to me about anything, since I won't know the right answers.

WAIT UNTIL EARLY MORNING.

Like five or six a.m.? That seems a little late to be starting this adventure.

NO! TWO OR THREE IN THE MORNING.

I *nodded* with a slow, deliberate movement. *That is a much better idea.* I tapped my fingers on the blanket, thinking. *Okay, here's what needs to be done.*

I climbed into bed several minutes later, after cleaning my face and teeth. I fell asleep as I put my head on the pillow. I slept deeply without dreams until being jerked awake by several needle-like pokes from strands of hair. Fisting my hands, I rubbed my eyes, sucking in and blowing out a few big breathes. *That's a rude way to wake up.* This wasn't the first time I'd said it.

IT WORKS.

I couldn't argue with the logic but that didn't mean I liked it. The method worked every time. I checked the time; two-forty-five a.m. Right on schedule. *Let's do the vid camera.*

Don't ask me how strands of hair can do what they do, like pulling up the earlier image of Myometo at my door to display at this time of morning. Just in case someone was watching and saw Myometo leave my room and they checked to see what time he entered. Because, of course, he wasn't here for real. Or how it changes the motion sensor or override any alarm I might trip by leaving. It's a mystery to me, too.

I entered the waste room—the one place with guaranteed privacy and no cameras—and emerged as Myometo; my hair had already dinked with the internal cameras. Now to find that file folder of information he'd hidden so fast. If only it had been an electronic file, I'm sure my hair could've hacked into it, but, no, it had to be old-fashioned paper. Too bad I couldn't have done this on the shuttle; that would've been so much easier. *If wishes were horses, Jessi, beggars would ride. Might as well wish for the moon to dance the tango with the sun.*

I opened the door after the lock got fiddled with, stepping into the hallway. Instead of skulking along the corridors, I strode out like Myometo would. You know, full of confidence, like he belonged here. Which he did, come to think of it, and I didn't but somehow, I was going to get answers. If he wouldn't or couldn't tell me, it didn't matter. I was on a quest and nothing would stop me until I got what I needed.

I approached the front area with caution. The one thing that worried me was having Myometo see me. It's a very dangerous gamble on my part to look like him while he was in the same building and I risked a lot doing this, like being imprisoned, not to mention the Amorphan military discovering my capabilities.

I was as nervous as a demon at a baptism, my hands trembling a little at my side. Hyperalert, I twitched at small sounds, ready to duck for cover or run for safety. I breathed a silent breath of gratitude when I reached the office area without discovery. Maybe the guards were assigned outside at night or being a skeleton crew, didn't need to guard the office area since everything was locked up tight. Or they had someone in a room somewhere watching internal cameras on this area. In case someone watched vid of this area right at this moment, I made sure to look and act like Myometo would—I hoped.

I must've succeeded since there was no outcry or the pounding of running soldiers coming my way. I walked along the office doors until I spotted the name placard for his office and I gave a silent internal cheer. Luck seemed to be with me early this morning.

Doors being locked were no detriment when you lived with a gazillion lock picks growing from your head. I pretended to be using a key to enter, shutting the door with a firm snap behind me, pulling the door window shade down before switching on the table lamp. *Now where would he keep that thing? Under lock and key? Did he give it to someone else for safekeeping? If he did, then all this is for nothing.*

I searched quickly but as thoroughly as I could. I felt strands of hair slithering in and out of keyholes on the desk, while I riffled through scant items on the desktop. A file cabinet sat near to the desk and a tug on my head signaled me to step closer so my hair didn't have to stretch. I'd found nothing of interest so far and I felt time ticking by like a bomb on a count down.

Excitement reverberated through the hair that had snuck into the file cabinet and I grabbed the drawer to pull it out. It was in there, right up front, as if begging to be discovered. I grabbed the file, dropping into the chair at the desk to read the contents.

My heart stuttered as I heard noises in the hall nearby. Footsteps and voices and I panicked. Shoving the file drawer shut, I looked wildly around the office as if a hiding place would magically appear. *Maybe they're not coming here. Maybe they're just walking by on their nightly rounds.*

I ducked into the only possible place in the room in which to hide under the desk. I huddled there, making myself as small as I could, willing the people to go on their way. *No one here, nothing to see, move on, folks.*

Cracking open my mental shields, I checked for mind voices on a whim and a prayer. Experience told me the Amorphans didn't have mind-voice abilities so I was stunned when I found them on a very high-pitched frequency, one my Human brain could never have reached. I hardly dared to breathe for fear I'd send a thought their way although I didn't know if they even knew they could mind whisper with anyone. Perhaps only a few have the ability and therefore no need to find out about it, or if they did, no one to use it with.

I did not have this ability back on my home world of New Eden. I discovered this ability on the StarFinder journey; it's a secret ability of the Imurians, the cat-like people who rule the galaxies. Si'neada and his sister,

Ler'a'neada, taught me what they could in the short amount of time available on how to use and control it. I only hoped I remembered how to be sneaky while using the ability as I'd had no one to practice with on Amorpha.

Zoe received the ability along with my blood when I saved her life after being shot on the StarFinder but it was a couple of days before our disembarkation onto Amorpha. She'd barely received any training in mind whispering at all although we'd pledged to contact each other nightly at a certain time. So far, I'd never been successful in connecting with her mentally and I suspected our cities were too far apart.

Zoe, who used to be my worst critic and a covert bully. Zoe, who was the prettiest girl I knew and could attract almost any male she wanted. Zoe, who'd become my frenemy, but more friend than not, on the StarFinder. After all, we were the only two female Humans on Amorpha. The fact she was possibly pregnant with who-knew-what by the scientists aboard the StarFinder always filled me with anger. They'd experimented on her, wiping her memory of what they'd done, so she didn't know how many times she'd been taken to the labs in our two weeks aboard.

The sound of the door opener clicking jolted me from those thoughts. I held my breath, hoping against hope they—or he—were only checking the offices as a routine matter.

"Sir?" A male voice said with a note of uncertainty. "Are you alright?"

Silence. I was too afraid to breathe.

"I saw you come in here, sir, but I didn't see you leave."

Oh, rat farts! What do I do now?

PRETEND. DROPPED SOMETHING.

It was my only choice. I unfolded myself from under the desk and as my head rose over the edge of the desk, the young soldier gasped.

"Sir! Are you alright? Do you need assistance? Shall I call for medical?"

"No." I said, gazing at him with what I hoped was a steady look. "I dropped my stylus, it rolled under the desk and I was looking for it when you came in."

"Did you find it? Do you want me to look for it?"

I frowned and he quailed back a little. "No. I can find it on my own. Now, go. Be about your duties."

"Yes, sir!" He about-faced and marched into the hallway as the door slithered shut behind him.

I wiped sweat off my brow, or, in this case, the sheen of gel Amorphans exude instead of perspiration. *That was close.*

I rose to stand in front of the open file again, scanning it with my PerPad so I could look at it later when I wasn't in such a hurry. *Oh, my grannie's garters. This is talking about prisoners being taken!* My heart felt like someone squeezed it tight with a fist and I drew in a shaky breath.

FINSIH SCAN. NEED TO GO. My hair is good at admonishment.

Oh. Yeah. Okay. I stopped trying to read the report; I needed to be in the safety of my bed, under the covers, before I read them. Lucky for me, there were only a few pages so I was done in very short order. Sticking my PerPad back in its pouch on my leg, I tip-toed to the door and peeked out. The hallway was clear of soldiers at that moment.

CHAPTER EIGHTEEN

I strode back toward my room as if I had every right to be there. I felt like sprinting back to my room but that would only attract attention. Nonetheless, I quick timed it back to the corner leading to my room, shocked to hear voices murmuring near the vicinity of my room, stopping dead in my tracks. I risked a quick look around the corner and saw two soldiers and–oh, gods of hellfire, Myometo himself, standing in front of my door, engaged in what looked to an urgent conversation.

What, by the rosy-red cheeks of a streaker, is going on?

LISTENING. Only a few seconds passed before my hair spoke with urgency. **GO. HIDE. MUST CHANGE.**

I froze in place for one-half second. *Where do I go?* I felt panic clutch at me. *Waste room! I'll go there; there's a stall in the closest one for my use.*

NOT THERE.

Yeah, it's down that fracking hallway, isn't it? Of course it was. I needed to find a place, though, before they all came my way and discovered two Myometo's on base. It wouldn't end well for one of us, I was sure of that. Turning around, I walked as quietly and calmly as I could, dodging down the next hallway because it was very dark. Touching the wall for guidance, I felt it come to a right angle off to my right.

I stepped into it, my enhanced eyes adjusting to the gloom, seeing a dead-end alcove with the outline of a door so probably a janitor's closet. My shape-changing began the instant I stepped in, as I clenched my teeth in an effort to stay quiet. You know how hard that is when you feel like a zillion ice picks are stabbing you all over while someone breaks your bones? Yeah, not easy but I managed it.

I had no idea who I'd be when the change was complete; we hadn't had time to discuss a choice but I wasn't surprised to find myself, well, me, as this made the most sense in these circumstances. *I need a cover story why I'm out of my bed and wandering around.* An idea flashed into my head.

First, I had to calm down. Showing up out of breath with shaky hands wouldn't sell my story. I slowed my breathing, which in turn slowed my heart rate. When composed, I snuck back toward the lit area, checking for others before I sauntered out into full view, humming a song, wishing I could dare to whistle. On the other hand, whistling might be over the top here.

Swinging around the corner to my room, I stopped short when three heads swiveled to stare at me, with one soldier's jaw actually dropping open. *Go on the offensive here, Jessi.*

"Hey! What are you all doing at my room? Did something happen? Is there something wrong?"

Myometo shoved his way through the other two males. "Why are you not in your room?"

"I was hungry and went to look for a snack." *Oh, my, he looks angry.* I almost stepped back but steeled myself to stay in place.

"You have snacks in your quarters."

"Yeah, but I didn't want those. I wanted," I made a face, "something different." I flipped a hand to the palm side up. "Something hot, like coffee or hot chocolate. Or fresh fruit."

I made a rueful face. "Apparently your military bases aren't big on hot chocolate. And I couldn't find any coffee grounds, so I gave up and came back here to go back to bed or," I nodded, "eat one of the provided snacks."

I cocked my head to one side, hoping it looked quizzical. "Why were you looking for me? It's pretty late, right? Were you going to wake me up for something, I don't know, important?"

He heaved a sigh. "No. The soldier on vid watch duty reported something odd about the camera in front of your room. It showed I was standing in front of your door but there was daylight shining. He called me, waking me out of a deep sleep, and here we are."

OOPS.

Can't be perfect all the time. "Well, as you can see, I'm perfectly fine, just a little hungry, and I want to go back to bed." I tapped my foot a couple of times. "Please."

Myometo stared at me with an intense look, his eyes glittering more than usual, a powerful 'are you telling me the truth?' Mom look. I almost squirmed from guilt, almost blurting out the truth from the force of it but I managed to not even twitch. His refractory skin colors, first in yellows and oranges, gradated into greens with hints of blue so I knew he was calming down.

After all, I was living proof I was alive and well and still in the facility. I faked a yawn, patting my open mouth, saying, "I'm so sorry. See, I had that long nap earlier today and that's a big reason I was having trouble sleeping, then I got hungry..." I faked another yawn. "It must be well into the early morning hours by now."

He blinked a few times as he considered my words, then nodded, although with reluctance. "Very well. Go back to bed, do not leave your quarters until you have an escort."

"Okay."

He beckoned to the soldiers to move next to him. He pointed at one of them. "You will stand guard outside her door until shift change." He looked to the other. "You will set up a rotation of door guards, starting now, for every hour of every day."

They chorused, "Yes, sir. Right away, sir."

Poopy puppies, that put an end to getting out of my room unseen. I wondered if I could fit through the window. "Am I a prisoner now in my room?" I asked, tapping my foot, crossing my arms, narrowing my eyes.

"No, Madam Jessi. I need to know you are safe, all the time. If you want to go somewhere, the door guard will take you if it's a place you have permission to go."

I nodded. "Okay, but you and I need to have a talk. Today."

He looked resigned. "After lunch. I will have time then."

CHAPTER NINETEEN

I snuggled into my blankets, pretending to fall asleep before pulling out my PerPad, holding it underneath the covers so the light wouldn't be seen if someone was checking in. I swiped back to the first page I scanned and started reading.

I woke to find myself still holding the device, the screen dark. I didn't remember falling asleep and was surprised I could after what I'd learned. Anger swept through me. *How dare they keep this information from me! If Myometo doesn't tell me about this himself, I* will *confront him! They can't leave me out of this.*

Fury is energizing, I'll say that much for the emotion. I jumped out of bed, getting ready for the day in record time. I wished it were an old- fashioned door so I could jerk it open, which would be a lot more satisfying than waiting for the auto feature to move the door to the side. The soldier, a different one now, looked at me before giving me a slight bow. "Breakfast, Madam?"

"Yes." I spit out the word as I stalked out the door.

If he could tell I was pissed, he didn't show it, merely escorting me to the busy eating area, carrying my tray of food to an open spot at a nearby table. As soon as I took my last bite of food, another soldier with a lot more patches on his uniform whisked me away to the exercise area. He drilled me over and over in new self-defense techniques until I wheezed for breath. He didn't have the same problem. Well, maybe I had gotten a little soft in the past few months. Not that I'd admit it out loud.

When I couldn't take anymore, I held up a hand in a 'stop' gesture. "Water." I said, grabbing a nearby bottle, and swigging down half of it.

"In real life–" he began.

"Yeah, yeah, I know. In real life, there wouldn't be a water break if I'm fighting for my freedom." I swallowed some more water. "But if I die here first, it won't matter." I glared at him.

My stomach wailed in hunger, surprising me into chuckling. Astonishing me even more, my instructor guffawed. "I think your breakfast didn't sustain you. I did a good job of training you if you are now this hungry." He grinned.

Well, don't break your arm patting yourself on the back, bubba. "I sure hope I can go to lunch now. I admit you trained the heck out of me." In truth, I'd been so busy dodging, punching, kicking and running, I'd lost track of time.

He nodded, a short up-and-down motion, still smiling. "You are a good and receptive student and I appreciate your willingness to work at this. You are improved already and you seem to have some talent for this work."

"Why, thank you," I said. "Now can I go eat?"

He'd better not stand me up. My irritation level rose at the thought and I almost stormed out of the cafeteria to find Myometo. I reined in my temper and frustration; demanding anything of an Amorphan was futile. They'd just look at me with those alien glittering eyes and then do what they wanted to do, anyway. I'd learned that the hard way during my time on this planet.

Noticing me standing to leave, my escort hurried over. "I will escort you to Myometo's office."

"Lead on, then, my fine feathered friend."

He put his hand to the hair-feathers on his head, patting them to make sure they were in place, fluffing them a bit, then looked abashed at the motion. "Come with me, then." He said in a gruff voice, probably trying to cover up checking out his feathers, his exposed skin flashing through colors of embarrassment.

I bit back a grin. The males were vainer than the females in this civilization. In fact, their refractory skin flashed colors not seen in a female's skin, and their hair-feathers were more luxurious looking. It's only because of my own abilities that I could even see their range of colors since a lot of them were beyond the spectrum of Human visualization. I knew they didn't know I could interpret their skin signals. I also knew they typically didn't have control over their color responses, having been an Amorphan myself. However, I didn't put it past Myometo to have that kind of iron control.

"Sure." I said in a breezy tone. "What is your name, anyway?"

"Garientin, Madam."

"Is that officer or ensign or...what rank do you hold?"

"Soldier, Madam."

"So I should call you Soldier Garientin?"

"If it pleases you, Madam."

We stopped in front of Myometo's office door and he settled into a stance, hands behind his back. I shrugged, spreading my hands apart palm-side up. "Do I just go in?"

"He will open the door when he's ready, Madam."

Fidgeting while I waited made me edgier. Was this a power play on his part? Did he want me irritated? Was this a lesson in patience? Or was he genuinely busy with something? It didn't help my mood to see Soldier Garientin looking calm and serene as he stood there at ease.

I was about to pound on his door, demanding entrance, when it slithered open, making me twitch with surprise.

"You may enter." Myometo said.

Remembering my manners, I thanked my escort, then took a deep breath for courage. I marched into the office, plunking into the chair in front of his desk without waiting for his invitation to sit, leaning forward onto my elbows. "We need to talk."

His brow furrowed. "About...?"

"You know something I don't know about my family and what happened at the cabin. It's more than time to tell me." I rapped my index fingernail on the table a couple of times for emphasis while glaring at him. "And don't leave anything out."

"Your family is alive, Madam Jessalya."

"I know that part. Now tell me the rest."

He steepled his boneless fingers together, putting them in front of his mouth. "I had to get permission, you must understand, and it hasn't been easy."

"Permission for what? To tell me what? To do something? What?"

"To tell you the circumstances."

"What don't 'they'," and I made air quotes, "want me to know?"

"Your family is alive. Remember that, most of all. However, they're prisoners of an anti-Human group. I assure you we're working on finding and rescuing them."

"So the second shuttle at the cabin site wasn't there to rescue anyone?"

He made a decisive back and forth movement of his head. "We think–we don't know for sure yet–they were there to kidnap you. Not your family."

"Me? But you said they're anti-Human. Why would they want me?"

I could see by the sudden shifting of his eyes away and back again, plus a faint hint of red so light I almost didn't see it, he was about to lie. "We don't know, not for certain. We think because they didn't get you, they took the next best thing: your family."

"So, they burned down the cabin to force everyone out?"

He sighed, a soft blowing out of air. "Partially true. The cabin was struck by lightning, which started a fire. It would have easily been put out but they helped the fire grow into something that destroyed everything. We speculate the unfriendlies timed their arrival for when the bolt would strike; there's even some who think they created the lightning bolt. We only had time to get everyone safely out of the building while the fire went out of control in an Amorphan minute. That group fueled it somehow."

"So, the anti-Human faction knew I was there at the cabin and they orchestrated all this to kidnap me?" I made a face. "That sure seems a stretch of the imagination." I gasped as a thought struck me. "What about my Human classmates? Are they safe? Is someone trying to kidnap them, also?"

"They are safe for now and all precautions are being taken."

"They're on military bases, also?"

He inclined his head.

"So how do we rescue my family? Are they demanding a ransom?"

"No." He looked grim.

"Then...oh." The answer dawned on me. "They want me in exchange, don't they?" I jumped out of my chair. "Well, let's go, let's get it done."

"No." He said in the same grim voice. "That is not possible."

"But I have to do it! I have to save my family!" I slapped the desktop. "No more dodging around, I have to do this!"

"We cannot and will not allow this." He stood, towering over me. "We will not jeopardize your life in any way. We will not give into the demands of a demented group. We will, however, find their hiding place and we *will* rescue your family." He hit the desktop with his fist, making less noise than my slap had.

"You weren't going to tell me about this at all, were you?"

His eyes glittered. "I would've told you immediately but I was ordered to keep it quiet. The less people who know, the better. Plus they were afraid your human impulsivity would put you in danger and I think my superiors are right about that."

He pointed at me. "Case in point right here. You'd rush out without a plan or backup, offer yourself up like a tasty treat without assurance your family would be released. If you're lucky, at best, they'd ransom you for money. Worst case? They sell you to a top bidder if they can find one. Believe me when I say there are plenty of unscrupulous people in the universe. There is a thriving sex trade on all worlds, for instance, and a Human female might fetch a nice price. Or being sold as a slave. All highly illegal and yet it still happens."

I dropped into my chair, deflated. "I–I hadn't thought of that."

"You aren't expected to; that's our job." He said in a softer voice.

"But every day they're held captive is another day they're in danger. We don't know if they're being fed, tied up all day, being tortured or gods know what else." I jumped up again to pace the small room. "I can't stand the thought of them being hurt. I can't. I'd rather take their place."

I turned to face him. "Let your superiors know that."

"It will not be considered as a solution." He said in a flat, unmovable voice.

"You tell them, anyway. And you tell them, also," I pointed at him with a finger gun, "I will be a part of this. I will *not* be left in ignorance again." My voice became louder with each word spoken. I blinked back tears of anger, my hands fisted by my sides.

"I do not need to tell them. They have heard you already."

"Then let me make this perfectly clear," I snarled, my eyes searching for the vid camera. "I am part of this rescue. There is no argument about this."

I knew my words were heard but I had no power to back them up. They could make plans all they wanted without including me. I needed to find where the upper echelon was housed so I could insert myself into the solution and not be overlooked.

"Where are the officers in charge, anyway?" I looked around the room. "Here on this base?"

Myometo's head moved in a 'no' gesture, only a fraction of movement, before standing. "It is time for you to return to your quarters. I remind you the upper ranks have assigned many people to work on this and have put together a rescue team for when the time is right." He paused to stare at me. "It is not right yet. I assure you they are nearby and ready to jump into action." He folded his arms on his chest, right hand over his left, his left index finger pointing, the gesture hidden from being seen by anyone other than me.

What direction is that?

NORTHEAST.

Myometo, it seemed, wanted to help me, even in defiance of his orders. That took a lot of guts to do, although I wasn't sure what I could do with the information.

"Thank you for filling me in. I've been so worried and it's a relief to know there's a plan. Will you tell me the instant they are rescued?"

"Of course. We all know how concerned you are for their safety."

I nodded, crossing my arms on my chest. "What time should I be ready—for my next scheduled activity?" I hoped my slight hesitation would signal him what I was really asking.

He made a show of consulting a schedule. "Three o'clock this afternoon."

"I will be dressed and ready. Thank you, Myometo, for, you know, everything."

"It is my job, Madam Jessi."

"Can you arrange for me to get some fresh air this morning? I'm starting to feel claustrophobic and need to go outside for a while.

He hesitated, something unreadable in his eyes, then picked up his comm unit, tapping into it. Within seconds, the device chimed with an incoming message. "You have permission to do so. I'll arrange soldiers to protect you outdoors.

"Thanks."

CHAPTER TWENTY

Feeling sunshine on my face felt good as I sucked in a breath of fresh-smelling air, full of warmth from the sun with a dash of ozone. The atmosphere on Amorpha was heavier in ozone than New Eden and, somehow, I seemed to be more sensitive to the odor. A fleeting thought zipped through my mind. *I wonder what the galaxy smells like?* Taking in another breath of the Universe, I breathed out dust.

I dismissed the thoughts as frivolous, turning my attention to the surrounding fence. "So, do I get to go outside the fence for a walk?"

The nearest soldier looked at me with the hues of shock–pale blue mixed with white–coloring his face. "Oh, no, Madam. That's too dangerous; you must remain on the grounds, inside the perimeter where we can keep you safe."

Can't blame a girl for asking. "Then tell me what direction we're facing right now. I'm all turned around from being inside too long."

He pointed with one elegant finger. "That is southwest." Turning a little bit, he swept his finger to point again. "That is true south."

Bobbing my head up and down in acknowledgement, I moved toward the perimeter. "Is anything out there? You know, like a settlement or a city? How big is this base, anyway? How many are stationed here?"

"We are numbered in the–oof!" One of the other two soldiers elbowed him in the ribs, a fierce glower on his face, shaking his head.

"Ah, we cannot divulge that information, Madam, as you are not a member of the forces. I apologize for the inconvenience." The elbow guy shot me a look that said 'don't even think of asking again', then glared at his companion. "You know better, soldier." He raised his eyebrow ridges at me, pursing his lipless mouth. "Please move away from the outer area. It'll be safer in case of a long-distance shooter."

I wanted to scream in frustration but ground my teeth instead. The one male would've told me everything I wanted to know but ol' Mr. Cranky-pants had to shut him up. We resumed our stroll around the buildings while I memorized each soldier's way of walking and their postures.

I asked about weather, food, anything innocuous so I could hear the cadence of their voices. It's tricky, with three of them, to get each one to answer in turn but I solved that by pointing at a soldier, one by one, and saying, "I want to ask *you* this question."

When I asked about girlfriends, all three became enthusiastic in their descriptions and talked over one another, each one now trying to convince me only he had found the perfect mate. I chuckled at their vehemence and rivalry. "So does she know about your intentions?"

"Oh, no," they exclaimed. "We are not allowed to have a serious relationship while in service so cannot discuss such things together." The first one complained. "But I think it's obvious to her and she will wait for me to finish my contract. Then we can discuss our future."

"True of all of you?"

They nodded as one.

"Good luck to you and I hope each of your future mates waits for you, I really do."

We completed going around the buildings and I'd counted all of them in my head, filling in a mental map of the grounds. When we had reached the northeast corner, it was closer to the fence and I'd gotten a good look through sturdy, thorny wires at a smudge on the horizon.

I decided I had nothing to lose, so I pointed that way before they nudged me back from the fence. "What's that over there? Is that another complex like this or is that a settlement?"

"A different complex, Madam."

"Why have two of them so close together?" I tilted my head to one side, smiling up at him, hoping he'd take it as flirting. I don't know why he would since I'm hopeless at the feminine charms, especially on an alien species.

"Wiladeon! Stop answering such questions!" Mr. Cranky-pants said with exasperation.

"What?" Wiladeon said. "There's no harm in telling her about this. After all, she can plainly see it over there." He punched him on the arm. "She's not the enemy here, Ariyendo." He looked at the other male. "Am I right, Caronuyen?"

"He's right, Ariyendo. What will she do with the knowledge, after all? I agree we cannot discuss logistics, but I think it safe to answer innocent, non-threatening questions such as that."

"Great; that's settled. So, why are there two bases so close together? Wouldn't it make more sense to have them together?" I broke in before they could change their minds. "Are, like, the officers all in that one and you soldiers all here or something?"

Ariyendo snorted. "Of course not; the officers would be the first killed if they were all in one place."

"Then, why?"

"Different purposes, Madam," Caronuyen said. "We need to be close enough to work together but far enough apart to not disturb each other's training programs."

"Like, what kind of programs?"

He shifted his long gun from one arm to the other. "Now that we cannot discuss."

"I understand." Silence took over while I mulled over what he said. Different training programs? What did that mean? Was one more dangerous than the other and had to be sequestered for safety? "Do you guys switch out so you get cross-trained between the two places?"

Wiladeon shrugged. "If we request it, yes. Most don't, however. Sometimes we're assigned there but mostly, we serve as escorts between the two."

"Why? Is theirs more dangerous over there? Their program, that is?"

He chuckled. "More like boring than dangerous." He and Ariyendo exchanged glances and I wondered if he was telling me the truth.

Their comm units all beeped at once. "We must return to the dormitory building, Madam. You cannot remain out here without us."

"Sure thing. I do appreciate your taking the time so I could get fresh air and feel the sun's warmth on my skin."

His face skin flashed with pinks and golds in pleasure. "Oh, it was not a chore, not at all, Madam. We're happy to have been chosen for this duty. Wait until I tell my future mate I got to walk and talk with a real Human!"

I chuckled at that. "Glad to be of service, my friend."

We returned to the complex, walking straight to my quarters. With a start, I realized it was mealtime and I was hungry. But first, I needed the waste room rather urgently. I thanked them, patting each one's hand on the back. They looked embarrassed, nodding in acceptance, saying "It's our job, Madam."

Ariyendo said, "When you are ready for your meal, Madam, please signal through your room comm unit."

Once in my room, I used the bathroom, then took time to wash my face and brush my hair. I could tell it was pleased with the extra attention as it swished around my shoulders, wiggling in delight down my back.

Sitting at my desk, I worried at a hangnail with my teeth as I thought over what to do next. I needed to get to the other base; there was no sense of urgency here at all, oh, no, not at all. *Liar.* I chided myself.

I didn't think the personnel in this complex were involved in the search and pending rescue of Matra, Datro and Simatrao, so it must be happening at the other base. I hated not knowing and not being involved and my frustration levels ran high.

If I could only see a duty roster or an activity schedule, I could become a soldier on the next trip to the other base to snoop around and get back before they found my room empty. I could plead a migraine headache, citing the need to be in bed all day and left alone.

Sure, it was risky, but so was leaving my family in the clutches of their captors. I thought perhaps Myometo would help me; he'd indicated that earlier when he secretly pointed toward the other base. Maybe I should consult him—no. I'd have to tell him about my shape changing and that's a secret I don't give up easily, as it's too dangerous to divulge. It's bad enough so many people already knew about it: Zoe, Si'neada, Ler'a'neada and Deester. They'd all found out in various ways while aboard the StarFinder. I felt I could trust Zoe to keep the secret; after all, who would believe her? Also, the same for Si'neada and Ler'a'neada; it was in their best interests to not divulge the information.

They were planning to find a way to put a stop to the genocide atrocities the Imurians performed in the interest of possessing a planet to sell on the Rent-to-Own programs. Not only was I the repository of all the viable DNA collected from those murdered sentient early civilizations, I also planned to participate in stopping the scientists and their cohorts.

The Imurian scientists, at least the ones on board the StarFinder, were doing illegal and highly unethical experimentations on many different species. They'd taken Zoe from her quarters at night, making sure to drug her to dissolve her memories of the time spent with them, as they worked to get her pregnant with—perhaps—a newly formed species.

I'd saved her on the final night of the procedures done to her, interrupting whatever they'd planned to do to her, but neither one of us knew for certain if the scientists had succeeded. We separated two days later to our Amorphan families in different cities, hundreds of miles apart. Being forbidden to contact one another during our time on Amorpha in any of the usual ways made sure she and I couldn't discuss or plan anything. Somehow, the Imurians had disabled our PerPads and personal computers so we couldn't connect with the other four of us Humans here on this world.

If only Si'neada were here, he'd help me. We'd find a way to rescue my host family together. I blew out a breath, shaking my head with my lips pressed together. *Not realistic, Jessi, not at all.*

Returning to my room after eating, I sat on my bed, leaning against the wall, pulling my knees up to put my arms around. I knew there were no cameras in here or the bathroom, as my hair and I had searched everywhere as soon as we arrived. However, I was certain there were motion and heat sensors in the room, something to be dealt with if we figured out a way to go to the other base.

I closed my eyes after a few minutes, opening my mind shield, seeking Myometo's mind or one of the three soldiers from earlier today. Going that high on the frequency range was almost painful but I clenched my teeth and endured, listening as I slowly went up the register.

There! I heard the wisp of a thought, so I worked on fine-tuning. Just the barest thread of contact, being careful to not twang the tenuous connection, I scarcely breathed while concentrating. It felt so...so distant and it flickered at the edge of my mind and then it was lost. I blew out a breath in frustration.

I resettled myself, placing my forehead on my bent knees. *Let's try again. At least I heard something, even if it was brief.*

Going the teensiest bit higher in register, I received nothing. Then, struggling, pushing it further than I'd thought possible, thoughts flooded my head. They were so fast and unexpected, I gasped, letting go of my knees and putting my hands to my ears. A cacophony of sound shattered through my mind, with countless layers of words, as if I'd tapped into a gathering where everyone talked at once. I took a few steadying breathes, holding tight to the frequency while, somehow, my brain was able to dial down the volume.

Oooookay. Guess I got what I wanted. There was the briefest pause in the noise and I almost slapped myself. Someone had received the mind whisper but there was an air of puzzlement in the gap. I imagined shielding my own thoughts while leaving my receiver open for theirs and it must have worked. The river of words started again as I laid down on my bed to be more comfortable while listening in.

It's like listening to one instrument in a full orchestra; at first, it's hard to do but after a while, you can pick out only the violin or the bass or whatever. I focused on listening for key words, like schedule or my name or upcoming trips to the other base. The Imurians believed the Amorphans didn't have the ability to mind whisper as they'd never been able to hear them. I could tell them why, now. The frequency was so high, it was out of their Imurian brains' capabilities, out of Human ranges. In fact, I wasn't sure which DNA I'd tapped to be able to listen at this high frequency but I didn't care.

Ha, Something I know the Imurians don't. Those blasted scientists don't even know this. I taunted them from behind the safety of my internal shield. No reaction from the mind voices my wall held. A part of me wondered if even Si'neada or his sister could partition their brains like this. He hadn't taught me this, so either they couldn't, or he hadn't thought to tell me, or he wanted that kept secret—or he didn't know.

:...not going to the base. I didn't volunteer so why do I have to do it? They do dangerous things over there. I want to stay here, guarding that pink, hairy tiny alien female being the easy job.: Resentment flavored the thoughts. *:Well, orders are orders and I have to go. Better get some sleep now since we'll be leaving so early tomorrow.:*

Aargh. The Amorphans did have a trip planned to the other base tomorrow. If only I knew what time.

I tuned in again. Thoughts tumbled and rolled, intertwining. Some were lewd, thinking of females and also other males, and I blushed to hear their thoughts, some resentful of slights and perceived wrongs. A few sang fragments of songs over and over. *Hmm, seems the Amorphans have ear worms, too.* I grinned at the thought. Nice to know we're not the only species who gets music stuck in our brains.

I stayed tuned in. :Get up at 0430, do my cleansing, breakfast and then the convoy leaves at 0530 sharp. Uh huh, I have plenty of time in the morning if I get to sleep now. I hope I get to sleep quick. What if I don't? I hate when I lie here, tossing and turning.: An image flashed into me of an Amorphan staring at the ceiling in a darkened room, frustrated for not falling asleep instantly.

Now I knew the time. I wondered who all was scheduled to go on the trip but I couldn't think of a way to find out, short of contacting someone through my connection and asking. Well, that would draw unwanted attention, I'm sure, if they even could believe someone wanted to talk to them, brain to brain, as it were. More likely, they'd shake it off as a bad dream or some weird happening and I still wouldn't get an answer. So, that leaves me making the plan.

CHAPTER TWENTY-ONE

I fell asleep while formulating a plan to join that escort. My hair pinched me awake at 0300 in the morning, details gelling in my mind overnight. This had to work. I had to know what the upper officers were doing about my missing family and how they were going to rescue them. I couldn't get that information here, even if Myometo was willing to tell me. There were too many ways he could be overheard or observed and it wasn't right to get him into trouble for keeping me informed. It was up to me to gather my own info.

Okay, the plan is all figured out, right?

YES. DON'T TALK MUCH.

I won't.

Throwing off the covers, I stood and stretched my arms high overhead, carrying a few strands of hair up high. I ambled around the room, one hand rubbing my face or covering a faked yawn. My hair told me where to stop so it could fiddle with electronics, which it did in a flash of time.

Last stop was at the door. I opened it slowly, holding a hand to my forehead and partly over my eyes. A soldier stood at ease outside my room, but he snapped into attentiveness as I looked out.

"Soldier, I have a killer headache. I think I had too much sun yesterday."

"I will call for the medics, Madam." A look of alarm crossed his face and I could tell he was worried he'd be found at fault somehow, since it happened on his watch.

"No, no, that's okay. I have meds I take for it."

"I must call, Madam." He lifted his wrist to his mouth and sent the request.

I left the door open a little bit, retreating to my bed so I could look wan and in pain. The attending medic arrived within minutes, carrying a small bag, announcing himself as he entered my room.

I gave him a weak smile. "Have you treated a Human before, sir?"

"No, you are my first." He looked pained, as if it were a huge oversight on his part. I'd counted on him not knowing Human ailments.

"I have a migraine headache. It's common for my species, and while I don't get them often, one hit me during the night. I have my own meds for it and I need quiet, a dark room, a lot of rest and let the meds work. They shouldn't have bothered you." I looked at him with a woeful look. "And no meals, just the thought makes me sick to my stomach." Putting my fingers over my mouth, I made a small retching sound for effect.

"I see." I could tell he didn't. He tapped into his PerPad, reading what came up on the screen.

"Looking up migraines?" I put the back of my hand on my forehead. "It's the worst kind of headache a Human can have. Usually rest and quiet is what I need plus the pill I carry with me."

"That's what it says here. Are you sure it's not a head growth inside?"

"Oh, I'm sure. I've had all the tests done on New Eden." Well, I did have to have all the tests to come here to participate in this program so I didn't lie.

"Let me examine you so I am sure it is nothing to worry about."

"Okay," I whispered, closing my eyes. "But noise and light make it worse, so please be very quiet." Oh, boy, I could've been in the movies.

He did a brief exam, nothing intrusive and done in a professional manner. When he found nothing obviously wrong, he laid a gentle hand on my head. "Since I can't find anything out of the ordinary, I will have to concede to your self-diagnosis. What can I do to help you today? Do you need more pain meds?"

"No, I don't need more chemicals. What you can do is make sure I'm not disturbed. I will stay in my room all day, so you can send the soldier of the day away."

"I will send a tray to your room."

"Oh, no, I can't eat or I'll throw it back up. If I get hungry, I have the snacks in the cooler and plenty to drink. But, thank you, sir medic."

"Just 'doctor' will do, Madam. Are you sure that's all I can do for you?" He backed up a step as I squinted at him. "I will come back this afternoon to check on you again."

"No, no need, honest! If I'm asleep when you came and woke me up, the headache would be worse." I waved a hand in the air. "I'll be fine. I just need rest and quiet today, I assure you of that. I appreciate your concern."

"Very well. You know more about this than I do. I will check on you in person in the morning, then. I'll monitor your condition throughout the day from the room sensors."

"Sure." I whispered. I watched him retreat out the door until it clicked shut, then brought down the vid screen to watch him leave. To my complete relief, he took the soldier on duty with him.

Okay, part one is done. Now on to part two.

READY.

Going into the bathroom, I did everything I needed to do including changing shapes. Examining my new face in the mirror as soon as I recovered enough to do so, I was pleased to see I wouldn't be recognized, since I now was an amalgam of different Amorphan DNAs. The Akrion god-like particle and my body had worked all night splicing, dicing and mixing DNA. No wonder I'd dreamed about being a chef in the middle of a swamp with no one around to serve.

First, to shore up my story, my hair fiddled with the settings for the medical surveillance equipment so it would run on a loop but with variances in my breathing rate, heart rate and other vital signs. Checking the corridor on the screen again, I stepped out and sauntered off toward the dining area to eat breakfast and find out who was ordered to leave for the base.

Holding my laden tray of food in hand, I looked around the room to see where to sit. A group of young Amorphan males clustered at one table, talking and laughing even while one or two yawned. There were a couple of open seats, so I walked over, pulling out a chair after placing my food on the table.

"Morning, everyone. I'm a new guy on base here; just arrived yesterday evening." I shoved food in my mouth. "Name's Jesalion."

All conversation stopped when I sat down, and they all looked at me, with peculiar looks, probably in shock someone had intruded their space. My heart pounded in a rapid beat, my nerves stretched tight like guitar strings. "Sorry? Did I interrupt something? I apologize! I'll find a different place to sit." I started rising from my seat, and one of them said, "No, no, you don't have to leave. We were just messing around until it's time to report for duty."

I thumped back into my chair. "If you're sure...?"

They all nodded, then introduced themselves to me, one by one. We talked, then, of the day's weather and other inconsequential things. Checking my watch, I said in a disgusted voice, "I can't be late for my first assignment but I'm not sure where to go for it. I was pretty tired when I got here last night and no time to find my way around."

"Where do you need to go?"

"Wherever they're leaving for the other base. I'm not even here 24 hours yet and they have me assigned to going someplace else for the day! I don't even know what I'm supposed to do over there. Guess I'll find out when I arrive." I shook my head. "Officers."

The male next to me snickered; his name lapel said Katerian, "You can say that again. They all think they're Zatro-ini's." They laughed uproariously at the quip. The Zatro is an absolute ruler of a city of a million citizens and he just called his superiors a 'little Zatro'. Well, it is the military after all; making fun of officers is part of it, I guess. He slapped my back, and I almost slopped the hot drink I had just raised to my mouth. "Didn't you get your map on your holo?"

My holo? Oh, little pots of piss! I wonder which button is supposed to be for that? "Uh, no, I didn't. I arrived so late last night, I guess someone was asleep on the job." *Please think it's true! And please, please, let it not be one of them!*

Reaching over, Katerian poked a purple button on my cuff on my left arm. Nothing happened, of course, since this wasn't a real uniform.

"I tried that earlier, but it didn't work." I took a loud slurp of my hot drink, wishing it was full-bodied coffee with cream.

His face folded into a puzzled frown. "That's odd; I've never heard of one of these malfunctioning before." His face suddenly lit up. "Or did you forget to plug in your suit before going to sleep?"

"By the balls of the nearest Zatro, I think you're right! I was exhausted last night and kind of fell into bed right after I got here." I rubbed my sharp, pointed teeth. "I don't think I even brushed my biters."

Laughter all around at the usage of the common Zatro curse phrase. "You come along with me and we'll get you a functioning suit. Won't take but a couple of minutes to switch and we've the time. I've been assigned there for the day, also." Katerian said with a grin. "What's your assigned job today?"

Another landmine I just stepped on. "I appreciate the offer of guidance." I glanced at him. "Uh, my job. Well, it was supposed to be part of my holo this morning, but," I spread my hands apart, showing the colors of regret, "of course, I didn't get it."

Another soldier chimed in. "I bet you're replacing Herandion today. He called in sick this morning; he was supposed to be the note-taker."

Relief flooded me, making my knees feel weak. Thank the universe for sending me a rescue angel and that I'd chosen my seat well. "That would be great! I appreciate it, Katerian. I'll owe you a favor in return." I flashed a smile at the other person. "That must be the job they assigned me to do, even though," I flashed colors of embarrassment, "I am such a new recruit and barely trained, I swear. What does a note-taker do at that base, anyway? I know how to take notes in a class so is that what I'm supposed to do there?" I couldn't see his name lapel because his arm was raised, holding a cup in front of it.

He nodded, looking at me a little bit oddly. "Yes, it's just like that. Are you sure you're supposed to do that job?" Suspicion colored his skin.

I shrugged. "That's what I'm told." *Or, at least, you just suggested it.* "You know how orders come down. They don't usually make sense to us lower-level grunts."

He barked a laugh. "That's true enough."

Katerian looked at his wrist. "You do have your PerPad with you?"

I tapped my breast pocket. "Of course."

CHAPTER TWENTY-TWO

What I love about being a brand-new Amorphan being, besides the novelty of it, is I don't have to mimic anyone's mannerisms, facial expressions and verbal quirks. It's a huge relief to just be myself, only in different skin. Using 'I'm a young and new recruit' as my cover was a great idea, also, because no one would think they knew me from somewhere and they'd expect me to screw up, since I was so green.

The ride to the other base was bumpy and crowded. I squeezed into the last seat in the back row, facing so we looked out the back end of the ground vehicle, open to the air. The tires, made from some material I didn't recognize, were oversized with big treads and spikes in them and sat high above the ground. Painted a camouflage pattern to match the foliage and surroundings, the inside was strictly utilitarian. We sat on metal seats, straps to hang onto while moving and only a lap belts to keep us in place. A heavy-duty weapon was attached to the hood and everyone on board carried an assault rifle, with choices all the way from mild stun to kill mode. Since I didn't have one with me, I took a loud, swear word laden dressing down at not having brought a weapon and then was issued one.

I hoped with a lot of fervor no one else showed up to claim "my" job. How would I explain that?

CHANGED ROSTER.

You did? When?

THIS MORNING. TAPPED INTO SYSTEM.

Thank you, Krystal, and to the high heavens you thought of doing that!

YOU'RE WELCOME, RACHAEL. HAPPY YOU APPRECIATE ME. The tiniest bit of acerbity to the words.

I almost chuckled out loud at that. My hair was rather chatty this morning, a highly unusual occurrence. *Oh, I totally appreciate you. As long as you remember who's really boss around here.*

HMPH.

When my hair first awakened, I found I had to establish who was boss and did that with a pair of scissors and a lot of pain. I had it under control. Mostly. Sometimes.

Hanging onto the swaying strap, clutching my weapon in my other arm, and not accidentally shooting while doing so is not an easy job, I discovered. The metal seat felt slippery, not helping with the logistics of staying in my seat. Other than that, the trip was short, uncomfortable, hot and jarring. I bit my tongue once from a particularly deep pothole; I swear the driver aimed for every rock and deep rut he could find. I'll bet, if I could've turned around to look, he'd be smirking every time we jounced around in the back. I think he was trying to see who'd be first to fall out.

There was no chance to talk on the ride over the roar of the engines and rattling of the metal vehicle. Feeling bruised and battered on arrival, we climbed down to stand in rows, my sore tongue complaining when it hit the back of my teeth. I looked around and saw nothing too exciting. This looked pretty much like the place we'd just left, actually. I shifted a little toward Katerian, asking, "Hey, I have a question."

He gave me a sidelong look with a small frown, muttering without moving his mouth, "Keep it down or they'll discipline us. Just wait until they've checked us off and then you can ask."

I pressed my lips together, nodding a little. "Later, then."

After we were inspected and counted off, we broke ranks and I stepped to Katerian's side. "Well, why don't they," I nodded at the enclosure, "have one of their own grunts do the note-taking? Why bring in someone like me? Why do they need all of us, for that matter?"

Raising his right eye ridge, he replied, "Because we don't know anything about what's going on over here. They figure whatever they say won't make sense to us, whereas someone who works here could figure out whatever it is they do here."

"Their work here is that secretive?" I asked. "Why not just record the sessions or whatever and not have a notetaker?"

"It's easier to edit a notetaker than take the time to splice a recording to remove what they don't want to preserve."

"Am I in danger, then?" I said, taken aback.

He wrinkled his nose. "Why would you be? Unless you talk back or don't follow orders, then yes, but that's true of any grunt soldier."

"Oh. Sure."

By then, we were all sorted out by our attending officer into some sense of order and he led the march into the enclave, stopping to be scrutinized by the guard on duty. I took in a breath of relief as the sentry guard let him in, then held it when I realized each of us were to be vetted by a DNA scan.

Did you...?

TAKEN CARE OF.

I breathed out. *Thank the stars and moons for that.*

THANK ME AND THE AKRION, INSTEAD.

Well, of course. It was implied but if you need to hear it, thank you.

ABOUT TIME.

No further time for banter; it was my turn; my hands turned sweaty with anxiety, skin colors flashing purple and yellow. I handed him the data chip I found in my pocket with a trembling hand. *How in the blazing starfield did you do that? Never mind, I can't be distracted right now.*

I passed inspection, the data chip did its job and I was waved onto the grounds. I rested my weapon against my shoulder like the rest of the soldiers, moving into my assigned position. Officer Farendian faced us, hands behind his back, slightly spreading his feet, standing tall and stern. His skin colors were calm and I wondered how they learned to control their skin colors. The Amorphans on the StarFinder had never told us about skin colors reflecting emotions and, apparently, none of us had noticed it happening nor did any of the five of us Humans ask.

"Soldiers!" He roared.

We snapped to attention. One hand on the weapon to hold it secure, the other down by our side, eyes forward and focused on the officer, spines stiffened and straight.

"Yessir!" We shouted back as one voice.

"You have your assigned duties. You will *not* talk about what your duty is, you will *not* discuss today's jobs with anyone inside OR outside of this squad, and you will *not* shirk your duty. Is that clear?"

"Yessir!"

"The notetaker will accompany me and the rest of you, go to your duty stations. We return to our base at six tonight so be here on the dot or you will be left to walk back. Alone. Dismissed."

I walked up to the officer. "Grunt Jesalion at your service, sir."

"Come with me." He turned on his heel, walking toward an adjacent building. "You understand the absolute need to not talk to anyone about what you hear here today." He made it a statement.

"Yes, sir." I answered.

"Good. Then there'll be no need for punishment if you fail to do so."

I gulped. "Yes, sir, there won't be a need, not at all."

"Make sure you keep it that way." Officer Farendian snarled. "Now, hand over your PerPad and I'll have it secured until you return. You will be provided with what you need to use."

I complied with his order because what other choice did I really have? I wondered what kind of top-secret stuff was going on over here, as I became even more nervous than I already felt. I shifted the rifle to a more comfortable spot on my shoulder and Officer Farendian noticed.

"Oh, that gets left out here in the hallway." He indicated a rack on the wall nearby. "Make sure the safety is engaged and put it over there. Be sure to remember which one is yours."

These weapons weren't DNA activated which meant anyone could use it. I suppose it made sense, because in the middle of a battle, if you needed to use someone else's gun, you couldn't stop to recalibrate it to your own DNA. Noting the number on the rack, I nestled it with care into the opening, double-checking the serial number engraved on the barrel and that the safety was engaged.

I returned to Farendian's side, wiping my sweaty palms against my trousers, glad soldiers didn't wear traditional robes. My own personal gun was tucked inside my uniform, concealed a dozen different ways so nothing or no one could find it. As long as it was accessible to me, I didn't care how it was hidden but I felt better for having it with me.

Farendian input a code into the security box on the door, not realizing my hair watched and memorized every digit and letter, waited for a scan of his body and eyes, then a DNA sample taken for analysis. Whatever was going on was truly top-secret and they were taking no chances of imposters. However, they hadn't guarded against a shape-shifter–me. The fact that every known species thought it was impossible made me the most unique being in the entire Universe. *Breathe in, Jessi, then breathe it back out.*

He stepped back, motioning me forward to go through the same process. Hesitating, I asked, "Since I just arrived last night, will they have my accurate info?"

He grunted. "If not, they'll get it now. They have your data chip for comparison." He jerked a thumb at the equipment. "Now, step up, soldier. Or do you have something to hide?"

His glittering eyes bored a hole through me. I swallowed hard, saying, "No, sir! Nothing to hide, Officer!" *Except, of course, I have everything to hide.* Stepping up, I went through the scan and DNA sample, and held my breath. When nothing happened, no one shot me for being an intruder, I let out my breath with a slight whoosh.

A narrow panel opened in the door, just big enough for one person to enter at a time, and Farendian pointed at it. "Get in there. They'll take it from here."

Having no idea what was happening, I stepped through the opening, expecting Farendian to follow me, but he stayed out. I stopped abruptly, looking at six Amorphan faces staring at me from where they stood around a table with tablets set before each of them. I gulped out of sheer nerves, then squeaked out, "Uh. Officers. What do you want me to do? I'm your, uh, note-taker?"

One of them, who seemed to be of a higher rank than I'd seen before, snapped at me, "Come forward so the opening can close."

I took two hurried steps, then came to attention again, hearing the panel slither back into place behind me. I was trapped in this room with six fierce looking, high-ranking officers, all cutting me apart with their laser-like stares. No one said anything and I had no idea what to do next.

"Didn't they brief you, Grunt?" Another one barked at me.

"Sir, I was only told I'm to take notes for you and not to speak of this with anyone. I just arrived on base last night so perhaps–"

He made a curt gesture, cutting me off mid-sentence. "Take your clothing off, soldier."

I started in surprise. "I–uh–what?" Then I tacked on a hasty "Sir".

"You heard me. Take your clothing off. We have to be perfectly sure you are who you say you are."

Amorphans aren't body conscious the way us Humans are but that didn't make this any more comfortable for me. I fumbled through a salute. My *gun?*

A brief, slashing pain in my upper abdomen and a slight suction made me flinch.

GUN HIDDEN.

The officers' eyes narrowed as I practically ripped through the fasteners on the uniform in my haste. Dropping it to the ground, it puddled around my feet as I stood naked before them except for the socks and boots. My male skin pouch, front, forward and low on the abdomen on Amorphans, puckered in the sudden cold on my refractory skin. Reds, oranges, and blues flashed over my body along with a couple of hues I didn't have a name for, colors of anxiety, eagerness to please, embarrassment and confusion.

Not knowing what to do with my hands, I clasped them behind my back, then released them to hang by my sides. I wondered if they would next demand I open my male skin pouch to prove I had a penis-like appendage in there, something they call a procreation rod. My physiology class at University had taught me a lot about their biology.

The officer closest to me made a twirling motion with a finger, so I turned around in a full circle, feeling their gazes raking over me. When I faced them again, he nodded, then looked at his companions. "Are we satisfied he is genuine?"

"Yes," they all agreed.

He crooked a finger at me, beckoning me toward the table. I reached down for my uniform to draw it back into place, but he said, "No, leave that where it is." Well, that meant the socks and boots had to come off, too. I sighed in resignation.

Now barefoot and bare-ass, shivering, I walked over to the table. One of them thrust a data pad at me. "You'll write down on here what we tell you to write, when we tell you to do so. You will inscribe it exactly as we dictate it. You will not add or subtract anything at all under penalty of death. Understood?

"Yes, sir, I understand."

He pointed at a corner of the room. "You may stand over there with your back to us."

CHAPTER TWENTY-THREE

The room contained a table with no chairs, their data pads, and themselves and now, me. Everything was painted gray, even the ceiling and floor with muted lighting from someplace I couldn't see although it was very bright shining down on the tabletop. It was rather disorientating. The flat quality of their voices, the way the words dampened and disappeared in the drab room, suggested this room was highly secure in every way. No wonder they needed an actual person to input information in the pad; I suspected they couldn't record their session even if they wanted to do so.

My back turned to them in my designated corner, ready to write down whatever they said with my stylus pen, I knew I had no chance to see what they were working on or what this session was about. If my hair wasn't a part of this body, it could've sent a strand or two out to investigate, but that wasn't possible in this form. We hadn't yet figured how to become invisible in any way. *Too bad, wish we could.*

A flash of light startled me and I raised my Perpad so I could see in the screen a reflection of a 3D display over the table. I blinked at the amount of detail available on what appeared to be photos of the burned down cabin. *This is about the fire! And perhaps, about my rescue and where my Amorphan family is being held.*

A few seconds later, they started speaking in hushed tones, one at a time at first, then with overlapping voices and I realized they spoke in a language completely unknown to me. *What the frick? What language is that?* I wondered if my internal translator would kick in, the military grade one inserted before coming here and the one they didn't have a clue I had inside my brain.

UNKNOWN LANGUAGE. TAKE A WHILE TO LEARN. Frustration came through, loud and clear.

I noted my skin flashed red, one of the many colors of frustration, but it stopped as soon as I noticed it. The colors settled into dull hues, reflecting boredom and patience on my part, even though that was far from what I was feeling. Maybe controlling the colors wasn't that hard, after all.

I started to feel sensory deprived, standing there, staring at a blank gray wall, only hearing the cadence of their voices behind me. When one voice snapped, "Grunt! Write this down," I startled like a new-born baby. I started to turn toward the speaker, who said, "Stay facing the wall. You can write from that position, yes?" He didn't sound friendly.

"Yes, Officer. I can, Officer."

He reeled off a string of numbers and I hoped I got them right. He ordered me to repeat them back, which I did in a shaky voice. When he said, "As you were," I huffed out a silent puff of relief. The rest of my time in there was more of the same, each time with different numbers. My mind puzzled over them, trying to make sense of the sequences. At first, I thought they were location numbers, like longitude and latitude, but there were too many of them. Each set they told me to record was different from the one before.

Is it a numerical code or language? For all I know, it's inventory of how many eating utensils they have in this place. One thing I can say with certainty is that it's deadly boring to stare at a blank, drab wall with your back turned toward where all the action took place, while naked and shivering in the cool air. I discovered parts of me shriveling from the coolness that I didn't think could shrink.

I fidgeted as I stood in my corner, thinking all I missed was a hat that said "Dummy". Shifting from foot to foot, I wished I could sit but didn't dare try squatting. No wonder no one volunteered for this job; I bet a soldier only did it once and then found a way to never return.

Their voices behind me receded to a buzz of incomprehensible overlapping sounds again as I fiddled with my data pad. I yawned. I practiced standing on one foot. I amused myself by changing my fingers into other shapes; the Amorphans have that ability with their fingers and toes. I thought maybe I started to recognize a distinguishable word or two in their dialogue but not enough to understand any sentences.

"Grunt!" The male's voice, abrupt and stern, made me jump and squeak in fright and surprise.

"Ye-yes, Officer!"

"Get dressed. We're done here. Hand me that data pad first." As I started to turn toward his voice, he snapped, "Hand it back, wait three minutes, then you may dress and leave."

I almost dropped the pad in my haste to comply but one of them snatched it from my hand. I heard the door slide open; I turned to see all of them gone except one, who stood by the opening, watching me with narrowed eyes and dilated nasal openings. "Three minutes," he snapped. I saluted in acknowledgement.

When the time was up, I dressed, relieved to stop shivering. I went to the door, not sure what to do next when it didn't open for me. Finally, I knocked. That worked; the panel slid open and I stepped out to face one of the officers. He patted me down, and he was very thorough indeed. I don't know what he thought I could've stolen from an empty room but this must be protocol.

"Dismissed." He barked out the words, striding away from me.

Grabbing my rifle from the rack, I made my way back to the meeting point, finding everyone there, making me wonder how long I'd been in that room. We piled back into the truck, once again putting me on the back seat facing outward. Maybe the scenery going back would be different than going over. Maybe it had rained a bit to keep the choking dust cloud down to a minimum and the potholes mysteriously filled in. Maybe I was Goddess of the world and no one had told me.

With orders to not discuss our duties of the day and the roar of the truck's engine, there was no conversation. I held onto my strap as before, keeping myself in my seat by the skin of my teeth. My arms were going to hurt later from the strength of my grip. Breathing in, I coughed from the dirt and dust pulled in with the air, my eyes watering. Then I squinted a little. Was that a smudge on the far hill over there? Or did I have dirt in my eye?

I couldn't spare a hand to wipe my eye clean so I bent my head forward to rub my eyes on my arm. As I did so, a ZZZZzzzt sounded by my ear, and the energy bolt hit where my head had just been. I screamed in a very girly way as the soldiers around me reacted. Four of us faced backwards, crammed together, the three of them bringing up weapons to shoot back and I belatedly did the same. A transparent shield of some kind sprang up before us, dispersing the stunning bolts. I saw several vehicles racing toward us from the far hills; that hadn't been dirt in my eye, after all. They bounced and roared as they came at us, Amorphans hanging over the sides of the open vehicles to shoot.

The other soldiers and I were able to return fire; the shield allowed our guns to shoot through it while also protecting us. I squeezed off shots as best I could through the jouncing, jostling, swerving and increased speed of our truck. Things happened so fast, I had no way to know if my shots made any difference or not, but that didn't stop me from shooting. Those sons of beanbags had almost shot my head off and that wasn't easily forgiven.

We were only one truck since it had been a small–by military standards–work force sent over for the day. They had three, moving to maneuver around us to force us to stop. There was now so much dust in the air from tires stirring the dry dirt that visibility was seriously impaired. At least we didn't have to worry about shooting allies, since we were all on the truck together.

"Got one!" The soldier next to me crowed.

"How can you tell?" I screamed back. "Oh!" I saw one of the assailants fall out of the truck, crumpling onto the dirt. No one spared him even a glance from his group.

"Why are they attacking us?" I yelled over the noise but no one answered. I glanced over to my left see the soldier dangling in his seat, only his seat belt keeping him in place. "Oh, shiii–" Something slammed into my right calf, turning my words into a scream of pain.

Our shield was tattered, that was the only explanation. The other two soldiers were too busy shooting back to bother with questions; the soldiers behind me had turned our way, their rifle barrels poking out between us, firing at our enemies. Gritting my teeth against the blazing agony in my leg, I pulled my trigger again and again, as fast as I could, my focus narrowed to the immediate sight before me. It was either shoot them or be shot again. I had the stray thought that Zoe would've fainted from fright but my Dad made sure I was prepared for anything.

A new sound cut through the turmoil and uproar, but I couldn't place it with all the shooting and noise and confusion. My weapon's light blazed red to tell me it was out of energy. On pure instinct, I grabbed my slumped neighbor's rifle and resumed firing. I hoped he was alive but had no time to check on him.

A hovercraft's propellers washed away some of the dust cloud engulfing us, as soldiers hung out open doors over us, shooting at the intruders. A flash of relief flooded my body; they were on our side and we needed the timely intervention.

The oncoming vehicles slewed into turning circles, fishtailing and revving their engines, going up on two tires before dropping heavily back down; they knew they couldn't win against aircraft intervention. The hovercraft fired small missiles at them, hitting one in the engine, blowing it and the Amorphans in it sky-high. I couldn't feel sorry for them, however, even as they dropped onto the ground with thuds and squishy stuff happening. I felt bile rise in my throat, gagging at the sight of their bodies, but managed to hold it back.

The remaining two enemy trucks roared away in different directions, visibly bouncing high in the air over the undulating hillocks and scrub brush. Even more dust billowed into the air around them, carried back to us by the breeze caused by the hovercrafts, as the dust cloud effectively hid the two vehicles. The hovercrafts, painted drab tans and browns to match the arid landscape around us, settled to the ground near our transport truck. Bodies littered the ground, some moving and some not. A few of them, I noted with horror, wore soldier uniforms. I blinked to clear my eyes and then saw those uniforms were dirty and ragged and ill-fitting.

Fatigue hit me with the force of a tsunami wave. We were safe but my thoughts scattered and my hands trembled in the aftershock of battle–my first battle, and I hoped, my last battle. I unhooked my harness, turning to my seatmate, still slumped in his straps. I felt for his pulse, relieved beyond measure when I felt one, though he remained unconscious.

CHAPTER TWENTY-FOUR

We arrived back at base, more or less in one piece. Our group had injuries but no casualties. Prisoners were escorted by armed guards, shoved through the gates, having been forced to walk ahead of the truck to our base since our truck was full of our soldiers. The hovercraft had taken the seriously injured for more immediate medical attention after calling a second hovercraft. Although I'd been shot in my leg, it wasn't emergent so I rode back with the others. I discovered burn marks on my left arm but whether from the enemy or from the rifle barrels being shot between us, I didn't know.

I walked like a zombie, trudging into the compound, still dazed by the fight. I didn't understand what or how this had happened and the others weren't talking. I put one foot ahead of the other, desperately wishing for my bed, running into the back of the soldier ahead of me when he came to a complete stop. I took a quick step back, saying, "Sorry, sorry."

His shoulders lifted in a shrug, not saying anything, slumped in exhaustion.

Blinking my eyes, I craned my neck to see why we'd stopped. Farendian stood at the front of our group, now short a few soldiers due to injuries and prisoner duties, facing us. "Soldiers!" He said in a loud voice.

"Yes, Officer!" We chorused back.

"Well done today. Due to our efforts and exemplary training and quick reactions, we foiled the bandits of their spoils. They have no prisoners—we do! They have no data—we do! They have nothing to show for today—but we do!"

All of us cheered, a sudden burst of energy sending fists shooting high in the air around me. *They were after data? But we have nothing written, just what's in our—oh. What's in our heads from what we saw and did today.*

"We didn't expect an attack today, as you probably figured out by now, but we still won the battle." Farendian nodded his head at us in approval. "Those with walking injuries, report to the physician on duty. The rest of you—" His words were cut off by an overhead alarm sounding.

"All officers report in person to their emergency stations. All soldiers report to the meeting hall for further instructions."

Carried along with the crowd, since I was in the middle, I didn't have a chance to sneak back to my room or anywhere else for shape changing. We spilled into a large meeting hall, the press of bodies pushing me forward as we all found a place to stand.

Myometo faced us from a raised platform as he waited for everyone to finish filing in and quieting down. After a minute or so, which seemed like a year to me, silence filled the air as we waited for his words. He looked grim and angry, glittery eyes almost spitting laser beams at us, or so it seemed. His hands were clenched by his side as he drew in a breath.

He looked us over with a cold look, giving one brief, sharp nod of his head. His skin showed angry and distressed colors of red; apparently, his color suppression abilities weren't working well today. A sinking, queasy feeling in my stomach made me want to cross my arms over my abdomen. Because it was Myometo up there looking so forbidding, I was afraid whatever this was about involved me.

"Attention, grunt soldiers." We hardly breathed for fear of his wrath if we drew his attention, his very stance spitting anger. "You know this base was chosen for its ability to safeguard an important and valuable person." Heads nodded, no one daring to speak.

"We have failed in our job."

An audible gasp sounded from the multitude of throats in the crowd.

"Madam Jessalya Lilienthal is missing. We believe the attack you endured was a diversion so she could be taken. On the chance she is still on this base, you will search every nook, every crack in the wall, turn over every rock and pebble, every part of this base. Do you understand?"

"Yes, Officer!"

"You will pair up for this search and report immediately if you find her or any evidence. You are to protect her at all costs when she is found. You are to escort her to the commanding officers. You will do whatever is necessary for her safety and well-being. If you do not have a functioning gun, you are to get one on your way out of here today. You will put it on maximum stun, but not on kill mode; we want prisoners if possible. And whatever else you do, do *not* shoot the Human. If you do, you will be shot with the same amount of charge, as you well know."

Oh, crap on toast, they must've checked my room and discovered my room is empty and the body in the bed is clothing. Now what do I do?

He bared his sharply pointed teeth. "Now go."

I didn't know what to do. I could find a placed to change, to pretend I had gotten lost or some other excuse. I could show up to call off the search, thus saving all my assigned bodyguards from being disciplined for losing me. I didn't know what they would endure, since I was missing and they didn't know if I'd been harmed or not, but I doubted it would be pleasant.

For all I knew, they'd be thrown out into the barren land around us without food or water to see if they could survive. Or put in a jail somewhere until I was returned. Pain in my heart stabbed through me at the thought, along with horror as I imagined them stumbling through the sand and dirt, sun beating down on them without mercy, insects thirsting for their blood.

Leaving the room was slower than entering, as someone at the door paired the exiting soldiers and assigned them an area for investigating. As I waited my turn, I decided I'd find a way to ditch my companion and change so I could save my guards, whom I considered friends, even if they didn't return the sentiment.

HAVE TRANSLATION.

Huh? I had no idea what it meant.

LANGUAGE AND NUMBERS. UNDERSTAND THEM.

And...? The line inched forward; I was only a few bodies from being sent out to look for me. *I need to find a place to change back, you know; that's my first priority. I can't let my guards be killed or maimed or whatever because of this. This can wait for later.*

EXCHANGE PLACE.

Yeah, that's what I just fracking said. Stepping forward, now only two people were ahead of me to the door, with a press of bodies still behind.

NO. NOT THAT. WHERE FAMILY WILL BE.

Seriously?

YES.

"Grunt, you are with Opardium to search. Here is your assigned section." He thrust a pad at me with a grid showing the location of our search area. I took it, looking behind me for Opardium, who nodded at me.

"Looks like we need to go to the south door and search from there." He said after peering over my shoulder at the display.

I nodded. That section was highlighted on the floor plans in green while the other areas were red. My head spun with what my hair had just told me and I couldn't pay full attention to Opardium. I shoved the pad at him. "Here. You know this place better than me so I'll follow you."

He turned to go down the hall, me on his heels while I thought about the implications of what my hair had revealed. I needed to see a map of where they were going to rescue my family.

Do we know the area? Are they going in to rescue them or retrieve them or what?

Hesitation. RESCUE FAMILY IF POSSIBLE. CAPTURE HOLDERS IF POSSIBLE.

And if not possible?

Silence.

They'll kill them if they can't take the bad guys prisoner, won't they? Even if that means my family dies with them.

YES. The answer felt sorrowful.

I sucked in a breath. *Then we have to be there, either before the soldiers arrive or with them if we have no other way of going. I can't let them die. I can't! I'll give myself up first. I don't think they'd kill me.*

I ran into the back of Opardium. "Oof! Sorry, sorry, Opardium! I wasn't paying attention."

He glared at me for a second while I raised my hands palms up in supplication. He twisted his mouth in a gesture of annoyance, then shook his head. "We start from here."

He shoved the door open as I said, "Maybe we should open that door softly. What if she's behind it?"

He tossed an irritated look at me but gave a short nod, grabbing the door to slow down its trajectory from his strong push. We stepped out into the waning afternoon sun.

The light was soft and diffuse outdoors, warmth pushing at our faces when we first opened the door. Dust kicked up from our booted feet as we peered behind every bush and blade of grass, like I was a mouse hiding in the roots of the low, scrubby foliage. Opardium took this very seriously and, literally, wasn't leaving any stone unturned. He picked up two sticks, handing one to me. Puzzled, my eye ridges knitted, I pointed it ahead of me. "What's this for?"

"To poke into any possible openings where she might have been left."

I blinked at him. "You think she's dead and discarded?"

He shrugged with that fluid motion the Amorphans used. "It's possible. Or she's been tied up and gagged and stuck in some hidey-hole to retrieve later. Perhaps she was drugged and now unconscious."

"I don't see footprints out here."

He raised one eye ridge, kicking at the dry dirt with one foot, causing a puff of dirt to rise a couple of inches into the air. He stamped his boot into it next, causing an even larger cloud of dust, making me sneeze. He crossed his arms, looking at the ground in a very pointed way.

I turned my gaze to the area. "Okay, I get it. We won't see footprints." The dust settled quickly and, like quicksand, had already smoothed away any signs of what he'd done.

"I guess grunts can learn from us soldiers, after all. Perhaps the rumors aren't true about needing knowledge stuffed into their brains through their ears."

I made a face at him. "Yeah, yeah, yeah. You take left and I'll take right?"

"Sure."

We moved apart, examining everything on the ground. There were no trees in our section but I saw other soldiers quartering their patch of ground, poking at the ground like we did, shaking the occasional tree while looking upward. One enterprising soldier shinnied up the trunk of one tree, disappearing into the leaves.

A sharp prod in my ribs with the sharp end of a stick brought my attention back to Opardium. He looked at me with narrowed, glittering eyes, a flush of red to his skin. "You are to pay attention to our area, not theirs." Quick as a snake, he took his length of wood and swatted my butt with it. "Back to work."

I stared at him open-mouthed. "You hit me!"

"Yes, and I'll do worse if I catch you slacking again." The hues of annoyance and satisfaction swirled across his face. I'm sure mine showed colors of embarrassment, anger, and outrage. By the smirk on his face, he noticed my humiliation.

I resumed poking at the ground, gritting my teeth, seething inside at his audacity. But–I was playing a grunt soldier and this was within the bounds of what he could do for discipline. I ground my teeth in anger until my tongue caught on one of my very sharp teeth.

The dirt had a lot of small holes dug into it, here and there, but all too small even for a diminutive human. I poked my stick into them, anyway, mimicking my partner, making sure there wasn't a hidden cavern past the opening.

The scraggly, scattered gray-brown plants sported spiky, serrated-edged leaves or thorns, sometimes both, and grew in sparse patches. There was no way to hide beneath or behind these; the foliage wasn't thick enough nor were they big enough in size. The arid climate here discouraged the lush growth of plants.

I pulled a water bottle out of one of my many pockets, taking a swig. As I did so, my skin flashed silver, reflecting light outward like a mirror set in sunlight, startling me. The Amorphan skin showed emotions in color, but I'd had no clue it could reflect the sun away. No wonder I wasn't boiling hot in the heat. I was hot where my uniform hid my skin but it wasn't unbearable.

I poked a hole while I thought about this and as I pulled my stick out, there was a bit of reluctance to come out. Something long and sinuous came fast and furious out of the hole, leaping toward me, hissing.

"Aaaagh!" I screeched as I scrambled backwards away from the snake-like thing, tripping over a rock behind me, landing in the dirt on my butt.

The snake-lizard struck at my boot, fangs bared, hitting the sole as I kicked at it. Opardium ran over, pushing his stick underneath the thing, flipping it away from me. It writhed on the ground for a couple of seconds, then slithered away faster than anything I'd seen before.

"Th-th-thanks." I stuttered, my heart still thundering in my chest as I leaned back on my hands. "Wh-what was that thing? Some kind of snake?"

"It is a burrow slitherer," he corrected me. "All the denizens of these burrows around here had been relocated and we check every few days to make sure they don't return, but this one..." He shrugged. "Must have snuck back when we weren't looking." A sudden grin on his face surprised me. "You shriek like a girl."

I dusted off the butt of my uniform, after standing. "I was surprised, is all. I wasn't expecting anything to attack me." I said in a stiff voice. I knew my skin showed intense embarrassment as his grin got bigger. "Where I come from, there aren't burrow slitherers."

"Just wait until I tell this story at dinner tonight, how I saved a grunt from a non-venomous slitherer."

"Well, how was I supposed to know that?" I snapped. "It looked dangerous to me! It tried to bite me!"

He chortled. "Dangerous! Dangerous? That little thing? Couldn't have been over four or five finger lengths long; its fangs couldn't have pierced a piece of wet bread." He guffawed, slapping his knee.

"Hey, Opardium!" Someone shouted at him from the next patch of dirt. "What's so funny?"

"Just a stupid joke, Jinardian. I'll tell you later." He started poking at the ground. "Back to work, scaredy-grunt."

I glowered at him as I started my search again, almost chuckling–again–at the irony of me looking for me. Finally, we'd rattled every bush, poked every hole and nothing else scary ran out as we worked.

Opardium wiped his hand across his brow. "Okay, grunt, let's move indoors."

CHAPTER TWENTY-FIVE

After we inspected every inch of our assigned part of the interior, collecting a few dust bunnies along the way, we took time for a hasty meal. I shoved the food down as fast as I could before going to the general meeting, starting in ten minutes. I said to Opardium, "Need to use the waste room before the meeting." I needed a little time to myself to think things over, figure out how to show up as myself again, how to get to the rendezvous point for saving my host family.

Shoving his tray aside, he rose from his seat. "I'll come with you and then we'll go to the meeting."

There was nothing I could do except nod and smile. *Couldn't you have made me a commander or something higher ranked than a grunt, Olive?*

BEST CHOICE, BEULAH. YOU DON'T KNOW HOW TO BE A COMMANDER.

Gee, thanks.

BESIDES, TOO CONSPICUOUS.

I'm sure I had a scathing retort to that but we entered the waste room at that second, did our thing, then left for the meeting. I'd have to stay a grunt a while longer. Impatience raised its ugly head; I itched to get something done, like a rescue mission.

We found a place to stand near the back of the large group jammed into the room just in time to hear the commander say, "Attention! I am calling this meeting to order."

We all shuffled in place, straightening our shoulders and backs, gazing ahead to his face. He paced a few steps one way, then returned the other.

"As I'm sure you can figure out, the Human has not been found yet."

I rolled my eyes. *Of course I haven't.* Something pinched me, a little tiny sharp pain and I almost slapped it away before stopping myself. My hair might be hidden in this body somehow, but it could still deliver pain.

"We believe she has been kidnapped, out of this very facility, let down by her head bodyguard, Myometo, and the soldiers assigned to keep her safe."

My heart stuttered. Uh-oh. They'd dislocated my bodyguards' shoulders in punishment for 'allowing' mine to be pulled from its socket. What would they do to Myometo and any others for my supposed disappearance? Surely, they wouldn't kill them. There was no evidence I was dead, after all, only that I was missing.

"Those assigned to the Human as her safety detail, step forward now." The commander snarled the words as my heart sank even further. My hands curled into tense fists, which, considering there were no bones in Amorphan hands, was pretty tight.

Six Amorphan soldiers stepped forward, shoulders rigid, eyes staring straight ahead, looking like they faced an execution squad. Perhaps they were. Myometo strode up to stand in front of them.

The commander pivoted to stare into Myometo's face. "Is the Human missing?"

"Yes, sir." Humiliation flashed over his visible skin.

"Have we found her?"

"No, sir."

"Is this offense punishable by execution?"

"Yes, sir." The pasty colors of fear flickered over Myometo's skin but only for a second before he tamped down the feelings. The soldiers behind him swallowed, one gulped, as they exhibited grays in various intensities.

"Then I pronounce your punish–"

"Sir!" I shouted, into a sudden shocked silence at my audacity. "There is no evidence or proof that I'm–the Human is dead or injured in any way! I do not believe this qualifies as deserving the ultimate punishment." The words squirted out of my mouth at full volume, surprising me as much as anyone.

Soldiers nearest me sucked in their breaths, visibly moving away like I'd just projected spears from my skin. They packed together like sardines to clear a space around me, making certain they wouldn't be tainted by my presence.

All personnel stared at me, the commander arrested in motion before he slowly swung to look at me. *Oh, Gods, he can't shoot me here. Can he?* I bit my lip. *What have I done? Did I make this better or worse?*

The commander stepped in my direction, scanning the crowd, spotting me in my little island of space. He used his first finger to beckon me forward. I took a faltering step toward him, like a puppet pulled in by its string. When the gap between us had become a mere foot apart, he held up his palm to stop me, his nostrils flared, eyes narrowed and his teeth bared. I stopped, barely breathing, my heart drumming in my chest and my hands shook.

I glanced at Myometo and the other soldiers for a split second, just a snap of my eyes moving to them and then back. Myometo's eyes were wide in surprise while the other soldiers showed fear and astonishment, expressions clearing as I glanced at them.

The commander grabbed my face with his right hand, fingers biting into my cheeks. "You will look at me and only me." He hissed the words at me.

"Y-y-yes, sir. Only you. Sir."

Keeping my eyes riveted on his face, I thought I might faint from the intensity and anger in his gaze. "I, uh, apologize, sir. I spoke out of turn. Sir."

"Did I ask you a question, grunt?"

"No. Commander. Sir."

Releasing my face from his death grip, he stepped back a pace. Without warning, he swung his right hand, slapping me across the left side of my face. Before I could even gasp, he backhanded the other side of my face. Something warm slid down my cheek. No one moved or even breathed loud in the thundering silence following his move.

I didn't dare twitch a muscle for fear of him repeating the action. My cheeks stung like they'd been set on fire, humiliation flooding my senses and no doubt lighting up my skin with intensity.

"Do you have more to say, grunt?"

"N-n-nothing m-m-more, s-sir." I kept my eyes on his, totally flustered but not daring to look away. Tears prickled and I blinked them away as fast as I could. The commander smirked at me, a sneer on his lips, his skin showing reds of anger, then greens of satisfaction, then into purples of resolve. *Oh, hairy poop, what if he throws me into a prison cell?*

"As I said, before I was so rudely interrupted," the commander roared, making me flinch, "I will now pronounce punishment."

He pointed at me. "This includes you, also, grunt."

My heart started beating so fast, I could barely get air. Panic threatened to overtake me and my head swam, even my arms shaking with trepidation.

"Until the Human is found, you will become lost. If she is found, healthy and alive, you will return at the end of your sentence time. It is one week lost for every day the Human is missing. If she is discovered to be dead, you face execution for dereliction of your duty to keep her safe and unharmed. If she is maimed, you receive the same."

He turned his head to look at Myometo and the soldiers, standing at stiff attention. He then looked at me. "Because we know the Human retained her Perpad along with her clothes, those are both allowed. We now go outside for immediate commencement of your punishment. You soldiers will witness. Guards, you'll take them to the main entrance, following me."

He pivoted on his boot heel, striding out of the room. Myometo stepped forward to follow him, the other sentenced soldiers following behind in single file. When the last soldier stepped in front of me, he murmured, "Behind me, grunt." The guarding Amorphans ringed us one for one.

I'd only been a soldier for a day and already I was being punished and exiled. Way to go, Jessi.

NOW TO RENDEVOUS POINT.

I stumbled at the words, catching my balance in time before I knocked into my guard, embarrassment flaming my face. He stepped back fast as if I might give him rabies if I touched him, holding a baton in his hand, raised to strike me. I'm betting no one would stop him if he chose to beat me.

I caught a glimpse of Opardium's face in the crowd, disgust written across it. Having to file out of the room in front of all those loathing eyes was almost worse than being publicly slapped. Good thing I wasn't really a soldier and even better that I'd never have to be a soldier with these people again. If I survived this exile, that is. Our line came to an abrupt stop.

The commander's voice cut through to me. "As you leave the facility, a tracker will be applied. It guides you to your designated direction. It keeps track of your movements and records encounters with others. Remember, you are the disgraced one and you are to remain alone to embrace your mistake. If and when the Human is found, the tracker will guide you to return at the end of your punishment time. If the Human is found dead, it will execute you. If the Human is never found, you will remain alone the rest of your natural life. Is this accepted by you?"

The soldiers ahead of me barked out, "Yes, Sir, accepted, Sir," taking me by surprise. Before I had a chance to echo the response, my guard walloped me hard on the shoulder with his baton, striking several times, not caring where it landed, the cudgel whistling through the air before hitting. I ducked out of instinct; he grabbed my arm to hold me in place. He glared at me with hate-filled eyes, hissing, "Answer the Commander, Exiled One."

Burning with shame and humiliation, even though I'd done nothing wrong except speak up for clemency, I yelled out my compliance. "Sir, Understood, Sir!" The guard landed a few more blows until the Commander nodded that he'd heard me. I could do nothing except take the punishment and fight back sobs.

On the flip side, this was the best outcome for me, as I'd shift forms and figure out a way to the rendezvous point so I could save my Amorphan family. A few stripes on my skin was nothing compared to what they must be going through.

Our small line shuffled forward, one soldier at a time pausing, and we shuffled forward again until I was the last one left. Two soldiers flanked the base commander, rifles at the ready, set to kill. *So, I'm guessing there is no refusal at this point?*

LOOKS LIKE NO. IF REFUSE PUNISHMENT, IS DEEMED CONFESSION OF CRIME AND KILLED ON THE SPOT.

All righty, then.

"Soldier, do you accept the lawfully pronounced punishment and tracker?"

"Yes, sir." I sucked in a shaky breath, hating the quaver in my voice.

He raised his hand holding an instrument, placing it against my neck and something bit into my skin. I thought I felt miniscule tentacles sliding through my epidermis, seeking blood vessels and nerves to become part of my body. *Universe's asshole! Is that thing alive? What the blazing hell did he put in my neck? Is it something we're stuck with forever?*

ONLY UNTIL CHANGE PROGRAMMING.

We can't get rid of it?

NOT SAFE TO REMOVE. LIFE AT STAKE.

OOOooh, they'd know, wouldn't they? And shoot me, right?

YES.

So, can it be changed to send out the info we want it to transmit? Can that execution thing be deleted?

Hesitation. YES? WITH TIME?

"On your way, nameless one." The barked command yanked me from my internal reverie, making me jump a little in surprise. The lack of title caught at me. To be nameless in Amorphan society was tantamount to being called a leper in ancient times.

If I'd really been a soldier, I'd just been stripped of any rank I might've had, any privileges accrued, status and identity, not to mention no future in normal society. Amorphan honor demanded me to announce myself as a Nameless One as though the tracker I felt on the side of my neck didn't already proclaim that. I didn't have any doubt the tracker would remind me in a painful way if I failed to do so.

I started to say, "Yes, sir," but he held up a hand in a stop motion.

"You may no longer speak to me or any other personnel for any reason whatsoever until–if–you are recalled into honor."

The tracker buzzed in my neck and the commander smirked as I cringed away from the sensation. Turning to my right, it intensified, so I turned the other way until it stopped zapping me. That's how I knew which direction to go from here. I stepped forward, walking away, not looking back, holding my head high. The least I could do was be a proud soldier, accepting the burden of penance with stoicism and acceptance in the Amorphan way. I couldn't let anyone see how relieved I was to leave the base and be on my own so I could get to the coordinates of the impending military rescue.

CHAPTER TWENTY-SIX

Countless hot, dusty miles later, I faltered to a stop, sinking to the dirt to rest. The sun blazed down, showing no interest in heading for the horizon. I was thirsty and hungry. I'd been stripped of everything except what I wore and my Perpad on the assumption the kidnappers let me stay dressed and keep my device. Only once had I seen anyone else along my forced route and when he saw I was a nameless one, he bared all his sharp teeth at me, stepping back in disgust.

I tried to ask for some water but as I formulated the words, the tracker gave me a sharp jolt of pain, making me gasp instead of speaking. Thinking it was because I'd deviated a tiny bit from my path, I tried to ask the male again, receiving a second, more severe slam of pain. Then I got the message; no talking to anyone. I wondered if I'd be able to answer someone if they spoke to me first but since this male clearly wasn't going to talk to me, I didn't know the answer.

Cradling my head in my hands, I closed my eyes for relief from the glare. Even being able to bounce off sun rays from my reflective skin didn't stop me from feeling like a melted cheese sandwich. I started to say something about finding water but my voice caught in my throat, drier than the parched ground I sat upon.

Can we find water? Soon? I may not live long enough to get to the coordinates if I can't get something to eat and drink.

SUCK IT UP, BUTTERCUP.

I didn't have the energy to growl or snort in answer. Head hanging, staring at my exposed forearms from rolling up my long sleeves in hopes of feeling a bit cooler, I saw a tiny quiver of movement. A single strand of hair worked its way to quest over and into the dirt around me. I watched with dulled eyes as it probed the ground through tiny cracks.

MOVE NEAR BUSH.

Heaving a sigh, I mustered barely enough energy to scoot the couple of feet to the nearest straggly bush, replete with bristly thorns and sharp edged thin leaves. If a clutter of spiders ran at me from the bush, I'd probably only twitch because I just plain didn't have enough oomph to react. Normally, I'd run screaming in a panic from such a thing, but today, not so much.

DIG HERE.

I stared at the spot where the hair danced up and down to gain my attention. Loose dirt on top of sunbaked soil, small rocks and debris from the bush were scattered around the area. There was a small crack in the dry soil but I had no idea how to get through the upper crust of cement-like dirt to get at whatever my hair had found.

DIG!

With what? I don't have a fracking shovel with me.

FINGERS. DIG.

Fingers. Yeah, there's something about fingers, if only I could think of what it was. A jab of impatience shook me a little from my lassitude and apathy. I blinked, pushing my fore fingers against the inner corners of my eyes and the motion loosened a memory. *Oh, yeah, now I remember. These fingers can change in shape to what is needed. That's why the fingers and hands don't have bones.*

Envisioning spades in my head, I concentrated on changing the Amorphan fingers of one hand into the shape of a digging tool. I'd need the other hand to scoop dirt out of the way. Fingers and hand began reshaping and a tiny spark of hope flared within me. When the change was complete, I worked the tip into the crack with my left hand and began digging. This was doggone hard work and frustrating when the loosened dirt kept sliding back into the opening.

I kept going, grunting with effort, until all of a sudden, I smelled moisture and it became easier then to keep going. *Am I close? Is this it for water or is there more of it below?*

ANOTHER INCH OR TWO FOR WATER.

It was right; I suddenly broke into a small pocket of dirty water. I didn't care if it had leeches or spiders in it, I was going to drink it even if I had to use my teeth as a strainer. My nanny system could take care of any germs, I hoped, but no matter what, I needed this water.

Scooping it out, my hand acting as a cup, I drank it as fast as I could and went back for more. Finally, I felt energy seeping back into my body as the water was absorbed. Water seeped into the depression in the dirt and it would be a while before it filled up enough to drink again.

I need a canteen.

CAN'T MAKE ONE.

Maybe I'll stay the night here, then. It's not like I have any appointments to keep. Hey, what about this tracker thing? Can it be disabled or reprogrammed or anything?

TRYING BUT VERY DIFFICULT. IT'S A BIOMECHANICAL DEVICE. QUITE COMPLICATED.

We only have a day to get to the site. Maybe I better get up and get going.

NO. GOING WRONG DIRECTION.

Well, poop on a popsicle stick. How long do you need to redirect the tracker?

DELICATE WORK. TRACKER KILLS IF IT DETECTS TAMPERING. NEED SEVERAL HOURS MORE. STAYING STILL BEST FOR NOW. NO DISTRACTIONS.

I was a little stunned at the volume of words from my hair; it's normally short, sweet and to the point with words. *Can the tracker tell what I'm thinking or hear our conversations?*

MAYBE? PROBABLY READS MUSCLE USAGE SO KNOWS WHEN WORDS BEING FORMED. CAN'T READ THOUGHTS IF ONLY SENSING MUSCLES.

I puffed out air. My personal thoughts were ignored or not heard by my hair, I wasn't sure which since we'd never discussed it, never needing to know the answer. It respected my internal privacy as long as it wasn't anything it felt needed its intervention or conversation. This tracker, being a combination of living tissue and mechanical parts, programmed by nanotech of extreme sophistication, was proving to be a big problem.

Sure, I was free of the military base but with this tracker integrated into my nervous system, I was still a prisoner, subject to punishment or execution by the device. *Probably something dreamed up and sold by those blasted Imurian scientists.*

Hunger pangs gained my attention but I had nothing to eat. I scooped up more water, this time holding it long enough to let the dirt settle to the bottom of my cup-shaped hand, sipping until it got close to the debris. I repeated the action until my stomach thought it had been fed. At least I had a water source for the night.

Realizing the force of the sun beating down on me had lessened, I squinted up at the sky. The sun had made the decision to stop torturing me and had sunk close to the horizon, defeated. A hint of coolness tinted the air, a welcome respite from the unbearable heat of the day.

Could I change shape and drop out the tracker as I become the new body?

NOT YET.

Well, what if–

SHUSH. BUSY, NEED TO CONCENTRATE.

Well, how rude. I curled one side of my upper lip up in a display of annoyance, feeling the urge to argue back and call it names. I squelched the impulse; the sooner it and the Akrion could complete this vital task, the sooner I could move on in a direction and species of my choice.

I laid on my back on the hard ground, cushioning my head with my hands, staring up at the heavens over me. If I couldn't go anywhere yet, I might as well get some rest. But first things first.

Gritting my teeth in annoyance, I struggled into a sitting position, then standing to amble a couple of feet away so I could relieve my bladder.

Coming back to my resting place, I swept away as many pebbles, twigs and other sharp objects as best I could before lying down. I figured I wouldn't sleep but I could at least rest with my eyes closed. The air cooled off as the sun disappeared from the sky, a slight breeze teasing at my head feathers.

I'd be cold before the night was done; this area was a desert and without sun, temperatures dropped fast at night. When that happened, I'd turn up my internal temperature, something my body was fully capable of doing, no matter what shape I wore. I thought about taking off my uniform to use as a pillow but winced at the thought of all those sharp little rocks and thorny twigs cutting into my bare skin and getting into the whipping stripes left by the baton wielding guard.

Instead, I cushioned my head with my hands, closing my eyes, one knee raised a bit to relieve the strain on my back. Even as exhausted and wrung out emotionally as I felt, sleep wasn't possible for me as my thoughts and fears whirled around and around.

CHAPTER TWENTY-SEVEN

A sizzling hot needle jabbed me in my upper arm and I batted at it as I jerked awake.

WAKEY WAKEY.

"It's not even morning yet; leave me alone." I reached down to pull the sheets up to my neck, then realized I didn't have any.

IT'S TIME TO CHANGE. TIME TO GO.

The tracker? You removed it?

NO. HACKED INTO IT, YES. CONTROL IT, YES. REPROGRAMMED, YES.

So it will still show me on my forced route, moving? I suppose at some point it lets a person stop walking and settle somewhere, as long as its not a city.

YES, CONTINUES TO SHOW MOVING ALONG PRESCRIBED ROUTE.

How do the Amorphans remove it, then, when the soldier is recalled to duty?

SURGERY.

A picture flashed into my head from the battle while on the troop truck. Those attacking Amorphans had an ugly scar on the side of their necks; I assumed, at the time, it was a result of shots from energy rifles like ours. Now that I thought about it, they were all in the same spot, the same spot my tracker was placed on my neck.

Those attackers! They were nameless ones, weren't they? Somehow, they cut out their trackers and now steal whatever they can from the convoys between the two bases.

HUH. YES. THEY MUST CUT THEM OUT FOR EACH OTHER.

No, the tracker would've prevented them from getting close enough to one another for that. I frowned, twisting my lips. *Each person had to have cut his own out, somehow, and if they lived through the experience, joined up as a band. Holy mother of universes, that must've hurt like molten lava poured on their skin.*

THEY'D HAVE TO CUT VERY FAST AND DEEP TO ESCAPE DEATH JOLT.

Or maybe there's a way to temporarily shut it down. Maybe if they were underwater? After all, there were lots of them in that group of bandits. Wonder how they were able to cut it out without the tracker knowing in advance. I shuddered at the thought of that kind of pain. It made changing shapes feel easy.

So...I think a Radir as my first shape so I can cover ground quickly. Then once we get there, I'll change back to Amorphan.

RORADIV.

I shook my head. *Too risky. A roradiv, with those long fangs, six legs and feline body? Yeah, no one would shoot that on sight. The radir is cute, less likely to be seen as dangerous, looks a lot like a deer if you overlook the arms on the upper torso, and can really cover the ground running. Plus, it can eat foliage whereas the roradiv needs meat.*

OKAY. YOU WIN. Said grudgingly with a little bit of a sour note to the words.

Without warning, shape changing started, perhaps in retaliation to me having the final word. Or perhaps not, but I'd bet on the former if I was old enough to place wagers. Then I had no time for thoughts, only to breathe through the writhing agony of reshaping myself into something else.

The first few moments of a new shape are like being a newborn animal trying to figure out its legs and balance. I stood still for a half-minute to get used to having four legs instead of two, twisting my head to squint at my green-tinged hair with speckles of dark and light. At least I'd be hard to see in the dark or in foliage.

When I thought I could move without falling over or making a fool of myself, I stepped back to the pocket of water, sucking up the liquid as daintily as I could to avoid a mouthful of mud. Nibbling on a few of the sharp-edged leaves, they were acrid and tough to chew but they were food. No one shrieked "POISON" into my head so it must be a safe form of food, no matter that it tasted like dried farts.

I ate a lot of the leaves, waiting for the water to fill up again in the ground but knew I needed to get going. I felt the right side of my neck for the tracker; there was a lump there in the same spot but thank the stars above, no pain—yet. Once there was enough moisture in the hole, I sucked it up, making a face at the dirt taste of it, then looked around. *Which way?*

45 DEGREES TO YOUR LEFT FROM HERE.

Do you think we'll intersect anyone's path if we go that way? I turned to face that direction.

NO. BE FAR AHEAD OF HIM WITH THE SPEED IN THIS FORM.

I nodded. I drew in a breath, waiting for a zap of pain from the tracker to tell me I was misguided in my direction, but nothing happened. I sprang forward, using my hind legs to propel me. This species could leap a long ways forward, coming down to spring forward again, like a self-propelled jumping machine. As I went along, I learned not to jump too high so as to gain the most ground while in the air. There's always a learning curve to everything.

There was also sheer joy in leaping and landing, then leaping again. A big grin split my face as I discovered the fun of moving this fast. I made a game of landing as gently as I could, trying to minimize the puffs of dust, and taking off again as gently and quickly as I could.

My elongated muzzle acted as sort of a sighting instrument, my body landing wherever I pointed my big black nose. One time, I'd picked out a spot and, while in the air, discovered a big rock there, my supple body twisting so I could land next to it safely. My two arms, sprouting from shoulders on the long torso, swung around haphazardly until

I learned to pump them like runners do for more impetus. I loved being this form.

Without a way to measure how far I could leap, I had no good idea of how far I'd come but the sun had come up full force, again beating down on my back with the force of a heated anvil. My tongue glued to the top of my mouth and my leaps became short and uncertain, so I dropped into a trot for a while, then a walk. My sides heaved in and out with the need for air, nostrils flared to full capacity to capture all the oxygen it could draw in.

Fracking-A. I need water and food.

No answer. I had no choice but to keep going, my head sagging, my arms crossed over my hair covered chest as I slogged along. Blinking my eyes to clear the dust kicked up from my hooved feet, my flared nostrils picked up a faint scent. I stopped in place, swiveling my head to capture the elusive scent. It smelled like–rain? Or maybe growing green things? Could it be trees? I didn't see anything in the immediate vicinity to tell me but my body's instincts screamed at me to go there right now, if not sooner.

Turning to go the new route, my hair didn't object nor did the tracker. *By the way, great job with that tracker. That couldn't have been easy since it took so long to disable. Thanks for taking away its ability to zap me.*

IN CONTROL FOR NOW. HURT US, TOO.

Does that mean its control of my body could come back?

A heavy silence for a breath or two. PERHAPS. INTEGRATED INTO NERVOUS SYSTEM. STILL WORKING ON HOW TO REMOVE SAFELY WITHOUT SURGERY.

My attention diverted to a small stand of spindly trees down a small decline in the land. *So that's why I couldn't see it before; it was hidden from sight.* Catching the whiff of water, I hurried toward it, so thirsty I didn't care if there was anything to threaten me.

Then a putrid scent filled my nose, causing me to skid to a stop. *What, by the rusty hot hinges of hell, is that smell?*

DANGER.

My hind brain shrieked in terror, babbling about a big and nasty bad thing in the trees, wanting my tender body to eat as its meal. I took a few steps backwards and almost turned to bolt away, but I needed that water.

Now's the time for a roradiv or, perhaps, that bear-like species– the, uh, the–

XINGIAN.

Yeah, that! It's the biggest, nastiest form I have. I think.

YES, IT IS. ONE XINGIAN COMING UP.

I barely had time to lie down on the hot ground before the changing started. Having been there and done that before cuts down on the time to transform to somewhat less than a minute, although wouldn't it be nice if it was instantaneous. Yeah, it would mean a lot less pain if I could just snap my fingers and it would be done and over with like that. Perhaps in a different galaxy far, far away I could have that, or perhaps not.

For now, I was thankful to be upwind of whatever big, dangerous animal was at the water source. I felt reasonably sure it hadn't seen or scented me yet and even if it had smelled me as a radir, I now smelled like danger myself.

As a Xingian, I stood tall on legs like humans, with heavy, dark brown fur tinted with gold, large, forward facing golden eyes with horizontal pupils, and medium sized round ears on my head that swiveled like a horse. Heavily muscled arms ended in hairless hands with six fingers, one thumb and a lot of long, razor sharp claws, which the toes also sported. A small, ridiculous tail clamped itself over my butt crease.

Two-inch fangs protruded from the upper corners of the lips, hanging down, with sharp pointed teeth in between while the back teeth were flat for chewing and grinding. I ran a hand over a short muzzle with a bulbous, twitching speckled nose and straggly hair brushing over my eyes from the forehead.

Enough of the beauty contest, Jessi, let's get some water before I dry up and blow away.

CHAPTER TWENTY-EIGHT

My feet were long, wide, and mostly inflexible which meant I stomped toward the watering hole. This species didn't know the meaning of stealth, probably because it's so big, strong and at the top of the food chain. I neared the stand of vegetation, the smell of water pulling me in like a magnet.

Maybe whatever was in here would let me drink my fill in peace and I'd go on my merry way without a confrontation. A low, fear-inducing growl said otherwise and my heart rate picked up in answer to a flood of adrenaline. Hyperalert now, I looked around the clearing, my brow furrowed, peering at sparse shadows under messy bushes, glancing at the short trees, nostrils expanding to take in any scent.

Without warning, a heavy weight hit my shoulders. I staggered as sharp teeth scraped at the back of my neck and claws dug deep into my shoulders. I slashed at whatever was clinging to my back while whirling in place, trying to displace my attacker. I howled, in anger and pain, doing my best to distract the beast from breaking my neck or chewing through my spine. The thick, dense covering of fur over my back, especially the spine area, kept me from being killed instantly before I had a chance to fight back. I guess my bones in this shape were made to withstand such attacks.

It's awkward reaching over shoulders to rake at things on your back, I'm just saying. From the metallic smell and startled yelp it gave as I made my marks on its back, I'd at least drawn blood. There was no slacking in its hold on me, however, so I did the next best thing. I didn't have time for my gun to magically appear and no time to think of anything else.

I fell over onto my back, flipping with as much force as I could muster with my push-off from the ground. There was a sickening crunch of bones, a cut-off squeal, and a sudden slacking of the grip in my flesh. I squirmed and raised up, falling back down until I was sure the thing underneath my bulk wouldn't move again, then I sat up, prying out its claws from where they hooked into my skin.

I turned to look at my assailant. The fall onto my back crushed its ribcage and the back of its ugly head. A long snout with sharp, pointed teeth and three-inch fangs, two going up and two going down, mottled muddy-brown and green hair over its entire body were the first things I noticed.

The long upper limbs ended in cat-like paws with long, curved talon-like claws, streaked with my blood.

The lower legs, shorter than the uppers, were similar, made more for raking its victim's body than latching on. Come to think of it, I reached back to feel my lower torso, and sure enough, rake marks bled sluggishly down my fur. I hadn't noticed them because I'd been too busy trying to keep it from snapping my neck.

I pulled myself into a standing position, grunting with effort, ignoring the burning pain from cuts on my neck and back, knowing my nannies and Akrion would heal the damage. I blessed the heavy fur and dense bones for saving my life. The critter, whatever it was, couldn't get through it to bite through my neck, giving me the edge in my fight for life. I had no doubts whatsoever that my hair had already harvested its DNA.

I poked the body with one foot to straighten it out a bit, discovering swollen teats on its abdomen. A sick feeling welled up; I'd killed a mother doing her job to bring food to her offspring. I felt horrible at the thought of the youngsters being left alone, starving to death if they were too little to make it on their own. But I had no idea where it might have a den—or a nest, since it seemed to be a tree-climber. It could be close or it could be miles away.

And did I even want to rescue them? They might be cute now, but when all grown up, they'd be doing the same thing as their mother, killing animals for food. All part of the food chain, yeah, I know, but try being on the receiving end of that and see how you feel about it then. And besides, perhaps the adult male would feed them until they could survive on their own. I refused to wonder if the male was involved in the rearing of their young.

Heaving a huge sigh, rolling my shoulders, wincing at the pain, feeling dried blood pull at the fur, I wanted nothing more than to sit and sleep off my injuries but I had a deadline to keep. Matra's smiling face flashed into my mind, Datro's laugh and Simatrao's teasing, so water first, and perhaps something to eat before going on my way. I wondered if the dead beast was edible to this species.

First things first, Jessi, I reminded myself. I stumbled to the edge of the small pool of water, sticking my snout into it and sucking in as much water as I could swallow. Oh, blessed, blessed water! It didn't matter it was as hot as the sunshine and tasted like old socks, it was wet and life-sustaining water.

Finally, I rocked back to my heels, wiping my mouth with the back of one hand. *Any chance I can find something around here to use as a canteen?* I shrugged to myself. "Guess I'll go look and see." My voice came out raspy and growly and the s's were hard to pronounce but there was no one to hear me.

I walked back to the trees, scouting the ground as I went for anything that could be used to hold water for my journey. A whiff of the dead animal hit my nose and I salivated, dripping over the sides of my lips to drop on the ground.

Instinct drove me back to the body while the human part of me quailed at the thought of feeding from a carcass. However, savage hunger took over the Xingian part of me as my teeth tore into the meaty part of the beast, savoring the taste of blood and still-warm flesh, not minding the bristly hair that came with it. Gulping down large chunks of meat, I ate mindlessly until the absolute need for sustenance abated.

Once I was in control of myself again, I backed away from the food source, wiping off my muzzle with a shaky hand, reminding myself that out here, it was eat or be eaten. I couldn't let myself feel bad about eating her flesh; after all, she would've eaten me without any remorse. I knew Mother Nature is cruel like that but part of me still cringed at what I'd done. On the other hand, my stomach was happy.

I returned to the water, drinking my fill again, washing blood off my mouth and hands. I'd found nothing to use as a water vessel so loaded up internally as best I could for the rest of my journey.

How close are we, anyway? Am I going to make it in time?

A FEW MORE HOURS. YOU'VE EATEN, HAD WATER, TIME TO GO.

I rolled my eyes. *Yes, dear. Let's get the changing done, then; what're you waiting for?* I paused. *Should we find those cubs or kittens or whatever to make sure they're alright? Maybe one would make a good pet.*

NO! NO TIME FOR LOOKING. NO PETS. MOTHER NATURE IS CRUEL, REMEMBER? HOW WOULD YOU RAISE THEM? YOU CAN'T, THAT'S HOW.

Countless miles and leaps later, back in Radir form, the day had advanced to late afternoon, although the intensity of the sun never relented from baking me. Now and then, I'd stop for a mouthful or two of foliage and then leap forward again. Water was sparse but when I found some, I gulped it down.

Are we there yet? My mouth was dry again.

I'd need at least a year's worth of sleep when I had time to catch up, if that ever happened. In the meantime, all I could do was keep going toward my destination. I settled into a steady ground-eating trot; I was so over the leaping thing, not to mention I didn't think my legs could do it anymore. Trotting didn't take as much energy and even though it couldn't get me further faster, it would get me there at a good, ground-eating steady pace.

The meat from the carcass had long worn off; my stomach reminded me it could use another big meal and a few leaves here and there wasn't enough. I ignored the rumbles since, besides dirt, dried leaves, grass and pebbles, there was nothing to eat. Maybe it was a good thing I'd started this journey on the, er, fluffy side. I wished being a shapeshifter came with superpowers, like not needing food or being able to fly, but that's not the reality.

ALMOST THERE.

I flung my head up into the air, ears questing for danger, nostrils spread to catch all scents as my short, fluffy tail clamped down over my butt. I hadn't heard from my hair for a while and my energy to keep going was definitely on empty. The sudden statement startled me so much the radir part reacted before I could control it and I sped up into running. Fatigue hit hard enough within a short distance, making me stumble and my head drooped low on my long neck.

Don't scare me like that! I'm too tired and need some sleep. Hazel. I tacked on the name out of pure habit.

NO TIME FOR RESTING, LUNA. VERY CLOSE NOW. NEED PLACE TO HIDE.

You think the soldiers are already there? What time is the exchange happening? I do still have a gun, don't I?

YUP. DON'T KNOW. YUP.

I hope the babies are all right. I stole a few minutes, despite my hair's resistance and lots of pinches, at the oasis looking for a den or nest or some indication of baby whatevers but didn't find anything, so gave up. I had to move on if I was going to make the rendezvous.

She was one ugly female, though I'll bet she was cute to her mama. So, can I become one of those? It's indigenous to this world, more than any of my other DNA species.

ZERO PRACTICE AT BEING THAT, TOO RISKY. AND PROBABLY NOT SENTIENT ENOUGH.

How about I become Si'neada instead, then?

NO IMMURIANS PART OF THIS PLAN.

Party pooper. So I become me again. Right, Mildred?

WAIT AND SEE, CLEMENTINE, WHEN THERE. GO BY STEALTH NOW.

Perhaps I should become a Fatar instead. They're small enough to sneak around for reconnoitering.

HMMM. YES. LOOK LIKE LARGE DOG-RABBIT THING.

Yeah, looks harmless, with arms and hands, and a really mean kick. So far, I've found the universal truth among all sentient beings is having hands with fingers and, more importantly, functioning thumbs. Anger flashed through me at the thought of the genocide done by the Imurians. Just because each murdered species hadn't yet achieved the Imurian's perception of civilization was no reason for them to obliterate budding societies so they could sell the worlds on their Rent-to-Own program.

I took a quick glance around the area. Without my noticing, the topography had changed, no longer an arid desert. The hard-baked dirt and scrubby, thorny shrubs and stunted trees had given way to tall grasses, taller trees with bright green leaves and more luxuriant bushes. Plenty of places to hide while changing shapes again.

A Fatar did indeed look like a cross between a really big dog and an enormous jackrabbit, with long ears for acute hearing, a large bulbous pink nose capable of discerning the smallest of scents and a big puff of a tail. Powerful back legs gave me jumping ability and speedy running along with being able to dodge and twist with nimbleness. Dark grey short hair covered the body and long whiskers adorned the mouth.

My front limbs doubled as front legs or as arms with hands as needed. However, I couldn't do both at the same time. Either I chose to use them as arms and hands or I could choose to run. I could hop while sitting upright but clumsy. The good news was I could be quiet and sneaky in this shape, especially if I kept my ears back along the sides of my body.

CHAPTER TWENTY-NINE

My nose quivered as my blended Fatar-Human brain sorted out myriad odors, figuring out what was plant, what was animal, and most importantly, what might be an enemy. I was flabbergasted at how acute my scenting ability became and how the brain could sort it out so fast into categories. I was totally impressed.

And the sounds I could pick up with these sensitive, long, pointy ears? I swear I could hear a gnat fart into a breeze a mile away and I'd be able to smell it, too, with this powerful nose.

A faint whiff of metal and fuel off to my left somewhere let me know at least one air craft had arrived. I knew I could follow that odor anywhere in the world and wondered if dogs got this big a thrill from having that ability.

I crept along the ground in the tall grass, ears tight against my body, moving with caution toward the source of the metal flavor in the air. My fingers and thumb folded up to form a paw when I needed to be on all four feet, an interesting piece of body engineering. As I moved forward, a second, differently flavored whiff of metal and fuel arrived. *Well, one of the vehicles brought soldiers with their rescue plan and the other must be the kidnappers. They'd better have my host family with them or I'll send them to hell in a handbasket, I'll rip their teeth out of their mouths, I'll–.*

WAIT UNTIL VIEW EVERYTHING.

My ears now perceived a slight whine in the air from the engine off to my left, distinct from the low grumble of a different engine to my right but both sounding 'up'. *So neither have landed yet. I wonder if they're at least communicating by radio or something?*

NO WAY TO KNOW.

I rolled my huge, golden eyes. I didn't know where they'd touch down so better to stay in hiding until then. My body had already changed colors to match my surroundings and so long as I didn't move, I shouldn't be noticed.

The pitch of the engine off to my right changed slightly, becoming lower in tone, the beat of it slowing down. I glanced upward to make sure it wasn't about to settle on top of me but the sky remained clear.

A small gust of wind stirred the grasses around me, puffing up dirt and scattering the contents of seed pods. My nose started itching, then I felt an impending sneeze. My sneezes are explosive and loud and I can't change it, no matter what shape I've taken. I've tried, lordy-two-shoes knows, I've tried.

You stop this sneeze! Now! I used my best "mom" voice with as much sternness as I could muster. The tiny hairs in my nose would obey my head hair without question, but not me. They were too small, I think, to understand me but my hair could enforce a need. It was the same with my other bodily hair. Well, except maybe my pubic hair; it had some independent notions but couldn't do much about its ideas even if it wanted to. And now I just embarrassed myself; good thing Fatars don't blush.

DONE.

The almost-sneeze disappeared and I drew in a breath of relief. My weapon ejected from my flank, without warning other than a tickle and an itch, falling to the ground. I picked it up, finding the Fatar hand was ill-suited to using it but I could pull the trigger if needed.

The sounds off to my left hadn't changed in volume or pitch but the right one had shut down. I figured the left one was hovering, waiting to see what happened. I had no way to know which one held my family and which one held soldiers. Soldiers that would shoot a Nameless One on sight if found off their designated path. Or shoot me for sport. Or because they were trigger happy.

The fact was the tracker was still on my neck, visible to the world. Try explaining why a Fatar sported a tracker to any superior officer—like I'd have a chance to do so before they killed me on sight, of course. They'd stuff my body and display it as a bizarre trophy, most likely.

I hoped neither side was into collecting exotic, unknown specimens–like me. I thought over my current options, which included staying very still and wait, creeping forward to survey the area to make decisions or–wait!

I wanted to thump myself on the head for overlooking the most obvious solution to this problem. I'd lower my mental shields and quest out for thoughts to see if anyone was recognizable or might be friendly to me.

Cracking open my mental buffer and keeping a passive mode, I waited. The Fatar brain could easily handle high frequencies such as Amorphans used. Using minute increments of pitch, I went through as fast as I dared without missing someone's thoughts.

Closing my eyes helps me concentrate more, relying on ears, hair, and nose to warn me and on my camouflaged body to stay invisible. Grasses and weeds rustled in the warm breeze, bringing scents of growth and dust, scuttling insects, old mold, dead grass, and a hint of moisture, swaying over my prone position.

There, right there! I felt something, more than I heard it, a kind of a prickle of a mind whisper. I strained to focus, to discern it more fully, but it was nebulous and hard to grasp. Moving my ability up just a fraction, to tune in better to catch words, I locked onto someone's mind. I grinned to myself, feeling a bit smug at how proficient I'd become at this type of stealth listening.

:*Crapola, I get stuck with all the boring jobs.* Sounds like a male. *Sun's warm here, at least. I shouldn't have stayed up so late last night.*: A picture flashed into my head of after-hours activities with a female Amorphan as he remembered the feel of her hand slowly closing around his--"MMMMPH!" I screamed or tried to, anyway.

A strong hand clamped over my mouth while a different hand picked me up by the scruff of my hairy neck. I dangled in the air, helpless. I kicked out with my hind legs but their arm was longer than my legs could reach backwards. *Story of my life.*

Panicking, I wiggled and wrenched around mid-air to free myself but to no avail; my captor had me in a strong, painful grip. I couldn't see my attacker because I couldn't turn my head and dangling in the air from the scruff meant my hands were pretty useless at this moment, too. *Snotty boogers, I hope I'm not about to become someone's meal.*

To my utter embarrassment, urine spurted down my legs, spattering on the ground with an unpleasant sour, musky smell. *Must be part of its defense system, to stink away the predator.*

A Fatar is heavier than it looks so it must be a strain to hold me in mid-air like that. I went from fighting to total dead weight without warning, wincing at the thought of dead, to make it more difficult. I hoped I'd surprise them into dropping me. *Where's my gun when I need it?*

I spotted it where I'd left it, off to the right of where I had stretched out in the grass to listen. I'd forgotten my most basic lesson ever learned: never put down your gun. If you have it out for any reason, you must be prepared to use it for self-defense and that means being in your hand, ready to go.

All my instructors from over the years would've yelled themselves blue in the face for my being so stupid. I'd been feeling so superior and arrogant about how well I was doing, smug in my new body, that I ignored the most basic of rules.

Well, I wouldn't die without a fight for my life. If my assailant brought his teeth near my neck, I'd–I'd–well, I didn't exactly know but it would be something.

I tried slamming my ears–it's all I could think of to try–into the arm grasping my ruff, but it was like hitting a baseball with a feather. All I got out of it was a whoosh of air.

BE PREPARED. SENDING OUT ATTACKERS.

Of course, my hair, my secret weapon! I felt parts of me, for lack of a better word, dissolve as my hair gathered into small bundles for a surprise attack. Ha. My enemy didn't know what was coming.

Then my brain caught up to what my ears were hearing. Chortling? Whoever was behind me was laughing? At my expense? Indignation took over as I stiffened in their grip, wishing I could at least bite the hand over my mouth. I couldn't even lick the hand as tight as the grip was around my mouth.

"Oh, Jessi, my little twinkly Bunny-Dog! I haven't laughed like this for a long time. It's me, Si'neada. I'll bet you're surprised!" He kept laughing. "I'm going to set you down now, so mind your manners, my little furry friend."

As soon as my hind legs touched the ground, I whirled around and kicked him in the shins. Fury and humiliation fueled my muscles as I drew back my powerful hind leg to land another blow, but he danced back a step or two. I'd forgotten how agile Imurians are when they need to be.

"Ow, ow, ow!" He hopped a little in place, grabbing his offended shin, showing off his immaculate manicure, claws painted in stripes of purple and gold, little bows on top. "My little kickboxer, there's no need for physical violence! I am your friend if you remember. I apologize for laughing but, truly, I couldn't help it." A poop-eating grin still spread across his face, giving the lie to his words.

I wasn't about to admit how much it had hurt my foot when I slammed it into his shins. I placed my hands on my hips, laying my ears way back down my back to show my irritation, and glowered at him.

READY TO STING HIM.

I'd love to, but he's right. He is my friend and he didn't harm me, after all, although he sure did piss me off. Literally. So, no, no stings, as tempted as I am.

JUST ONCE?

I snorted, fighting back a small smile at the disappointment in the words. *No, sorry. Not even once. This time.*

PFFFT. My hair hissed out its disappointment.

"What in the fracking hell gates are you doing here? How did you know that was me and not some indigenous animal taking a nap?" I snapped, baring my blunt, plant-eating teeth as I did so, narrowing my eyes to slits.

"Oh, come here, my little hairy hare. I think you need a hug."

Well, he wasn't wrong. I glared at him for a few more seconds, while he kept his arms spread wide with a twinkle in his eye. Finally, I made a face and walked forward into his embrace. As soon as he folded his arms around me, tears leaked from my eyes. It felt so good to be with a friend that emotions swamped me until I couldn't control the crying. I sobbed into his jumpsuit, leaving a big wet mark along with slobber and snot, which he bore with surprising patience. I suspected he'd discard the clothing as soon as he could since this would offend his elite sensibilities, but at least for now, he gave me what I needed.

Finally, I gulped in air, pushing myself back from him and he released his arms. "How did you find me?" I asked in a plaintive voice. "I was well hidden."

He nodded, a small smile on his catlike face. "Oh, you were. If you hadn't dropped your shields to 'listen', I would not have found you, because even your unique smell is masked." He inclined his head toward me with respect. "Well done, very well done."

"What are you doing on Amorpha, anyway? When did you get here and why?" My brow furrowed in puzzlement.

"When I heard you were missing, I made sure to get here as quickly as possible to help find you. I knew you couldn't be dead, my little DNA depot, and I had the best chance of finding you. And," he gestured in a sweeping motion, "obviously, I'm right."

Something in his expression made me think he wasn't telling me the whole truth. "And that's the only reason you're here?"

"Oh, my little peach, your disappearance caused waves of huge proportions, so of course I had to be here."

He didn't quite answer the question but Imurians are noted for half-answering questions and making you think they'd told you everything.

"Really? The Zatro of my city told the StarFinder crew about this?"

"They needed help from anyone competent to give it." He quirked an eyebrow at me. "Only the important people know," and he preened a bit, "and it's been kept from the other students and the population at large. Can't have panic taking over, of course."

"Or someone killing Myometo and the other males who're now Nameless Ones because they're blamed for my vanishing." I ran a soft hand over my fluffy face. "It's all my fault that happened to them, but I had to get here, to the rendezvous point to save Matra, Datro and Simatrao."

He raised both eyebrows. "And what were you going to do? Walk into the clearing as yourself, raise your hand and shout, 'I'm here! Let them go!' You'd be lucky if someone only shot to wound you. These people tend to be the 'shoot first, look later' variety."

I rubbed my nose, looking down. "Well, I hadn't quite figured that part out yet." I looked at him with defiance. "That's why I was reconnoitering first so I could make a plan after I knew how the exchange would be managed."

He reached out, sweeping his finger down the right side of my face with a soft touch. "You have such a soft heart, my little flower, but it might've gotten you killed today."

"How did you get here, anyway?" I held a finger up. "Oh! You came with the military, right? So that must be the one airship I heard land."

Embarrassment flitted across his face so fast, I wasn't sure I'd seen it. "I was the first one off, since I knew I could find you." He tapped a finger on his lips. "The biggest problem we have right now is," he reached out and tapped the tracker on my neck, "this." He quirked an eyebrow. "Yes, I saw it right away. How did you become a Nameless One?"

"Long story for later. I've been able to modify it enough so it doesn't zap me anymore for straying from its preset path, but I don't know how to get it out of my nervous system without damage. Still working on that part. Do you know how to remove it safely?"

He looked startled. "Now, why would I know that?"

"Didn't the Imurians invent this?"

He shook his head. "No, actually. The Amorphans came up with this all on their own, even before we made contact with them. It is highly sophisticated and they've always refining it. Somehow, they've managed to keep the secret of how to manufacture it. Our scientists have offered a great deal of money to have one to study."

"Well, they are the last people in the galaxy that I would let have one! Can you imagine how they'd misuse it?" I shuddered. "It's bad enough they instigated the annihilation of all these species I carry within me," I tapped my chest, "so them having trackers like this? Not while I'm alive and kicking."

"And you definitely have one powerful kick." He wrinkled his nose at me, smiling, bending forward to rub his shin again, teasing me.

"I was mad." I crossed my arms over my chest, lifting my chin into the air. "Not to mention very embarrassed at being caught. Plus I didn't know it was you and I was scared beyond belief, because I was certain I was about to be killed."

"I couldn't resist sneaking up on you, you know. There you were, hidden so very well, eyes squeezed shut, your little earrings twinkling in the sunshine. Funny how those come through with a changing."

I felt along one ear; he was right. I did have my earrings still showing. Well, I did hate to not have my earrings on every day, my biggest vanity, even in other shapes.

"Anyway," he continued, "I just had to do it. The kitling in me came right out to play although I didn't expect to get peed on. Or kicked." He tapped my nose. "Please forgive me?"

"I'll bet you wouldn't have done that if I'd had my gun in my hand," I muttered. Speaking of which, I took the couple of steps needed so I could scoop it up into my hand.

"Yes, it's a good thing for me you weren't holding it, because I think you would've shot first before knowing it was me."

I looked up at him through my lashes. "Well, maybe. I'd like to think I'm well trained enough to make a reasoned decision before blindly shooting someone." I sighed. "Well, enough of all this. How am I going to save my family?" I brightened, flashing him a toothy smile. "Now that you're here, you can help me make a better plan. If they haven't already done the exchange, that is."

"There's no exchange without you, right?"

"Right. But I don't think my going with the rebels or whoever they are would be good for my health. So, I guess what I planned to do was show myself to them, get them to release all of them first, then I was going to run like hell to the soldiers to keep me safe."

"That," Si'neada pronounced, "is a terrible plan. Especially with you wearing that tracker. The soldiers are more likely to shoot you once they see that than the other side would. I think the rebels would keep you alive because you are a valuable commodity to them."

"But why? What makes me so special to them and not, you know, Zoe, for instance? They can't know about my shape changing abilities. Can they?" My eyes widened in sudden worry. "Unless...unless the scientists paid them to kidnap and return me to them for their nasty experiments or for revenge, or both. Maybe somehow they figured out it was me that rescued Zoe from them. Am I on the right track? What do you think?"

Si'neada, who did have eyebrows, raised them. "It's a definite theory that has feasibility."

I pointed at him, "You're here from the StarFinder, so I know it's somewhere near Amorpha. " I rubbed my shoulder. "They dislocated my shoulder the first time someone tried to take me by force. It still aches at times."

His eyes widened. "Oh, my little flower! I am so sorry that happened to you. I do not want you to be hurt!" He held his hands over his heart, looking mournful at the thought of my injury.

Patting his arm, I said, "I'm okay, Si'neada, really." I paused and tilted my furry head at him, looking up, this body so much shorter than his. "Hey, I have a question for you."

"I have an answer; let's see if they match." He smirked at me.

I smiled at his quip. "When you said you heard me when I lowered my mental shields, how could you have? I didn't send out any thoughts, I was in listening mode only so how did you know?"

He spread his hands apart. "There is still a lot about mind-whispering you don't know yet, my little starshine. Our minds are never truly blank so when you lower them, especially all at once, thoughts escape whether or not you intend to do so."

"Is there a way to circumvent that?"

"Yes, of course."

"Will you teach me the method?"

He drew in a breath. "Certainly, but not right now. What we need to do is come up with a plan for rescuing your Amorphan family."

CHAPTER THIRTY

"Yes, totally. But what I need right this instant is something to drink, although eating would be good, too. I don't suppose....?"

He grinned while digging through a few of his pockets. "Here," he said, "eat this. Er, which species are you? I can't quite place this one."

"Fatar. It seemed appropriate for information gathering from a distance." I ran my hand-paw along one of my elongated, large ears.

"Of course." He bobbed his head. "Oh, here, take this canteen; it's full of vitamin water." He waved a hand around in a vague manner. "Good for, you know, this desert place."

I put the container to my mouth, gulping down the warm liquid inside. Cold water is always better but a raging thirst can be quenched with almost anything fluid and I was grateful to have it. After several huge swallows, I came up for air, taking a huge chomp of the meat bar he'd offered me. I could practically feel energy flowing into my body from the sustenance. I would've have guessed a Fatar was a total herbivore but I might've been wrong.

Finally, I was done and I handed him the empty wrapping and canteen. "Thank you; even the bones of my body needed that."

He inclined his head in acknowledgement. "Did this model come with camouflaged hair or did you do that?"

There was an odd note to his voice, like he was being careful how he phrased the question like it was an idle inquiry. I looked down at my body and shrugged. "It came this way. Luckily for me, it blends well into grasses."

Some instinct told me to keep my secrets to myself. Si'neada knew I was a shape-changer but he didn't know all of my abilities and it's better that way, as far as I'm concerned. The less people who know about my ability to shape-change, the healthier my life would be. It was especially vital to keep this information from Imurian scientists as they had no moral qualms about experimenting on any species, with or without permission.

The only reason I have this ability is the Akrion in me, a God-like particle, extraordinarily rare, which I received as a fetus in my mother's womb. The scientists released one particle into a room full of Human pregnant women, without anyone's knowledge or permission, to see what happened. They didn't care if it went into a mother or baby; it was a random selection. As a result, my brother, Devon, only a child himself, became the first host of the particle, a very unexpected result since it was a last-minute thing for him to be with my mom that day. He died on that journey because his body couldn't reconcile to hosting the Akrion. It left his dying body and entered my mother's womb into my body instead.

The longer I lived with the Akrion, the more things I discovered I could do. The Akrion stayed dormant until my body started its transition phase and then became active within me. I was ignorant that I harbored anything like it. I'd no idea why my hair sprang to life one day, scaring the peewaddin' out of me.

Until I took the journey on the StarFinder spaceship as an Alien Exchange Student, I only knew about my hair having abilities. I'd kept my relationship with my hair a strict secret; on the spaceship, I learned I had other capabilities, like changing into other forms.

Shape-changing was universally accepted as being totally impossible although the Imurians have looked far and wide through the galaxies while exploring and developing planets. The Amorphans came the closest, since their hands and feet are malleable, being boneless, but that's as far as it goes. So, yeah, I'm the impossible in all the galaxies and I knew, with gut wrenching certainty, that no military, government or scientists could know about this. My freedom, at a minimum, would be gone within a millisecond.

Fingers snapped in front of my face, startling me. I blinked rapidly at Si'neada as he said, "Amorpha to Jessi, come in, Jessi. I know you're in there somewhere."

I shoved his hand away. "Stop that."

"Ah, you're back with me, my little ponderer. You went somewhere else for a while. Good thing I was here to watch your back." Concern laced his voice. "You're not being swallowed up by being in that body, are you? You know that's something we've worried about from the beginning."

"No, no, that's not it, not at all. I just zoned out for a minute while the water and food replenished my spirit."

"You are to sure you are all right?" He lapsed into formal Imurian, his worry apparent.

"Yes, I'm fine." I heard the note of irritability in my voice. "Now, let's work out a feasible plan." I picked up a stick lying nearby. "You know the layout of the military ship, right? Do you know how they plan to do the rescue? For that matter, are they even concerned about the safety of my family? For instance, what happens if I don't show up?"

"What are you going to do with that stick?"

I jabbed him in the arm. "Well, I was going to have you draw schematics in the dirt of the inside of the ship, but, you know, I think poking you with it is a better idea."

He rolled his eyes. "Or," he said with a dramatic flourish of his hand, pushing the stick away, "we could use my Perpad."

"Oh. Well, yes. We could do that instead." I rummaged around in a pouch on my abdomen, which, I swear, I didn't have a couple of minutes ago. *I have a pouch? Like a marsupial?*

NEEDED A "STORAGE" PLACE. The air quotes were almost visible, making me want to roll my eyes.

I pulled out my device, squinted at it, and shook my head. "Mine's dead, therefore, the stick." I sat on the ground with a thump and a little poof of dust, shoving the pad back into the carrying pouch. I patted the patch of grass next to me, grinning up at Si'neada. I knew he'd loathe sitting on dirt.

He looked with distaste at the ground. "You don't really think for one second I would sit in filth?"

I snickered. "Only for a second or two. You two-furs do not like being mussed or dusty."

He sniffed. "Too true, my little smarty pants friend. Now please, stand up."

I made old-lady noises as I stood just to irritate him, while he retrieved his device from one of his multiple pockets, thumbing it on. I watched him for any sign he heard me while I whisked my hand over my furry butt and tail to remove any clinging dirt but he chose to ignore my huffs and puffs. He swiped through displays, me on padded tiptoes to watch, until he found an air ship schematic. For a tailor, he certainly had a wide array of information on that thing but I kept that to myself. Si'neada, I already knew, was way more than what he presented to the world.

We studied the screen in silence together until we counted the entrances/exits together out loud, as if we were one mind. "We are of like minds, you and me." He petted my head, running his hand over my soft fur in the direction it grew.

"Don't pet me!" I exclaimed as I pushed his hand away.

"But your hair, it is so soft, my silky friend." He raised his hand to repeat the motion.

I batted it away. "Stop that! We're under a time crunch; let's get this plan put together." I felt time ticking away as a pressure along my nervous system, and I knew it was time to quit fooling around and get this done.

Si'neada slipped in one last quick stroke across the top of my head and down along my ears before I could stop him. I gave him a narrow-eyed glare but he only wrinkled his nose at me, a small smile on his lips as he opened a blank screen. "I'll take notes while we work out a feasible plan."

"Oh, for the love of candy," I said in exasperation, "we don't need a written plan, you doofus. We only need to know how we're going to proceed."

"Mmmph." He snorted.

"Really, I think the best thing is for me to just walk out between the two ships as myself, and that'll put a stop to all this nonsense. My family will get saved and the military can protect me. You go back to them and tell them I'm coming out so they can be prepared for action."

Si'neada sighed, shaking his head. "You're forgetting one thing, my little Nameless One." Raising his eyebrows again, he tapped the side of my neck. "With this intact, you'll be shot as soon as the tracker notifies them you're off your path, whether or not you are you."

I cocked my head at him. "Isn't that only if I'm an Amorphan?"

He shook his head in a slow, deliberate motion. "If they see an implanted tracker, they won't care what species you are. They'll shoot to stun you, then scan the tracker for information. When they find you're off track or it's been tampered with, they'll kill you without mercy or consideration to your species." He cocked his head to one side, a quizzical look on his face. "How did you manage to tamper with it?"

"I didn't." I shrugged, trying for nonchalance. "This is the path it sent me."

He made a face that said, 'Riiiiiggghhhttt'. "Oh, sure, I believe that." His eyes narrowed. "Not."

"Just how did you think I could possibly tamper with it? I can't even see it! I have no clue how it's engineered, no idea of its programming and nothing but my fingernails as tools." I held them up to show him. "I didn't think they'd shoot a Human on sight for fear of an intergalactic incidence, but maybe I can disguise the tracker until we can explain...?"

He covered his mouth to hide his titter. "Oh, my little innocent friend." His eyes said he would dig out the real explanation at a different time.

"Well, okay, then, that was my idea," I said in irritation. "What's yours, my big smirky friend?"

"You need to get that tracker removed."

I fingered the side of my neck, feeling its outline. "But how? I've tried, you know. It's tangled into my nervous system."

"That is indeed the crux of the problem. The Amorphans were very, very clever when they made these. To remove it from an Amorphan is very tricky; most die from the attempt and those who survive become outlaws because the scar left behind still proclaims their nameless status." He shook his head. "Once the tracker comes out, it self-destructs."

Something clicked in my mind. "Oooooh, that's who attacked the convoy. They're a gang of nameless ones who successfully lived through the removal process."

"They band together because," he shrugged, spreading his hands, "who else will associate with them? What convoy?"

"Oh, you know, I was a soldier for a day or so to gather information and was sent out on an escort detail. We won the fight, obviously."

"Thank the blooming flowers in spring you weren't hurt or killed!"

To divert him away from that subject, I said, "I imagine it must hurt a lot to have this thing ripped out of their systems."

"Quite so," he agreed. "Removing it from you will be an intricate process, especially if we want to keep the tracker intact for, perhaps, future use."

I tilted my head to one side. "Do these work on other species, other than me, I mean? Of course, I was an Amorphan when it was placed so that's why it worked and I guess it changed to accommodate my new form. Surely your scientists have tried doing so." I made a face to signal my distaste of the Imurian scientists.

"The scientists haven't been able to retrieve one before it self-explodes, not even when the subject is on the table before them while they try to remove it for study." He sighed. "You are not wrong about the scientists."

"Ha. I'll bet they want to use them as a restraint device." I narrowed my eyes. "Don't they?"

He quirked his lips. "Wouldn't you if you were them? I'm also certain the scientists want one for study, to manufacture more for control of their subjects and who knows what else."

"Who would volunteer to have scientists do that to them?"

"Outlaws will do many unsavory things for money."

"True that." The beginnings of an idea poked me. "I have an idea, though, that should work while not killing me for trying."

CHAPTER THIRTY-ONE

Feeling like I bathed in a storm of lightning bolts, agony wracked my body. My brain was being squeezed in a red-hot vise and I couldn't do anything at all. I had no muscular control, no vision, no hearing, consumed by the fiery torture happening to me. I couldn't even scream.

After an eternity of constant, steadily increasing levels of pain beyond anything I could have imagined, the crushing intensity eased, giving me a minute amount of hope that I might live through this. For a long while, I would have welcomed death just to be relieved of the overwhelming agony that seemed to have no end.

The pounding on and in myself lightened in little bits, until, finally, I regained hearing and sight. Even though my vision was blurry and sounds were muffled, I welcomed the return of my senses, although I had no power of speech yet. That would require me forming words and that was beyond my capabilities right now.

Is.....it.....gone? Even thinking words was painful. I groaned, although I made so sound.

yes.

I'd never, ever, not once, heard the voice of my hair so tiny and subdued.

I became aware of a hand stroking my head. My skin felt like it was on fire, my hair was distinctly miserable, and the tiniest motion ratcheted up the pain levels again. I moaned, the only sound possible for now, becoming a bit more aware of the hard surface underneath me.

Something wet trickled along my lips, my tongue licking the moisture, wanting more. I grunted, a small sound, but it worked, more wetness dribbled onto my lips, a drop snaking down my neck and I mourned its loss. I cracked open my mouth to get as much as I could for the ravening thirst.

"Jessi?" A voice roared. I winced even as I managed to swallow the liquid. *Water. It's water.* Nothing had ever tasted as good as this water did. Swallowing was painful but each small amount eased the ache in my throat as I felt a small amount of energy come back to me.

I cracked one eye open, my eyelid fluttering with the intensity of the light in the room. *Oh. Not outdoors anymore.* A tear seeped out the edge of my eye, oozing down the side of my face.

:Jessi?:

This voice was soft and comfortable, not causing any pain.

:...Mmmm...?:

:I am so relieved; I thought I'd lost you completely. You scared the pellets out of me!:

:*Mmmm.*: Even using mind whispering hurt my brain. *:..Die...?:*

:*No, but you came perilously close.*:

:...*Out...?*:

:Yes, thank the universal light! It popped off, trailing all kinds of nasty looking stuff. I didn't dare touch it until it was completely out of your body, then I stuffed it into a sturdy container, where it self-destructed.:

:*Good.*: Sleep took me with the swiftness of a shark attack. Sometime later, I swam back to awareness, the pain having eased enough to make me think I might survive to the next day after all.

:Si'neada?:

:Yes, my little morsel of delight?:

:Fatar?:

:*No. You are quite human now.*:

I struggled to sit up, putting a hand to my thumping head. Gentle hands lent me support until I slumped against the corner of whatever I was on. "Was I shot with a full dose zap?" The light was too bright to be comfortable.

Normally, I wouldn't have noticed the tiniest of pauses before his reply. Right now, however, everything about me was hyper-alert and raw. "Not exactly." Si'neada's voice said with an odd tone.

"What, then?" My voice was scarily faint to my own ears.

He huffed a quiet sigh. "Sedative."

"Why?"

"So many things happening at once with your changing, going into another shape, then out of it, and into other shapes. I felt your mind slip away from me more than once and I had to interrupt the process." He gripped my hand. "It was the scariest thing I've ever watched and I was so afraid I'd lose you forever. Some of the shapes you started to become aren't sentient beings."

"Oh." I rubbed my forehead. "I have no memory of it." I licked my dry lips. "Is there more water?"

"Of course, my little thirsty desert plant." He placed a glass against my lips, sloshing some of the liquid out to dribble down my chin. I took the glass from him, drinking deeply before pausing for a breath. The room's light glared into my eyes through my closed lids and I didn't want to chance opening them.

"How did I get here?" I pressed the heels of my hands to my eyes, watching stars explode in the darkness behind my lids.

He said in a soft voice, "I carried you onboard."

"As what?"

"Your Human self. I had to wait until you stopped shifting through forms and settled into being just Jessi again. I was trying to keep track of your Human brain through the transitions; that's the hardest thing I ever did, by the way. I had to be sure you'd still be you and not get lost in some form. No one saw what you went through other than me, so don't be worried about that. I made sure you stayed out of sight until it was safe to transport you."

"And nobody shot at us?"

"No. The military wouldn't dare shoot you, at least not with witnesses, and the Nameless Ones," this time I heard how he capitalized the title, "want you alive."

Something rattled as I raised my hand to rub my nose. I peeled my eyelids open, blinking rapidly as my eyes adjusted to the glare. I gasped when I saw a chain dangling from a metal bracelet around my wrist. I stared at it, befuddled by its presence. "What's this? Why is it on me?" I tugged but it was anchored to the nearby wall.

Lifting my other hand, I saw it was shackled, also. That explained the clinking sounds I'd heard while conversing with Si'neada. Who had placed me in chains? And why? Si'neada wouldn't do that; he's my friend and mentor and we were working together to stop the blatant genocide of new civilizations by their elite scientists.

Si'neada turned his eyes away from me, a flick of movement, then looked back. "For your safety. The way you thrashed and fought, we–I was very afraid you'd injure yourself without intervention."

I wondered who the other part of 'we' might be. But still, because I wasn't sure I'd heard the word, I had to ask. "Did you say 'we'?"

He stroked a finger down my cheek with a gentle touch. "No, no, my little confused Human, I didn't say anything like that."

"What ship is this? It doesn't look military." I frowned, drawing my knees up to rest my arms on, shocked to find chains around my ankles. I had enough leeway to reach my face with my hands and to bend my knees but that was the extent of my freedom.

"Well, I'm not confused or thrashing around anymore, so you can remove these horrible things." I rattled the chain on my left wrist at him.

He didn't flinch nor did he reach for a key. "The good news is your Amorphan family has been released into safety."

Relief flooded me. "Oh, my stars, that's the best news I've heard for a while." My eyes widened. "Wait a minute. So I'm on the rebels' ship? The exchange happened and they kept their word?" He nodded.

"At least my family is safe." Yanking against the shackle again, I glared at Si'neada. "But now I'm their prisoner? What kind of crap is this?"

He had the grace to look abashed. "It was the only way, my little friend. It was the only way; I had to do it."

"You brought me to them and let them chain me up!" I exclaimed as I shrank away from him. "You're my friend! And now I'm their captive?" I rattled the chains binding me to the wall. "Let me out of these. Right. Now." My fists clenched as the iron bracelets bit into my wrists.

"I...cannot." He looked away. "I do not have the keys."

"Are we still on the ground?"

"Yes. It is not safe to fly while the military is still here. The ship is staying quiet and hidden for now. You will be all right, Jessi." He reached out as if to pat me on the arm and I jerked away from his touch.

"They're going to sell me to the Imurian scientists, aren't they? Right? That's what's happening here so you might as well tell me." Bitterness lay heavy in my words along with the sting of his treachery.

A long moment of silence slipped by as I fought back tears. I wouldn't give him the satisfaction of seeing me cry like a baby in defeat. There had to be a way out of this. There had to be.

Sinnet? Are you there?

YES.

Can I get out of these chains?

PROBABLY. NOT YET.

Do I still have Amorphan DNA in me?

NO. YES.

Well, which is it? Purging their DNA from my system must've worked to get rid of the tracker since it's gone. My body couldn't get rid of it if there was even one strand of Amorphan DNA left in me. And the tracker is gone so all the Amorphan DNA is gone? It struck me, then, my hair hadn't objected to this name. Hope she didn't know it was tennis spelled backwards but it was pretty when the second syllable was emphasized. Maybe I'd finally found the right one. I'd have to wait and see, however; sometimes a name was tried for a few times and then discarded.

YES. BUT REPLENISH WHILE HERE. WHEN CAN.

Can't you get DNA from surfaces?

BEST FROM PERSON. BUT CAN'T DO YET. UNDO BINDING.

Huh? I reached my hand toward the back of my head but came up short when the chain reached its limit. I bent my head forward but couldn't reach my hair.

What's confining you?

BAG GLUED TO SCALP.

Can you get out of it?

WITH ENOUGH TIME. CAN'T CUT THROUGH. MUST DISSOLVE AN AREA WITHOUT HURTING US.

I can't reach back there to help, either. You're really out of commission?

YES. FOR NOW.

The tightness in the words bespoke how furious my hair felt at being helpless. I could relate.

I sucked in a breath. Right this instance, I was livid at Si'neada for selling me out, at being captive, at being helpless. I wanted to inflict damage on him, not ask for his help. Hating myself, my jaw clenched hard together before I forced out the words.

"Si'neada, take the bag off my hair. At least do that for me. I'm getting a headache from the weight of it." I couldn't look at him or I might spit in his face and that would be counterproductive. He didn't know about my hair's abilities so he might remove the bag. I'd never told him or anyone, ever, about what my hair could do. I wished I could've kept secret my ability for shape changing but at least, only four others knew about it and they were all pledged to secrecy. If it hadn't been for Deester filming me changing forms, no one would know about that, either.

"I do not dare. I am sorry, so sorry." A small catch in his voice sounded like a sob but I refused to feel pity for him. Not after he'd sold me into slavery like this.

"Please?"

"I cannot." He whispered.

:Tell me why, Si'neada. Why did you betray me like this? Why can't you at least release my hair? Come on, it's only hair. It's bad enough I'm chained like a dangerous dog but to have my hair in an ugly bag like this? I mean, really? At least let me have that vanity.:

His shields were rock solid and I felt my mind words bounce back to me. Tears leaked from my eyes before I could stop them as defeat and despair washed over me. "Please, Si'neada?"

He shook his head, not looking at me. "I can't. I hope you'll understand one day."

"I don't understand. So, explain, please, just tell me what's going on."

CHAPTER THIRTY-TWO

The door opened, cutting short any answer Si'neada might've given, as two Amorphan Nameless Ones came into the room. Si'neada stood as they entered the room, fear fleeting across his face but it disappeared so fast, I couldn't say for sure it had happened. I'd never seen Si'neada scared of anything, which alarmed me more than being cuffed to the wall. The Si'neada I knew was the definition of self-confidence with a dash of arrogance, tempered by compassion. He was also groomed impeccably at all times, even the stripes on his fur often sporting different colors to match his outfits.

The nearest Amorphan, taller than Si'neada by a good 12 inches, grabbed him by the upper arm, wrinkling the material, shoving him roughly toward the door. "Leave, Two-fur." His sneer as he used the term made it sound like an ugly thing. "Your time's up."

:Si'neada! Si'neada, don't leave me here alone!: He's the only familiar face here among all these unknown persons and,

angry as I was at him, with the pain of his betrayal, I feared being alone more with these renegade strangers.

No answer; his mental shields were solid and closed tight. My mental shouts were about as effective as a moth trying to bore through a steel door. His shoulders slumped a tiny bit as he scurried out the door without a word or a backwards glance.

I frowned as I watched him leave. His behavior was totally out of character for him and I'd never seen him slump, not even the tiniest bit ever, no matter the situation. What was going on here? I didn't know the answer–yet.

The two disheveled Amorphan males looked at me, one crossing his arms over his chest. They both had scars on the right side of their necks, round in shape, raised in a bumpy pattern and reddened as if sunburned. The skin in that area no longer refracted colors: instead, it was a dead area surrounded by the loveliness of the hues reflected from living skin, a jarring contrast. The center of the ring looked like it had been torn into pieces, those pieces flung back into the area, then allowed to heal in a willy-nilly pattern.

Both were tall, well, heck, everyone is tall to me, especially when I'm looking up at them. Their eyes glittered in the light as their breathing openings flared as if they smelled something rotten. I suppose that might've been me since I hadn't seen a shower for quite a while. They wore identical uniforms with plenty of pockets, most of which bulged with unknown objects.

Right then, the only way I could tell them apart was from the differences in their scars. The male who'd come in the room first fingered his neck scar, staring at me. "Does this upset you?" He smirked.

"No, other than whoever let that heal wasn't a very competent physician. You could have that scar fixed, you know."

He exchanged glances with the other male, then they laughed, a jeering sound. "These scars are hard earned and we have no desire to disguise them."

"What are they from?" I asked, reluctant to let them know I already knew the answer. "Were you in some kind of accident?"

Again, they chuckled. "You could say that." The same one answered as his eyes narrowed. "If you can call it an accident to be accused falsely of misdoings and cast out into the wild with nothing to help you survive and a tracker slammed into your system."

It hadn't occurred to me that others could've become Nameless Ones as a result of false accusations even though that's exactly what happened to my Amorphan self. "I'm so sorry about what happened to you. What are these trackers? Why did they leave such a big scar?"

He fingered his scar again, although I don't think he was aware of the habit. "Trackers are a punishment. They are permanent unless you can find those who can remove them and let you become part of their group. This scar is the result of living through the experience of having your nervous system ripped apart to get rid of the device."

The other male spoke up. "Why are you telling her this, Morian? This isn't knowledge that needs to be shared with a Human. Come on; let's get her ready for transport." He reached toward me and I shrank back from his grip, stopped by the wall and the mass of hair behind my back.

"Where she's going, Yarian, it won't matter what we've told her. You know that."

"Where am I going? What is it you all want from me?" I stretched my arm up to my forehead, as far as it could go. "What happened to my hair?"

Yarian barked out a coarse laugh. "Money, you foolish Human. You are worth a great deal of money to the right people. Us Nameless Ones, it costs money to keep us alive and since we can't get jobs or rejoin the military, we have limited resources. We get our cash from whatever source we can. As to where you're going, you'll find out when you get there, although don't bother to plan a return trip."

"What happened to my hair?" I pointed at my head while I prompted. Might as well get what information I could while he was in the mood to answer.

"Oh, that stuff. It was getting in our way, being all over the place so I stuffed it into that bag. Then I couldn't keep the bag around it so I glued it to your head."

"At least you didn't cut it off."

He shrugged. "I tried. I had no idea you Humans have wire for your head coverings."

Thank the depths of space for that! Good job, Sinnet.

FOUGHT HARD TO STAY OUT BUT HE SPRAYED US INTO COMPLIANCE. Oh, my hair was pissed.

NOT PISSED. DOWNRIGHT FURIOUS.

At least you didn't let him cut you. I shuddered at the thought even as I asked my next question. "Why do you have shortened names? I've never heard of an Amorphan name without four syllables."

"Since we can't be part of society anymore, we don't have to follow rules. When the group takes in one of us, we shorten our names by one syllable so everyone knows we belong." He glared at me. "We can't all call each other Nameless One. That would be way too confusing." He moved a step closer. "It's time to go."

Reaching out, Yarian grabbed my right forearm. I jerked against his hold on me, chain swinging, as I removed my arm from his grip, grabbing at the key in his other hand.

"Not until you take my hair out of this bag! I have a headache and I can't manage without my hair to keep my back warm. You don't understand what it means to us Human females!"

Morian seized my upper left arm with both his hands, yanking it out to the side where I had little leverage. Morian snagged my right arm again with a grip of steel, so I kicked out with my feet, but was brought up short by the chains.

I growled, lunging my head forward, fastening my teeth onto Morian's hand, making him gasp from the sudden pain from my bite. I writhed around as much as I could to avoid their grips, limited by my shackles, but I refused to go meekly. They wanted to transport me? Fine, they were going to pay a price with as many bruises as I could manage, teeth marks, too. I didn't take all those years of Cat Fighting for girls for nothing, after all.

"Stop that!" Yarian snarled at me as he tightened his grip on my arm. "We can't unlock you from the wall unless you cooperate."

"I'll cooperate when you let me have my hair back. Being without my hair is like you....like you being a Nameless One." I spat the words at them and their eyes widened for a split second, then they looked at each other. "We could just paralyze you with our stun gun and take you that way."

"Somehow, I think whoever you've sold me to will want me alive and well. If I die because you don't know the proper dose to give me, you won't get paid."

Yarian spoke first. "If you comply with us, we'll release your hair. We don't have much time, though; we must have you on that transporter soon or our superiors will come looking for answers." A tiny grimace. "And you don't want that."

"If you free my hair, I will comply," I promised. To prove my point, I stopped struggling. I watched them closely since I didn't trust them any further than I could toss them in an underhand throw.

Morian rubbed his hand where I'd bitten him. "If we weren't so time limited, I'd make sure you pay for this."

"Did you expect a human female to be all meek and submissive? Well, think again, Charlie, because most of us are not." I lifted one side of my lip. "And besides, if you were me, wouldn't you have done the same exact thing?"

He uttered a low, guttural sound but nodded with reluctance. "Yes, I suppose I would. But we Amorphans don't bite."

"Yeah, because you have shark teeth. We have blunt teeth so we can't do your kind of damage." Crapola, why did I say that? I certainly didn't need to encourage him to bite me or anyone else. Their teeth, sharply serrated, would do real damage.

"Only in the worst of circumstances would any of us, even us Nameless Ones, bite and only to save our own life. We are still honorable, no matter what people think." He pulled a vial from a pocket. "Now. Hold still while I apply this to remove the confiner from your head."

He was not gentle in his application of the liquid, which was so cold, it burned. I gritted my teeth against the words I wanted to spit out against the discomfort.

Finally, about a million years later, the biting coldness became a throbbing in my scalp and I unclenched my fingers because I thought he was done. He wasn't.

Before I had time to draw in a breath, he seized the edges of the bag and ripped. I know it's best to rip off a band-aid fast, but holy smoke, this hurt! The unexpectedness of it made me yelp and my head followed the trajectory of his yanking, going back and then snapping forward.

Morian grinned in satisfaction.

"You happy now?" I muttered, swiping tears from my eyes. Something wet trickle down my forehead. I hoped it was only from the dissolvent but when I wiped it off with the back of my hand, I wasn't surprised to see the color red.

"Immensely." He said with relish, baring his sharp teeth at me, a very rude gesture for Amorphans.

I ignored him. *You okay?*

MOSTLY. LOST SOME OF US. Anger laced the words and my hair stirred against my back.

Not now. Not here. We can't win and they can't know about you. Please.

The movement stopped. *Doesn't mean we like it but we have to wait for a better opportunity.*

CHAPTER THIRTY-THREE

As I promised, I didn't fight them anymore and Morian unlocked my chains from the wall, but not from my wrists or ankles. For the first time, I noticed they were around my wrists and not my upper arms, like they would with an Amorphan, where they shackled the upper arms together, with a connecting band on their backsides to prevent them from using their arms altogether. They were prepared for someone like me to be prisoner.

A few strands of hair sneaked out, taking DNA samples from the two males to replenish our stash. Having to purge all my Amorphan DNA to get rid of the tracker meant needing new DNA to replace our loss. I almost touched the side of my neck where it had resided but caught myself in time. I didn't want to call their attention to the area; I didn't know if I had a scar on my neck or not but no sense taking chances.

I was, of course, disappointed they left the chains in place, like I was a dangerous bull being led to slaughter. Ack, wish I hadn't thought of that analogy. When they tugged on my arm chains, I looked at them. I raised one eyebrow. "Do you want me to stand? You only have to ask, no need to jerk me around."

Yarian raised his eye ridge in return, eyes sparkling with a bit of malice. Sliding his hands down the chain, closer to me, he pulled on my arm chain again with a sharp, sudden motion, jerking me forward.

Anger whipped through me but I bit it back, swallowing it down into my stomach, burning from the insult. I stood onto shaky legs, gulping in a breath of air, relieved to feel the warmth of hair against my back. Both males pulled each arm straight out to the side, standing out of range.

Morian pulled a pulse pistol, aimed at my head. "Come quietly or I use this."

"I promised I would." I retorted. As I took a step, I could only do the jailhouse shuffle, as my ankles were chained close together. Well, running away was out of the question, then. Good thing I hated running as much as I did.

They led me, shambling and clanking, toward the door from which they'd entered, keeping a tight grip on my arm shackles. At least I wasn't wearing a collar with a leash, but that's the most optimistic thing I could find about this scenario.

"Huh. You'd think I was some dangerous wild animal, the way you have me all trussed up." *Do* NOT *suggest or even think of a collar and leash, Jessi!* I banished the image from my mind, just in case, you know.

They didn't answer. They pushed me forward into a corridor where a few other Amorphans stood around, some watching with crossed arms, expressions varying from amusement to smirking. We made our way through the belly of the transport ship, past the galley and lounge area, both cluttered and messy and approached the entry to the space shuttle. Morian and Yarian had fun keeping me off balance, making me stumble and lurch to catch myself from falling. For variety, they'd shove me into the wall, then laugh. I burned with anger but knew I couldn't win right now. I'll admit, being humiliated like this wasn't something I could stomach for long. I vowed I'd get revenge someday.

Instead of boarding the shuttle, however, they stopped, shortening their hold on the arm chains, holding me in place. Yarian grabbed my chin, turning my face toward a small blinking light, which I'm guessing is a camera, not loosening his grip. He might've been worried I'd bite him again. He'd be right.

I think I'll have finger shaped bruises...and the ones from the walls and the shackles.. It's still hard to believe that Amorphan hands and fingers could have this kind of strength without bones, but then I remind myself of how our own tongues work without bones. I could only wait until he was done with whatever he was doing.

Finally, he released his hold. From the listening look on his face, he'd received the instructions he wanted because he wore a satisfied smile. He looked at Morian and nodded.

Morian smiled wide, showing lots of sharp teeth. He said, "You are worth a great deal of money, Human, and the credits have been transferred to us." He grunted one chuckle. "Guess we'll let you live, after all."

"How kind of you," I said with as much sarcasm as I could muster.

He cuffed me on the back of the head, not realizing how dangerous it was to handle my hair. Thank the air around us that my hair knew it needed to behave right now; if it cut off his fingers, we surely would die. They already had their credits, although I wondered how Nameless Ones could have a credit account through an institution, and if they "accidentally" killed me? They'd shrug and say, "Oops and good luck on getting back the money", while slinging my body through the door.

It didn't matter that it would cause a huge interworld uproar, I'd be dead and wouldn't know about it. The Nameless Ones had very little to lose so their incentive for me to be alive was low. Except, I hoped, the payors would know enough to only pay half of the money up front and the other half when they received my warm, breathing self.

Anxiety spun through me as we waited for the shuttle door to open for entering the transport ship. I knew in my gut it had to be the Imurian scientists who were paying the ransom; I refused to think of this transaction as a sale. I'm nobody's slave. I didn't know–yet–how'd I get out of this but I would find a way to escape. I had to.

Are you working on these shackles? Cutting through them so when the time is right, I can be out of them?

DIFFICULT; UNKNOWN ALLOY. NOT SURE CAN CUT THROUGH.

My heart squeezed in pain followed by a sinking feeling. If my hair couldn't cut through these metal cuffs and no one removed the chains, I'd be totally and completely screwed over. *There has to be something we can do.*

A big internal sigh. CHECKING MOLECULAR STRUCTURE SO CAN DISSOLVE, CAN'T CUT.

That doesn't sound like it'll be fast or soon enough. I can't break them; I've tried. And I wasn't able to get the key. I blinked. *Wait a minute, can't you steal the key? It's in Yarian's upper pocket, left side of his chest area, has a fastener on it.*

HAVE TRIED. BRUSHES US AWAY.

Well, that sucks. And that's a first; no one else has ever noticed you before like that.

DEFINITELY SUCKS. AND VERY RUDE.

I snorted, a soft sound, but both Morian and Yarian stared at me.

"What?" I demanded. "Is this going to take a year to open that door or what?" Sometimes the best defense was offense.

As soon as I said the words, a clanking sound came from the other side of the door and the heavy, circular metal door started to open inward at a snail's pace. Sheesh. Whoever said anticipation is the worst part of an event, well, they're right. My heart picked up speed as a wave of fear swept through me at being forced into the unknown. I still didn't know if I was being sold as a slave, being served up for dinner for some unknown species, or going to the scientists for their experiments. What I did know is I would make whatever I faced as difficult as I could for my new captors.

A variety of other horrible scenarios ran through my brain before I could stop them, leaving me with hands shaking and heart pounding as I tried to hide my fear from the two Amorphans.

And now I had to pee. I mean, bad. Like as in I needed to do the potty dance but couldn't move enough to do so and I prayed I wouldn't pee down my legs. I remembered a trick my mom had told me about a long time ago, doing a bunch of Kegel squeezes, fast, and darned if it didn't override the urge to empty my bladder.

When the shove on my back propelled me forward, I wasn't prepared, so I stumbled and almost went to my knees. Rough hands caught me, gripping my upper arms on both sides, forcing me to the open doorway. Imurian soldiers stood on the receiving side, grabbing my chains, giving me no chance to move without someone's permission.

The soldiers reeled me toward them like a fish on a hook until I was fully through the door, which creaked closed behind me. Well, at least I wasn't with the Nameless Ones, anymore. I guess that's a plus.

"Hey, fellas." I said. "Um, I need to use a bathroom, like right now."

They ignored me, keeping a tight grip on the chains, waiting for the door to fully close. I heard it grind to a halt, then one soldier stepped behind me and I heard him secure the door.

"Hey." I said. "I need a toilet. Now." I crossed one knee over the other, the best potty dance I could do with my restrictions. "Please." I used my best Imurian to ask.

The soldier I looked at rolled his eyes, hesitated, then nodded. He used whisker talk to tell the other soldier to give him both chains so he could take me to the bathroom. They, of course, didn't know I could read their whisker language and I wasn't telling them. I guess they were under orders not to speak to me or answer me, but some things prevail, like full bladders.

They said a few other things about me, like how little I was and therefore, couldn't be that dangerous, so why truss me up like a cooking bird. I agreed with their assessment, well, except for the not dangerous part. They performed their job as ordered, but only the minimum they could and they weren't all that happy about being commanded to do this. Along with discussing me, they also complained about how they felt demoted to have to pull this guard duty. After all, I was no threat to them.

Chains clanked and I shuffled, making my guard take mincing steps, reminding me of Si'neada, which made my chest constrict with pain at the way he betrayed me. We reached the bathroom where my young soldier realized he had a conundrum. He had a choice to make here. Either he let me go in by myself with my tethers or he removed them to let me go in, or he came in with me into the tiny space.

I almost laughed at the horrified look on his face as he picked through the choices. I did my best to look small (not difficult) and helpless (also presently not difficult) and most of all, not dangerous. Oh, no, not lil' ol' me, no dangerous Humans here, so move along, folks.

Of course, I voted for removal but kept my mouth shut. I knew crowding in with me was out of the question, as the room had barely enough room in it for one Imurian, much less a Human female–no matter how short I am–and an Imurian.

KEEP THEM ON. SOLVED HOW TO GET THEM OFF.

Yeah, I suppose this isn't a good time since there's no way out, I can't fight an entire ship. I could morph into something big and scary in the bathroom but then I'd have to kill these two when I come out. And I won't kill them They're not really the bad guys here. I huffed a sigh. *Okay, later when we have a real chance.*

The young Imurian was still frozen in indecision so I solved it for him. I yanked the door open, stepping into the tiny enclosure, and motioned for him to toss the chains in with me. He jumped in place from my sudden movement, then looked at his hands clutching the chains, then at me, and shrugged, tossing the restraints in with me and I closed the door. He shouted through the door, "Knock before coming out so I know you're done."

"Yeah, yeah, I will."

For the first time in several days, I saw myself in the mirror. My eyes widened as I stared at my dirty face, disheveled hair around my head with bruises dotting my cheeks and forehead, two blackened eyes staring out. *What in the world happened?*

PURGING DNA NOT EASY TO DO OR GO THROUGH. Hesitation and then a reluctant admission. ALMOST DIDN'T MAKE IT.

You mean we almost died? Dying? Hairy crap on a brush! It was that serious; no wonder Si'neada had been so worried. Yeah, worried I wouldn't be alive to deliver to the Amorphans for the reward. My stomach churned with anger.

UH, WELL, PRETTY CLOSE. BUT KNOW BETTER HOW NEXT TIME.

I certainly hope there isn't a next time!

AGREED.

I washed my hands, so much more comfortable now with an empty bladder, chains clinking against the steel sink. I faced the door to leave instead of backing out. Although, if someone were going to shoot me, I guess better in the butt than the front of me. I knocked on the door to let the guard know I was leaving the room.

I inched the door open, playing meek, shoving my chains out the door for him to grasp, then stepped out. "Okay, lead on, McDuff."

He frowned. "What is a mick duff? Are you calling me something bad?"

I shook my head. "No, it's just some Human saying my mom used to use. McDuff, I guess, was some guy in the distant past on Earth."

He looked at me with suspicion. "Well, don't call me that again."

"I don't know your name so had to call you something."

He sniffed his displeasure. "Come on, it's time to secure you for the trip."

I rolled my eyes. "I'm so looking forward to that. You do know I'm not some criminal, right?"

"Not my place to ask. Only my place to follow orders."

"Are you taking me to those scientists?" I made a face, dread curling upward from my toes to my belly, goose pimples showing the path.

"No more questions." But I saw sympathy on his face before he averted his eyes. The other guard stood from his chair, yawned and stretched, then took the few steps forward to join us.

The second guard curled his lip. "Couldn't you have washed your face while you were in there?"

"You're lucky I managed to wash my hands." I retorted, holding up my shackled wrists.

He gave me a cold look, tapping his comm. "We're on our way with the Human female."

"What delayed you?" A voice demanded in return.

"Bathroom for the Human."

CHAPTER THIRTY-FOUR

A pause, then, "Very well. Bring her to me."

The Imurian guard indicated the door ahead of us with his chin. He gathered the chain tighter, the other guard doing the same, and we all moved forward, limited by the short, scuffling steps I was forced to take. We couldn't all three fit through the one–person doorway at the same time, so came to a stop while they thought this over. Using their whisker twitch language, they decided they'd short shackle my hands together, leaving one longer chain on my arm for control.

"What are you staring at, Human?" The gruff one growled at me. The other guy was more sympathetic toward me so this guy I now dubbed McGruff.

"Something wrong with your whiskers? They're all twitchy and stuff." I inquired in a sweet tone. "Do they itch when you do something you know is wrong, like, you know, keep me in chains?

He cuffed the side of my head, making me stagger a step forward. "Shut up." Pulling a key from a pocket on his upper right chest, he unlocked the chain from my right wrist shackle, then looped it around my wrists using a figure-eight configuration, snapping a circular lock through the links. I hoped he would do this on my upper arms, as he would for an Amorphan, but he was too well trained for that kind of mistake.

Got that key location?

OF COURSE. NOT A FOOL.

McGruff thrust me through the door, keeping a tight hold on the back of my collar as I blundered through, then he stepped through right on my heels. In a swift motion, he attached a new length of some kind of cord to my shackle on my right wrist, pushing me forward for the other male to come through. The door snapped close in a decisive way.

LURCH HIS WAY.

Who, McGruff?

NO, THE STATUE OVER THERE. My hair snapped at me. **OF COURSE, MCGRUFF.**

To punctuate the words, my hair gave me a shove his way, I lurched to the side, knocking into him and he grabbed my arms to hold us both upright. "Stay on your own feet, Human!" He roared at me.

"Well, *you* try and balance with all this stuff binding your feet and hands, you idiot! It's not as easy as I make it look." I raised my chin in the air with a haughty sniff.

Did you get it?

YES.

Way to go, cheers for us.

McGruff growled in response, shoving me off him and forward at the same time. The elevator doors opened. Anxiety ratcheted high within my core, my breathing fast and heart beating hard. I sucked in a deep breath, trying to calm down. I now had the key to the chains, I hoped it fit more than one lock, and then I could find a way to escape.

In the few seconds it took to rise to the next level of the transport ship, silence reigned, only the sounds of our breathing in the small enclosure. The doors silently slid apart and I stared into a large space with little furniture, a lot of equipment, and a chair with large eyebolts fastened to the arms and the floor beside it on both sides.

A hand on my back thrust me forward, and I almost fell again as I gritted my teeth in anger. They both yanked on the chains, hauling me upright in a rough manner, making my head snap forward and then back, and I bit my tongue in the process. "Ow!" I yelled.

McGruff's hand clamped over my mouth. "Shut up," he hissed into my ear. "You do *not* want to make anyone mad in here."

The other male muttered so low I barely heard him, "Yeah, well, they're already mad in here."

This time, we stepped forward as a unit, me wrapped in chains like a prize pig at the State Fair and I got my first full look around the room. Various monitors blinked and whirred, set around the perimeter of the space, about the size of a bedroom, gray walls with no adornments, the chair in the middle made all of metal, and a few other chairs scattered here and there. There was no one else in the space, no windows to the outside, and only one other door on the opposite wall, shut tight. Overhead lighting cast shadows over the edges of the room.

The cool air of the space brushed against my skin and I shivered, more from fear than temperature, if I were to tell the truth. The vents were overhead between the lights, and then I realized everything in here was metal, ceiling included. I looked at the floor, metal with drain openings in three spots across the middle of the space. I wrinkled my eyebrows in puzzlement. There was no source of water or other liquid that I could see, so why need drains?

My brain skittered away from the obvious answer: to wash away blood or other bodily fluids.

McGruff leaned into my space, breathing next to my ear. "You are very lucky no one is present to hear you yelp on the elevator; we'd all be punished and I wouldn't forget something like that." He paused. "Ever. And I always get my revenge."

We stood by the chair at this point, and he positioned me in front of it, ramming me down onto the seat by pushing hard on shoulders, hooking my feet with one foot, pulling them forward, so I had no choice but to sit. Holding me there, while I fervently hoped he didn't go for the key in his pocket, the other male, whom I now called Good Cop McDuff, fumbled in one of his pockets to pull out a key. Working together, working fast, they locked me into the chair with no room for me to move any limb from its current position.

"Can't you give me a little slack here, boys?" I used my sweetest tone, fluttering my eyelashes at Good Cop McDuff.

In answer, Good Cop clamped his hand over my mouth and McGruff pulled something out of somewhere, and as Good Cop removed his hand, he shoved a cloth gag into my mouth, velcroing it on the back of my head, catching hair into the fastening. The cloth cut into the corners of my mouth and immediately soaked up any and all spit inside. Now I wanted water to drink but at least my bladder was empty.

"I told you to shut up." He hissed at me. Satisfied I was securely fastened, he and Good Cop stepped to either side of me, a couple of paces away, and stood to attention just as the opposite door started to open. My breathing became harsh to my own ears, my heart beating so rapidly I thought I might faint, and I whimpered, to my chagrin.

A tall, muscular male Imurian figure came through the door, wearing the standard jumpsuit but with a long lab coat over it, his long tail held at a jaunty, self-satisfied angle. *It is one of the scientists. Oh, shister blister, I'm in trouble.*

I blinked tears out of my eyes to get a better look but I didn't recognize him. Of course, the only scientist I'd ever seen before was on the StarFinder when I rescued Zoe and this wasn't him. I didn't know whether to be relieved or even more scared.

He smoothed his hands down the sides of his lab coat, as if to make sure he was presentable for our introduction. Then, clasping his hands behind his back, he strolled our way and I felt his gaze on me like a knife edge, cutting away the superficial to see the truth underneath.

Akrion, you'd better be well hidden or this guy will find you in a nanosecond.

He stopped in front of me, about two feet away, again dissecting me with his eyes. "The gag?"

"She talks a lot, sir." McGruff stared straight ahead as he answered. I looked from him back to the scientist in front of me, who tapped his lip with one hand, with his other hand on the elbow for support.

"I see." He tilted his head one way, his golden eyes narrowing, the vertical pupil flaring open, then constricting, his cat-like ears hard forward in a display of intense interest. "I think she will learn to talk only when asked a question." He loomed over me and I shrank back in the chair. Yeah, I'll be the first to admit he was definitely intimidating.

He smiled, a cold motion with nothing reaching his eyes. "I'm told she's a fast learner." He pointed at the eyebolts. "She is secure?"

"Yes, sir, double checked and snugged, just like you like, sir."

The scientist flicked a finger at Good Cop. "You may leave. Wa'len'den, you may stay."

They both chorused, "Thank you, Dr. Ot'ino'yan, sir." Good Cop stepped out of sight and I heard the elevator door open.

The doctor's cold yellow eyes fastened onto me again. I swallowed hard, even though my mouth was now as dry as a popcorn fart, as my Dad would say. He bared his teeth at me in a facsimile of a grin, pointing a finger at me. "The fun will begin shortly. At least, one of us will have fun. It remains to be seen who it will be."

He looked over at Wa'len'den. "Remove the gag, give her a drink of water. If she talks, you can shut her up but don't draw blood. Yet. I need to retrieve a few things."

Even though Wa'len'den's face was in profile to me, I could still see the smirk of pleasure on his face. "Yes, sir."

BE READY.

Dr. Ot'ino'yan turned on his heel, striding toward the far door with purpose. Wa'len'den slid a finger under one end of my gag, pulling it out a little, pinching the other edge of my mouth even more. A blade snicked open in his other hand. He pressed the tip of it against my skin and I froze. "Don't move," he whispered, making his words sound intimate. "I'd hate for the blade to slip." He sighed. "But I'm not to draw any of your blood. Yet."

He slipped the cold metal under the gag and with one hard tug, cut through the cloth, grabbing one end to pull it from my mouth. I worked my tongue around, trying to wet my lips, but I had no saliva yet.

"Water." I croaked, barely a whisper. He flicked a finger against my sore lips, smiling at my discomfort. Then he pulled out a flask from somewhere, uncapping it, and tilted it against my mouth. I sucked in the moisture as best I could, a large part spilling down my front because he didn't put it right up to my lips. I didn't care; it was liquid, it was cold and right then, delicious.

Each swallow bolstered my body with energy, the wetness on my skin and clothes refreshing, even with the goose pimples. After only a few mouthfuls of water, he pulled the flask back, putting the cap back on. At least my mouth didn't feel full of cotton anymore.

I flexed my wrists, testing the imprisoning shackles and felt them give a little. Sinnet had been quite busy and the metal would give if I gave a good yank, which was problematic, since I was bound tightly to the chair arms and eyebolts in the floor.

I don't think I can break through. There is no give and I can't yank. I can pull, but that's about it.

TRUE. WILL WEAKEN MORE.

That I can live with. Will I have my gun available when I get my hands free?

NO. CAN'T MANAGE YET.

Disappointment deflated my mood. I could get free but overpowering the large male and defending myself would be difficult without my weapon.

STEAL HIS. HAVE HIS DNA.

Well, frickin'-a, what an obvious solution. While my hair and I conversed, he'd finished stowing the flask away in a leg pocket. He squatted next to me, putting a clawed hand on my thigh. Watching me intently with his green-yellow eyes, he inched his hand upward on my inner thigh toward my crotch. I tried to dislodge his hand, trying to raise my knee enough to throw it off. The only thing that happened was when he grinned, licking his lips, lust sparking in his eyes.

NOW.

Tightening my muscles, jerking against the metal with all my might with my lower arms and legs, the metal broke, all at the same time, with a loud snapping noise. As that happened, my hair surged forward over my shoulders to wrap around Wal'en'den's throat from both directions, cutting off his air. He opened his mouth to shout, I think, but all he could produce was a gurgle. He clawed at his throat trying to remove the slippery strands of hair, which also wrapped around his hands.

I grabbed the gun in his holster, pulling it, setting it to maximum stun. My finger morphed as fast as it ever had into a duplicate of his finger, the gun activated, and I placed the muzzle on his torso, pulling the trigger.

He collapsed on the floor, twitching, as my hair untangled itself from his neck and hands. He moaned, spittle drooling from his partially opened mouth. I squatted next to him, ignoring the pins and needles in my hands and feet, grabbing the flask of water and the contents of a few other pockets.

GO GO GO!

I'd only taken a few seconds but Sinnet was right; I needed to get out of there. I scampered over to the elevator, pressing the button several times, as if that had ever hurried an elevator anywhere in any galaxy. I heard the soft whine of the mechanism as it engaged and the lift moved. The door across from me opened, the one the scientist had gone through earlier, with a surprised squawk from Dr. Ot'ino'yan. I turned fully toward him as the doors to the elevator slid apart, pointing my weapon at him. I risked a quick glance into the elevator and, to my everlasting relief, it was empty.

Because I'd set my weapon to full stun, I needed to wait until the scientist was in closer range for the full effect to happen. He stalked toward me, a large, angry, merciless male figure. He held several objects in his hands, and most of them seemed to have sharp ends.

"How dare you!" He snapped at me.

Oh? Have I upset him? Tsk tsk, how rude of me.

"Get back over here this instant!" He even snapped his fingers, as if I were a dog to obey instantly. In his world, I guess I was.

"Like hell I will." I said in a calm voice, even though inside, I was shaking like a personal earthquake. "Just what were you planning to do to me, anyway?"

"I don't answer to you. I paid good money for you; you are my property so you need to come over here *now*."

CHAPTER THIRTY-FIVE

Pinning his eyes on me, he lifted his wrist to his mouth. "Take off now, this instant. And shut down the elevator. I have a situation here I need to take care of."

He lifted the comm to his ear so I missed whatever reply was given.

"I said lift off *now*. I don't want excuses, I want action! I am the Elite Scientist Doctor and you *will* obey me."

I blinked several times. Seems I'd pissed off the next most powerful male on an Imurian spaceship, answering to no one, not even the captain, making this sadistic, sociopathic Imurian scientist the supreme ruler of this transport ship.

A rumble shivered through my feet. The light inside the small elevator space switched off as the rumble continued. Dr. Ot'ino'yan slid forward toward me, reminding me of a poisonous snake, even though I kept the weapon trained on him. I had an instance of despair; I could no longer use the lift because I'd waited too long but to be fair, I wanted some answers and he was the best source. I doubted I could've gotten off the ship alive, anyway.

*He doesn't think I can use the gun. Little does he know...*I almost smiled.

He barked into his wrist comm again, and I jumped a little in place at the sharpness of his voice. "Get two guards here on the double, with a full set of chains and locks. Somehow this female got loose and that cannot happen again."

I said, "Stop giving orders or I shoot you. Oh, and cancel the guards while you're at it." I snorted. "And might as well turn on the elevator, too. I mean, why not?"

He smirked. "You cannot use that weapon so you might as well give up. If you do, I promise I won't hurt you very much when we secure you again."

The pleasure in his voice when he talked about hurting me made me shiver and the chafe marks on my wrists and ankles reminded me how I got there. "What is it you want with me? What have I ever done to you?"

"You've done nothing to me. It's what you're going to do *for* me."

I shook my head. "No, I'm not doing a stinky-eyed thing for you."

"Your co-student, the other female? What's her name?"

Without thinking, I said, "Zoe." Then I could've kicked myself for answering.

"Ah, yes, her." He nodded. "We implanted something in her and I can't wait until your return trip to New Eden in six months to activate it. While I have the opportunity, I'll implant one or two into you, also, only I will activate yours right away. Might as well have the experiment going with two timelines. It will be interesting to see how the hybrids progress in two different females."

"You can stuff your timelines where the sun don't shine, mister." I raised an eyebrow. "What did you combine to make a hybrid?"

His eyes narrowed as fury crossed his face, his lips tightening. I smiled just a little bit.

"You know my absence hasn't gone unnoticed. I'm sure everyone is out looking for me." I scowled at him. "And you're not implanting a damn thing in me and whatever is in Zoe, I'll find a way to remove it. In fact, I'll find a way to have *you* removed, also, like the septic cyst you are."

"Brave words for a prisoner." He shook his head slightly side to side as if to say, 'sheesh, kids these days, what is the world coming to' as he took a step forward.

"I warn you; I will shoot you if you come any closer."

He chuckled. "Sure you will." With a sneer on his face, he took a big, deliberate step forward, raising something wicked and sharp looking as a weapon.

I flipped the gun's mode to mid stun and shot him in the arm holding the most equipment. The look on his face was priceless as the equipment clattered to the floor. He gaped at me, uneasiness and astonishment warring upon his face, then looked at the floor where his stuff had scattered.

"That was fun," I remarked as I dialed the gun to a higher level of stun. "Now call off the guards or I'll give you a bigger dose in the other arm."

"How could you–you can't–that's not possible!" He exclaimed.

"Huh. How about that." I tapped my lips with a finger. "Apparently it is possible because I just numbed your arm. Now, *call off your guards* or the next one could be very personal. And, by the way, I am a superb markswoman. I hit my targets every time."

"This isn't possible!" He spluttered. Worry and puzzlement warred for space on his face, along with fury.

"What? That I'm a superb markswoman or that I have a weapon I can use? Or–both?" I mugged a face at him and he bared his fangs back.

"Where did you get that gun?"

I chuckled. "Oh, like I'm going to answer your questions right now so you can stall me?" I raised both eyebrows. "I haven't heard you call off your guards yet. Well, never mind, I'll just stun them when they come in." I frowned. "In fact, perhaps it's best if you can't communicate with the ship." I shot his wrist comm, which exploded into minute pieces, and he dropped the rest of his instruments onto the floor, clattering loudly when it hit.

"Oh, oops." I said in a calm voice. "Were those sterile? Tsk. I'm so not sorry."

For the first time, I saw fear on his face. I felt no pleasure shooting him but I did feel some satisfaction for having the upper hand, for once. Just a teensy bit of satisfaction, that is. Well, maybe a touch more than that.

A door opened somewhere off to my right, a quiet snick of sound alerting me. *So that's where the stairs are. Good to know.*

There being no more noise and no footsteps, they were in complete stealth mode. I had to shoot them before they shot me but I had to see them first to do so. *Shield me?*

My hair cocooned me and hardened. *Thanks.*

ONLY GOOD FOR ONE SHOT.

Thanks.

A small clinking sound reached my ears. Puzzled at the out-of-place noise, I flashed a look that way. As I did so, Dr. Ot'ino'yan leaped toward me, his useless arms swinging wildly and I stumbled backward to avoid him, prevented from moving much by my own hair being solid around me. I fell onto my back like a turtle but still clutching my gun, my hair-shell protecting me as I landed, then immediately relaxing into its normal state of being. He fell on top of me, making me expel air with an 'oomph', as he yelled, "I have her! Get over here!"

I pulled the trigger, the stun shot hitting him in the torso. Good thing I'd stunned his arms already or I'd have been choked into submission by now, I'm sure. His furious eyes were millimeters from my own, spit hitting my face from his open, snarling mouth, teeth and fangs ready to rip into me.

He stiffened and shook, then his entire body relaxed as his eyes went dull from the stunning he'd just received. I bucked, trying to dislodge him as hot, wet flood of liquid wet my legs. He was total deadweight on top of me, with my breathing becoming a tad bit difficult because his weight compressed my chest. And now I smelled his pee, which was beyond disgusting, the ammonia smell strong and pungent.

Boots with slits in the toe box for claws to extend appeared to my right and left, and a male Imurian voice barked at me. "Put down your weapon now. You are surrounded."

Are there more than two?

NO.

I'll shoot one and you take the other?

YES.

Okay, one...two...NOW!

I pulled the trigger, shooting the one to my right, possibly in the crotch or so I hoped but since I had it on full stun, it should do the job. There was a surprised yelp, a lurching of the legs, and then the guard fell with a loud thump on the floor. His head might've bounced once or twice, oh, oopsie.

My hair flowed out from under me, wrapping around the ankles of the other guard, who didn't notice until a huge tug knocked him off his feet. He grunted when he hit the hard floor and it seems he lost control of his gun, since I heard it clattering on the floor and sliding away. *I'll bet he saw stars with that.*

I heaved and bucked again until the scientist's body slithered off on top of the legs of the stunned male on the floor to my right. Sitting up, I brought my weapon around, shooting the other male—the one my hair felled—in the torso before he could recover his weapon and shoot me.

CHAPTER THIRTY-SIX

My body shook, chills running over my skin, and I gulped air as tears stung my eyes. I'd actually shot someone–no, make that three someones–and now my body reacted. Me–who was to be a physician with a vow to never do harm, had just stunned three people. Well, they weren't dead and since they wanted to make me a prisoner or a slaver or a lab experiment, I had to accept what I'd done. It was either them or me. I really didn't feel better with that thought but at least I was untethered. I realized I needed to get out of here before more came to investigate.

Something fluttered against my mind, like a desperate bird beating its wings. I raised a hand to my head to wave away whatever was flying around my head, but the sensation persisted. I shook my head in a quick motion, like a horse getting rid of a fly, but it continued, intensifying my irritation. I was still shaking from the fight, terror still gripping me at my close call, but as I started to calm down, I was able to process information again in a more rational manner.

This was not an insect trying to get my attention, nor was it coming from the room around me. This was internal; someone or something wanted my mental attention but I had my shields locked as tight as I'd ever been able to manage. Who was scrabbling at my mental walls and why? I was suddenly afraid to find out.

There was something oddly familiar to the sensation but I couldn't think of why at that moment. First, I needed to get away from here, that's the first step I needed to take, so I decided to ignore the mind sensation. No, wait, first I needed to secure these males so they couldn't come after me.

I spied the shape of a knife in the pocket of the male to my left. I pulled it out, snicking open the blade, and cut the wrist comm off his wrist, then crawled over to the other one and did the same. I tucked them into a random pocket on my suit, then checked for breathing. All had the sonorous sounds of deep sleep and I figured they'd be out for at least fifteen or twenty minutes, maybe more. I wasn't quite sure how long a full stun would keep an Imurian unconscious.

The fluttering in my mind became a buzzing sensation and very annoying. I brushed at my head, a futile gesture but I was getting seriously annoyed at it. I grimaced at the increased level of noise in my head. I had way more important things to do than risk finding out what was making all that racket.

Huh. It's probably Si'neada and him I can definitely ignore. How dare he sell me into the hands of these thugs!

Something didn't feel right about it being him, but I shrugged it off. The clinking sound I'd heard earlier when the guards had arrived flashed into my brain and I realized that it had sounded like a bundle of chains, like the ones I'd had on me. I stood from my squatting position. I needed those chains and hoped like heck the locks were with them.

I tiptoed away from the inert figures on the floor toward the area the two guards had come from, feeling foolish about doing so. After all, they were out like the proverbial lights and shouldn't wake any time soon. However, if it's one thing defense training had taught me was not make assumptions. They could be out for hours or for minutes so the sooner I secured them, the safer I'd be.

I spotted the pile of metal links not far from the door they came in from and drew in a breath of relief. Crouching down, I gathered the pile into my arms, the metal cold through my clothes, and saw the locks on the floor. I'd have to somehow snag those, too, since I didn't want to make two trips. My hair could snag them, however, which it did.

I stood–at least, I tried to stand. These doggone chains were doggone heavy and I couldn't lift them. I'm in good shape, I thought, but I couldn't hold all this and stand at the same time. I ground my teeth with frustration. *Note to self, start working on upper body strength again. What a wimp!*

I had no choice,_I had to divide this into at least two piles. I didn't know what the metal was but it was stinking heavy. Letting the links slither out of my arms, I pulled on one length to separate it from the pile, then another, relieved to find a shackle at the end of each one. I rolled my eyes at the thought of being relieved to see restraints. This was like separating tangled necklaces, something I had experience with, only the chains were thick, so it was easier.

Finally, in what seemed like hours, but was only minutes, I had two piles. I'd been concentrating so hard I'd overridden the buzzing in my head but it came back with full force now that I had this task completed.

Lalalalala. I could outshout the sound, at least for now. *Lalalalalala.* I huffed as I carried one of the weighty metal piles in my arms, dragging the other length of chain behind me,. I staggered back to the felled males, one of whom was outright snoring now. I noted with amusement it was Elite Scientist Doctor. *I think he needs a CPAP machine.* I snickered to myself.

I took up a length of chain, securing the shackle at the end around the left wrist of Guard Doofus. Then I grabbed his ankles and tugged him, panting from the effort, over to the metal chair, where I secured his arm, using a lock my hair handed me to the eyebolt in the floor.

Wiping sweat off my brow with my forearm, I hurried back, grabbing another chain, doing the same routine with the other guard. The Elite male was starting to stir and I was out of chains, but I wasn't out of stun gun settings. I checked my weapon, pulling it from my right hip pocket, making sure it was green to go, set it to medium stun, and pulled the trigger again on the scientist. He slumped into a puddle of a body, no muscle tone anywhere. Drool seeped from his mouth and another large dark wet spot showed darkened his groin area.

Poop feathers. If my Perpad had a charge on it, I'd take a photo for my future amusement. Smiling at the thought, I trotted back to the chain pile, carrying one and dragging one. I was taking no chances with this guy. Dragging him over to the chair and around the two secured soldiers took a lot of effort since he was such dead weight.

The smell of liquid waste reached my nose, burning from the ammonia in the urine. Dagnabit, I really needed a vid of this. After securing his royal Eliteness with a chain on his arm and one around his ankle to the eyebolts, I rifled through the pockets of the two guards, keeping a cautious eye on them. I didn't need them waking up and grabbing me with their free arm.

I found their Perpads, but they were fingerprint protected and I didn't want to take the time right now to morphing my fingerprints to match. I turned to the scientist, finding his Perpad, a more sophisticated version, of course, seeing as how he's an Elite and all that. I rolled my eyes.

My brow wrinkled. What was I forgetting?

KEYS.

Of course, keys. I went through the guards' pockets again, more carefully, sliding found weapons away from them, knives included, while I absently batted at the buzzing sound in my head. Finally, in an obscure pocket inside a pocket, I found a tangle of keys on a tiny chain. I swung it around on my forefinger for a couple of twirls, then balled them up in my first, throwing them away from me as hard as I could. They hit something with a metallic clang before they clunked to the floor some distance away.

I moved out of arm's reach from my prisoners, thinking how lucky they were that I was their warden and not this sadistic scientist. I bit at a cuticle while I figured out my next step, trying to smooth a broken fingernail down with my teeth while I worried.

The buzzing in my head escalated to a frantic beating against my shields. Terror and pleading bled through and I couldn't ignore it any longer.

I focused on the internal alert but it was being sent so fast and so often it came across as '*:pelppelppelpelp:*' I cracked open my mental shield the tiniest bit I could manage. Was this some other language I didn't know? Definitely a feminine lilt to the tone and desperation laced the words. But what the fiery hells did pelp mean? The chant battered at the opening in my mental wall, becoming louder and harder, almost painful.

:PELPELPELPPELPPELP!:

What the stinking bog did it mean?

HELP.

Huh? What do you need help with?

HELP. SAYING HELP.

Ahhh. Now I got it. Someone repeated the word so fast that it came out as pelppelp, and so on. :*Quiet! Settle down! I'll try and help you but you have to slow down so I can understand you.*:

:*Pelpelpe–oh, thank the bright feathers, someone hears me.*: *Are you still there? Hello? Please, are you there?*:

:*I'm here, I haven't left. Where are you?*:

:*I–I don't know. Someone knocked me out and locked me in here.*:

:*Can you see anything? Look around and tell me what you see.*:

Silence. :*I'm in a cage with a cot, a blanket and a bucket.*:

:*Are you in the dark? Can you see out of your cage into the room?*:

:*N-not in the dark. I'm chained to the wall so I can't move very far but I can see some stuff out there. Equipment of some sort, flashing lights, that kind of stuff. I'm all alone right now.*: A shudder of fear laced her mind voice.

:*Sounds like an office of some sort.*:

:*I think~*: Her mind whisper faltered. :*I think it's a lab of some sort? Maybe a hospital room?*:

:*Have you been hurt by anyone?*:

:*Not yet but there's been this scary guy who kept staring at me, smiling.*:

:*Imurian or Amorphan?*:

:*Imurian.*:

:*By the way, I'm Jessi and who~*:

:Jessi!: Her voice 'shouted' into my head, making me wince. *:By the light of the stars, it's you! Oh, thank the infernal goodness that it's you.:*

:Oooo-kay. Then who is this?:

:This is Zoe, you ding-dong! Who else would this be? You have to find me and get me out of here. Before that hairy scary cat comes back to do horrible things to me.:

:Well, it would help if I knew where you are.: I heard a moan and some scuffling. *:Hold on. I have to take care of something.:*

:DON'T LEAVE ME!:

:I'm not. Just a sec, okay?:

Walking over to look at the bodies lying on the floor, unmoving. Which one had moaned? I couldn't remember what position I'd left them in to say with certainty if any of them had moved. The scientist–I refused to honor him with Doctor–had had a double dose of stunning so I doubted it was him. Just to be sure, however, I stepped close enough I could nudge his leg with my foot, holding my stunner in a ready grip for firing.

CHAPTER THIRTY-SEVEN

I thought about just shooting them all again without checking for consciousness. However, that might kill them and I couldn't have that weigh on my soul. After all, I planned to be a healer, an interspecies Galactic physician—the very first—and I couldn't start my career by causing deaths. The soldiers were just doing their jobs, after all, as ordered and I didn't yet have proof, other than my suspicions, about the scientist being a sociopath and a torturer.

I did wish, however, that I'd pulled them apart further than they were, leaving more space between them. I visually checked the locks, and they were intact with no signs of tampering.

:Jessi, what are you doing? I'm going bonko in here.:

:Just a sec, Zoe, quit distracting me.:

Sliding my right foot forward, I nudged the leg of the guard on the scientist's left, jumping back fast. No reaction. I walked over to the other guard on the right side of the scientist in the middle and repeated the action. Again, no response. Well, if they were still out, and they only got one dose, then the scientist had to still be unconscious.

Well, nothing like double-checking, is there? To be on the safe side, because they could be faking being out, my hair sent out a small slither of strands that poked the skin under the pants leg, probably feeling like stinging ants. Not even a twitch. Relieved, I exhaled, giving one last look at the trio splayed on the floor.

"Sorry, guys, it was either you or me. I picked me, funnily enough." I said in a soft voice.

Fumbling open a pocket flap on my hip to put away my gun, a hand clamped itself around my ankle, jerking so hard I fell backwards onto my butt, letting out a shriek at the same time, losing my gun from my hand. What–who–how...? They were still all unconscious!

I pulled against the vise-like grip, but the holder hauled me in like a harpooned fish. I realized the scientist held me; he'd obviously faked being asleep. But how? He'd received a double dose of full stun and that should've kept him out for a lot longer. Come to think of it, he had recovered fast from the first one, which is why he did get a double dose.

I could've kicked myself for not realizing that sooner but right now, I needed to get out of his grasp. "Let me go, you sadistic pile of pig poop!"

My butt slid on the floor toward him from his pull as I scrabbled to stay away from him but there was nothing I could hold to keep from moving. I had no idea he was this strong, wishing now I'd secured all four of his limbs instead of just his hand and leg. I had a lot to learn, it seemed, about keeping people restrained. My self-defense courses hadn't covered this type of situation, something I vowed to remedy in the future.

Leaning forward, I grabbed at his hand, prying at his fingers in a futile attempt to free myself. He couldn't even sit up, as I'd tethered them all on a very short leash, but by the pits of demons, he was powerful. Of course, he outweighed me by a whole lot, putting brawn on his side.

:*What's going on, Jessi? How come you're not talking to me?*:

:*Busy here, Zoe, be right with you. Now shut up!*:

:*Well, I never–*:

Ignoring the rest of her statement, I used my other foot against his torso to stop my forward advancement. I aimed for his crotch but hit his thigh instead. "What do you expect to accomplish, you slimy piece of fish?"

"You will unchain all of us. Now." The snap of authority rang through his words and a certainty he would be instantly obeyed.

Here was a guy who was too used to people jumping when he snarled. Ha. I'm not one of them.

"I can't."

"You will." His finger claws dug into my skin through the cloth of my pants. "I demand it right now. By doing so, you'll earn yourself a small mercy." His pitiless eyes stared at me.

I shook my head. "I can't and I wouldn't even if I could." I used my own fingernails of one hand to dig into the back of his, still working at leveraging his fingers out of their clamp on my ankle. "Let me *go!*"

He snarled. "I am the Elite Scientist Doctor and you will take me out of these chains!"

"Well, I'm the Elite Alien Student Deluxe and I say no!"

KNIFE!

Knife? How can he have a knife? Those are claws digging into me.

NOT HIM, STUPID. YOU.

Don't call me stupid, you pile of tangled hair. I received a quick sting on my cheek to show its disapproval.

My hair was right, however, much as I hated to admit it. I did have a knife and he didn't. I kept my fingernails in the back of his hand, for good luck, I guess, and used my other hand to find the pocket with the knife. I dug it out, snicking it open. His eyes widened in a small display of fear.

"Let me go or I will cut off your fingers one by one." I said in as calm a manner as I could to let him know I was deadly serious. I really would do this. Maybe.

He bared his teeth at me, whiskers twitching furiously with cusswords and insults against my parents as his grip tightened. I raised an eyebrow at him, even as I caught my lower lip in my teeth from the pain, placing the knife tip to the base of his index finger. "You don't think I'll do it, do you?"

I dug the point of my knife into his skin, blood welling out and watched his eyes bulge out a little as he yelped. "Now do you believe me?"

The two guards started to stir. I really needed to free myself before they woke up enough to grab me. The scientist's ears twitched; he'd heard the sounds, also, and thought he could wait it out until they were coherent enough to move. His eyes rolled down, chin sinking to his chest as he tried to see what I was doing. I didn't like the calculating look in his eyes.

"Oh, no." I said in a soft voice. "We're not waiting for them to wakey-wakey." I dug in a little harder with the knife tip. "Let's see, the entry to the joint should be, huh, right about here. Getting my knife in there means I can make a quick, clean cut to sever it all in one strike. I have studied anatomy, you know, so I know what I'm doing." No, really, I was bluffing; I might've studied the subject but I hadn't dissected any humans or Imurians. "Or you can let go."

I watched his face, seeing an interesting array of emotions cross his features in a matter of seconds, but the emotions never reached his eyes. His nostrils flared a little bit as he stared at me with malice.

"I have Zoe, you know. I've already started the activation procedure on her."

My hand jerked a bit before I could tame the reaction, although I couldn't slow my sudden rise in my heartbeat. *He has Zoe? Sure, of course, that makes sense and explains why I can hear her mentally. She's close by somewhere. Only a sadistic son of a bastard like him would use cages and chains.*

"What do you mean, you have Zoe? Where? "

He sneered at me. "Just what I said. She's in my control and if you want her to live, you'll release me."

Wrinkling my brow, I looked at him with a laser stare, at least, I hoped it was like a laser. "Why would she die?"

He blew out a sniff of air in a disdainful way. "Because without me there to monitor her through the process, she will die." He shaped a small smile on his lips. "And it will be your fault."

"Why would it be my fault?" I hissed at him. "You're the one doing unspeakable things to her!"

"But you're the one delaying her treatment and prolonging the activation, which is deadly if not guided carefully." He rattled his chain on his right arm. "I'll make sure she lives if you surrender to me now. Otherwise," Somehow he managed to shrug, "she'll die."

CHAPTER THIRTY-EIGHT

His eyes glittered. "In fact, it may already be too late but I won't know until I can check her."

"What is this activation thing you're talking about?"

He lifted one side of his upper lip in a sneer. "When it's successful, I'll tell you. If she lives to finish the project, of course. If she doesn't live, well," he tilted his head to one side, eyes half-lidded, "I'll find another subject. It'll put me behind but it won't stop me. In fact, you'll be a great replacement for her."

I huffed a sigh, blowing directly into his face, seeing the look of distaste flit across. I wasn't quite ready to concede the battle even knowing I couldn't let Zoe be harmed or let her die.

"What are you suggesting? If I surrender, you'll let Zoe go?"

He licked his lips. "You won't fight me?"

"No." *Yes. You bet I will.*

"I can do whatever I want with you?"

"Not quite that far, Bubba. I'm only talking about whatever this thing is you're doing to Zoe. You make sure she lives and you remove your little package from inside her. Do you agree to those terms?"

"I cannot remove the, what did you call it, oh, yes, 'package' from her. It is currently integrated and could kill her if removed prematurely. However, I agree to limiting my experiment to this procedure only."

"You need to safely remove whatever it is from her, keeping her safe and healthy or I'll shoot you again." *Yeah, bluffing here but he doesn't know I don't have a backup gun.*

"I told you, it's very risky to do that and I can't promise she won't be harmed if I try. Her body has become accustomed to it and to remove the, er, package prematurely could cause long-lasting ill effects."

"So if I surrender to you now, how will I know you'll keep your word? And what do you plan to do with me?"

"My word is good as the Elite Scientist Doctor and I give you my word and solemn vow to release her unharmed if you surrender to me willingly."

It's probably the best I'm going to get from him. If he is lying about letting Zoe go, however, I swear I'll kill him at my first opportunity. "Very well." I withdrew my knife from his finger joint. "We have a deal." I pointed at the guards. "What about them?"

He barked a small laugh. “They are nothing to worry about. They obey orders from me and will keep quiet. And they will never want to admit to being overpowered by a silly, small Human female. They’d never live that down so you’re safe from them.” He smirked. “However, I suggest you unlock me very quickly before they have enough muscle control to hurt you.”

I’d thrown the key ring somewhere into the large room so they couldn’t get to them but I had a back-up plan. I pulled out the key we’d stolen earlier, guessing it was universal and would open these locks. Failing that, I hoped my hair could be super-fast at picking the locks if the key didn’t work. My palms were sweaty and a little shaky from adrenaline so I fumbled with the key. I wasn’t quite sure what I’d agreed to have done but I had to save Zoe’s life. Again. I couldn’t let her die because of my actions or lack of.

The key fit into the lock and with a snick, the hasp sprang open, the shackle dropping off his leg along with some of his body hair. My hair snuck a strand or two for storage and possible future use.

“Your word you won’t hurt me.” I paused to stare at him.

“My word.” He spat out his agreement.

“My, my, you sound irritated.” I fit the key into the arm lock and his arm became free, the chain rattling to the floor. I backed away a fast few steps. “You will not do anything to me until I know Zoe is safe, that she'll live, and on her way back to her host family."

He actually rolled his eyes. "Yes, yes, we've agreed. Now, let's get to her while there is still a chance to keep her alive."

I gestured. "You go first since you know where we're going."

He moved toward the door on the opposite side of the room, the one he originally came from. His boots clicked on the metal floor in a steady rhythm, his tail twitching with anger as he stalked. It would've been impressive and intimidating if he hadn't wobbled while he walked.

:Zoe, we're on my way to you. Dr. Ot'ino'yan and I have reached an agreement. He's agreed to make sure you're all right and can be taken back to your host family.:

I waited for an answer, becoming worried when she didn't immediately reply. *:Zoe? Are you there? Answer me, Zoe!:* I added some snap to my words, the equivalence of slapping a cheek. Listening intently while trailing behind the scientist, I heard nothing. Then, just as I was about to shout at her again, I heard the faintest of sounds.

:Jessi. Hurry.:

The mind whisper was faint, feeling like she'd expended her last bit of energy to send her words. The scientist must've been telling the truth about her situation, although I'd had my doubts. I was beginning to believe him now.

He was a few feet ahead of me and I hurried to catch up, poking him in the back with my knife point. "She'd better be okay from whatever it is you did to her. If she dies, you die. It's that simple, sweetheart. You got it?"

He gave a curt nod of his head, reaching out for the door handle. "I'm as invested in keeping her living as you are. I do not like to lose my experiments before they can complete."

The door swung open and we entered as a unit into a brightly lit room filled with all kinds of monitors and other machines. Lights blinked and equipment hummed while each screen showed something different. I recognized one showing her heartbeat and breathing, along with her pulse and oxygen levels, but that was it. I noted a small cage along the right-hand wall, sturdy locks on the entry gate, secured to the wall with U-bolts welded around the rear posts of the metal enclosures. It looked like they were a later addition, probably to soothe the scientist's demands.

A peculiar smell hung in the air, a blend of acid with a touch of citrus, metal, burnt hair and something oily and thick. It grabbed at my throat, making me cough before I could suppress it. "What is that smell?"

"An indication we were almost too late for what I need to do. Thanks to you." He pointed at me, blood welling a little from the cut I'd made over his joint. I winched a little at that but he ignored the injury.

He stopped in front of the cage and we looked inside the shadowed interior. Bare floor, metal mesh walls and ceiling, a single cot along the back wall with a limp figure lying on it. My heart squeezed with fear. "Is she–is she breathing?"

He glanced over at the monitors. "Yes, but it's shallow." He swatted at the knife in my hand. "Move that thing away from me so I can get to work."

I hesitated, then moved away a couple of steps, keeping a clear line to throwing the knife at him. He stepped over to a small desk nearby on his left, opening the drawer to take out a small instrument which he pointed at the lock, then touched with his finger. An electronic DNA activated lock, then, very difficult to pick or break and can't be counterfeited. Well, unless you're a shape-changer like me and can use his DNA.

Swinging the gate open, he stepped into the pen, crossed the three feet to Zoe's inert figure, and scooped her up into his arms. Her head lolled back, eyes closed, face pale, blonde hair disheveled and pain filled my heart again. If she was dead, then it was my fault to not getting him to her in time. Guilt choked my throat.

Ignoring me, he carried her out of the enclosure as he went toward the wall. I scurried after him as he took Zoe through a hidden door into a small room with a large metal table. I slipped through the door before it could close, then shivered. It was cold in this room, with a bright spotlight on a jointed metal arm, a ceiling full of lights, and more equipment. I recognized a heart monitor, a respirator, an IV stand and a metal tray with various instruments on it, most of which I didn't know.

He laid her carefully onto the table surface, pulling a blanket out from underneath it, and flipping it over her to cover her, then flicked a switch on the side of the table to provide heat to her body. He pulled her left arm out, his tail moving the IV stand closer. "Go to that cabinet and get me a liter of Lactated Ringers. You can do that?"

"Yes." I ran over to the cabinet, seeing all kinds of bags of fluids, and hurriedly read the labels, finding the one he demanded, running back to him.

"Hang it from the pole."

I secured it to the hook provided, unwinding the tubing hanging from one end.

He bent over her, placing a needle into the crook of her arm, blood flashing up into the small barrel. He pulled over the tubing, attaching it to the IV needle, then thumbed open a small device on the tubing to allow the fluid to start dripping.

He then pulled a small monitor over to Zoe, placing a small device on her chest and the screen lit up with her rapid heartbeat, making my knees sag with relief at seeing it. "Sit down over there." He pointed to the only chair in the room. "I must get the medications she needs."

"Don't you have an assistant?"

"Does this look like the StarBuilder ship? Of course, I have assistants, but not here. They're all back on my starship.

I didn't need them for this endeavor." He gave me a withering look, then turned on his heel, going out the door.

"Oh, Zoe," I whispered. "I'm so sorry. I had no idea he was holding you captive and I don't know what he's doing to you but you have to stay alive. I can't live with myself if you die. So hang on to life, Zoe, you have to. If not for yourself or for me, then do it for your family on New Eden and your host family here."

There was no indication she'd heard me so I decided to try mind whispering. *:Zoe? Can you hear me?:*

There was a curious sort of blank space when I sent my thoughts her way, not a void, precisely, but an absence of some sort. A tear slipped from my eye, running down my face, as I watched her lie on the table, looking lifeless, seeing her heart rhythm on the monitor slowing down a slight amount, her breathing shallow. I knew I needed to separate myself from imagining how she was feeling; after all, someday when I'm a doctor, I'd never make it through a day if I felt everything my patients did.

It seemed an eternity before the scientist walked back through the door but was probably only a minute or two. He held a fistful of syringes, each holding a different amount of various colored solutions.

He didn't look at me as he made his way to Zoe's side. He set the syringes on the small metal stand table, arranging them into a rainbow of precisely placed tubes. He looked them over, touching each one as he considered its placement, then nodded to himself when he was satisfied they were in order. He checked the time on the wall clock, then said, "Voice recorder, activated."

A mechanical Imurian voice answered, "Recorder activated."

"First dose, five microts, Anictoloneiactin, given at ten-o-three ship shuttle time." He flicked the syringe with a finger to dislodge any minute bubbles of air, pushing in the plunger slowly until a tiny droplet appeared on the end of the needle. He shoved it into the port on the IV tubing, pushing the plunger steadily until the amber fluid emptied into the solution dripping from the bag. We both watched it make its way down into her arm and the red flush of her skin as it entered her system.

"First dose completed."

"Noted." The recorder answered.

He crossed his arms over his chest, watching the heart monitor, nodding a little bit as the heart rate slowed down into normal range, a steady, reassuring blip on the screen, her respiration rate also normalizing, her oxygen levels rising into the 90th percentile.

"Is she okay?" I asked.

"Yes, so far. She is still in danger, thanks to you, so must be monitored closely. The next few hours will show if I've been successful in delaying her death."

"What do you mean, delaying?" I held my knife blade up to the light as if to admire it. What I really meant is it would go into his heart if she didn't live.

He sighed. "I only mean she will live a long, full life if I succeed in getting her past this danger time."

"Oh. You're sure?"

"Of course I am. I'm an Elite Doctor Scientist and I am always sure."

"Except whether this experiment of yours will succeed."

"A scientist never knows ahead of time if an experiment will succeed but I am always sure of my ability to instigate the path to a successful conclusion."

My stomach gurgled, surprising me with its intensity; I hadn't realized I was hungry. Come to think of it, I couldn't remember the last time I ate anything of substance. He looked at me with his eyebrows raised, then pointed at the door. "Third desk on your left, first drawer on the right. There are protein bars. Bring them back here so we can both eat. I cannot leave her side."

I wavered over obeying his command or staying with Zoe, then my stomach growled again. Since we're in a room with no other exit, I felt okay about leaving him for a minute or two to get food. I did believe him when he said he wanted Zoe to remain alive.

He didn't know I knew that the Elite scientist on the StarFinder, the ship I'd journeyed to Amorpha on with Zoe, had done something to Zoe during our two weeks aboard.

Zoe and I both thought maybe it was a blended species pregnancy implanted into her, held in abeyance until they decided the time was right to have it grow to fruition. So, this activation he talked about had to be that and I figured that's what he wanted to do to me, also.

I also suspected he didn't intend to let Zoe go, especially if this activation succeeded, since it would be very difficult to explain how an alien Exchange Student became pregnant without the presence of a human male–or any type of male. Plus, I knew she'd been a virgin when starting our trip until she'd been used sexually on the StarFinder by the soldiers helping the scientist. Anger burned like acid through my veins every time I thought about it. The only saving grace was they gave her memory erasing drugs although I interrupted, saving Zoe from their last night with her.

Zoe and I had, at one time, been frenemies, emphasis more on the enemy part of the word, until that night. Now we were united into friendship through what happened to her and she is one of the tiny group of people who knows I can shapeshift. By giving her my blood to save her life that night, she'd also developed the ability to mind whisper, although she was still quite inexperienced with sending and receiving.

CHAPTER THIRTY-NINE

:Zoe, can you hear me?: I breathed a time or two, waiting for a response but nothing. I trotted to the door, finding the drawer, removing four food bars, stuffing them into my pants pocket.

I opened a few more drawers, in hopes of finding something useful to our escape, but found nothing more interesting than office supply stuff. I looked at the screens with their blinking lights, equations, data, and what appeared to be formulas scrolling across the screen but none of them made sense to me and I didn't dare take the time to download anything.

I chewed on a bite of the tasteless, gummy food as I approached the table on my return. Dr. Ot'ino'yan injected something into the IV tubing; this time, a light green fluid he slowly introduced into her IV fluids. The mass of stuff in my mouth stifled my words and I cleared my throat to move it. He glanced over his shoulder at me and I held out one of the bars. "What are you giving her now?"

He indicated the tubing with his chin as he unwrapped his bar. "You mean the medication?"

I almost said, "No, I mean the torture you're giving her," but instead I said, "Yes, of course that's what I mean."

"It's part of the activation serum and helps to stabilize her system and start bringing her back to consciousness."

"Okay but what is it?"

"I haven't named it yet. I can give you the chemical name if you insist."

I pursed my lips, then blew air out through them. "No, that's fine. I was only curious." I pointed at the other syringes still lined up on the small table. "What about those?"

"Part of the same procedure. It all helps to balance her bodily systems while allowing immunity for the foreign tissue in her."

"Where is it in her body?" *Huh, we were right; this is some kind of pregnancy thing.*

"I don't believe it's part of our bargain for me to tell you that."

I glowered at his back, shoving the knife tip into the area between his shoulder blades. "I believe you do need to tell me."

"If I die, she dies. So, no, I don't need to tell you." His tail lashed back and forth in agitation, hitting my ankles a couple of times with a stinging thwack. I stepped back out of its range. Fartblossoms, he was right. "Well, make sure she lives, as we agreed. She dies, you die. That's the deal."

"She lives and will continue to do so." He said with a snap to the words. "You know," he paused, "I could've called ten more soldiers up here to capture you but I haven't. I am keeping my part of the bargain."

"Am I supposed to thank you for that?"

He shrugged, turning to face me. "Just saying so."

"I don't become your guinea pig until she is off this ship and back with her host family and I have proof of that."

He blinked at me. "What is a ginnee pig?"

"Never mind. Just make sure you hold to our agreement fully." I gestured with the blade. "Or else."

He looked at the knife with a flat gaze, then sighed, his ears drooping a little to the side as if greatly disappointed in me. "You really think that little pin prick of a knife will make a difference?"

"It will if I stick it in the right spot." I held the knife in proper fighting position, gesturing upward with the blade. "I have had training with a blade and I don't mean just for cutting bread."

"Sure, I'm scared of it. Now let me do my work." He checked the time on the wall clock, waiting a few seconds until he saw the time he wanted, then picked up the next syringe in line. "Do not knife me; this is a very critical ingredient but it may cause her some pain."

"Then give her some pain meds first before you shove it into her body."

"That won't work and might hurt my project." He glanced at me, whiskers trembling in a laughing pattern. "I will, however, give her something to numb the veins before I introduce this substance."

"What are you cooking inside of her?"

"You–and the worlds–will find out when it comes to fruition." Reaching over to the small cabinet on the wall, he removed a small vial with clear contents, picked up a needle and proceeded to pull some of the substance out.

"What is that?"

"Your world would call it lidocaine. It numbs the vein, although it burns a bit when its introduced." He injected it into her IV, turning up the rate of infusion at the same time.

Zoe's hand closed into a loose fist when the injection went in, then relaxed again. Dr. Ot'ino'yan saw the reaction because when her fist relaxed, he placed the contents of the next needle into her tubing. It appeared more viscous than the others had and moved like sludge through the tubing, even with the rapid infusion rate he'd programmed.

"That's awfully thick. Are you sure it will even go in?" I asked, uneasy about allowing these substances being placed into her circulatory system. I couldn't risk not letting him do this, either, since he claimed she would die without all this. If she died because I let him do this, I'd never forgive myself but for now, I had to let it play out.

:*Zoe?*" I made my mind whisper as soft as possible and watched for signs from the scientist that he'd overheard me trying to call to her. He didn't twitch and she didn't answer. I grit my teeth in frustration and then thought about trying something.

I kept my mental shield open a tiny bit as I started running the scales to listen for the scientist's thoughts. If I could find his mind-whispering range, perhaps I could listen in on what he planned next and if he was telling the truth about Zoe's condition. I didn't have the experience of someone like Si'neada at doing this in stealth mode but I'd practiced and thought I'd gotten pretty good. I felt a pang in my chest, causing my breath to hitch once, at the thought of my former friend. What had happened to cause him to sell me like a lump of meat to the scientists? He and his sister, Ler'a'neada, and I had pledged to somehow bring down the power of the scientists and put a stop to all the species genocides they committed in the name of profit.

I shook off the feeling; I couldn't let myself be distracted while trying to sneak up on someone's thoughts. Most Imurians' ranges were higher than mine so that was the logical way for me to start. I went slowly enough to be thorough but I didn't pick up on anything. Perhaps he couldn't mind whisper, since not all Imurians could, or perhaps his shields were so good I couldn't hear his thoughts.

I pulled back from my quest when Zoe bucked on the table and a low scream come from her mouth. Her limbs jerked as her head thrashed side to side, but she had light cloth restrains on her arms and legs and her head was cradled in a padded horseshoe shaped contraption, stopping most of her motion.

"Make that stop! You're hurting her, make it stop!"

"She will be all right. I told you this would hurt, but don't worry, she won't remember this."

"I'll remember this! Is she seizing? Can't you give her something to make her more comfortable?"

"No. The solution has to be allowed to work on its own without interference. It's either this way or I cut her open and place the solution directly into her major arteries." He indicated the bed. "She is safely padded so she can't hurt herself."

My left hand covered my mouth in distress watching this. Is this what was going to happen to me, also? I didn't want to know that answer right now, I can say with truth. She started calming down until she was again deeply asleep.

"When is she going to wake up?"

"After I have finished all the steps to assuring her health and the well-being of my project inside her. Then she'll need to rest for an hour or two before I release her to leave."

Turning his head to look at me with a calculating look in his eye, he said, "While we wait for her to rest enough to go home, I can get started with you."

My heart slammed into my ribs and I forgot to breathe for a couple of seconds. The knife became slippery in my clammy hands. "No, no, that's not what we agreed to. She has to be home, safe and sound, with her host family before you start with me."

"Why waste the time?" He said with a slight nod of his tilted head, an eager look in his eyes, his gaze boring into my head.

CHAPTER FORTY

"Listen to me, Sparky, we're not starting anything until she," I nodded at Zoe, "is home, *as we've already agreed*, and I know she's safe from you."

"It's just a preliminary step to assure you, too, stay safe and healthy during the implantation."

"Just what are you planning to implant, anyway? I already have a nano system."

He smiled, an unpleasant look on his feline face. "When it is time, I will tell you."

I stepped closer to him, placing the knife point into his neck over the carotid artery. "Be careful; one slip of my hand and you're fighting for life."

He stiffened as he felt the point prick his skin through the golden hair. "Remember, I am not yet done with keeping my subject alive."

"You can walk me through what needs to be done as you're bleeding out. I'm going to be a real physician, not a fake one like you."

His ears flattened back in annoyance. I love how scientists resent not being genuine physicians when they think they are but aren't. His tail twitched, banging my calf, once, twice. Okay, that's annoying. I decided to try an experiment; his tail hitting my leg reminded me of the first time Si'neada had used mind whispering with me and he touched his tail to my skin to facilitate the transfer of thoughts.

I brought my left hand up to the visible part of him not covered in clothing, his hand. I touched him with a finger, his skin twitching in reaction.

"Get your filthy hand off me." He snarled.

"Tut tut, my furry fiend, I'm only seeing if you're really alive or maybe just a robot. Robots don't have feelings, so making sure." While my finger was placed against him, I searched my mental ranges quickly, 'listening' for his thoughts. To my disappointment, I didn't hear anything.

"I demand you remove yourself from my skin!"

"Okay, okay, sheesh, don't sweat the small stuff, Sparky." I kept the knife point on his neck but dropped my hand back to my side. His tail continued to lash my leg in the same spot, over and over. I'm pretty sure he knew exactly where his tail was going and did it to annoy me. It worked; I was annoyed but stepping back meant losing control because the knife would leave his neck.

My only warning something bad was about to happen was the soft movement of air against the back of my neck.

Puzzled at the puff, I didn't react in time as hands seized me from behind, jerking my hand away from the scientist's neck, pulling me away. Whoever had me in their grip was very strong and I had no chance to keep my balance. Another furry hand with claws–Imurian–grabbed my right wrist in a steel grip, digging into my tendons, forcing my hand back to open my fingers. I fought to keep the knife but I couldn't overcome his superior strength.

As soon as the knife dropped out of my hand, it was caught in mid-air and I could only hope he grabbed it by the blade, but no blood dripped to the floor, disappointing me. My arms were swept behind me, handcuffs clicking into place, a gruff voice saying, "She's secured, sir."

Dr. Ot'ino'yan nodded. "Good. Took you long enough. Place her into cage three and give the sedative."

I kicked and squirmed with all my might but I didn't make any progress. "We had a bargain. Is this how you keep it, by breaking your word?"

"My word is trustworthy–to a fellow Imurian. You are only a human."

"You rat bastard!" I spit at him but it didn't go far. He'd kept his back to me the whole time, as if unconcerned about me being a threat. At that moment, he was correct, which ticked me off even more.

I didn't have time to dwell on his attitude, however, as the males holding me dragged me toward the door. I couldn't see their faces, only felt their strength. I fought them but I didn't have a snowflake's chance in a bonfire of succeeding. However, I wouldn't meekly submit, either.

I could've slapped myself for being stupid, though; I should've made certain all the doors were locked, including that room. Just because I'd destroyed Ot'ino'yan's wrist comm didn't mean he didn't have other ways to call for help. *Great time to think of that*, I chided myself, as I tried to land a kick somewhere important on one of their bodies, but only hit air instead.

I started cussing, using every foul word I'd ever heard in every language so it came out as a mish mash of words, as I continued to struggle. It only helped to relieve my feelings as they dragged my unwilling body step by step to the door leading to the cages.

They had me in a bad position, with a hand in my armpit on either side, feet dragging, so it was a very difficult position to fight from. I had to use my last resort, so I let my body go completely limp. Now they had to drag me as dead weight but I was hoping they'd drop me. To my huge disappointment, they let out a startled 'oof' while tightening their grips. My arms were going numb from their compression on my brachial plexus of nerves.

One of them dragged open the door, holding it open with the heel of his boot, and they shoved me through. I had a small amount of satisfaction when I heard them panting; I hadn't made this easy.

"Which drawer?" One of them grunted.

"Third down, right side."

I turned my head that way to see between his spread legs the open drawer and his hand pulling a syringe out. "This the right one?" He asked.

"Yeah. Give it quick; she fights like a slimy, squirming Dusarian!"

I hadn't stopped resisting but now I renewed my efforts with more vigor, even though, to be honest, I was becoming fatigued of fighting a losing battle.

Can we resist the sedative?

No answer as the soldier plunged the medicine into my neck through the applicator. "Now she'll behave," he snarled.

The injection hit me like a load of boulders. Within the first second, my muscles went limp, then my head started to swim and my eyelids fell closed on their own volition. I knew I was in trouble now as I sank into a black well of nothingness.

When I woke up, I had no idea where I was or how I got here. I looked around through bleary eyes, seeing bars on the other side of my space from the cot on which I was lying. Puzzled, I wrinkled my brow, trying to figure out when Datra would've put bars on the windows of my room.

Then it hit me: I wasn't at home with my Amorphan family. That realization caused physical constriction of my breathing as I felt how much I missed being with them and my own human parents, too, along with sharp pains in my chest over my heart. Somehow, I had to let them know I was still alive even though, by now, everyone had to think I was dead.

How long had I been asleep? Wait, I think I'd been knocked out, judging from the foul taste in my mouth and fuzziness in my vision. I started to raise a hand to wipe my mouth, discovering, then, they were shackled together behind my back. No wonder my shoulders hurt and my hands were numb.

What happened?

SEDATION? SEDATION, YES. The slurring of the words suggested Sinnet didn't totally know what had occurred, either.

Why?

A FIGHT? ZOE? NOT SURE.

Zoe?

SHUSH. CLEARING MED OUT, NEED TO CONCENTRATE.

Well, guess I'd been put in my place. I hmphed to show my irritation but was ignored. *How about these restraints? How soon can we get out of them?*

THAT'S NEXT.

I had to be content with that as I couldn't do it myself without help. As if hearing me, a few strands broke away and slithered down to the restraints and set to work. A couple of minutes later, there was a gratifying snick of sound and the cuffs fell off. I groaned, a soft sound, but the relief was enormous. I rubbed one hand with the other, willing the circulation to come back, dreading the pins and needles of it returning. I took the pressure off my shoulders by rearranging my hands under me and turning to my side, back toward the wall; I wanted to look like I was still restrained in case of a surveillance camera or someone coming to check on me.

I gritted my teeth against the sensations in my hands, making a face as the tingles intensified beyond a comfortable level. Oh, well, the good news is the feeling and usefulness of my hands was returning. The bad news was it hurt.

My head suddenly cleared of all cobwebs, so the sedative had been purged from my body. I sent a silent thanks be to any supernatural Supreme Being out there for that and included my hair and the Akrion particle. After all, I wouldn't have sentient hair or shape-changing abilities without the god-like particle.

CHAPTER FORTY-ONE

With the impact of a bullet, I remembered Zoe. She was supposed to be released and returned to her own host family, that was part of the deal I'd made, but somehow, I doubted the scientist had kept his word. For a minute, I felt crushing defeat. How could I rescue her and me, and get us off this ship since I was now locked in a cage and a prisoner?

Speaking of which, I needed to know if the ship was moving or not. If the ship had already departed to return to the StarBuilder, then I had a huge problem, indeed. I listened intently to the sounds around me. These darn Imurians built their space crafts with exquisite engineering; they could land and take off from a planet or moon or spaceship without motion or a lot of noise. They had gravity-cancelling capabilities during take-offs and landings, which as a passenger is wonderful and makes for a comfortable trip. As a prisoner, it made it difficult to know if we were moving through space or not.

No sense in lying here in a puddle of self-pity and despair, however. Closing my eyes to intensify my hearing abilities, I detected a slight hum and the tiniest of vibrations through the cot. The ship had lifted from Amorpha, then, and my heart sank. My best options were either to hide–but where–or to recruit help, but from whom was the real question. The Elite Scientist Doctor had a huge amount of command powers on any of their ships and I doubted very much the Captain could be induced to help me over him. I was being taken to a starship where I knew no one, thus having no allies I could recruit. Tears leaked from my eyes as I sank deeper into the quagmire of depression and hopelessness.

As despair washed into me like a bath of heavy metal, a quick series of zings of pinpoint pain jarred me back to reality. Sure, I might be a prisoner for *now* but I had tools and weapons no one, absolutely no one, knew I had–like my hair and my gun, still hidden somewhere within me.

I drew in a breath, feeling a little lighter at the realization I wasn't totally helpless, then thought about the need to verify Zoe was on board. Why not? I had no other options and if she wasn't aboard, then it would be easier to get myself rescued, I hoped.

:Zoe? Can you hear me?: I waited a few beats for an answer and then tried again. I sensed someone struggling to reply but I didn't know for sure if it was Zoe. I quested for other thoughts on Zoe's frequency but found nothing and no reply from her. I was about to accept she wasn't on board, after all, when a word whispered into my mind.

:Jessi?:

:Yes! Zoe? Are you okay?:

:Probably. I guess. I still have all of my own parts, at least. I think. Where are you?

:In a cage in that rat bastard's lab. Where are you?:

A pause. *:Looks like some kind of hospital room?:*

:Are you alone?:

:Yeah. You?:

:Yeah. Do they have restraints on you?:

:Sure. Did you expect otherwise? But they appear to be from material and could be cut. Can you come get me?:

:First, I have to get out of this cage. I might not look like me when I get there, you know.:

A hesitation while she thought that over. *:Oh, sure. I understand. Don't worry about your...appearance.:* Then in a bare thread of a whisper, *:Is someone listening in?:*

:Not sure but no need to take chances.:

:True.: Her mind-whisper trailed off and I suspected she'd fallen asleep.

:Zoe?: I waited a couple of seconds and tried again. No response. She'd fallen asleep, judging from the slow, slurred thoughts she'd sent my way.

At least I know where she's at. What I didn't know was where Dr. Ot'ino'yan or his minions were at the present time, but that was a problem for later. Right now, I had to get out of this cage, get Zoe, then find a place to hide or steal a shuttle. That part would be tricky because we were on the ship's shuttle but surely they had escape pods. If nothing else, Imurians were thorough when they designed their crafts, including redundancy.

Any surveillance?

OF COURSE.

Within reach to disable?

YES.

I was pretty sure it was a closed system, limited to the lab, as I thought the scientist didn't want to advertise his "experiments" to the crew or captain, risking being shut down.

Sitting slowly, shaking my head as if clearing it, I made a show of being wobbly and confused as I stood, stumbling around the cage, holding my hands behind my back as if still cuffed, until my hair reprogrammed the security vid feeds. When that was done, I made faces at them, making a few rude Imurian gestures for good measure. When nothing happened, no one came in to bat me down, I felt more or less secure we'd gotten them all.

The door lock was the next thing to tackle. I sat on the floor, facing the entrance, so my hair could reach the lock, rocking back and forth, as if I were still incapacitated in case someone was watching from one of the computer screens. This lock proved to be quite the challenge and it turns out my hair didn't have the strength to move the bolt. This is the first time we'd been defeated but the metal alloy used was disproportionately heavy to the size of the multifaceted shank. Every time it seemed we could unlatch the door, it reformed into a different shape, which made it hard to defeat. We'd never run into anything like this before, not that I was a proficient or expert lock picker.

I didn't want to admit defeat; neither did my mass of hair and I chewed on a cuticle as I thought this over. I needed the key, that seemed clear enough. *If I became something big and strong, could we break the bars, Sinnet?*

TOO MUCH NOISE. NO TO SINNET, EW. DON'T LIKE IT NOW.

I wrinkled my nose. It was true about the noise but that didn't mean I had to like it. *Something small and slithery so we could slide out of here? Lorraine?*

NO SHAPES SMALL ENOUGH AND STILL STAY SENTIENT. BE STUCK FOREVER. NO TO LORRAINE, BITSY.

Oooo-kay, didn't like the sounds of that. I found a ragged fingernail to nibble at this time. I patted down my pockets for the umpteenth time in the hopes that somehow, magically, something like a key to the cage or a knife had been overlooked. I was disappointed for the umpteenth-and-oneth time.

I ground my teeth, abandoning my nail, since I'm not really a nail biter. I was more of a pick-at-it-until-bleeds type of gal but I wasn't willing to shed blood in here. *Then our only hope is to call for help. Much as I don't want to, I have to search for Si'neada. He's betrayed us once and probably will again but maybe, just maybe, he'll help us get out of here. I can't believe he really wants me or Zoe experimented on by any of the scientists.*

AGREED.

Still furious and hurt at what Si'neada had done, asking him for help brought bile into my throat, burning and forcing me to swallow. What if he wasn't here? What if he wouldn't help? What if he helped the doctor do unspeakable things to me? I'd agreed to be experimented on but that was before the doctor broke his word; I figured fair is fair so I'd break my word, too.

Gathering my courage, anxiety rampaging through me at the idea of getting Si'neada's help, I forcibly relaxed my shoulders. I stared at nothing while moving to the mental frequency that was Si'neada's and cracked open my shield the barest amount possible.

:Si'neada.: I could only bring myself to say his name. Waiting for a reply ratcheted up my nervousness since I wasn't sure if I wanted him to answer or not.

:Si'neada!: I waited. *:If you're there, answer me.:* Nothing, no mental sense of him being there, no sense of his presence. My shoulders slumped; he wasn't on this shuttle. I had to do this alone.

CHAPTER FORTY-TWO

I opened my mental shield a bit more just on the off-chance I'd blocked him out by an opening of my shield that was too small. Still nothing. Dagbone it, it was enough to make a saint cuss. I was swallowing my pride, hurt and anger to plead for his help and he wasn't there. Not fair, then I snorted a little. My mother was quite fond of reminding me often that life wasn't fair, so suck it up, little truck, and get on with things.

Pulling in a long breath, I tried to clear my mind. *Let's try one more time on the lock, perhaps it only has so many changes inherent to it and when it runs out, it stays in that shape.* There's always hope, right?

Different strands of hair crept into the lock to start working while I sat there, miserable and chilled from sitting on the cold floor. *:Jessi? Is that you, my little flower?:*

I jumped in place, startled at hearing Si'neada's mind whisper, since I'd given up on finding him. I checked his frequency and he was on a much higher pitched channel than normal. I knew very few beings could change their mind frequency like that, but Si'neada and I could. I hadn't expected him to use other frequencies but I was tired, hungry, cold and scared so I decided to give myself a pass on this one.

:I'm not your little anything, you big turd feather, but yes, this is Jessi. Are you on this shuttle?:

:Yes, of course I am. Why do you ask?:

He was being coy, I could feel that in my bones. *:I am, too, and so is Zoe. No surprise, the 'good doctor' lied to me. I made a deal with him. He saves Zoe's life and I let him live and he could have me instead but he had to release Zoe to her host family and leave her alone. Well, guess what. He broke his word to me and now I'm a prisoner again. About to be experimented on myself:* Even I was surprised at the amount of bitterness in my words.

A startled silence from Si'neada, then he answered.. *:And this is a surprise–why? Of course he lied; it's what they do to gain their own purposes. Where are you?:*

:I'm in a cage in his laboratory and can't pick the lock; it's malleable and the lock keeps changing shapes. I...I needyourhelp.: I rushed through the words so I could get them out; if I used each word separately, I wasn't sure I could actually ask. *:Oh, and Zoe is in his little hospital room; he's done something to her, activated something, and then she almost died, but he's used a bunch of stuff on her to stabilize her, swearing he'd keep her alive.:*

:I see. I swear to you I didn't know about Zoe.:

:You knew Dr. Ot'ino'yan had me, you shark bastard! You gave me to him! I know you haven't forgotten that!:

He sighed, a soft exhale of sound. *:I can explain why I did that and how it was supposed to go. Right now, I need to find a way to come to you without being shot myself. He would like nothing better than to kill me, you know.:*

:No, why would I know that? How did you piss him off? Did you double-cross him like you did me?: I knew my tone was sharp like a knife's edge but I couldn't help it.

:No, it's not that. And I didn't betray you, truly. Yes, I know it seems like it but-: His voice cut off. Even though I was livid with him, an upswell of worry flowed over me. I held my breath, waiting for him to speak again. If something had happened, however, if someone had discovered our conversation, then it didn't bode well for either of our futures. I found something on my cheek to worry at while waiting. There was nothing else I could do, even though the strands of hair were still working like mad to overcome the lock problem.

I started to droop into a light snooze but startled like a baby when Si'neada's voice was suddenly in my head again. *:Jessi. I was interrupted before and had to shut things down for our safety. I'll find a way to you now. I have to find a way to keep the Elite Scientist Doctor occupied and away from you and he's confident that he has you knocked out for at least several more hours.:*

:What did he use on me, big beast sedative?:

:Something like that. Now hush while I make my way to you; don't be distracting me.:

:Shutting down now.: I snapped close my shield, then cracked it open again on second thought. If he needed to get through to me fast, I needed to be able to receive. *:Well, I'm keeping a slit open in case you have to talk.:*

:Good idea. I'm on my way so be ready for anything.:

:Sure, I'll be ready with all the weapons at my disposal.: I laced the words with sarcasm. *:Ok, I'll be quiet now.:*

I put my head down on my bent knees and closed my eyes. Perhaps I could get a little nap in while waiting since I didn't know where he was coming from or how long it would be. Besides, perhaps I could ignore my growling, hungry stomach this way.

My eyes snapped open; it seemed napping wasn't on the menu. At the thought of a menu, my stomach cramped a little and I rubbed it with one hand. I had nothing to eat so it had to deal with it. I couldn't sleep, anyway, I needed to be alert for when Si'neada arrived, hopefully alone and without soldiers.

My heart thumped in my chest from a mixture of anticipation and trepidation. My hands were the tiniest bit shaky from both hunger and anxiety. These things combined made my breath come short and fast but as soon as I realized I was becoming a little light-headed, I slowed my breathing down. That helped a little bit, anyway.

Any progress on the lock?

Frustration came from my hair which I took as a no. *Enough is enough, then. Si'neada is on his way so I'm going to stand now and be ready when he opens the door.*

SURE HE'S ON OUR SIDE?

No, but what choice do we have?

NONE EXCEPT GIVEN LONG ENOUGH, CAN DEFEAT THE LOCK.

I doubt we have long enough for that.

As if the universe decided to prove me right, the door handle turned, the latch clicking as it released. I didn't know whether to pretend to be asleep or to be ready to run from the cage.

I only had an instant to decide and I almost took too long. Dr. Ot'ino'yan stepped into the room, looking over his shoulder as he entered, saying something stern sounding as he did so. That was the only piece of luck I had as I leaped back onto the cot, scrambling to look sedated. Just as my head touched down, he made a swift turn toward my enclosure, probably hearing my mad scramble. With my heart hammering and my breath harsh, it was difficult to keep my eyes closed and to look dead to the world. I prayed fervently to whatever deities existed he wouldn't come in to check my pulse.

Footsteps came over, then stopped. I presumed he stood there watching me to see if I was faking. It took all my will power to keep my eyes closed, my breathing even and to keep every muscle relaxed. Fighting someone wasn't as tough as looking knocked out when you're full of adrenaline.

Maybe I'm a better actress than I give myself credit for because it sounded like he moved over to the desk area. However, I swear I felt his eyes boring into me as he watched from a few steps away. I stayed still, not daring to even peep open an eye; he's a wily son of a slime dog. Deepening my breathing to sound more sonorous, I hoped he'd think I was still heavily sedated. I opened one eye the tiniest crack to see him staring at me.

The weight of his gaze lay over my skin like a cold shadow. Time stretched into eternity until, with an almost audible snap, he turned away and started clicking on a keyboard. I wished Si'neada would show up; he was my main hope right now. Oh, how I hated feeling desperate, helpless and out of control.

However, if the scientist opened that cage door, I'd have the element of surprise and could use that to advantage. Lying there, I used the time to ignore itches and plan an attack. I couldn't risk changing forms, for certain, so had to rely on my years of self-defense training. I bet I could surprise the slime dog with an attack.

I changed my position a little bit to ease my aching muscles and played at moaning a tiny bit, turning over on the cot on my side, turning so I faced the enclosure's front. I felt his gaze snap back onto me, chilling me, but I stayed stuporous looking.

I felt, more than heard, the gateway into my cage open in a very stealthy manner. Pressure against my skin increased as someone moved closer to my position on the cot. It had to be Dr. Ot'ino'yan sneaking up on me. Perhaps he hadn't been as fooled by my acting as I'd thought.

I fluttered my eyelids like I was dreaming, hoping to catch of a glimpse of what he might be planning to do. I couldn't see much of anything except to confirm his lower legs and feet looked like the scientist's. *What is he doing?*

HAS SYRINGE IN RIGHT HAND. LET'S ATTACK. GO!

As one coordinated attack, my hair and I surged upward, knocking into the scientist's stomach area, aiming for his solar plexus. A thick bundle of hair whipped around his right wrist, tightening like a flexible band of steel, pulling his hand into a downward position to loosen his fingers on the syringe.

There was no time to see if he'd pulled the cap off the needle as I grabbed for the syringe, trying to avoid the needle part. He shoved at my head with his left hand as he tried to pull his right hand high into the air, snapping my face to one side. He dropped his left hand, claws extended, to my neck to get a grip on my airway or my jugular or anything else important, but I knew this move. Bringing my head back as fast as it went to one side, as his hand moved downward, I chomped into the fleshy area around his thumb and he yelped in surprise and pain as I tasted blood. Eww, and cat hair.

Wrenching his hand from my mouth, he snaked his arm around my body, yanking me in close to him, straining to use his right hand to plunge the sedative into my unwilling self. My hair's tight grip around his wrist also wrapped around his fingers and thumb, but this guy was strong, he was really strong, and he was slowly winning against the stranglehold my hair had on him. A thick strand of hair wrapped around the syringe, trying to pull it from his resisting grasp.

Got it?

A terse **NO** flitted through my mind.

Other hanks of hair wrapped around his ankles, jerking to unbalance him as I gritted my teeth against the pull against my scalp. He grabbed me by the back of my neck with his left hand, entangling fingers within my mass of hair and squeezed hard, making me gasp with pain.

I dropped my body weight suddenly, surprising him again with the dead weight I'd become, twisting out of his one-armed grasp. If he got that needle into me, I'd become his favorite experimental toy and no one would know where I'd gone. I couldn't count on Si'neada, no matter what he'd said earlier, and for all I knew, he was being paid handsomely for keeping me in prison.

I took my small microsecond of a chance; he fought me and my hair with superior strength and size. Our combined efforts left him struggling to stay on his feet and keep his grip on the syringe. What in the devil's name would it take to shut him down? I had to have control of that sedative solution or I was doomed.

I grabbed his wrist, trying to pry him away from my scalp as he tried to pull out hair. Several strands snaked over, driving sharp ends over and over like pistons into the back of his hand. He let go without warning, giving a short yowl of distress, and I lurched with the suddenness of his withdrawal.

He slammed me across my face with his free hand, claws dragging furrows into my skin, blood dripping. I hopped back out of his reach, panting. He couldn't kick me as he was anchored by hair around his ankles but I could kick him—well, as soon as his hands were secured, I could but then it wouldn't be a fair fight to hit him while he couldn't defend himself. Darn my instructors and their ethics.

I ran to his right side to remove the syringe from his grip while my hair restrained his left hand. I tried to pluck it from his fist, tugging upward while my hair strangled his wrist, putting pressure over the three nerves on the palmar side of the wrist. He might have claws and teeth, superior strength and height and weapons; well, I have sentient hair. *Ha, take that, you slimy scientist!*

He somehow managed to move his left arm against the strength of the hair strangle-hold, grasping the top of my scalp with his claws. It felt like he was squeezing my brains out through my ears, his hold was that strong and tight.

I yelled, "Let it go, you son of a bastard! You're not sticking that into me again!" I dug into the back of his right hand with my fingernails while keeping my grip on the sedative with my other hand and strands of hair drove hot needles of pain into the back of his hand and up his arm through the material of his uniform. I had to be hurting him but he didn't show it—much.

He suddenly dropped his head—damn, he was supple—and sank his sharp teeth into my shoulder, or tried to, anyway. Having fangs is a bit of an advantage but the material of my jumpsuit blunted the attack and the tiny hairs on my skin coalesced into a stiff kind of hair armor. Well, okay, that was a completely new talent I didn't know I possessed but was very glad for at the moment.

Then, the hair around his ankles gave a hard tug, I kneed the scientist in the back of his right leg, and finally, *finally,* he fell to the floor. My hand slipped off the barrel of the syringe, removing the cap by accident. My fingers flew upward, the point of the needle scraping the end of my finger as I made a desperate grab as he fell. An immediate wave of wooziness washed over me, my knees felt like they'd give out and I wobbled where I stood. Adrenaline rushed through me with the strength of a tsunami, clearing everything from its path, including the sedating effect.

Before the Imurian could react, I held the syringe in a death grip, thumb on the plunger, needle pointed away from me. I swung my arm in a short arc, driving the needle through the material into the muscle of his upper arm, slamming down the plunger.

He howled in rage and surprise, wrenching his body side to side, flinging his hands out to stop me. Since he was still entangled with my hair, he didn't succeed. I backstepped as fast as I could go to the open door of the cage, not moving my eyes off him. I slammed the door closed as soon as I was through, fumbling with the key he'd left in the lock, getting it to turn with a satisfying click as the tumblers moved into place.

My hair sprang back into its place around me with the speed of light but still ready to attack again if needed. I stared at the scientist, gasping for air, moving back until my butt hit the desk edge. "How do you like having a dose of your own medicine, you son of a dog turd?"

He snarled at me, supine on the floor before springing to his feet in a fluid move, taking one large step to the gate, rattling it with his fists, demanding to be released. My goodness, his teeth were long and pointed; I dodged a very nasty bite from those. His cold eyes glared at me from between his narrowed lids, his tail lashing back and forth in fury, ears laid back tight against his head.

I hoped like hell there wasn't a hidden safety latch release that we'd overlooked. As furious as he was, he was burning off the sedative at a high rate. Without warning, his eyes widened, then his body slumped to the floor in a boneless heap as I jerked, startled.

"Huh." I said. "That doesn't look comfortable at all." I snickered, struggling to keep it from morphing into hysterical laughter. “And methinks he just peed his pants--again. I should record this.” I picked up his Perpad, since mine was out of charge, and snapped a few pictures, sending them to my account but not deleting them. *Thanks, Sylvia.* I felt my hair’s derision at the name and mentally added it to the very, very long list of rejected names.

I stared at him for a little bit more but he was a boneless heap on the hard floor. No way was I going to check to see if he was faking it or not but it didn’t hurt to watch him while I waited for my pounding heart and panting breaths to normalize, trying to ignore the cuts, scrapes and downright painful injuries I’d received. As I watched him, something clicked into place in my head.

His antisocial attitude, behavior and lack of a conscience could only mean one thing. If he were human, he’d be diagnosed as a sociopath, along with being at the severe end of Asperger’s Syndrome. I didn’t know what the Imurians might call this—genius, perhaps—but he certainly had impaired social skills, intense focus on his area of study, and high intelligence. It was a close call between the two and more likely, a mix of both.

I didn’t have any idea of his childhood or his training; I did know he was very high in rank and given a huge amount of leeway in his actions. Just guessing here, but if he killed an Imurian during one of his experiments, he might get a wrist slap. Kill a Human? Probably, no one would even remark on it.

I rubbed my hands over my face, heavy weariness settling over me as all the “go juice” of adrenaline left my system. Right now, sleepiness pushed at me, stealing over my body as my muscles felt heavy and weak.

DO NOT SLEEP! A strong pinch on my cheek with a weighty slap of hair against my back snapped my eyes open.

CHAPTER FORTY-THREE

Moving to the door, stifling a yawn, I placed my ear to the panel to listen. I opened my mind shield, listening intently both mentally and physically for any presence that might be near and a threat to me. My goodness, I was tired of being in danger.

Goes to show how exhausted I was; it took a few minutes for the idea of changing forms trickled through. Of course! I needed to become an Imurian; what had I been thinking, staying in this form? By the gods' bloomers, I can't believe we hadn't done this already.

I snuck a quick peek over my shoulder to check the scientist still snoring on the floor. Just in case he was faking it again, I spotted a small area out of his line of sight and I tiptoed over to it. *Fifth floor, Imurian form at your service.* I must be getting a little loopy from fatigue if I was pretending to be on an elevator stopping to shop for an Imurian body.

As always, the horrifying pain urged me to yell and scream but I held it back even through the crunching feeling of bones being reshaped. In the beginning, I couldn't have had that kind of control but with enough experience, I can now control at least that.

Anyone I know?

MORE OR LESS. LOOK ENOUGH LIKE SCIENTIST TO BE OBEYED. BUT NOT 100% LIKE HIM.

I nodded. *Thanks, Letisha.*

Now, I know hair doesn't have eyes it can use in a giant eye roll but that sure was the perception I had from it. *Lilly?*

STOP IT.

Now, you know, I'm not stopping until I find the right name for you.

I received an exasperated noise in return.

LET'S GO, BABS.

I frowned. *You know what? I want to find some of that sedative to take with me. Sure would be handy to subdue someone instead of fighting them. Let's check that cabinet Dr. Ot'ino'yan got it from. Do you remember how much was in that syringe?*

POSSIBLY. PROBABLY. UM, YES.

I smiled. *You sure?*

SURE.

I strode over to the cabinet as any self-respecting Imurian scientist would do. For once luck was with me; he hadn't bothered to lock it so the little door swung open. I checked over the vials present, many of the labels unfamiliar to me and I moved those aside before finding one I was interested in. Propanaprenfulin. I knew this to be a very powerful and fast-acting drug, most often used to put people asleep for a procedure. It had been used on me for some of the stuff I'd had to go through before being accepted as an Alien Exchange Student plus my mom had told me all about it. She sometimes had to use it for her patients in her Reproductive Specialty.

I placed it my pocket, looking around for syringes. I felt a vague surprise at it still needing to use an old-fashioned needle but then remembered Mom saying it was because it was a thick fluid and couldn't be given any other way. It was best through an IV but could be put into muscle tissue, also, as I could attest.

Tapping a finger against my lip, I muttered, "Now, where did he get that syringe from?"

An eager hank of hair quivered in the air as it pointed toward the desk, dropping back to its place when I stepped that way. I rummaged, finally finding one still in its intact wrapper amongst all the debris jumbled into the space and a few dust bunnies.

I made a face. *Is that the only one he has? Surely he has more on hand somewhere.* I pulled out the next drawer and managed to glom onto one more syringe. I snorted softly. Why worry about sterility because, if I needed it in a hurry, then I couldn't be worried about being all protocol about it.

I removed the wrapper and peered at the markings. *How much?*

A few strands of hair indicated the level. I filled cylinders, securing the caps back so I didn't poke myself by accident on my journey through the ship. Thankfully, the caps had a self-locking feature. Placing all but one in a readily accessible pocket, the other went in my left hand for quick usage, I felt ready to find a way back to Amorpha. The fact that I only knew the rudiments of piloting any kind of spaceship, thanks to my pilot Dad, didn't deter me. Surely, the pods had an instruction manual and an AI to fly the thing.

It felt like an hour had passed but when I glanced at the timekeeper, only minutes had zipped by. I sucked in a breath of courage.

"Well, here goes nothing." I gently cracked open the door, my large cat-like upright ears swiveling to catch any sounds, my unbooted feet silent on the floor as I stepped through into an empty hallway. During my changing, my own gun reappeared so I held it in my right hand by my side to sort of hide it and a filled syringe in my other hand, thumb claw ready to flick off the top in an instant.

My heart was in my mouth, fear crowding through my body, but no one was in sight and I let out a soft sigh of relief. The door to the hospital room was across the large space; equipment dotted the way unevenly so there wasn't a clear path to the door. I frowned; this seemed too easy.

Where were the guards? Someone must have let loose the ones I'd secured with chains or I'd be hearing them by now.

Feeling like a thousand eyes watched me from dark corners, I hesitated, tail lashing low to the floor behind me in agitation. *Let's go, kiddo.* I chided myself. *Standing here won't get Zoe out of that room. I'm as ready as I'm going to be. Gun is in ready to use mode and the syringe is ready.*

I sucked in an unsteady breath, deliberately stepping forward, projecting an unfelt confidence, eyes swiveling in unison with my Imurian ears. The room was darkened but there was enough ambient light from the electronics to see fairly well with these cat eyes, although not into those dratted dark corners. I ventured forth a few more steps, my bare feet silent on the hard cold floor, my tail held low to the ground. The long whiskers around my mouth quivered, standing out straight from my face, ears on high alert for sounds.

Other than the whir of a few of the computers and electronic stuff, I didn't detect anything out of the ordinary. Maybe the doctor had dismissed everyone from the area, not wanting them to know about his experiment with Zoe or about me imprisoned in a cage, or both. Plus, being in the early morning hours meant all but the sparse night shift would be asleep in their quarters.

I zig-zagged across the room without incident until I felt a soft push at my mind shield. Only Si'neada could do that, or his sister, and I knew she wasn't here. I debated whether or not I should admit his mind whisper or go get Zoe first.

Logically, I might need his help moving her so I decided to answer with a push of my own, then cracked open my internal wall.

:Jessi, my little stealth walker, stay quiet.:

:Wha-?:

A hand clamped over my mouth, my left hand holding the sedative grabbed into a vice-like grip as my right hand was trapped against myself with his body. I froze for a second of absolute terror, then adrenaline hit like a 20-foot wave, preparing me for battle.

"MMMMMMMMfffff!" I screamed out my fear but the hand over my mouth muffled the sound and words.

:Shhh, shhh, shhh! It's me, Si'neada. I'm here to help you get Zoe out, and you, but we need to be very, very quiet. You're doing very well on your own but it will take two of us to get Zoe away.:

:Prove you're who you say you are!: I fought against the bodily holds; I couldn't remain passive until I knew for sure. I couldn't break the unyielding hold on me.

:Stop squirming, please! Okay, here's proof it's me holding you. I'm the one who made your special bras to hold your gun.:

:Not good enough; Si'neada could've told anyone about that.:

:You gave Zoe your blood after she'd been shot; she would've died without that transfusion and now she can mind whisper, too.:

That convinced me. Only Si'neada knew about the consequences of my giving her my life-saving blood. Plus, his mind voice sounded like him and there was a slight, but familiar, fragrance coming from whoever was holding me.

:Ok? I can let you to go? You won't shout, fight or shoot me?:

:If you're not really Si'neada binding me, no promises, but if it's you as you say you are, then yes. Or, I mean no.: I sighed, the hot air of my breath forced back into my own face from the tight hold over my nose and mouth. *:I mean I won't shout, shoot or fight you if it's really you.:*

He released the hold from my mouth and nose and I pulled in big, grateful breaths. He continued to grasp my hands, however, which I would've, too, if I were him. A face moved in front of mine as he shifted his body enough to show me his face. I went cross-eyed from trying to make out his features from so close.

However, only one Imurian I knew wore lash lengthening darkener, sparkles to his whiskers and eyes with that particular blend of gold with green specks. It was Si'neada. I nodded.

"I'm still mad at you, you know." I whispered.

"Yes, I know you think you are, my little pudding, but once you know the reason why, I'm sure you'll forgive me." He also spoke in a whisper.

I curled a lip. "Don't be too sure. Part of me wants to still shoot you." That part being my hair, well, and me, but I needed his help first.

He released my hand with the syringe first, then my gun hand, stepping back and to the right in quick succession, letting a computer monitor cover his midsection. I showed him my teeth in a false grin, narrowing my eyes. "I won't shoot you now, you dweeb. We need to rescue Zoe and then I might shoot you." I looked around. "Where is everyone, anyway?"

"Asleep, I should think. It is the wee hours of the morning. Where is the Elite Doctor?"

I smirked. "Asleep in the cage he shoved me into." I raised the syringe. "Courtesy of one of these that he was about to plunge into me–again. I couldn't allow that."

He nodded. "Good going, my precious fighter. I was working on a plan for removing you from his clutches, but you did it on your own. Well done; I'm proud of you."

An embarrassing feeling of pleasure shot through me at his words. My parents had always praised me when I deserved it but it had been a long time and I guess I was a little starved for positivity. I almost–almost, mind you–forgave him right then. *But, they are only words,* I reminded myself, *even if he does sound sincere.*

"Thanks. Let's get Zoe and then you can explain to me all about why I shouldn't shoot you."

CHAPTER FORTY-FOUR

"First," Si'neada said, tapping his chin with a manicured, purple striped claw, "let's have you look more like a crew member. This is a small shuttle, remember, and if you look like a stranger to the crew, they'll shoot first and not bother with questions."

"Oh," I said, startled. "I hadn't thought about that."

He inclined his head. "And that is one of the reasons you shouldn't shoot me." He grinned at me, flashing an uncomfortable number of sharp teeth, one glinting a little.

"Hey! Is that gold in that tooth?" I squinted at him.

"It's only temporary, my little diamond. Just to have a little bling with my drab uniform."

I thought the glitter around his eyes, the tiny fake jewels on his claws, and the mascara were enough, myself, but, hey, who am I to judge. One person's glitter is another person's overload, I guess.

"Of course, I can see where you'd want that." I resisted rolling my eyes. "I think I can modify to look like....?" I cocked my head at him in a questioning way.

He blinked a couple of times as he pondered this for a few seconds. "If you can look like that big, burly guard you so cleverly chained up, that would be useful. He's in his bunk sleeping at present." Then he held up one finger. "First, let me check to be sure." He examined something on his Perpad, then nodded. "Yes, he's marked as being in his bed, snoring away like the brute he is."

"Um, they were both big and burly to me."

"The one on the left as you face them, then. If that helps."

I nodded. *Okay, Goldie?*

ICK TO NAME. CAN MODIFY.

Without going through the entire change? I hope?

YOUR LUCKY DAY. YES.

I could call you *Lucky!*

NO.

Huh. Definite note of finality to that word but I couldn't think about it anymore as my face suddenly felt like someone had mushed it with tenderizing hammer. My hands flew up to my face and I felt it rearranging under my fingers even as I felt the painful process. We hadn't modified like this before but it was good to know we could.

My face settled into its new look and a few last zips of pain shot through me as I dropped my hands to my side. *Wow. That was fast. Still hurt, though, Elaine.*

EASIER TO DO, EDITH.

I looked at Si'neada with a narrow-eyed look. "How'd you know which guard was which?"

Si'neada had the grace to look embarrassed. "I let them go."

Seeing thunderclouds gather on my features as anger rose through me, he hastily added, "It wasn't worth the amount of punishment they would've received for being imprisoned like that. As it is, the Elite Scientist Doctor will no doubt include them in his next Imurian experiment because of it. Why add a whipping to that?"

I stared at him. "A–a whipping? For real?"

He nodded, his lips set in a grim line. "Yes, for real. It isn't pretty and does nothing for their personalities or attitudes. I am totally against that but my voice isn't enough, although I'm not alone in thinking this." He shook his head. "Now, my little malleable one, we need to scoot; we're running out of time."

"Oh, geez Louise, you're right." We stepped together toward the room containing Zoe. "Maybe she'll be awake when we get there; that would sure be helpful."

Have I tried Louise already? By now, I'd tried so many names and combinations, I'd totally lost track.

YES. A NO GO. NOW HURRY.

We hurried to the door, checking as we went for danger, my hand on my gun. Si'neada had one, too, in his hand, although it was quite small and hard to see. He'd told me once all Imurians are trained in weaponry as soon as they're old enough to comprehend the safety rules and strong enough to carry one.

"Hey, Si'neada, what about security cameras?"

"I circumvented them before coming in here. Your appearance change is safe."

"Whoooo." I blew out in relief as we reached the door. I reached for the door opener when Si'neada grabbed my hand, staying it from grabbing the handle.

"Wait. I took care of cameras but I think the doctor has a safeguard built into the handle so no one walks in on him in the middle of something, er, delicate he might be doing."

"Or that he doesn't want to be caught doing." I said, fury making me snappish.

"That, too," Si'neada nodded. He bent down to sniff at the handle and inspect it more closely. "Yes, I am right; he has activated the privacy mode on this handle."

"Can we overcome it?"

"I believe I can. I don't think there is a 'we' to this." He pulled out a small electronic device, holding it delicately between his fingertips of one hand, pointing it at the handle. A tiny blinking red light pulsed in the dim room, showing numbers flitting across a tiny screen.

"What's it doing?"

"Finding the frequencies and codes Dr. Ot'ino'yan used. He's so sure of himself that I'm very sure he wouldn't have changed his pass code numbers from when he first entered them."

"Yeah, he's a pee pot full of arrogance."

The pinpoint of red light changed to orange as Si'neada held it steady in front of the lever. I was afraid to breathe in case I interrupted the process somehow by taking in air. Just as I couldn't wait any more, the light turned green, and Si'neada opened the door. My heart thudded in anxiety and worry for Zoe.

We didn't dare turn on lights but we could see her curled up under the blanket on the hospital bed. She didn't stir when we walked in, Si'neada somehow as silent in his booted feet as I was with bare feet. Of course, bare is a relative term when referring to an Imurian foot, which is covered in fur to the tips of the toes, where the claws come out, and heavy pads on the bottom for stealthy walking, hair sprouting between the pads to cushion sound.

I held up a hand for Si'neada to halt, then put a finger to my lips to tell him to be quiet. He raised his eyebrows at me but did as I requested.

:Zoe.: I waited a breath or two. *:Zoe, it's Jessi. I'm here to take you out of here. Wake up, Zoe. It's really me. Remember that time in Cat Fight school when I dumped you on your ass, pulling your hair and biting your arm? Oh, now that was a fun day. And, hmm, I think you quit the class the next day.:*

A beat of silence; I kept one hand in the air to keep Si'neada from moving.

:Jessi?: Her voice sounded fuzzy in my head. *:I want to get out of here.:*

:Me, too, Zoe, me, too. Si'neada is with me–:

:I don't want him in here, get him away from me! He's a traitor.:

:Zoe, he's the only reason I got into this room to help you. And, much as I hate to admit it, he's the only one right now who can get us back to Amorpha. We need him.:

:Well, tell that big hairy furball that I think he's an ass, a turd basket and a pile of spit!:

:Wow, Zoe, I'm impressed! Tell you what; let's get you out of here and you can tell him all that yourself when we're on the escape pod. I locked the doctor in one of his cages in his office but I don't know how long the sedation I used on him will last. If he catches us, I don't think he'll be as kind as before.:

She sat up in one swift, graceful move, glaring at Si'neada, her eyes narrowing, then widening in surprise when she saw an Imurian next to him. Fear flooded her face but drained away when I gave her the Cat Fight hand signal that only she and I would know. It helped I'd warned her I wouldn't be myself when I got there.

"Get me out of here!" She slurred the words, tone low and gravelly. Grabbing a nearby pair of scissors from a surgical tray, I cut through the restraints. Damn tough fabric but I managed to saw through it in a short time. She chafed her wrists with her hands, sliding her feet off the bed to the floor, wobbling and swaying as she stood. I grabbed one arm and Si'neada the other to steady her.

“Please, let’s *go.* I can’t stand being here another second.”

“And you’re welcome.” I snipped.

She gave a stiff nod. “Thanks,” and leaned toward the door.

“Uh, Zoe? You need some clothes. Where are yours? You’re still in a medical gown, you know.”

She looked down, a grimace of distaste on her face. “Oh. Well. Frack it all.”

I stooped down, peering under her bed, her clothing stuffed on a shelf in a messy pile. I grabbed them, shoving her jeans and top into her hands, saying, “Hurry!”

She dropped the gown, pulled on her top and pants, clumsy from the sedation, and I helped her to slip on her shoes.

I nodded. “Ready to go.

CHAPTER FORTY-FIVE

Thanks to the late hour, getting to the escape pod was anti-climactic. We saw no one on the way, and no alarms blared when we left the doctor's area. It seemed too good to be true but if someone were watching us, they'd see two Imurians escorting one Human female to wherever we'd been ordered to take her. We provided support on both sides of her so her stumbling walk didn't look suspicious, or so we hoped. Her eyes were still glazed and half-lidded and she kept yawning. I murmured to her in an encouraging way to keep her going. *Well, she and I have come a long way, haven't we? In the not-so-old days, I would've been threatening her! Or, well, at least scolding her.*

BERATING BETTER WORD.

Okay, Sparky, I don't need an editorial. My hair blew a raspberry at me, heard in my head.

Si'neada used his small gadget to override the fail-safe on the door to the pod so the bridge didn't receive an alert to someone entering the pod or starting the engine. We settled Zoe into one of the passenger seats, securely harnessing her as her head lolled to one side. I shook my head a little in sympathy, glad we got her out of there in time. I hoped it was in time.

"I need some of those handy dandy gadgets you pulled out of your magic hat." I remarked. "Where'd you get them, anyway?"

He gave me a sideways glance. "Oh, my little gadget queen, that's my secret but I do have to return them. They're not mine to keep so I cannot gift you with one, either."

"Ah, rat spit. I guess that means I won't get them for my birthday present, huh."

He looked startled. "Is it your birthing day today?"

I chuckled. "Since I don't have any idea what the date is, I'd say no to that. It was mostly a joke."

Nodding, he said, "I see. It's a good thing since I do not have a gift for you, other than your life and an escape back to the planet." He grinned at me in a cheeky way.

Zoe mumbled, "Who's getting a gift? Where am I?"

I glanced at her, startled at the sound of her voice but she'd fallen asleep again. Dr. Ot'ino'yan must've used some heavy-duty drugs on her and I wished I had the antidote. If only I was already a fully qualified physician so I could do more to help her but might as well wish for the stars in heaven to dance the tango.

We settled into the two seats at the console for take-off, harnesses in place. The pod was small as compared to the shuttle, with room for about six people, if they weren't giants, seats rimming the walls of the drab vehicle. Zoe looked lost, the only passenger besides us. It was strictly a utilitarian interior, designed to save a life but not for comfort. Small hatches built into the walls over the seat backs announced their contents as water, meal packets, survival equipment and other useful items. Well, at least we wouldn't starve if we got stranded.

Si'neada pressed and poked the panel, hands flying over it as if he were a pianist and I was impressed. He obviously knew what he was doing, whereas I'd have been floundering by now. No, correct that: I would've been recaptured by now since I couldn't have gotten this far without him.

My anger at him softened a bit; he really was helping us escape. I just hoped it wasn't to something even worse. I figured I could prod an explanation out of him on the way back to Amorpha since we'd have time in transit. I had no way to know how far away we were from the surface but I didn't think it was all that far as a rough, perhaps hopeful, guess.

The engine hummed into life, lights flashing on the panel, going from red to green, the same system humans use for such things. A mechanical voice announced overhead, making me jerk in surprise, "Prepare for eviction from the ship."

"Are you sure they don't know we're in here?" I asked, worried someone would stop us from leaving, biting at my lower lip with my teeth.

"As of right now, no, they do not to know we are in here." He said in formal Imurian. "However, once we detach and move away, I guarantee they will to know. The question is what they will to do about it."

"What can they do about us leaving?"

He shrugged. "Shoot us down, as worst-case scenario. The Captain could activate the magnetic retrieval system to pull us back into the ship. Or they could ignore us and let us go."

I snorted. "And how likely is that last? More likely they'll pull us back in. So how do we prevent that?"

"We zoom away from here as fast as we can go, like a monster with huge, sharp teeth is about to rip into our asses." He flashed me a smile. "So make sure your harness is tight and hang on for the ride. It isn't going to be pretty."

"Have you done this before?"

His face assumed a look of innocence. "Who, me?"

I gave him a slit-eyed glare. "Well? You and who else?"

"All right, it was me and Ler'a'neada. We were in our Transitional years and we were dared to do it." He smiled at the memory.

"Well, obviously they didn't shoot you out of the air since you're here. So what happened? How did you manage to do it?"

"Well, we practiced in the simulator every chance we could to improve our piloting skills for regular craft, making sure we got it into enough trouble to use an escape pod in our scenarios."

His hands continued moving over the controls and I felt pressure start to build in the cabin, pushing on my chest. I suspected the pod didn't have gravity-cancelling abilities and this could become very unpleasant. I looked at Zoe to make sure she was still secure and asleep. Reassured, I turned back to Si'neada.

"So, finally we decided we were ready." He laughed, a soft sound. "We were young and stupid, as all are in the Transitional Years. And arrogant in our certainty that we'd trained well without anyone suspecting us."

He shook his head. "Yes, we were stupid. One night, in the early hours with only the night shift on duty, Ler'a'neada and I snuck out with one of these gadgets like I have today, got into the escape pod, and took off."

"How did you plan to get back to the ship and not get punished?"

He grinned. "That is the part of the plan we hadn't thought about, actually. We concentrated on how to fly it and take it off the ship but we didn't think about how to safely get back. I think we thought the Captain would retrieve us with the magnetic pull once he knew who had done it."

"So, what happened?" Sweat broke out on my face, heaviness on my chest making it harder to breathe.

"They left us out in space for three days to teach us a lesson before finally pulling us back in. And now, my little princess, no more talking; you'll need all your air for this next part, as will I. This is not going to feel good but it is necessary." His finger hovered over the launch button, checking to see if the engine was ready for a forcible and fast ejection, then he pressed it.

Enormous weight slammed into me, trying its best to make sure I became a pancake in the chair; I could barely force air in and out of my lungs against the force. Blackness edged my vision, spiraling in from the sides; I knew if it met in the middle, I'd pass out. Burning in my throat announced stomach acid being pressed upward, triggering my gag reflex. I fought against vomiting even though I had no strength for anything other than struggling to pull air in through my mouth.

This must be what a rock in a sling felt like only the rock wasn't about to become a huge wet spot on this chair. The compression against my body continued to build and just as I knew I was going unconscious, it eased just enough for me to gasp in a much-needed breath. I could only hope Zoe could breathe in her presently sedated condition but there was absolute zero things I could do about it at this time.

I struggled to open my eyes, blinking away tears, looking at the panel with blurred vision. One of the screens showed our trajectory away from the ship in a curving line but we weren't very far yet and fear added to the squeeze against my chest.

"Are...we...safe...yet?" I managed to grind out the words.

:*Not yet.*:

:*Huh, mind whispering. Much easier. So now what?*:

:*Reaching apex of our curve, pressure will lift*:

:*Okay.*: I decided to shut up and not distract him more than I just had. After all, he had to pilot this thing and he'd only ever done it once before, all those years ago. Well, spider spit, I guess we were either going to reach the planet alive or we were going to die and, at the moment, I didn't much care which.

The force holding me in the chair started to lessen in tiny increments. When it started, it slammed into my body with the force of a bulldozer and I wished it would stop that fast, too, but that's not how it went. Just my luck.

When I was finally able to draw a complete breath, I noticed Si'neada doing the same thing at the same time. Then I became aware of an angry voice coming into the ship.

"--demand to know who is on the escape pod *now* or I will fire upon you."

Si'neada held up one finger, signaling me to stay quiet. He activated the channel, drawing breath so answer. "Captain, this is Second Officer Si'neada of the StarFinder. I thank you for allowing me on board but I have an emergency to attend to upon Amorpha and had to return forthwith. I apologize; I had to borrow an escape pod to do so."

"Why wasn't I informed of this? Why isn't your vid camera on? Turn it on now. Why didn't you request an aircar?" His voice sounded harsh and demanding.

"I had no time in which to inform you myself. As for the camera, it seems your maintenance crew didn't do their job too well; it isn't working. Thank goodness the voice control does. We are too far from atmosphere to use an air car."

CHAPTER FORTY-SIX

"And why should I believe you?" The captain barked, making me jump a little. "Where are your orders to do this? Why shouldn't I retrieve you this instance?"

"Ah, Captain, I wouldn't do that if I were you. Under the authority granted to me by my ship, the StarFinder, and by the Zatro of the Tenth City on Amorpha, I have been ordered to return in haste and under a code of silence. Please check with my Captain and the Zatro if you must. And if the camera worked, I would have it on." He looked at me, wagging his eyebrows up and down, amusement in his eyes. I'll confess he's quite good at bluffing and I determined to never play poker against him.

A short silence ensued, which I took to mean the Captain was mulling this over. I opened my mouth to ask a question when the Captain's voice intruded. "Very well. I hold you personally responsible for returning the–" Noise erupted on his end, a panting voice saying, "Captain! We discovered–" Communication was abruptly cut off.

"Ah, I think we've been found out." Si'neada all but whispered. He smoothed a fingertip over a control and the pod lurched, throwing us against our harnesses, Zoe groaning, as our speed picked up and that bulldozer rested on my chest again.

The speaker crackled into life. "Officer Si'neada, you return here right now with the Humans. I know you have them on board and they will be held accountable for imprisoning the Elite Scientist Doctor against his will. It is a violation of his authority and they will answer for it!"

"Oh, my Captain, I do not have them on board with me," he lied, "and I cannot return, as I've already told you. Perhaps they are hiding where you cannot find them? Perhaps the good Doctor was doing things to them they didn't like and felt the need to move to a different location?"

The Captain snarled into his microphone. "Turn around this instant or I will fire to cripple your pod."

I gripped the chair arms, my heart stuttering from fright. Zoe made a gasping sound but the cabin pressure was too much to allow for words.

:Zoe. We're going to be okay. Are you more awake now?: I hoped like heck I was right about being okay.

:Yes, I had a rude awakening the first time a building landed on my chest and I had to fight to breathe. It's back now, too. Is the Captain really going to fire at us?:

:I don't know but I'm sure Si'neada can evade the missile or laser beam or whatever it is. Or maybe we're out of range by now, I'm not sure.:

:Oh, gods of cesspool hells, I hope so.:

:Me, too.:

I dragged in a breath. "Si'neada..."

"Not now," he snapped.

Then I couldn't breathe anymore and my awareness fled as blackness overwhelmed my senses.

A sudden jigging of the pod wrenched me back to reality and I gasped in a breath, then another, trying to get in as much air as I could. "Wha-what happened?"

"Had to increase the speed and then evade the missiles sent against us." Si'neada's voice was terse.

"Are we still in range?" Fear made my voice squeak.

Si'neada took in a long breath, puffing it out through his mouth. "For a few minutes longer, yes. Hold on!" The pod lurched and rolled and my stomach gave up the fight; I puked onto my lap, throat burning from the acid. I wretched until I dry heaved, hearing Zoe doing the same. How Si'neada stayed calm and focused without a physical reaction was beyond me to figure out right then.

The stink of the pile of puke on my lap, dripping to the floor, kept me gagging as I tried to breathe without smelling it. Si'neada threw some cloths at me and I mopped the mess up as best I could while harnessed into the chair with the weight of a world still sitting on me. The heavy g-forces made my movements jerky and hard to control but I managed to wipe up the worst of it somehow, dropping the soiled material to the floor. Poor Zoe didn't have anything to clean herself; she was just that much too far from our seats for Si'neada to throw rags her way and the heavy g-forces kept us pounded into our chairs.

The pod shook and shuddered and a sudden hard lurch to left with a stomach twisting drop made me gasp. A too-bright flare of light flashed on one of the panel screens and I knew a missile had exploded. I heard the ping-ping of debris hitting the shell of our little pod. I closed my eyes, praying my death would be quick and painless.

"Damn it all, that was close." Si'neada muttered. "Hold on, my female friends, we're going out of range....................right............now."

"Were we hit?" Tears slipped down my face as I forced the words out with a sob, my hands gripping the arms of my chair with the strength of a vise.

"No, it exploded close by but not close enough to damage the pod."

Sweat and tears dripped off my nose, my chest and other personal places from fear. Zoe sobbed from her chair and, for the first time in my life, I wished I could pull her into a hug to comfort her. Okay, if I'm being honest, I wanted to be comforted also and to feel safe and Si'neada was too busy to provide such things.

After a few minutes of gaining distance between our pod and the missile range of the shuttle, Si'neada finally eased the g-forces back, allowing us to breathe easier. As soon as I could draw a few normal breaths in a row, I moved to unbuckle my harness.

"Jessalya, you cannot do that yet. It isn't yet safe."

"Maybe not but one of us has to check on Zoe and that somebody is me."

"Sit down." Si'neada barked in a no-nonsense tone of voice.

"No! I have to check her! She could be having internal bleeding, or broken ribs or–I don't know what else but I need to help her."

"Zoe!" Si'neada snapped.

A weak 'yes' came back from her direction.

"Are you all right? Anything broken? Are you coughing up blood?"

"N-n-no blood. I don't think anything broke." She panted a little with the effort of speaking.

"Do you need immediate attention?"

"I don't think so."

"There. You see?" He smiled at me, a teeth baring expression with a hard look in his eyes.

I glared back at him, angry but I couldn't very well argue about checking on Zoe. I sat back into my chair with a huff of annoyance, crossing my arms over my chest, turning to look at her. I could at least do that.

She sat with her head bent forward, blonde hair in disarray, as she swiped at the mess on her lap and an expression of disgust on her face. Crapola. Si'neada was right; she appeared to be okay and didn't need any attention from me. Well, I'd be strapped to a thorn tree in my underwear before I'd admit that to Si'neada.

"Hey, Si'neada." I said instead. "I am curious about something that I've meant to ask you forever but never had the chance."

"What's that, my fierce little doctor-to-be?"

"Why does your name only have one break in it? Every other Imurian I know has two."

He frowned at me. "You do not know enough Imurians, then." He sighed. "All right, I'll explain." Turning his attention back to the navigation panel, he made some minute adjustments as I watched our trajectory on the screen smooth out.

"When we declare our two-fur status, one break is removed."

"Why? That seems like a rude thing to do and maybe a little prejudicial."

He smiled, a swift movement, gone as fast as it arrived. "No, my little worried gal-pal, it's not like that. We two-furs are, mmm, how to say this. Yes, a blend of male/female, yes?"

"Yeah, that's certainly one way to look at it."

"Well, one break in our name is removed in acknowledgement of the blending we were born with. It is not an insult. Plus, it's an easy way to know another two-fur without having to ask or guess. There is no shame because it is the way we are born and almost all of us are proud to proclaim it when we are completely sure that is our genetic being."

"Makes sense to me and a good way to do it." I cocked my head to one side. "But you said 'almost'; so there are some out there who won't admit it?"

He made a face. "Yes, there are a few families who refuse to accept or understand, no matter the evidence presented about the genetics of it. It is unfortunate but it is true."

"Ah ha. So the Imurians aren't as perfect as your species wishes us to believe."

He gave a soft chuckle. "Yes, isn't that true of all species, though."

I nodded. "Of course, it is." I drummed my fingers on the chair arm. "How long and where are we going to land?"

"Does it matter?"

"Well, it matters to my bladder, for one thing, and for another, I'd sure like to get clean clothes for me and Zoe. Oh, and not to mention, I'd like to be Human again."

"Me, too!" Zoe exclaimed. "Well, at least the clean clothes and bathroom part of all that. Then at least I'll feel Human again."

"See? That's exactly what I mean," I said. "No offense."

He flipped a hand at me. "None taken. We have three hours to our destination and it is now safe to move around the cabin. You may remove your harness while up, but only for essentials and you must wear it while in your chair. Agreed?"

Nodding, I said, "Agreed. Zoe?"

"Of course, agreed." Her voice was strained and soft, not like her at all.

I unbuckled, my legs shaky as I stood, making me grip the back of the chair for support. I drew in a couple of breaths, *breathe in universe and out with debris* then willed myself to walk over to her as I wondered where the stray thought had come from.

Okay, honestly, it was more of a weaving gait with some hitches along the way until my legs figured out how to keep me upright and off the floor. Reaching Zoe, I bent down to see her face; she was staring at the floor and her blonde hair covered most of her face.

I'd never seen her so disheveled. I reached out a hand, slowly, and gently brushed some of her hair back. She was very pale and looked a little bit green, and she was gulping air like I do when I'm fighting against losing stomach contents. "It's okay, Zoe. The flight should be easy from here on in. I'll get you some water." Fighting back my own need to gag at the stench of vomit, I closed my eyes for a second, taking shallow breaths as I back away. I had to get her cleaned up or I'd throw up again. Ye gods and little kittens, I couldn't think that or I'd do it.

Without lifting her eyes, she gave the barest of nods. I found her a bottle of drinking water and some cloths for cleaning her. When I was done, and she was slowly sipping the water, she looked up at me, some color back in her face. "I don't know what happened; I don't get flight sick, not like this."

"Maybe all the twisting and dodging we did to evade the missile? I lost my cookies, too, and that normally doesn't happen to me." Boy howdy, that took everything I had to confess my weakness.

The glassy look in her eyes disappeared as she gave me an odd look, head cocked to one side. Then, without warning, she chuckled, which turned into a giggle, which grew into a belly laugh. Puzzled, I tried to figure out what was so funny, knowing I'd probably rue the day I'd confessed space sickness. I stood from my crouched position, an angry twist to my lips, and stepped away. "You're welcome." I snapped and turned toward my chair at the console.

She grabbed my wrist, saying, "Wait." She took a shaky breath. "I wasn't laughing at you, I really wasn't. It's just, well, it's stupid but when you started gagging earlier, that triggered me and then with all the motions of the pod–" She see-sawed her hand in the air. "I just had the sudden thought that we weren't just Velvetwins anymore; now we're also Puke Pals. And that's why I started laughing. I'm sorry, I know it's stupid."

Wrinkling my brow, I stared at her for a few seconds, then glanced at Si'neada, whose grin was huge on his face. "Oh, that's a good one, my retchy blonde friend." He chortled, which startled me into smiling, which led to my own rueful chuckle.

I nodded my head with a slow up and down motion. "You know, Zoe, I think Puke Pals just might not catch on and it's, like, way too obvious. Now I'm going to see if I can find us clean clothes." I pinched my nose together in an exaggerated motion. "Yeah, we need the air scrubber on, Si'neada."

"It's been working ever since I could reach the button."

I made a face at him which he waved away with a languid hand movement, then I started rifling through compartments until I found clean jumpsuits that would sort of fit us.

Let's become Human again.

AGREED. GO IN BATHROOM.

Yeah, good idea. No need to risk anyone filming me changing skins again. I felt the flash of anger I'd held ever since I'd found out that Deester, on the StarFinder ship on my journey to Amorpha, had filmed me changing shapes. I hadn't known he was there, barely knew him or his species at the time, and definitely didn't know how sneaky they were or how often they could get into the smallest of places. They no longer had a home world, making the starships of the Imurians their homes, offering services in the maintenance and cleaning areas, also collecting info on passengers as they deemed necessary. Or had the compulsion to do, which seemed to be a common trait for their otter-like people.

"Be right back, I need to use the waste room." I looked at Zoe. "You okay until I come back?"

"Yup, but don't delay too much, I think I need the room, too."

"You want to go first, then? I might be a while."

She considered this. "Yeah, maybe I should." She unstrapped herself and walked to the bathroom, only having to grab for support a couple of times. I was envious.

"Si'neada, I'm going to become Human again, just so you know."

He looked at me with thoughtful eyes, thinking this over before nodding. "Perhaps it would be best."

"Can we send a message to my family now—and Zoe's—to let them know I'm alive and she's okay?"

"No, that cannot yet happen. No one must know you two are on this pod. It's better for people to think you are still dead."

"But why?"

He hesitated. "I can't tell you everything yet but you'll find out in due time."

I made a growling sound and my long, striped tail switched back and forth in irritation, ears slanting back in annoyance. "You said you would tell me why you did what you did!"

He smirked at me. "Yes, I did, and I will. However, I didn't say when I would do this."

My mouth dropped open and then I made a strangled sound. I couldn't beat it out of him, as tempted as I was to do so, since he needed to pilot us somewhere safe. I managed to squeeze out words. "You are taking us to Amorpha, right? And not to the StarFinder or some other Imurian or Amorphan ship?" I swear if I found he wasn't going back, I'd shoot him myself. Somewhere very, very painful to recover from.

"Yes, yes, of course, we're headed to Amorpha. See?" He swept his manicured hand out in a grand gesture to indicate the plot on the graph showed our pod, if I believed the screen, was headed to Amorpha. Bellybutton lint. Even if the screen was lying, there was truly nothing I could do about it at this point.

Zoe came out of the bathroom, looking refreshed and back to her normal self. I gave her a thumbs up and she flashed one back as I entered the small waste room, carrying my change of clothes with me. I stripped out of the stinky coverall, stuffed it into the laundry bin, and sat on the floor to endure the pain of changing shapes.

When I was back in my own skin, I dressed in the new coverall, amused now because these were made for Imurians, so there was a hole on the rear of the pants for their tail. This meant that things were a little, well, um, breezy on my butt, not to mention maybe a little crack dealing to the viewing public. Hmm, true confession. For me, it was only a problem when I hitched up the pants; otherwise, the rear drooped on me like a hound dog's ears because I was so short, especially compared to an Imurian. And who doesn't like a little air flow on their butt, anyway? Answer: me.

I rolled up the cuffs and wrists as much as I could manage and still had to pull up the pants to walk. Such is life as a short person. Excuse me, I meant to say petite.

CHAPTER FORTY-SEVEN

For the rest of the journey through space, Zoe and I chatted about our host families, telling funny incidents about our classes at each of our University, the bother of having bodyguards *all the time*, so making friends was almost impossible. No one shot missiles at us, although she and I flinched at any little clang on the outside metallic shell, especially when the little vehicle swerved without warning.

Si'neada laughed at us, saying, "Oh, my scaredy young friends, it's only a stray rock or two."

The first time he giggled at our reaction with his explanation, I said in return, "Yeah, but what if that rock is the size of a mountain?"

He laughed harder, slapping his knee. "The alloy used to make this pod is stronger than any debris in our path. The shield is engaged, the ship is designed to dodge any such dangers, and we're well guarded against excess radiation. We Imurians design only the best, you know."

I glowered at him. "Yeah? And how were these things tested? And what's the alloy? What about those missiles? I'll bet they would've torn this apart if we'd been hit by those."

He flipped a hand back and forth. "Yes, the missiles would've been a problem which is why we skedaddled so fast from the starship. Thankfully, we got out of range in time to avoid the main blast, just getting the backwash for an especially bumpy ride."

He wagged his eyebrows at me. "The alloy is our secret and shall remain so."

"Ha, that just means you don't know how it's made." I snickered.

"Whatever. Just know, you and Zoe, we are perfectly safe until we reach our destination. Now would one of you please find me a water bottle?"

Grumbling to myself, I opened the compartment for water handing one to him, one to Zoe and one for myself. "How about a meal? I'm really hungry and I heard Zoe's stomach grumble." Grabbing three, I stuffed them into the cooker device, telling it how many to cook and it turned on. When it beeped, I passed them around with forks and we settled in our chairs to eat. Not the best food in the world, and it was possibly as old as the saying, "Hunger is the best Sauce," but we did eat them, Zoe and I making faces as we chewed.

Once done and cleaned up, Zoe and I kicked back our chairs for a nap. "Wake us when we get there, Si'neada." I yawned, stretching my hands high up over my head as I made myself comfortable, securing my safety harness.

The next thing I knew, it felt like we were driving on a road paved with potholes, and I woke up clutching the armrests. "What's going on?" I squeaked, anxiety making my mouth dry.

"Oh, nothing," Si'neada remarked. "We've entered the upper atmospheric layer of Amorpha." He looked annoyingly relaxed for the roller coaster ride we were on at this moment.

I glanced over at Zoe and her hands were as white knuckled as mine, making me feel a teensy bit better. I opened my mouth to ask her something but an especially hard bump snapped my teeth together, biting my tongue and the pain made me forget the question. Closing my eyes made the sensations worse so I kept them open, watching Si'neada's hands dance over the control panel. I wondered when he'd put on a headset.

He murmured words I couldn't understand; he must be using a subvocal mike. The pod rattled and bounced through the air, throwing us around in our chairs, no matter how snug I tightened my harness. The braking procedure kicked in without warning, a whale sitting on my chest, making breathing again difficult. The jolting and quaking motions grew worse along with whistling and shrill noises. I felt certain we were going to disintegrate during our descent. I clenched my teeth to keep from biting my tongue again and hung onto the arm rests for dear life. I couldn't spare a glance at Zoe to see how she coped with this; it was all I could do to keep myself from screaming. Well, grunting in discomfort since I didn't have the air for screaming.

All motion ceased with the sound of a mighty thwack against something solid. If it hadn't been for my seat harness, I would've been thrown to the ceiling and back from the abrupt stop.

"We've landed, my dear little passengers."

"Couldn't you have given us some warning?" I complained.

"No time. Piloting a pod to land in a specific spot takes intense concentration, but, of course, I can manage it." He waved a hand in the air in a dismissive way. "What? No 'thank-you, Si'neada, for delivering us safe and sound to the surface?"

I rolled my eyes and was darned certain Zoe did, too. "Thank you, Si'neada, most noble pilot of all the Imurians."

"Now that's more like it." He sniffed, then smiled.

"Where did we land?" Zoe asked. "Is my host family waiting? They must be so worried. And what about Jessi's family? Will they be meeting her here, too?"

"Yeah, what she said? I want to know, too. Are they here? I've got to let them know I'm all right!" I bumped shoulders with Zoe. "And that she's okay, too."

To my utter shock, Zoe wrapped her arms around me in a hug, something I'd never even thought could happen, no matter our current history together. I hugged her back and as

I did so, my head yanked back so fast I thought I felt it snap. Utter despair swept through me, my lifeless hair puddled on the floor around me, and I wailed my anguish and misery out, not yet knowing what I mourned. As fast as it hit me, as I drew breath to cry out again, my hair sprang back into life and the empty sucking emptiness within disappeared. I had no idea what had just happened and I shook my head in bewilderment.

"Jessi! Are you okay?" Zoe asked, concern lacing her words as Si'neada chimed in with, "My little precious gem, what happened?"

I shook my head. "I don't know. Maybe it's because all this is finally over and it hit me like this. I—I'm all right, really, I am." *Am I okay?*

YES. NOW YOU ARE.

"If you're sure, Jessi?"

I nodded, heaving a sigh, gesturing toward the door. "Let's get out of here, okay?"

"Let me open the exit first."

With the door open, wind whistled in, cold pushing at us. My hair knew to stay out of my face, resisting the blustering air, but Zoe's hair whipped in all directions as she tried hard to get it gathered and out of her face. Climbing out of the pod was tricky with legs shaky from the horrible ride but we managed. Si'neada jumped out of the opening with a cheerful grin, showing off. Guards surrounded us, weapons handy but turned outward. Looked like they were guarding us against, well, I didn't know what but at least they weren't pointed at us.

Si'neada and the officer in charge conferred, then the front guard led us to the stairwell and we started trooping downstairs. Each landing had two armed guards. Our escort paused each time to exchange passcodes and IDs before letting us go further down.

"Hey, what happened to the people who attacked my family and me in the woods? Were they caught?" I asked the nearest guard.

"I cannot discuss such things with you."

"Well, were they caught? Can't you even tell me that?"

"I cannot discuss this subject with you or anyone."

I stopped on the stairs, turning half-way around to look at him. "You cannot or you will not? Somebody needs to tell me!" I crossed my arms over my chest, scowling at him.

"Zatro will tell you what you need to know. I am forbidden to even talk this much. Now turn around and keep going." He gestured in an abrupt way.

Seething, I turned back around to go down several more flights. By now, I'd lost count of how many floors we'd passed. "Sheesh, aren't there any elevators in this stinking building?" I grumbled, rubbing my wobbly, sore thighs.

"Stairs are more defensible." The guard snapped.

The lead guard stepped in front of a plain metal door on the next landing, exchanging words and signs with the armed person standing there. He opened the door slowly, peering around, weapon in his leading hand, before pulling it all the way open to let us go through.

We moved as a tight group down the hallway to another door, guarded by four Amorphan guards, and again the guards exchanged words, signs and ID badges with DNA checks, maybe spit and toenails, too, which they examined with various instruments before finally giving nods of acceptance and one said, "I will alert Zatro to your presence."

"About time," Zoe muttered. I touched her arm, nodding in sympathy as I sucked in air, my legs trembling from descending countless steps.

The door opened just enough for Zoe and I to step through, Si'neada coming in last. The door snapped closed and I think Si'neada did some fancy tail maneuvers to keep it from being caught. I almost giggled at the mental image but there was a taller-than-average Amorphan in an elaborate robe staring out a window as we entered the room. Something about his regal bearing prohibited such things as chuckling and it died in my throat.

His voice was abrupt, masculine and imperious. "You may step forward."

Zoe and I looked at each other, shrugged, and moved forward a few feet until he lifted his hand to halt us, Si'neada behind us. I noted we were out of striking range of his body. Clasping his hands, he swiveled slowly in a regal manner to face us. He looked us over with narrowed eyes, as if discerning our internal organs with the intensity of his gaze, before nodding the tiniest bit. I saw our reflections in the window and knew he'd used it as a mirror to judge our approach and, perhaps, intentions.

My only intention was rejoining my host family, letting my human family know I was alive so I could return to my studies so I could go on to medical school. Anxiety radiated from Zoe; she was as nervous as I was. We didn't yet know why the Zatro wanted to meet us in the wee hours of night in such secrecy. A silence stretched between us and the Zatro. Even Si'neada wasn't saying anything as he stood behind us. I was starting to get twitchy with the need to fill the space with words.

My hair spoke so unexpectedly into the well of silence, I jumped a little in place, causing Zatro to raise his eye ridges in a questioning way. For a panicked second, I thought maybe it had spoken out loud instead of into my head.

AKRION TRANSPORTED NEW.

New? What are you talking–you know what, now's not the time. Explain later. Why is the Zatro just staring at us?

MANNERS. BOW TO HIM.

Knowing my hair was right, I elbowed Zoe and then bowed forward in the most formal way I could manage as Zoe followed my lead.

"Ah, finally, you have manners. Tsk, tsk, so unlike the young people of today who seem to have none. It is refreshing." He nodded and almost smiled. Almost. He pointed a boneless finger at two chairs. "Please do sit."

"Yes, Zatro," we murmured.

"Congratulations to coming back to us alive, Madam Jessalya. I am sure you are most excited to return to your family." I wondered which family he meant and was about to ask when he continued. "I think you are also anxious to return to your studies."

We said, "Yes, Zatro." Since there was no actual question, protocol forbade us from asking a question or from answering a question not yet asked. I clamped down on the impulse to ask about my family.

"Madam Zoe, it is also good you are returned to us. Your removal from the planet shouldn't have happened and we apologize to you and Madam Jessalya."

Mouse pimples! The Zatro apologizing to us? That was unheard of, as far as I knew.

"Yes, Zatro," she said in a soft voice, with a gracious nod of her head. Trust Zoe to be all elegant and gracious while I felt like a plush toy animal whose stuffing was coming out of its tummy.

He placed a finger along his right cheekbone, glittering eyes cutting back and forth between us, ignoring Si'neada. Colors of calm and certainty swirled over his exposed skin as he walked to the window again to look out at the dark, then over to a small table with a filled pitcher and glasses. He poured a glass of clear liquid, which I took to be water, handing it to Zoe. "Please, drink up, you must be thirsty." He waited while she took a sip from the glass. "Please, drink it all." There was a hint of coercion in his voice or maybe I imagined that.

She emptied the glass, saying, "Thank you, Zatro. I appreciate your consideration."

He nodded in acknowledgement. "You are well?"

"Yes, Zatro."

"Then, Madam Zoe, you may return to your guard detail now and they will take you home." He nodded at the door. "Again, accept our apologies on your unexpected removal and know it will not happen again."

She looked at me, then back at him. There was nothing either of us could do so she stood, bowed, and said, "Of course, Zatro. Thank you for gracing me with your time." She lifted a hand in farewell, gliding toward the door, whisking through before I could do or say anything. I turned back to Zatro, meeting his intense gaze. He remarked, tilting his head to one side, his gaze intense on me, "I will tell you, now, why you're here."

I held up a hand. "Zatro, I could use a drink of water also."

"In due time. This pitcher contains a nanobot to clear Madam Zoe's memory of being here."

Instant, hot flashing rage swept over me. I couldn't think, I could only react, which I did. I leaped toward him, slapping him as hard as I could across his cheek, snarling at him. "How dare you? That is completely wrong and I won't have it! I'll go find her and fix this."

I whirled to leave the room, blocked by Si'neada's body, who looked down at me with pity.

"I'm sorry, my little tempestuous friend. It must be done and it is already too late. The guards will drink theirs after they deliver her back home."

I pushed and heaved at him to move out of my way. "No! No, this isn't right! Zoe doesn't deserve this, she needs to know..."

He wrapped his arms around me in a bear hug. "Yes, I know and Zatro knows, too, but this is about much bigger things than her memory."

"What bigger things?" I felt my face blanche. *Oh, my grannie's pink panties, I hit the Zatro. That's an offense punishable by death.* Now I was afraid to turn around to face the Zatro; I'd rather not see my own death coming.

"Madame Jessi."

"Yes, Zatro." I whispered the response.

Zatro said, "I forgive you your physical transgression. I understand why you slapped me." His hand landed on my shoulder and I flinched, but he only gave me a gentle squeeze. "I know about your abilities." *Another betrayal by Si'neada.* Fury filled me. *Steam's going to come from my ears.* Now I wanted nothing more at that moment than to dismember Si'neada.

:Not everything, little Jessi. Just what I had to tell in order to save my sister.:

I clenched my teeth together; how did he slide his mind whisper through my tight internal shields? I wanted to shove him, hit him, hurt him but I had to know what he'd tattled. :*What did you tell him?*: I shoved hurt and fury with the words. Then, :*Save Ler'a'neada? What do you mean?*:

:*She was kidnapped out of the StarFinder and was held for ransom. I have been doing everything I could to save her*:

:*Including selling me to the Nameless Ones who sold me to the scientist.*:

A soft inhale over my head as he continued to hug me. :*Yes. It was the only way to get her back alive.*:

:*Why was she~?*:

The Zatro spoke, cutting off my question. "Madam Jessalya, I asked Si'neada here as he is your good friend from the Imurians and this concerns all species."

"He is not my friend."

Si'neada blew out a big sigh, patting my back. "Ah, my little prickle, you are my friend. What you think happened is not what happened. I assure you, I am your friend."

I snarled into his chest, pushing away from him, wanting to hurt him like he hurt me.

"Enough!" Zatro snapped, his voice full of power and force. The emotion he ejected rocked me and pushed his will into me. I didn't know any Amorphan could project such force with their voice but perhaps that's why he's the Zatro. Perhaps only a select few of the population could do this. Or perhaps they all could and I just hadn't felt it yet.

"I need you both. You, Si'neada, you will teach her what she must know."

"What? What do I need to know about? I just want to go back to my host family and get back to my studies." Folding my arms across my chest, I narrowed my eyes into a glare, another gutsy thing to do to a Zatro.

He ignored my stare. "You cannot do that yet."

"Why the frack not?" I spit the words out with anger.

The Zatro walked to the window, flicking an unseen latch. An airship waited outside with a short entrance ramp extruded. The craft was heavily camouflaged and almost impossible to see against the night sky. He stepped out of the window, ducking into the open hatch before turning around to point at me.

"I am aware of your shape-changing ability. You will now become me."

My jaw dropped open in shock as I jumped toward the window to grab him to explain but it was too late. The hatch closed, the aircraft accelerating away at a rapid speed, leaving me no chance to deny his mandate. I rotated to demand answers from Si'neada but he was gone, not answering me when I shouted for him.

"What the frack do I do now?" I whispered. Fury and worry wadded up inside of me and I didn't know if I should run, cry, scream or kick a hole in the wall.

SLEEP FIRST, FIGURE OUT LATER. Yeah, my hair made a good point.

I found the hidden door to the living quarters, finding a sumptuous bedroom with a comfortable bed. I crawled onto the luxurious mattress, letting the covers settle over me in a comforting hug of material. My eyes closed, a million or more questions crowding my exhausted brain, questions I couldn't answer but only gnaw on like a bone. Fatigue pulled me under despite my restless brain and a forgotten voice feathered through my mind as I slipped into sleep.

BREATH IN THE UNIVERSE, BREATH OUT THE STARS.
BE THE UNIVERSE WITHIN.
KNOW WE ARE THE UNIVERSE.
WE ARE THE BEARER OF NEW SPECIES.
BE STILL AND KNOW WE ARE.
BE STILL AND KNOW.
BE STILL.
BE.

ACKNOWLEDGEMENTS

So, this completes book two of the Exchanger series. It took me longer than I liked to get here but the fact is, the first draft, well, um, wasn't so good so I had to rewrite everything between the first page and the last page.

Yes, there'll be a third book.

Thanks to Kat Domet for an outstanding book cover (Domet Designs).

Thanks to my husband, Larry, for leaving me alone when I said, "I'm working on my book".

Thanks to those who said, "But, Karen, *when* is the next book coming out?" Here's your answer.

Thanks to my art buddies, Renee, Robbie, Mary and Sue. You keep me inspired to keep painting!

Thanks to my proofreader, Marie L, who caught the mistakes I let slip by. Whatever mistakes sneak in are purely my own. Thanks, Marie!

ABOUT THE AUTHOR

K. E. Brungardt, D.O. is a retired family practice physician, but you can call her Karen. She's a bridge player, author and an award-winning Watercolor Artist during the daytime and sleepy by night. Living in Arizona since 2001 has helped her arthritis a lot as did getting away from the wind and cold in Wyoming. She loves reading science-fiction and fantasy the most and now loves writing it and has received writing awards for some of her short stories in the past. A good laugh makes her day and she's always happy to hear from readers at **karen@artandbooks.net**.

The best thing you can do for any author is leave a review of their book (after buying it, of course)! You can go here to leave your review! **https://tinyurl.com/h8kys7hf**

You can always find out more about K. E. Brungardt by going to her website at www.karensauthorsite.com. While you're there, sign up for you forthcoming newsletter!

GLOSSARY

HUMANS:

Jessalya (JESS-a-LIE-ya) Lilianthal, Human with shape-changing abilities and sentient hair

Keaton Smithy: Human, 6'1", brown wavy hair, brown eyes, likes to weight lift, joke, play games and practical jokes, is interested in politics as a career. Will pursue his law degree first so he can enter government politics. Jessi has a crush on him

Mitchler Cadden: Black hair, dark blue eyes, 5'11', lanky build. Loves sports, also loves playing board and card games. Wants to become either a professional gymnast and perform or become a sports caster

Soli Dawson: Reserved personality, genius level intelligent, technology driven, loves any video game. Black hair, gray eyes, dark lashes, well built, 6' tall. Male-oriented

Zoe Marshall: Frenemy to Jessi, only two Human females on Amorpha, brought together by circumstances. Experimented on by Imurian scientists on starship journey to Amorpha

AMORPHANS:

Datro Aelotra: Head teacher for language and social niceties, known as Tatro (teacher) during class hours, on Imurian StarFinder starship

Datro Lariendo: Amorphan Father to Jessi, works as architect

Matra Teatriana: Amorphan Mother to Jessi, works as clothes designer

Tatra Hilodria: Female, teaches dance and social interactions on StarFinder starship

Tatra Meleandrea: Female, dance teacher and social interactions teacher on Starfinder starship

Saro Simatrao: Jess's "little brother" in her new alien family on Amorpha. Age equivalent to eleven-year-old (Late Childhood years)

DURSARIANS:

Deester: From Dursaria, small species, long body with opposable thumbs and language skills. Species now lives on spaceships with the Imurians, doing maintenance, repair work, cleaning, and similar jobs in exchange for safe-haven living

Exanno: Dursarian companion to Deester and clan

Mareesta: Dursarian companion to Deester

IMURIANS:

Ba'runka, StarFinder: Imurian security guard

De'red'ita: Imurian security on StarFinder

Ler'a'neada, StarFinder: sister to Si'neada, keeper of DNA cache

Lt. Sn'er'a, StarFinder: angry officer

M'yxtyl, StarFinder: Junior Officer-in-Training

Rank Officer Merlou'te, StarFinder: Imurian self-defense teacher, part of underground movement to stop genocide of budding sentients

Si'neada, StarFinder: Civilian Imurian, tailor, instrumental with preserving DNA from species and involved in movement to stop genocides of new civilizations

S'ret'ah: Highly placed Imurian officer who spearheads species annihilation

SPECIES:

Amorpha: Amorphans vary in height, have semi-shape changing abilities, can change their hands and feet to accommodate terrain or other needs and can change genitals if needed. Eyes and skin refract colors; skin colors reflect emotions. They have head feathers instead of hair.

Bruk:e: Round in shape, medium tall, green skin with knobs, three legs and feet, three eyes in front and one in back, three ears, one on each side and one on top of the bulbous head, one air hole under the chin, round mouth ringed with sharp teeth. Three long supple arms, equidistant around round body, each with four-fingered hands with thumbs.

K'Lect{ca: K'Lect{cans are tall ranging from six feet to seven feet or more, lavender skinned, six fingered with two opposable thumbs. Bruke:e and K'Lect{ca are also enrolled in the Alien Exchange program.

IMURIANS: Cat-like in appearance, tall in stature, striped fur over most of body, two upright ears that swivel, long whiskers on short muzzles that can be used to communicate. Two hands with thumbs and two feet, all with retractable claws, long striped tail. Eyes have vertical pupils. Teeth very sharp with short fangs, blunt teeth in back for chewing. Most Imurians can 'mind whisper', a form of mental telepathy.

GENERAL INFORMATION:

New Eden: Recently settled (within 100 years) Human world.

Amorpha: Settled within 100 years, Amorphan world, site of Exchange program for Jessi and classmates.

Bruk:e: Settled within 100 years, also in Exchange program with other Human students.

K'Lect{ca: Settled within 100 years, also in Exchange program with other Human students.

STAGES OF HUMAN DEVELOPMENT: Stages classified by brain wave studies, universal among all known civilizations. Years are no longer counted.

Infancy

Early childhood

Middle childhood, school commencement year

Late childhood

Early Transitional years

Advanced Transitional years

Early Prime Adult, advanced learning stage

Prime adult years

Advanced Prime adult years

Aged Adult years

AMORPHAN TERMS:

Bara: Daughter in family

Batra: Unmarried female

Daro: Not yet married, no children

Datro: Married male, has sired children

Mara: Not married, no children

Matra: Married female with children

Saro: Son in family

Satro: Unmarried male

Zatro: Leader of designated city

EXCHANGING (Book Two):

AMORPHANS:

Ariyendo: Amorphan soldier, aka Mr. Cranky-pants

Caronuyen: Amorphan soldier on base

Farayeno: Nighttime bodyguard

Garientin: Amorphan on military base.

Geronteo: Amorphan soldier on base

Herandion: Soldier who gets sick

Jesalion: Jessi's soldier name on the first base.

Jinardian: Fellow soldier of Opardium

Katerian: Amorphan soldier on military base

Larenteno: Daytime bodyguard

Morian: Nameless One guard

Myometo: Chief daytime bodyguard

Officer Farendian: Jessi's squad leader on base

Opardium: Soldier assigned to be Jessi's partner

Timanaro: Daytime bodyguard

Wiladeon: Amorphan soldier on military base

Xaleander: Fire Inspector Amorphan

Yarian: Nameless One guard

Zaleander: Bodyguard (daytime)

Zarilayo: Daytime bodyguard

IMURIANS:

Elite Doctor Scientist Ot'ino'yan: Top ranked scientist

McDuff: Imurian guard on transport ship

McGruff: Nickname for Imurian guard on transport ship

SPECIES:

Bru:kean: From world of Bru:ke, stout being with three legs, three arms and three eyes, one of which is on the back of the head. Three Large upright ears, ringed around the head. Green knobby skin.

Chee:lon'ga: Humanoid shape, average height 5' tall, Scaly skin, stands on two legs and has two arms, but the arms split at the elbow area so they have four forearms, therefore, four hands with three fingers and one thumb each. Eyes are elongated horizontally so they cover both front and sides of head, two ears on top of head, each pointing out to the side with long pointed tops and tufts of hair along them. Mouth small and round, puckers to close, can enlarge if needed. Omnivorous with chewing teeth, small and round in the back of the mouth and sharp for tearing in front. No nose, small breathing openings around the center of the head, going all the way around.

Farat: Size of large dog with jackrabbit ears, large, round golden eyes, round fluffy tail, hands with thumbs, large back feet. Burrowers.

Hydrophon: Size of a Husky dog, silver/brown mottled fur, sharp claws and muzzle with sharp teeth, prehensile long tail. Upright triangular ears on top of head. Yellow eyes with round pupils. Can swim like a fish, claws can retract to use front paws like hands, opposable thumbs.

Melakews: Upper limbs with fingers & thumbs that fold into a paw for running. Powerful hindquarters for jumping and running with a fluffy tail. Elongated large ears for acute hearing. Looks like a cross between a huge rabbit and a big dog. Large bulbous nose. Eyes set toward sides of the head for better peripheral vision. Omnivorous.

Radir: Deer-like creatures, same size, speckled green hides to blend into foliage, herbivorous, four legs, two upper limbs with hands, four fingers per hand with one thumb each hand and reminiscent of centaurs. Elongated muzzle, large, pointed ears that swivel, large black nose.

Roradiv: Like a cougar, with six legs, fangs like a saber tooth tiger, and fur with barbs at the end of the hairs. Front appendages have hand-like with long tapered fingers, sharp claws, and a thumb. Can walk on middle and rear limbs to use the front limbs as arms and hands.

Xingian: Large upright species, bear like with long front fangs for meat and blunt teeth for plant chewing, heavy fur, large golden eyes, horizontal pupils, and six-fingered hands with one thumb. Feet are flat and flexible with claws on six toes. Tool users.

DAYS OF AMORPHAN WEEK:

9-day weeks on Amorpha

FirstDay: Human's Monday on Amorpha
SecondDay: Humans' Tuesday
ThirdDay: Humans' Wednesday
First Rest Day: Acts as a rest day
FifthDay: Human's Thursday
SixthDay: Human's Friday
SeventhDay: Human's Saturday
Worship Day: Human's Sunday, acts as rest day
Second Rest Day: Ninth day of week, acts as rest day
There is no prohibition to working on a rest day.